Eastman Was Here

Alex Gilvarry

• • • • •

Eastman Was Here

VIKING

VIKING
An imprint of Penguin Random House LLC
375 Hudson Street
New York, New York 10014
penguin.com

Copyright © 2017 by Alex Gilvarry

LIBRARY OF CONGRESS CATALOGING-IN-PUBLICATION DATA AVAILABLE
ISBN: 978-1-101-98150-4

Printed in the United States of America
1 3 5 7 9 10 8 6 4 2

Set in Bodoni LT Pro Book
Designed by Francesca Belanger

For Alexandra Kleeman

I
The Call

Eastman, the timid bastard, look at him! Seated in his reading chair, all worn and tousled, face behind a book (*The Metaphysical Poets*, an anthology), hiding from a world he had come to fear. The month was May in the year of the polymorphous perverse, 1973. This is Eastman at the beginning of his journey, not the end. And what was he doing? Paralyzed? Hardly. Eastman was cowardly ducking. His legs were tightly crossed in poor man's corduroys (once brown)—the pants he had been sleeping in for four nights—his right leg atop his left, a protective barrier of what remained between his crotch. He had all the distinguished signs of middle age. A well-formed belly, testament to better years, smiling out of a shrunken T-shirt; his white back hair peeking out of the shirt's neck; that mess of overgrown curls atop his head (once jet black). Eastman did not even possess the will to shave, to wash, to eat, only to sit, to read, to hide behind a book of poetry.

The poem that held his attention presently: "Mediocritie in love rejected," Thomas Carew.

Give me more love, or more disdaine.

He did not know how he felt about either.

Four nights ago, Alan Eastman, beaten husband, lover, and devout father of three, one from a previous marriage, was informed by his current wife of ten years, Penny, that he had fallen out of love with her (news to him) and that he was no longer the proud bearer of her love, nor would he be the recipient of her sex. There would be no more waving around of his proud, uncircumcised flag, humping in every corner of the house, deep in the throes of marriage, or love (the two often fell out of sync).

And who would be the recipient of her sex now? Eastman wondered. *Who will have my Penny in his arms?* He did not really want to know, nor did he have any substantial proof of an affair, but experience had taught him that no man or woman made such a jump out of love without another flaming hoop to jump through.

Four nights ago, when Penny had informed him of this new development in their marriage, in the kitchen (how domestic!), the thought of their sex crept up on Eastman and triggered a tempered panic. How awful to admit here that he fell into the male stereotype championed and conceptualized by women's liberators. He did not think of himself as the stereotypical man, in fact, he fought hard against it.

The sex with Penny was often good; perhaps this is why it came to him at that moment in the kitchen, possibly at the very second of her attack upon him. He still desired Penny. Penny standing before him, half clothed (*pessimist, Eastman!*), her undergarments on the kitchen counter next to the breadbox and crumbs from the children, and her wonderful ass bouncing atop his lap as he sat in their kitchen chair, her hands gripping beneath his knees, his face looking down at what transpired between his cock and her cunt, the very odor of sex, of bodies, rising into his breath. Only this was a memory, an illusion of love. For instead, she stood before Eastman informing him of her plans to depart that very evening. The children were already at her mother's. Would he take her there in his car? His car, *the* children, not ours, though he knew he would be helpless were they left in his care alone. Assets were being divided, her plan had already been set in motion, and he had not been the least bit aware. He was used to doing what she told him, it suited his disposition, and this time it was no different. She was leaving. So Eastman waited in his study among his books while she gathered an assortment of personal belongings in the upstairs bedroom. He had been sitting in the same reading chair he was sitting in now, wearing the same corduroy pants, thinking of the sex with her—as he was now—and when she had finished packing and come downstairs with two suitcases, he dutifully carried them to the car and drove his wife to her mother's in Pequannock, New Jersey, Platonic Parkway due west.

Eastman ruminated on the event of four nights ago. He paged through his book of poets with ambivalence. He entertained taking his own life. Sex, violence, the two seemed, to Eastman, inherently connected, the poets knew it. There was so much despair and death in love. Both sex and violence provided Eastman with guilt. Did one starve or feed the other? Would he become a murderer of himself now that she was gone? He did not know whether the thought of suicide was real or simply an idea, a gut reaction to the loss. In fact, he was not imagining ways to do himself in, only the language of the idea drew on him. There was a penknife in his desk drawer, and for a second he imagined the dull blade that he so often used to open his mail, and the object frightened him. No, he knew then that he was not suicidal. He had not lost the will to live. Only to act alive.

A call came. To hear each of the lines in the empty house go off at once, the phone in the kitchen, the line in the hall, the new one he had installed in the upstairs bedroom, and the phone before him in his study, couldn't have been more lonely. The chimes throughout the house terrified him, made him aware of his loneliness. He still hid behind the metaphysical poets. It occurred to Eastman that it might be Penny calling to say that it was now over, and she was coming home. Or it would be the children. God, his boys; he had put them aside to brood.

"Yes?" he answered, clothing his voice with a little sorrow.

But it was not his wife on the other end, or the boys. It was Baxter Broadwater of the defunct *New York Herald,* now the *International Herald.* Eastman knew Broadwater from Harvard. The two were both on the staff of the *Advocate.* Broadwater was Pegasus, and for years Eastman despised him for his refusal to print one of Eastman's poems in 1942, "Of What May Ne'er Come to Pass," an elegy for Pearl Harbor. Eastman maintained the notion that if Broadwater wanted to run the same muck of mannered short stories and odes to prep school, then let it be his own mediocre funeral. The grudge lasted ten years, up until the day Broadwater married Elaine Pottsdam, younger sister to Eastman's first wife, Barbara. Eastman and Broadwater set aside their bad blood because they had become themselves blood, and on a cold evening in November 1952, at the rehearsal dinner at a restaurant lodge in New Hampshire, they reconciled.

"Broadwater, is that you? How's my favorite sister-in-law doing?"

"Just fine, Alan. Just fine. It's so nice that you still consider us family. We still think of you as family, I hope you've always known that."

"That must be why we haven't spoken for a decade."

"Oh, come now, Alan, it hasn't been that long."

"Okay, cut the crap, Broadwater. What is it you want? Your timing is impeccable, as always."

Broadwater, likewise, dropped his affectations. "Why, Alan, I'm amazed that you even picked up the phone. I have half a mind to think this is some sort of miracle."

"I'm expecting a call from someone important. And you, Broadwater, lack even a smidgen of importance."

"Now don't you want to know why I'm calling?" There it was, thought Eastman, Broadwater's prep school lilt (Deerfield) coming to the surface. He was not treating Broadwater indecently, for Eastman had learned to keep his guard up when dealing with the type of Harvard men he knew so intimately.

"Not in the least," Eastman said.

"Oh, come now. You're not still sore about that poem, are you?"

The poem in question had been written by Eastman as an undergraduate in 1941 when the news hit that the Japanese had bombed the American naval base. Young Eastman was coming back from the library, bundled in a peacoat, scarf, mittens, all sent by his mother. He walked across the frozen grass heading for Dunster House, his redbrick dormitory along the Charles. Martin Lutz, his roommate, had CBS radio turned up. The boy had been listening for the New York Philharmonic when the announcement overtook the airwaves. Eastman dropped his books to the floor once the report registered with him. *"The Japanese have today attacked Pearl Harbor."* Lutz, another Brooklynite from a similar middle-class background, had an older brother in the army. Arnold, a true fuckup, as Lutz described him. But Eastman knew, perhaps before Lutz did (that's how intuitive he was even at that age), this could be the final tussle that tipped America into war. Arnold's fate would be determined. Eastman saw the fear in Lutz's face. Something called to him between his roommate's despair and the posters of Virginia Bruce and Joan Blondell. The event alone became Eastman's political awakening, even though he hadn't any familial connections to the military like Lutz. For months he had been ambivalent to the prowar sentiment around campus that began with

Hitler's invasion of Russia. He took no stand next to the leftist Student Union protesting in the Commons. But this, this was Lutz, good old Lutz, staring off with thoughts of Arnie. Eastman sat down next to him on the bed. The boys said nothing, only listened to what transpired live. When darkness fell, an eruption began in the Commons, but Eastman stayed in. He took out the notebook he used for advanced composition and wrote the poem Broadwater referenced now. It would become Eastman's first bit of war writing, and it wasn't half bad either.

"Goddamnit, no," Eastman said into the phone. "I'm not still sore about that poem. I thought we put it behind us. But now that you bring it up, I should be sore about that poem, shouldn't I? You wouldn't have brought it up if you didn't want to hang it over my goddamn head."

Eastman continued to berate Broadwater. And it wasn't just meaningless lambasting against Broadwater's masculinity, although Eastman did fit in that he always thought Broadwater a homosexual at Harvard and wasn't the least bit convinced when Broadwater married Elaine Pottsdam. The two old classmates exchanged recollections of the controversy surrounding the poem's candidacy for publication in the *Advocate*. Eastman wanted the poem in the January issue, immediately following the attack on Pearl Harbor. Yet Broadwater found the poem exploitative, and far too leftist at a time when the *Crimson* had even shifted its stance to prowar. Broadwater's rank as Pegasus gave him seniority at the *Advocate*, and even though most of the staff knew Eastman as someone with literary flair and a good bit of talent, they took Broadwater's side, deciding not to run Eastman's poem. Eastman blamed Broadwater solely, though the decision against him was unanimous.

They continued to argue, circuitously perhaps, about what was respectable to print in those years. Eastman brought up the exclusion he felt he endured for four years among the WASPs of Cambridge as a Jew from Brooklyn. But now this was Eastman blowing off steam. Broadwater was the first person he was speaking to in the four nights since Penny's departure. Something had been building up in him, sitting at home, grieving, and Broadwater's timing, as Eastman had admitted freely, was indeed impeccable.

"Now, Eastman, listen to me here. Let's get serious a minute. I'm calling with a proposition for you."

"A proposition? You sound like a pimp."

"Now just a minute."

"Or should I say a madam," Eastman countered.

"Alan, they want to send you to Vietnam."

Right away Eastman perked his stance. Was it the rebellious sound of the word that got him? The foreignness that had infiltrated the American lexicon?

"Who? Who wants to send me to Vietnam? You're still as cryptic as you were thirty years ago."

"The higher-ups," said Broadwater. "Jay Husskler suggested sending someone big into Vietnam now that we've pulled out. You know, get the feeling on the ground, the sentiment. Get both sides of the thing. First name out of Husskler's mouth is you, Alan. Believe me, I nearly shat myself. That's why I'm calling."

"To tell me that you nearly shit your slacks, or that Husskler would think of me, the most important war journalist of our generation?"

"You're still pretty important, Alan. Around here you are, I admit that. Then we suggested someone a little more proven than you, currently. But Husskler, well, Husskler just shot it down."

"Fuck you. Moreover, who the hell do you think is more proven than me?"

"Now this is all said in confidence, Alan. Some of us feel you haven't done anything in a while, but Husskler still wants you. He said that. And I'm on your side on this. That's why I'm calling."

"I *am* important, you ten-cent pimp."

Eastman looked around his study and couldn't help feeling rather unimportant. His family was gone. His love, Penny, whom he drove to New Jersey willingly. *Coward, Eastman.*

"What day is it?" he asked Broadwater.

"Thursday, of course."

"Then it's been four nights."

"What has?"

"Never mind that now, Broadwater. I'm assuming you have a foreign bureau in Saigon."

"Yes, that's right."

"So why the hell are you calling me?"

"Between you and me, Alan, the paper's in trouble. I tell you openly because we have a history. A lot is at stake now, and, and, and . . ."

"You're stammering, Broadwater."

"Fuck you, Alan. Fact of the matter is a washed-up writer such as yourself, who may still have a few thousand words left in him, sending dispatches from Saigon and Hanoi is something that Husskler wants to print, and that, we can only *hope*, people want to read. Provided they give a shit. It's about selling papers, Alan. As Husskler called it, it'd be a revenue booster. I thought it would interest you since you might be able to get a book out of it."

"So Husskler wants to send me into certain death. Have me write a dispatch on getting my ass shot off, maybe stepping on a VC mine? I know what he's up to. He despises me as much as you do."

"I don't despise you, Alan. No one here despises you. Where do you get such notions? To be honest I haven't thought of you in years until Husskler suggested your name."

"Are you sorry you never ran my poem?"

"Jesus, Alan. Now we're back to that again."

"Well, are you?"

"We've cleared this up."

"Well?"

"No, I'm not sorry I never ran your damn poem. It was unfit for print. We determined that then. The atmosphere was too precarious."

"Precarious? There's nothing precarious about it. Broadwater, you've never been able to put yourself aside for the greater good. I'm afraid you can tell your boy Husskler to stick it up his ass. Tell him I was contemplating it. No. Tell him I was seriously considering his offer. I want you to relay that to him. 'Seriously considering.' And that you fucked it up over a silly little thing that happened to us thirty years ago."

"Eastman—"

Eastman hung up. Through the course of their conversation, he had never truly considered taking Broadwater up on his offer to report on Vietnam. He had been against the war from the beginning and had made it known. He appeared on television next to left-wing intellectuals and draft dodgers. He did not consider himself among the liberals, though he felt he was indeed a champion of the poor and a combatant to the conservative wing. To Eastman, America's involvement in Asia was nothing more than a misguided panic, an aggression without merit against an idea that, if spread, had zero consequences. Vietnam was merely a symbol to stop the idea in the Orient, a desperate act of fear, a refusal to admit defeat. It was an evil war that had brought every horror in America bubbling up from the sewer. Eastman said as much on television whenever they would grant him an appearance. So why would Husskler want him for the job? Eastman had gone to war himself, it was true. He knew the military mind intimately. Maybe it was precisely his discomforting feelings about Vietnam that made Husskler think of him. Though this would just make Eastman a walking target, and a bullet would just as likely come from Uncle Sam's chamber as it would a VC sniper.

The current situation in his study was Eastman himself. It was now Thursday. He had been in hiding for four days' time. He had eaten very little but wasn't yet hungry. He looked down at his worn pants, he could smell his odor, his rank. Each day he got older, his odor became more prominent, more unpleasant. It shed itself upon his reading chair, stuck itself to the wallpaper, stained sheets, folded itself into the closing of books. There was a time when he admired the way he aged, but now that he was alone, and could very well be alone for an undetermined amount of time, there was a panic apropos of aging. How would he attract another woman of Penny's stature? Who would accept his phallus, love his belly, crave his scent, which was quickly souring into a stench? No one, not in his state. He had spent his forties, his most attractive decade, with the love of his life. Now he felt old, fat, tired. His body was put aside for the sake of his marriage and children. Who would love him now? Who would bear him more children? Not that he could afford more. Eastman caught a glimpse of himself in the mirror above his desk. *Shameful.*

He waddled back to his reading chair. At his feet he found the book, *The Metaphysical Poets*, facedown on his Oriental carpet. He bent over to pick it up, feeling the age in his knees, and that's precisely when a most livid pain entered the small of his back. It felt as if he had been struck by a billy club. A club swung by Penny, this unforeseeable turn of events, and Broadwater, too. "Oh, fuck it!" he said as he toppled over onto the carpet. His arms were still taut and quick enough to prevent a head injury in the fall. Eastman slowly turned on his back, which was now riddled with pain. He was helpless and knew he hadn't the strength to move. After a few deep breaths, Eastman settled down. He reached for the book of poetry next to his head and found it opened to a most unfortunate poem ("Mortification"), which began with a most unfortunate phrase.

How soon doth man decay!

2

Eastman had purchased the Oriental rug on the Upper East Side of Manhattan from a private dealer. This was before they were married, when they were moving in together after an eight-month courtship. Penny, a PhD candidate in psychology at NYU, and Eastman, ten years her senior. He was a free-floating journalist, public intellectual, accidental cultural critic, and author of several books about America. For the book about war, which made his reputation in 1953, he was a finalist for the Pulitzer. (It went to his rival, Norman Heimish, a complete downer for journalism.) When he met Penny, he was still disillusioned about marriage from his first outing with Barbara. His daughter Helen's childhood had been ruined. But with a woman like Penny, a poisonous divorce would never rear its head.

Who was this woman of vibrancy and intelligence and sensuality? Her presence was that of a savior to him, for his finances were in turmoil, his first marriage was in the dumps, and with too many awful affairs behind him, he thought of love as a disadvantageous chess game where men were pawns to be sacrificed. For the rest of the fifties life took on a tinge of complete unfairness. Then he met Penny, a thirty-two-year-old brunette of Polish heritage, a quarter of that Latin, barely noticeable except in the summer, when she bronzed exceptionally. She was on the tall side and thin, quite the opposite of Eastman's tight-end flank. She was Penelope Domowitz. Once they were married, she was happy to take his surname. She even considered replacing her maiden name with King, from her grandmother's name Krol, all because Eastman had read in *Life* magazine that "Krol" meant "King" in Polish. He thought it would make her sound more dignified. "Oh, you don't think Penelope Eastman will sound dignified? Try it with this at the end." And she wrote out for him on a scrap of paper, *Penelope Domowitz Eastman, PhD.* "It's just a silly idea," he said to her. "Besides, it comes from a true place. You're a woman of immense power and I want my wife to be seen as such." "Well, you hold the chalice for the both of us, hon. I'm quite proud of the Domowitzes of New Jersey."

Still on his back, Eastman thought of the day he had gone with Penny to purchase the Oriental rug. This was how memory worked. One had to fall facedown into an object such as a dusty, worn carpet, and soon the unconscious, the navigator of the mind, automatically recalled how it all came to be. The carpet, too, not just the man lying on it.

The lovers, then unwed, had borrowed his cousin Sy's Volkswagen van in order to transport the rug.

They arrived at the address of a townhouse on East Seventy-seventh Street, an inconspicuous home that had been turned into a private showroom. Carpets were rolled and piled in every room of the townhouse; others were stacked and laid out knee high, smaller Afghani rugs adorning the walls. Eastman's allergy to dust had kicked in and right away he left the decision making to Penny, the soon-to-be woman of his house. They were rug shopping because he had just asked her to move in with him, and she expressed her feeling that his brick townhouse was too cold and bare for her taste. He'd buy her anything she wanted to make her comfortable. She would be giving up her small, sun-filled studio in Greenwich Village, and Eastman had lamented the moments he would dearly miss, the mornings bathed in bright light, feeling her hand slipping below the sheets to wake him. Those open-mouthed kisses, Penny's salt-lick skin, her small breasts, the musky scent of her cunt. Eastman knew how lucky he was to be with Penny. She was his unicorn, an intoxicating creature of myth. Before him, she had been engaged to a linguistics professor, Don Bradford. She was, in fact, still engaged to Bradford when she met Eastman at a Vietnam protest in Washington Square Park. Though Eastman wasn't aware of the engagement until after they'd slept together. First he followed her to a café, then they had a drink at a bar she liked, then a slice of twenty-five-cent pizza. The next night he called her and they met again. He spent that night at her apartment, which smelled to him of night creams and laundry detergent. "I have to tell you something," she said. She was sitting up in the moonlight with one foot on his bare chest. "I'm engaged to a man named Don. He's a linguistics professor."

He took in the information while trying not to show a flicker of jealousy. She looked to him for a reaction, some sign of how they were to proceed. As she awaited his answer, he thought that she was not only beautiful and brilliant, but that she had gotten herself into some hot water by going to bed with him and she was trying hard to be fair, which told Eastman that she was not confessing to being a liar but was looking to him for guidance. She wanted to be true. So he said back to her, "You want to invite me to the wedding," which took some air out of the situation and Penny let loose a big relief-filled laugh.

She didn't marry Don Bradford. She left Bradford for him, and soon enough Eastman was coming around daily to spend the night with her.

Those morning romps in her Greenwich Village apartment usu-ally lasted just a few minutes before Eastman burst inside of her with the intention to impregnate, to own her forever through some biological promise, a child, even though he already had one from his previous marriage and couldn't bear to take on any more debt. It was on one such morning, the two of them lying bare in the sun, spooning postcoitally, that Eastman snuggled his nose into the crevice of her neck and asked Penny to move in with him.

So they chose the rugs together, Eastman with his handkerchief over his nose, sneezing as if he were in a field of pollen, and Penny searching the townhouse decisively. She was adept at making good decisions, and this is what he felt he needed as he watched her through his glassy, allergic eyes. She lifted the heavy carpets around and spread them out with help from the dealer, a Russian. Eastman knew the accent well. It matched his mother's Russian-Jewish inflections. Then Penny found what she was looking for. "This one." She turned to Eastman, who was cowering a small distance away. "What do you think? For your study."

"Is it expensive?"

"I give you good deal," said the old Russian. "For this price you won't find better."

"Then we'll take it," Eastman said. Penny smiled delightfully at her lover across the room. It was a smile to make a man feel a sense of accomplishment. God, he loved her taste for the finer things, something he knew he lacked.

He'd like to say that it was precisely at this moment that he loved her, but he had loved her before then. Eastman couldn't say when he first knew he loved Penny. Wasn't it days or weeks or months before one confessed to being in love that one knew?

They ended up buying three rugs, in fact. Two more than expected. One for the upstairs bedroom and another runner from Turkey for the downstairs hallway. Once home, they rolled out the rugs in their respective places, the largest in his study. Penny tackled him atop the rug and they tumbled around the floor in each other's arms with dust from another continent peppering the air. He was a virile man then, strong, able to make her happy. Penny got on top of Eastman, kissed his forehead sweetly, his cheeks, then his lips. He sensed her playfulness turn into desire. She called to him with her tongue, her breath. Aroused, Eastman slid his hands beneath her summer dress, felt the smoothness of her hips, her sides, her whole body. Her scent filled his belly. She continued to kiss his mouth and he moved to rubbing her dark bush through her panties. He found her clit, how it easily soaked through the fabric. Penny unbuttoned his shirt and hiked herself up so that he could slip off her underwear. Like a gymnast she elegantly moved out of them. With his one hand beneath her dress he massaged her cunt. Penny called his name and hoisted herself over Eastman's face for him to perform cunnilingus, her knees on the carpet, her crevice over his face. She came easily. He wanted only to give her pleasure and let her rest, to lie in satisfaction. Penny was always a most considerate lover, and he drove her wild with desire. Unbuckling his pants, she asked if he had a preference. Would he like to come in her mouth or inside of her? He didn't know, he simply wanted to make her happy. "This will make me happy," she said, and brought his hard phallus into her mouth, returning a most delightful orgasm.

They were married within a year of moving in together.

Another call came, thank heavens. It broke his fantasy and he wouldn't die on the carpet after all. Though if he did, he'd want Penny to find him lying on a memory they both shared. The phone continued its toll. If it was Penny, she would come to his aid. But he wouldn't call her. Never would he admit defeat. Pride was too purposeful in a breakup.

He didn't want to appear before her on his knees, begging, but as the attractive man she had fallen for.

Eastman rolled onto his stomach, forgetting to buckle his pants, which had come undone during the thought of the rug purchase and the frolicking they once did on this very floor. His calloused elbows to the floor, Eastman willed himself across the study. He did a crawl just like he had learned as a young marine in Texas, crawling forth under barbed wire through dirt and dust, cradling his rifle. The pain, excruciating. The phone hung on and Eastman, red faced, vein protruding through his neck, hurried his snail pace to his desk, where the phone was. "Don't hang up, you son of a bitch."

He made it across the carpet all the way to the foot of his desk. The phone, still ringing, couldn't be reached from his position on the floor. He put out an arm along the desk's side and attempted to grasp the phone wire. He had short, albeit muscular, arms, and at moments like these they made him feel castrated. He reached out in pain along the desk's depth until he could feel the phone's cord. Now in his hand! he pulled gently, moving the phone to the desk's edge. *Pain is a state of mere discomfort,* Eastman scolded himself. He knew this through his military training. He was still in top command of his mind, at least he had that, and all the lower back pain in the world couldn't stop him from getting something done. Eastman took in a deep breath on his stomach. With his belly out, he rolled from side to side. The pain worsened. Using the roundness of his stomach as a ramp, he excruciatingly turned over onto his back. It was a small victory. Beads of sweat dripped down through the thicket of his eyebrows along the contours of his face, stopped by his handsome, prominent nose, the one he got from his dear mother. The ringing continued.

He once again took the phone wire in his hand and devised that he would pull the cord off the edge of the desk so that as the phone fell he would catch the receiver and the box separately, answer the call, and save himself from dying on the Oriental carpet. And if it was his unicorn on the other line, his one true love, he would tell her: *Look. Look what you've done. Here I am on our carpet. The blue-hued one in the study. Don't you remember, my dear?*

At the ready, Eastman gently tugged the cord off the desk. *Now!* He timed it correctly, the receiver he answered midair with his hand. However, the female part of the contraption, the box, came down and struck him direct in the eye. He tried to shield himself; his back seized. How could he have been so slow to defend himself against an appliance?

Nonetheless, the phone had been answered.

"Eastman? Are you there?"

It wasn't Penny. It was the sound of a man who had been recently neutered.

Eastman breathed a heated breath into the receiver. "I'm here."

"Eastman, now let me apologize." Again it was Baxter Broadwater. "I think we both lost our cool there and I want to be the first to say I'm truly sorry. I am truly and deeply sorry and I just feel terrible about it."

"Broadwater, listen to me."

"No, now you listen to me, Alan. I lost my cool there, and I want you to know that I apologize. Vietnam aside now. I'm being sincere. The fact that you humiliated me, I'm willing to put that aside."

"Broadwater, will you shut up for a minute and let me speak."

"Yes. Now go ahead, Alan, I'm listening."

"I need you to come over here."

Broadwater squirmed on the other end. "Oh, I don't know about that, Alan. If this is another one of your tricks, well now, I'm just not going to fall for it."

"Broadwater, shut up. I need help. My back has gone out and I'm laid out like a goddamn cripple on the floor. I'm in pain, you understand?"

"Now, Eastman, I'm not going to fall for any of your deceptions when I'm sincerely apologizing here. I'm being real now. All I ask is that you be real."

"I'm not deceiving you, you son of a bitch. I'm laid out on the floor of my study. I can't move. I've thrown out my back."

"That sounds terrible, Alan. I wish I could help."

"What do you mean you *wish*? *Wish*? I'm asking for your help, Broadwater."

"When is your wife due home? You must have someone coming."

Eastman was at a loss. There was no one coming for him, no one returning home. He had driven his unicorn away four nights ago and had been dwelling in his own misery. He had trouble answering Broadwater because the question was new to him. He hadn't a response, and on a whim, he had to create one.

"Broadwater, if you must know, my family is out of town."

"Where?"

"My mother-in-law's. I can't call there, they'll panic." It wasn't untrue.

"Well, Alan, you've caught me at a bad moment, I'm afraid. We're in the midst of preparing for the Watergate hearings."

"Up your ass, Broadwater."

"Now that's uncalled for, Alan."

Eastman knew he needed Broadwater's help. Anyone's help, and Broadwater was the only person who had the mind to call Eastman in four days' time. Maybe this was a sign that whatever was between them should be patched up. His back struck pain once again and it did not recede. Tears began to form in Eastman's eyes. He let out a whimper.

"Jesus, Alan, are you in that much pain?"

"My unicorn," he sobbed. "Baxter. My unicorn."

"What on Earth are you talking about?"

"She's gone."

"Alan, get ahold of yourself, will you?"

Broadwater stifled his laughter at the offices of the *International Herald*. That's when Eastman, laid out on his back, broken, defeated, really began to sob.

"Hold on, Alan," Broadwater said. "I'm sending someone straight away."

It was approximately two hours before Broadwater arrived with Dr. Wilhelm Spritz, a general practitioner who gave shots to the reporters at the *Herald* before they were due overseas. Spritz had just finished his rounds at the office, pricking various correspondents with needles, when Broadwater was able to persuade him to make a house call. "For whom?" Spritz inquired. "Alan Eastman. We're trying to get him to Vietnam. He's having some kind of nervous breakdown. Though I'll warn you. He could be full of shit." Spritz had read *The American War* in his native German (*Der Krieg im Pazifik*), a book based on Eastman's experience in the Pacific during the Japanese occupation. It was published when Eastman was just twenty-six, and it announced the emergence of a new talent. The book was a precursor to a new type of journalism: a novelistic history, full of character and voice and color and movement like the Russian novels Eastman so admired—*Anna Karenina* and *The Brothers Karamazov*, et cetera. His literary reputation was solidified, at least for the rest of his twenties, where the book sat on the best-seller list for fourteen consecutive months.

It was in the opinion of Broadwater and most of the American reading public that Eastman had squandered both his gifts and reputation in the intervening decades. But it was not an opinion shared by the good doctor, Spritz, a German by way of Dusseldorf, who came to aid a fallen American hero.

The two men, doctor and nemesis, hustled into the house, where they found Eastman at the foot of his desk, next to the phone, on his back. His pants were down around his ankles, his hair was wild, his odor was rank.

"Jesus, Alan," said Broadwater. "You need a bath."

"Are you here to help me, Broadwater?" Eastman said.

Broadwater put out a cautious hand, as if he had no intention of helping at all.

"I can barely move," he said. "Who's this? He better be a medic."

The doctor placed his valise down on the floor and opened it, extracting his stethoscope for an examination.

"I'm Dr. Spritz. Can you tell me where it hurts you?"

"My back. I've thrown it out. When I move the pain shoots into my groin."

"It could be psychosomatic," said Broadwater.

"Sit on it," said Eastman. The sight of Broadwater after ten years was like a punch to Eastman's stomach. He became enraged, forgetting the men had come here to help. "You should have published my poem, you son of a bitch." Eastman tried to grab Broadwater but winced from the pain as soon as he tried to move.

"Do not move, please," said the doctor, lifting Eastman's shirt. He placed his cold stethoscope on Eastman's chest and listened to his heart.

"Am I broken, Doc?"

"Quiet," said Spritz. "Have you had the trouble with the back before?"

"No. Most of the year I'm in good shape. Summers I tend to gain a little weight."

"What's wrong with his eye?" Broadwater said. Eastman's eye was half closed and red from the impact of the phone.

"The phone came down off the desk and hit me while I was trying to answer your goddamn call."

"Okay. Don't get so excited," said Broadwater. He shuffled through the papers on Eastman's desk.

"Where are you from, Doc?"

"Germany. Dusseldorf. Have you gained weight recently?"

"Twenty-five pounds, give or take. Like I said, I let go a little in the summer."

"You still have your place on the Cape?" asked Broadwater.

Eastman ignored him. The house, a dune shack on Cape Cod that he had expanded into a two-bedroom, was being rented by a former colleague of Penny's, a professor of Oriental studies, because the endeavor had become unaffordable. The only reason they didn't sell was because of its historic literary value (Eugene O'Neill, Tennessee Williams—dune-goers all). Eastman himself had written a good portion of a novel there, before the renovation. But it was a horrible investment that would soon be overtaken by the ocean. His place on the Cape was not a topic fit for discussion.

"We're going to sit you up, now," said the doctor.

Broadwater snickered. Eastman shot him a scowling look. The doctor left the room to look for a few pillows. He returned with the large decorative shams from the living room. The fabric had been picked out by Penny when they had the living room furniture reupholstered. Spritz placed the pillows at Eastman's side and indicated to Broadwater that it was now time to prop him up. "On three?" said Broadwater. The doctor acknowledged and counted off. "A one, a two, a three."

They lifted Eastman's heavy upper half as he yelled something incomprehensible. The doctor quickly propped him up on the pillows and allowed the patient to settle into the pain.

"Maybe we should pull up his pants?" Broadwater said. Then he came in close and spoke into Eastman's ear: "Eastman, do you want your pants on?"

"I'm not deaf, you idiot."

"Bring him some water, please," said Spritz.

Broadwater went to the kitchen to fetch a glass and Spritz went into his valise for some sedatives.

"I'm a great admirer of your books," Spritz said.

"That's nice of you to say."

His career was the furthest thing from his mind. He would banish all of his success if Penny would just come back to him.

Broadwater returned with the water and the doctor gave Eastman the sedatives. He slugged back two with the water.

"What was this you mentioned on the phone again?" asked Broadwater. "Something about a unicorn."

"I was in pain, I barely remember."

"You said 'My unicorn has left.' You went on and on about it."

"It was pain like I have never felt. Excruciating pain."

"You do know that unicorns don't exist. You do know that?"

"I was hallucinating from the pain. That's how bad it was."

"How is it now?" asked the doctor.

"I think the pills are working. You better leave the bottle. There's money in the top drawer. Take what you need."

"That's not necessary. I'll write you a prescription."

"Do you have some kind of fascination with unicorns, East-man?" asked Broadwater. "I mean, if you were hallucinating from pain, as you say, and you saw this mythical animal . . . I'm just thinking out loud. It comes from Greek mythology. Zeus was nursed by the she-god Amalthea. She was half a goat. In Christianity the unicorn became associated with Christ. Only you're not a Christian. She makes an appearance in Hebrew Scripture. A biblical beast. But then, your Jewish heritage doesn't interest you either. Were you having a vision?"

Eastman ignored Broadwater's musings. "Can we just leave it as a lapsed moment to be forgotten?"

"Astrology?" Broadwater snapped his finger. "Were you born a Capricorn?"

"I'm an Aries. It's bullshit."

"When was your wife born?"

"Stop this."

"January? February?"

"Sure."

"Capricorn. Your wife."

"Enough."

"Penelope. Capricorn. Unicorn. Your wife was not here to help. You were in pain. You were hallucinating, as you say. Tears. Your wit's end. Penelope, your wife, she's your unicorn."

"I'm at my wit's end now. And if you don't shut up, I'm going to come over there and snap your neck."

"It is a goat, the astrological symbol," said the doctor, "not a uni-corn." The two men ignored him.

"You said something else to me," Broadwater continued. "On the phone. My unicorn, you said. She's gone."

"Doctor, I'll pay you five thousand dollars if you coldcock this man in the face."

"So much violence. Enough, you two!" said Spritz.

"Hmm. But you said she's at your mother-in-law's. So that's it. She left. She's gone. Gone away to her mother's. Not much of a mystery."

Eastman was not full of rage. If he was not laid out, yes, it's true, he would have resorted to violence. To slugging Broadwater in his mouth, perhaps wrestling him to the ground, neutering the man he had already humiliated over the phone. But Eastman was not full of rage. Broadwater, running his mouth, had pushed a button in Eastman so deep that it shut off any emotion he could feel, and instead he felt emptiness, hollowness, darkness.

"So," said Broadwater, "how are your children?"

3

The two men were gone now. Broadwater, the Dusseldorfer Spritz. Once the pain medication set in, they were able to help him on his feet and took him upstairs to bed. They set him up with a pitcher of water, crackers, a jar of peanut butter, country jam, a rounded spreading knife. No sharp objects, he instructed, lest he resort to suicidal thoughts once again. He wasn't at the stage to consider the children, because he was not giving up. He was still possessed by the missing variables in Penny's equation.

There were always signals when dealing with the disruption of two mates—lovers so confident and set in their ways and in their bond that they neglected to talk about the particular ailment until it shaped itself into a cancer and spread. Decisions were put into question. Signs manifested.

But what were the signs? And was he too self-absorbed to notice? Had his Penny been hiding her discontent? How could he have been so clouded to overlook her unhappiness?

Weeks ago, in the very bed where he now lay dormant, there was an incident during their lovemaking. Penny had been away for a weekend conference in Boston, leaving Eastman in New York to care for the boys. It was their routine to fuck on the night when one returned, even if it wasn't particularly desirable. That night she began by sucking his cock for a short period, and once he was hard enough, she got on top to ride him. He grasped for her breasts, but she pushed his hands down in a way that could be described as irritable. She then held his hands against the mattress. Eastman didn't think anything of it. He liked to be dominated, he encouraged it. But the restraint seemed out of place during this routine fuck. His hard-on began to recede as she continued to thrust atop him. That's when Penny uncharacteristically guided one of his hands to her throat. Her neck was long, like her torso. On it she wore a pendant he had given her many years ago for her birthday, a jade stone on an elegant gold chain. Eastman did not think anything of the movement and returned his hand to one of her breasts, but she reached for his hand again and placed it at the base of her neck. He did not know what to do. Could he be so prudish to shy away from what she wanted? He had once been eager to try everything, to fuck however he pleased, however she pleased, and he, in fact, thought of himself as a man who had tried everything. At his age, he knew what he wanted from sex. To come inside her mouth or her cunt (usually from behind), and if the mood struck them both as it did a few occasions a year, inside her anus. So he casually left his hand there as she continued to ride him, and he held her gently by the neck, keeping her aloft, as it were. Her long thrusts transitioned into tight squirms, a sign she was getting ready to do her final push into orgasm. "Do it," she said. "Do what?" he said. "Squeeze." "Squeeze?" He removed his hand from her neck and placed both hands on her ass where he proceeded to squeeze. She became irritated with him. She took his hand once again and placed it directly on her throat, not at the base of her neck any longer, but over her larynx. He was sure now of what she wanted. And as if it couldn't be any clearer, she said, "Choke me." Would he get any pleasure out of this? Strangling his unicorn? But Eastman did what she asked. He squeezed. And as he squeezed his cock expanded to its full capacity. Yes, he had a raging hard-on from this violent fantasy of hers. Eastman was afraid of this. Therefore he loosened his grip and merely kept his hand on her neck. "Harder . . . Choke me! Fuck me! Choke me! Fuck me!" "Penny," he said. But at the risk that she would stop fucking him, he tightened his grip, felt her glands, throat, muscle, the parts beneath her delicate surface. Her panting was silenced and she fucked him harder. He was stifling her from the neck up. Was this the passion she wanted? Her beautiful flushed cheeks began to turn a purple of sorts. She opened her mouth as if she were to dry heave. She couldn't breathe. He loosened his grip slightly, retaining some pressure, lax enough so that she could breathe. "Tighter," she said once she caught her breath. And he did, only his hand was tired, so he placed two hands upon his Penny's throat and tightened. She was being strangled (Eastman, the strangler), and as she took pleasure in this erotic asphyxiation, she rubbed her clit rapidly, harder and with more purpose than he'd ever seen, and she burst into an aching orgasm, still with his cock inside her, though he was unsure whether she needed it. She sat on top of him for a moment and refused to look into his eyes. She collapsed on his sweaty chest; his erection receded. And then she rolled off him onto her side of the bed. She had no intention of finishing him off. The two of them didn't speak, nor did they speak about it in the days and weeks that followed.

He had no appetite. When had he eaten last? He didn't know. He felt as he did when he fasted with Penny, like on their trip to India in 1965. They stayed on the grounds of an old temple that a healer put Penny in touch with. They took a bus that traveled on dirt roads from Bangalore to Mysore, through impoverished shantytowns, children barefoot and begging wherever they stopped, all the way to the ancient temple on the hill. The stench of garbage would carry over the gates of the temple and breach the sacred grounds. Penny had been practicing yoga under the guidance of a Rupert Vaz, a healer to the upper echelon of Manhattan. She was successful in getting Eastman to follow her all the way to India. He thought of her yoga as a quick fad popularized by the Beatles and movie stars, though he enjoyed watching Penny bend over in her underwear at home, doing leg splits on the hardwood floors that made her ass look like a puddle of dreams. There was also a bit of jealousy in him, and so when she went to study with Vaz, he thought no one man would get to see her spread-eagle without Eastman in the room. So they practiced a few months together. There was sexual energy in yoga and Eastman felt it a good match for his creativity, health, mind, and phallus. Then a weekend in India. Mysore. They fasted, meditated, stood on their heads; by the end of the day they were too tired to fuck. Candles kept the garbage stench at bay. He liked living in his Indian garb, the roominess of a white bed dress. He experienced the delight of what it must be like to be a woman in women's clothing.

The lack of food provided clarity. Eastman could move from memory to memory without overlapping anxiety. He strained to locate the course of their problems, which he believed was locked inside his memory, and only then would he eat and allow himself to rest.

He thought back to the night in question. Penny, standing in his study, confronting him about their happiness. She had come in guns blazing, late that night for dinner. He thought they would go out once she arrived. She was not herself, entering the house late, transformed, a devious bitch, possessed by the idea to flee his hold. In the kitchen she took a meek but accusatory stance. She had told him earlier in the day that the boys would be at the Stevensons', a lie. She had taken the car and driven them all the way to her mother's in New Jersey. His own children knew the score before he did.

"I'm leaving you, Alan," she said.

He thought he heard wrong, and so he said to her, "But where do you want to go to dinner?"

"You didn't hear me, Alan. I said I'm leaving you."

He demanded why, and the usual stock answers that he had once heard from Barbara came tumbling out. She didn't have a good enough reason and so they accused one another, unleashing the history of their infidelities. Infidelity, in Eastman's eyes, wasn't a sound reason to split up a marriage. He had his share of affairs over the course of their ten years, but in Penny he had met his match, and that night it came out that she, too, had her own set of lovers. A colleague in the Anthropology Department, before Toby, their first child, was born. A subway musician, a busker, who found her irresistible. And then Rupert Vaz, the yogi healer, who could do a full split on the floor. He suspected that limber devil, but he could never confirm it. Eight in total, she had said. Eight in ten years. Double his number. He knew about some of the men before, it wasn't news. They didn't bother him for more than a few days at a time because she was his. Plus nothing carried on for too long. He understood those moments when a partner strayed, for he had placed himself in similar circumstances, with other women. Monogamy was an insincere ideal, though he had always wanted it. So what were a few sour nights in a decade?

"I'm not leaving you because of your behavior, Alan. I knew who you were when I married you. You had your reputation. I saw the way women treated you. All those little publishing whores."

"Then why, Penny?"

"You've fallen out of love with me. Don't you see?"

"That's completely false. I do, in fact, love you."

"*In fact?* You're confirming a forgotten feeling. You're no longer passionate. Not about me. Not about anything at all."

"That's nonsense. I feel passionate about plenty. Our children, for one."

"But you won't fight for me. You lack the passion to do it."

"I am fighting. What the hell do you call this?"

"No. You're not fighting for me, Alan."

"If it's a counterattack you mean, that is because you're ambushing me, Penny. I've had no idea how you felt, you've given me no notice."

"You're blind."

"Do you still love me, Penny?"

She didn't answer. He took her hand; she pulled it away. He held it with both hands, trying to communicate his desire for her. He was telling her the truth. She looked to the floor, her hands cold. If it was another man, he suggested, they could try an open marriage for a period, to keep up appearances for the children. He knew what divorce was. His first daughter, Helen, now nineteen, he hardly saw. She grew up with Barbara and her new husband in Mexico. Divorce would estrange him from his boys. He didn't want a repeat of what he felt he'd done to Helen.

Penny dismissed the open marriage. Referring to the infidelities, she said, "That's what we've already had, isn't it?"

No, he didn't want the open marriage either, of course not. I want you!

"Prolonging this into an open marriage will only delay the inevitable," she said.

"And what is the inevitable?"

That is when he knew there was another man. Someone who had stolen Penny's affection, love, mind, and body. Stolen it from him when he was at his weakest and least attractive.

He wanted a name. "What's his name?"

After all the honesty about the affairs that they had confessed, she was now lying to him. She wouldn't tell him who it was, or how it happened, because she was ashamed. He saw this clearly now.

"There's someone else," he said.

"There isn't." She was a terrible liar, unable to hide from her desires. Then she admitted, "There's the idea of someone else."

"So what we're talking about is that you've fallen out of love with me. And you stand here accusatory, blaming me, when it is you, after all."

"You won't fight for me." She was in tears. Again, she stuck to her lie, that another man was just an idea. But Eastman knew differently.

"Mother of my children, I'm not going to beg you. But it's not me who isn't fighting. It's you. You quit fighting. Remember that. When you're sucking his dick, whoever he is, I want you to remember that."

"You're a pig."

"I'm a realist. I see the reality even when you can't. You call it the idea of someone else. I call it a whore."

Penny slapped him. He had crossed a line. They hadn't fought like this in years. Never had he called her anything but his love, his treasure, his Penny, his unicorn. Was this not the fighting she so assuredly accused him of not doing?

He deeply regretted his attack. The slap to his face made him subservient. Perhaps this is what she was driving at. If she could get him to lose his cool then she would have every reason to walk out the door. Eastman felt ashamed, and he was scared of himself now. This was the start of the depression that would set in for four nights. She had two suitcases packed upstairs, hidden in her closet, and like the good husband so eager to assume his role as ex, he carried the bags outside and loaded the car. The rest of the night played out as if he were watching himself go through a series of mistakes. He no longer saw her through his loving, deeply engaged eyes, but through the eyes of the omniscient.

The drive to New Jersey they made in silence.

Now alone, Eastman ate in bed a dinner of stale crackers and peanut butter. The jam, after opening it to find crumbs and butter coagulating at the top from the boys' breakfast, he dropped to the floor in frustration. He did not want anything so sweet. He drank a glass of water and took two painkillers, which alleviated the returning ache in his back. And then he took an additional half to alleviate all the other pain, and very soon he fell off into a deep sleep.

He awoke midway through the night, talking to himself. What he was dreaming of he could not remember. But he woke with a powerless feeling, as if in the dream he had been harassed, beaten, perhaps even sodomized. The dream was truncated by an overwhelming urge to pee. All that water. All those pills. If he had let go in bed, he truly would have felt at his lowest. Eastman got up. His back was not as bad as before, the Dusseldorfer's magic was working. Rest had been good for him. He made his way through the dark hallway to the bathroom, finding the light switch. The toilet seat was still down from Penny's last use. He had been using the downstairs bathroom for the past four nights. Too tired to lift the seat, Eastman carefully urinated between it but his aim was not what it used to be and he quickly soiled the porcelain U. Then once he sprayed his urine on the seat he decided, who the hell cares, and painted the seat and bowl in urine.

It occurred to him that if he couldn't have her, if he was indeed losing her to another man, then he would resort to getting her back into the house. The boys needed their home. They couldn't be taken out of school because she selfishly wanted to be with her *idea* of someone else. How ridiculous! He would get her back into the house, tell her he was moving out, that she should be here, in her home, the boys near their friends, in school.

Over the years the four Eastmans had developed into quite the traditional family. They had dinner every night at seven. Penny did most of the cooking, but he handled the shopping before she returned from work. The boys set the table each night and helped their mother dry dishes after the meal, while Eastman went to the den to fire up the television. The clacking of the dishes and the laughter and voices coming from the kitchen were comforting.

Both he and Penny had respectable careers that gave each of them some recognition on a national scale. Penny, in her field of psychology, had been publishing papers consistently in *Psychological Science* and *Social Perspectives,* and she taught three classes a semester at NYU, where she was building a fast case for tenure. Her work sometimes called her away to give lectures at academic conferences. All of which was okay by Eastman, because he worked out of his study at home and was there when the boys got home from school.

Toby and Lee went to a Quaker school in Brooklyn, where many of the teachers were young men and women of the counterculture scene. Both Eastman and Penny were happy with the progressive approach to education, though he was not altogether satisfied with their lax ideas on grading, for the school stressed creativity over grades and this irked him somewhat. Eastman had excelled in school because he was motivated by grades. Grades created competition. How else could a poor Jewish boy have measured himself against the more physically gifted boys? He certainly couldn't measure up physically—he was a short stack, like his children.

Recently over dinner, Toby and Lee showed their parents their report cards and Eastman always looked forward to this time in the year. For every A, he paid them. If the school wasn't going to stress the importance of grades, then he would. "Stop spoiling them," Penny said. "They shouldn't be driven by money in order to do well. They should be driven by knowledge. The desire to learn is enough." "What's a little incentive?" he told her. She rolled her eyes as he gave each of them two dollars. It made them happy. Before they went to their rooms to put the cash in a sock drawer, Penny gave them each a big kiss on the cheek. "From me, you get a kiss," she said. Then Toby and Lee ran upstairs. "Penny," he said, "it's my own way of showing I appreciate them. I did the same thing with Helen, and look how she turned out. She's at Vassar with a partial scholarship." "Okay," Penny said. "We'll keep them on the payroll if we must."

Eastman flushed the toilet and ran his hands under the faucet in the dark. He shuffled down the hallway and stopped in the doorway of the boys' shared bedroom. The orange streetlight came through their window and he could see the two made beds, empty. Their kids would pay in the end for her lack of judgment.

Were Penny to move back in the house, they could both work together on a proper separation. They hadn't yet talked about divorce. The ink wasn't dry on the papers yet. "The ink, the ink, the ink," he said, walking back to his room. He needed to talk to her about moving back. Call her. It was five-thirty in the morning. Penny would just be waking up for her morning yoga. Call her. Do it. Get her back in the house. You'll move out. You'll get a hotel. You'll make something up. But if you can get her back in here, then there will be a discussion.

Call her.

Eastman got his address book then went to the phone on her nightstand. He hated having a phone in their room. To be reached at all hours was an unnecessary luxury and an incessant pest. But now he saw why she had insisted they have it in the boudoir. "For emergencies, Alan. For whenever we are apart." He looked up the number for Cathy Domowitz, his mother-in-law, and dialed the rotary.

"Oh, hello?" It was Cathy, barely awake. Now that it was 1973, did everyone have a phone beside the bed?

"Cathy, it's Alan. I need to speak to Penny. Is she awake?"

"Alan, what time is it?"

"It's still early. I'm sorry for waking you."

"Can't this wait till morning, Alan? I'm sure she's still asleep."

"I'm sorry, it can't, Cathy. It's a matter of life and death."

"You can't be serious."

"I'm sorry for the disturbance, but you have a phone by your bed-side, yes?"

"Of course."

"And it is for times of emergency, I assume? Or is it to ask people to call back later? This, Cathy, is one of those times."

"Hold on, Alan. I'll wake her."

Was she not already awake? It occurred to Eastman maybe for the first time that Penny was just as depressed and desperate as he was. He should have called earlier, days earlier, but he had been too stubborn. He wanted to punish her, to allow her to see what life was like without the man she'd spoken to every day for the past decade.

Penny took the phone. "Yes, Alan." Her voice was tired, asleep. Intimations of her in bed next to him. The plan, the one he conjured in the bathroom as he urinated on their floor, was escaping him. Her voice was paralyzing. It had this effect on him, turned him into a little puppy, dying to please.

"Penny."

"What is it? What's wrong?"

"Everything."

"Can this wait a few hours? You've woken me up."

"No."

She paused and told her mother to go back to bed, that she would be taking the call.

"I want to apologize, Penny. For my behavior the other night when we fought. I said some things I regret, and that wasn't right."

"I understand, Alan. I understand what I'm doing to you."

"So you feel it, too."

"Yes, of course. I feel terrible."

"Then you must come home. This is your house as much as it is mine. You've overreacted. And I have come to the conclusion that I must respect what you want, as you want it. The boys need to be home, they can't be moved. And so you will live in our home, not me. I will leave. For the sake of the boys, Penny. You can't just pull them out of school."

"It's summer, Alan. They don't have school."

"You can't take them away from their friends, then."

"You don't know what's going on with them, and you certainly don't know what's going on with me."

"Because you haven't told me, Penny. You must talk to me."

She was silent. It was a silence that could have lasted into the morning hours. It was the start of the fifth day; more had been accomplished in less time. Peace treaties, wars fought and won. But she was silent. She wasn't going to explain anything to him. She hadn't the energy at this time of the morning. And so Eastman, faced with a desperate silence, a black silence that could determine the rest of his life, decided to act, to fight, to push against darkness.

"They're sending me to Vietnam, Penny."

"Who? What are you saying?"

"The *Herald*. Baxter Broadwater and the boys upstairs. They're sending me to Vietnam. I'll be embedding with the few marines left. It's a mission that could very well reverse the course of the war. A very dangerous mission. Men will die. But if they are successful, and if the story is told properly, in my way, it could have a true impact on the way the country sees this awful pig fuck of a war."

"But Alan, you've been against the war from the start. You've demonstrated. You've given speeches. You've been arrested. They probably have a file on you."

"I'm not fighting in it, Penny. I'm going as a correspondent. Although I'll probably have to carry a firearm for protection. It'll be a hairy mission. That's for sure. Saigon. The field. Then to the north. Hanoi. Possibly covering a subsequent surrender. But if I make it through alive then I'll be home free."

"Alan, you're not thinking this through."

"There's nothing to think about, Penny." He wanted to say to her, *You've left me! You've left me no choice! It's you who haven't thought this through!* But in order for a story to have true effect and merit, one must allow the reader to discover the implications on her own. And at all costs hide personal ambition. It is a story. It has no ownership. And so he allowed the words to resonate. He would be fighting for her. Just not in the way she thought.

"When are you leaving?"

"A matter of weeks. Sooner possibly. Days. I'm waiting for my visas. A fixer. A translator. But I'd like to see you before I go. I'd like to spend time with you and the boys."

"Alan," she said, as if she wouldn't give in. And so he pressed.

"Just in case," he said.

"Just in case of what?"

"You know."

"What are you saying?"

"It's a war, Penny, anything can happen in a war."

"Oh my God, Alan." She began to cry. It was an opening to deeply affect her, to change her mind once and for all.

"So will you come, Penny? Will you move back so I can spend these last few days with my family?"

"Alan, you're making this impossible. I can't do this right now. I just can't."

"I know this is a lot to take in at the hour. But sleep on it and call me in a day or two. I'll keep you abreast of the situation as it happens. I don't have a lot of time, but I have some. Will you be at your mother's? Is that where I'll be able to reach you?"

"What? Yes."

"Is there another number? If I need to get in touch with you."

"This is the number you will call."

"I would need to move quickly for the sake of the mission. Things could be expedited in my situation. I need to be able to reach you if that happens."

"Jesus Christ, Alan."

There. He was putting the brakes on Penny's affair in the making. Let it be just a simple idea for the time being. Let her get her stubborn head around the situation before she could move on. She was not only leaving him but breaking up a family, it was a disaster already, so why not wield the disaster.

"I will be here, at my mother's," she said. They ended the conversation and she didn't say I love you and neither did he.

After the call, Eastman went into Penny's bedside drawer, looking for answers. The drawer smelled of old teak and jasmine. There were her night creams, hairpins, massage oils, perfume, a dildo wrapped in a velvet cloth. And then a summer scarf, paisley and purple, that he had given to her on her birthday a few years ago. He remembered picking it out, searching all the top department stores in New York until he found the perfect item that reminded him of her.

He picked up the scarf, determined to smell it, to recall all the times she wore it with him. And just as he did, a matchbook fell out of its center onto his lap. It had been carefully folded into the scarf. It was a matchbook from the Waverly Inn, a restaurant they'd never been to together. He was a little hurt that she'd left the scarf, something he gave her, but he was more curious as to why she had hidden a matchbook in it. He opened the matchbook and discovered a phone number scribbled on the inside flap in someone else's hand. Drawn next to the number was a little heart. Her new lover, perhaps? He convinced himself it was. So an affair had already started. His suspicions were confirmed.

Eastman gritted his teeth and tried to remain calm. There was a rage in the pit of his belly, he could tear out somebody's throat, kill a man with his bare hands. His thoughts turned bloody, primal.

It was invigorating, a feeling Eastman had not felt in days, months, years. Hatred, beastly violence. It made him feel alive. And with matchbook in hand, Eastman stood from the bed with no pain in his back to speak of.

Broadwater was right. It had been psychosomatic.

4

Eastman set off that morning with good intentions, focused on becoming someone he once was. He felt Penny was giving him a chance. Despite what he had said to her over the phone, Eastman still had no intention of going to Vietnam for the *Herald*. It was a lie. Penny would be relieved to know that Eastman was, in fact, not going to Vietnam, and this is what he wanted to avoid at all costs. A lie, a good one, was duplicitous. Once Penny began negotiations to get him to stay he could barter for his marriage.

It was certainly not the worst lie told over the course of the war.

Upon leaving the house, Eastman had placed in his breast pocket the matchbook from the Waverly Inn, the thief's number, so he presumed, written on the inside flap. He patted his breast every few blocks to make sure it was there.

He took the subway into Manhattan and got off at Union Square. A protest was in progress at the foot of the park. Young men and women with guitars, beads, bandannas. Hippies, dopers, vets, students, and dropouts. They sat around cross-legged. Some of them, it seemed, had been camping out in the park. The nights had been warm enough. But this sudden encounter with youth gave him an intimation of tiredness. He could smell their fatigue through the musk and body odor and marijuana smoke. This generation was tired. They had been spit out, abused, drafted for a decade. Still, they were determined to keep their lives.

A sign hung over the southwest park entrance.

Among the soldiers who died:
12 were seventeen
3,092 were eighteen
14,057 were twenty
9,662 were twenty-one

He took his notepad out of his hip pocket and wrote the figures down. He would check them later against the records he kept of the war, the news clippings stored in a file in his desk.

As he walked deeper into the park, he found men sleeping on benches. They were veterans in their twenties, looking much closer to death than he did. Some homecoming. He had a point of comparison. Back in the winter of 1945, he had returned from war to his wife, Barbara, his college sweetheart. She was devastated to hear that he would only be home for a month's time before he was to return to the Philippines to begin a job with the Associated Press.

His first few days back, they stayed with his parents in Brooklyn Heights. The apartment was too loud and too small. His mother, Frances, scolded his father, Bert, until his father became irate, fleeing the apartment for the track. He remembered being home with his wife and feeling like he was thirteen. Fran would be washing dishes in the kitchen, the clinking sound of the china, the pots against pans. He couldn't think there, he felt he had more room in the belly of an aircraft carrier among a fleet of marines. He fled with Barbara to the Catskill Mountains, rented a cottage, where they caught up on much of the lovemaking he had missed while deployed. It was a celebratory time, postwar. After a few weeks of country living, which relaxed his mood, they returned to Brooklyn. He left her with his parents and flew back to Manila. She was willing to let him go for the purpose of starting a career as a correspondent and to begin the book he spoke about constantly.

Half of Eastman's time as a correspondent was spent in Manila, reporting on the rebuilding of a Japanese-occupied city. Because of his service he gained access the other correspondents didn't have. He frequented the Officers' Club at the Manila Hotel, had drinks with lieutenants and generals. They trusted him not to write anything too tell-all. Eastman was fine with it. He was not after a story for the AP, he was interested in talking to people for his book—the men who were still stationed in the Philippines and their stories of patrols and ambushes in a jungle thicket of death. He got them talking, under the guise of being a reporter writing about reconstruction. He had a tremendous memory then and would retain whole conversations until he returned to his hotel room to expel them onto paper. He wrote Barbara five times a week, and after thirteen months with the AP he quit and returned home. Eastman had made enough cash, including his military severance, to support his wife. They lived cheaply in Brooklyn in a small one-room apartment, spent summers on the Cape, and after two years of writing and living off his savings and Barbara's salary, he had completed the manuscript that would become *The American War.*

His generation had their share of shell shock and misspent youth, but Vietnam had changed the dialogue.

Eastman left the park and the singing and chanting behind him. He walked south along Fourth Avenue, where the booksellers were just opening their doors. So many of them were gone now—Gilman's, Loon Kramer's, Schultes'. Weiser's was still standing on the corner. Eastman stopped in front of the window to gaze at their selection. He saw a Norman Heimish title, his nemesis for the Pulitzer in 1953. He recognized most of the authors, none of note. Then a young woman, not old Sam Weiser, wheeled out a cart of discounted titles to be placed on the twenty-cent rack. She smiled at Eastman then unloaded the books hurriedly and without care. She went back inside and turned over the sign on the glass door to OPEN. Eastman flipped through the fresh stack of used dreck. He had an appointment with his manager in an hour. Maybe he'd find something to read at a café to kill the time. Shuffling through the used paperbacks, he desperately searched for a copy of a Norman Heimish title in order to gloat. He could send it over to Heimish with a note. *Sticking out of the twenty-cent bin, plain as day. Good ol' Weiser's! Your pal, Eastman.* Instead he pulled a copy that was familiar. It was the movie edition of his *American War*, generically retitled *The Pacific*. The producers of the film had demanded a title change, and his publisher released this horrific edition with the movie's poster on the cover. Palm trees, biplanes, tanks, and illustrations of the actors on a poster-white backdrop. For less than a subway token, a masterpiece. Worse still, he was responsible for penning the screenplay in six months' time in a Hollywood Hills bungalow back in 1958. That damn movie reversed his credibility. But in those years he was too far into fame, pussy, marijuana, Seconal, and bourbon to realize it. Eastman looked around the street as if there had been some mistake. Even the movie edition didn't deserve to be remaindered into the outdoors.

He stormed into the shop, where the young woman sat behind a desk reading the *Herald*. "Can I have your pen?" he asked.

She didn't even look up when she handed him a ballpoint. He took it from her and opened it to the title page, crossed out the dummy title, and restored the original.

The American War

"Man, you're buying that, right?" The woman's attention had been gotten.

"No, young lady. I'm restoring it." He signed the copy with anger, nearly tearing through the page. "Now it's worth more than two dimes." He went to the window and reached over the display to pull the copy of Norman Heimish's book, *A Winter in May.* What dreck. He threw it over his shoulder and put his book in the window.

The shopkeeper got up from the desk. "What do you think you're doing, man?"

"I told you. Restoring a masterpiece. Now it's signed. Sell it for more so you can have an abortion."

"What the fuck are you even saying?"

He didn't know. A slight embarrassment overtook him. She was just a lowly bookseller, possibly a student at NYU. His Helen's age. She hadn't plucked his book from their shelves to place in the twenty-cent bin. He shouldn't have taken offense. It was too late now. Eastman stormed out of Weiser's and continued down the street past the other bookshops. Fourth Avenue Bookstore, Pageant, Raven, Stammer's. He remembered the fifties, suddenly. When his book had just been released, his friend Claude Forché threw him a party in Claude's large apartment on Twelfth Street overlooking Book Row: his debut into the New York literary world, a party in his honor, a book of hard labor. His parents were there. His sister, Carla. Aunts and uncles from Brooklyn and New Jersey. Friends from Harvard. His old roommate Lutz came with a date. Elaine Pottsdam, his sister-in-law, who hadn't yet met Baxter Broadwater. Only Barbara was absent. She was home sick with the flu, and the baby, Helen, had stayed with her.

Eastman wore a three-piece suit for the occasion and got drunk on red wine. People he didn't know came to congratulate him. He appeared to this new world not the married man he was, but a bachelor. And so that's the role he played. Women at the party gravitated toward him. They were flirtatious. Once the members of his family left, the party continued into the early morning hours and Eastman continued to drink and flirt, even with his sister-in-law, until Claude put Elaine in a cab. By the bar table he got drunk off bourbon. In the bathroom he smoked marijuana with a hip girl who took her dress off and allowed him to feel her breasts, then threw him out. Later that night, the editor Meredith Chase propositioned him. He was rather drunk and incoherent, lounging on Claude's sofa. She said she wanted to go to bed with him on the night of his debut. "Let's make it a night never to be forgotten." "But I have a wife," he said. "Where?" "She's home with the flu." "Then you're free. Come over and fuck me. I'll call in sick. In the morning, you can have me again." She took his hand and ran it between her legs, where he found only darkness.

In a night, the tone of his life had changed. He had his first affair. Meredith Chase was a powerful, free-spirited woman who commanded attention. She had been piercing him with looks the whole evening. Had she seduced him into it? No, he wanted her. He wanted her from the moment he saw her that night. Moreover, he wanted what she represented. Literary promise. A world he felt he deserved. But in her parkside apartment, somewhat sobered, he had trouble getting a full erection. The phallus was still under the mind's rule. She was attractive and exciting and knew how to turn a man on. And he was in the wrong, he knew it. He could have stopped himself. But Eastman was helpless to fame. And so he worked against his own conscience in order to achieve what an affair granted. A night of humping. *I'm angry. I'm angry, goddamnit. Angry that Barbara wasn't here to share my success. Damn them! Damn them all!* His blood was hot. He convinced himself he needed to be in Meredith's bedroom and all the bedrooms that fame would demand of him. He was hateful. He fucked Meredith with such abhorrence. His anger eventually helped him achieve an erection. If he fell asleep he was woken by her hand, her mouth, the bristles of her cunt. It all seemed clean, exciting, naughty, defiant, and of course, absent of love.

A thing had died in Eastman. Something he had not even known to protect.

A year later the marriage to Barbara was over.

5

He would not be put down by a silly used-book store that was just a limb on a dying animal. Weiser's would soon be gone like the others. And if Norman Heimish was who they were using to bait customers in the door, then he wished them death. He was twice the writer Heimish was. It was a simple fact! Eastman walked north for twenty blocks, hatred spewing out of his mouth like a backed-up sewer. He muttered on about Penny, Heimish, the whole lot of them.

He stopped along the way and entered a phone booth.

Who was the man she was seeing? Who was the man inside the matchbook? He imagined Penny with her lips wrapped halfway around a stranger's cock and Eastman's face quivered with repulsion. This most intimate act had happened already, right under his nose. He felt stupid suddenly, for not anticipating it.

He took the matchbook out of his breast pocket. The logo of the Waverly Inn. They had never been there together and he assumed she had gone there with him, the phantom. He imagined them seated across from each other, drinking wine, deciding together on a meal, the beginning of an affair. He opened the matchbook to his phantom's scribble. The phone number and little heart. He picked up the receiver, put two dimes in the phone, then listened to the dial tone. He hadn't thought of what to say. Most of the anger was dedicated to Penny, not the mystery man. How could he channel it now and put in a call that would change the course of events? He was always able to rely on his ability to degrade, after which it wasn't uncommon for his target to take a swing at his furry head. But no . . . a call wouldn't do. There would be no satisfaction in it. An operator came on the line and said, "City and state please."

He hung up the phone and retrieved his change. He was scared in that cramped phone booth. Men and women seemed to soar by around him, each one of them faceless. He let the possibility that she wasn't coming back sink in. Penny's most persuasive quality was her absence.

There was a dinner party at his publisher's home that evening, which for weeks he had been intent on avoiding. David Lazlo had been unnecessarily kind when extending a deadline on Eastman's next book, the book Eastman had promised himself would be "major." (Yet the topic of this "major" book still eluded him.) Eastman had taken further advantage of Lazlo by requesting advance payments against his royalties. Lazlo submitted to the request without much hesitation. He liked Eastman, and must have thought it rather fulfilling to have such a controversial figure on his list. The second point of contention regarding the party thrown by Lazlo: Eastman had been with Lazlo's wife, Meredith, formerly Ms. Meredith Chase of the old Rhinehart Publishing Company. In fact, it could be said that Mrs. Lazlo, formerly Ms. Chase, was Eastman's fair-weather mistress.

Now, it was not an affair carried on in the normal fashion. When they were first together back in 1953, the sex did not excite Eastman enough to continue it. He tried to fulfill his obligation as a husband to Barbara and as a father to Helen, and when he failed at this he developed a reputation as a womanizer. The reputation that followed him around suited his new idea of himself.

By the end of the fifties he was coming into his own as a public intellectual. He wrote essays on politics, literature, art, sex, and society. Many of his larger writing projects he put on hold, often indefinitely. In the spring of 1961, Eastman traveled to Munich to give a talk at the German Academy of Fine Arts, something or other on the intellectual situation in America. The academy put him up at the Hotel Laimer Hof, where a literary conference was being held. All the foreign publishers had convened in Munich to exchange manuscripts, and Eastman had set a meeting with his German publisher. It was while talking with his publisher over tea in the hotel lounge that he caught sight of Meredith Chase in the doorway of the hotel lobby. She stopped to look around and then went on to the concierge desk. He wasn't sure it was Meredith—his eyesight had been getting worse—so he politely excused himself for a moment and went to the lobby, where he carefully approached the concierge desk. He lightly stepped in closer, sideways, close enough for his ear to recognize her voice. When he was certain that this was indeed the Meredith he had once known, it was as if his chest began to inflate with a sense of pride, and he waited for her with contentment. Meredith turned around; her expression at recognizing Eastman registered a welcome surprise. Using a Texas accent he said, "Well, li'l lady, you comin' or goin'?" They exchanged pleasantries, he dropped the Texan act, and he learned she was indeed there for the literary conference. He playfully called her Miss Chase and she endearingly brought to his attention the ring around her finger, wiggling it in the air. "It's Mrs. Lazlo, now."

Eastman explained that he was in town for a talk at the Academy of Fine Arts, and had finished with his obligations. So the two friends made arrangements for dinner. He was pleased to see a friendly face after all these years. He returned to the lounge, where his German publisher was waiting patiently.

"Who was that, Alan?" his publisher asked.

"A very dear acquaintance of mine, chief."

"American?"

"Yes. She's an editor. Used to be with the old Rhinehart Company. To be honest I didn't catch where she is now."

"Was that Meredith Lazlo?"

Eastman snapped his finger and his hand formed a pistol. With a wink, he brought his thumb down like the hammer and shot his German publisher with what he felt was considerable American charm. "Bang."

Dinner was simple, the hotel restaurant. They were both due to leave the next day.

He wound up speaking of Barbara much more than he had wanted to. Her moving to Mexico with her new husband, Castle Martinez, a man Eastman liked and trusted. His worries were of Helen growing up in Mexico City. "If I wanted her to grow up in Mexico, I would have brought her there myself. She should be . . ." He stopped himself. "She should be with her mother. That's fine. I just want her in the same country. A little closer would be nice. I'm not made of money, where I can fly everywhere at any time. Don't let my being here in Germany fool you. I'm working. This is paid for by the German academy. I live a modest lifestyle."

"There's nothing modest about you, Alan."

"Watch your tongue."

Apropos of nothing, she said, "I've been thinking about that evening we spent together. It was so many years ago now."

He was struck by her directness. He would never have addressed the night they slept together. Perhaps he would have danced around it a bit and made subtle intimations. But they were having a good time and they were both getting a little drunk. Since that afternoon, when he'd run into her in the lobby, his memory had been going over and over that night in 1953. He had spent the afternoon in his hotel room recalling it with immense pleasure. Meredith was tall, full bodied, with nice breasts and a round, healthy stomach. She once had a bush that was full and mouse colored. They had fucked three times in the course of that night. He remembered her taking his penis and rubbing it around the exterior of her mouth, over her nose and cheeks, between her breasts and over them. She was highly experienced, more so than he had been, and this, perhaps, was intimidating at the time. She had insisted on being the aggressor and would sit on top of him and move her lower torso in a steady rhythm. With the advantage of time, he was no longer guilty about the affair and could enjoy the memory for its details.

"Oh, I remember it well," he said. "I don't know why I never called you again. It was perhaps for the benefit of my marriage, which I was trying to patch up. But I thought of you often. It was thrilling. Do you remember how many times?"

She held up three fingers. The alcohol was making her flirty.

"If only you had chased after me like you did the night we met," he said.

"You dog! It was you who went after me! I liked you, sure. Who didn't in those days?"

"What do you mean *in those days*? People like me now."

"Oh, you know what I mean. I remember being so attracted to the way you treated everyone. And the way everyone treated you. They loved you. But you pursued *me* that night. You begged me to take you home."

"That's simply not true, Meredith." He smiled and looked away from her, motioned to the waiter to bring him another whiskey. When he brought his gaze back to the table, she was still smiling at him, now with blush in her cheeks.

"You want to hear the truth?" he said.

"Please." She swigged her wine, spilling a little as she put the glass back down, which made them both erupt into laughter.

"The truth is I had only ever been with one woman before you." He had used this line on many women as an effective mode of flattery, but in Meredith's case it was true.

"Oh sure, Alan. And no man had ever made me come before you. I won't fall for it."

"No, it's true. It was 1953. I married the first woman I'd ever been with. And then you came along. I think it's true if I say that in regard to monogamy . . . you turned me."

She laughed.

"Go on," she pleaded. "I adore this topic. But I still don't believe you."

"I still think about you. I thought about it this afternoon. It was an awakening to fuck you." He could tell she was enjoying rehashing their past, and she was telling him what he wanted to hear just the same. The waiter came and refilled their drinks. "*Dang-ke*," he said, using his Texas twang. Meredith was in stitches.

"Now it's your turn," he said. "What did you think of me then?"

"Why, I told you. Everyone loved you. It was attractive. I watched you from across a crowded room. I desired you."

"See, you admit it. It wasn't me who convinced you. Your mind was made up. The difference between a man and a woman, the woman knows if she's going to fuck. She decides. You decided one night in 1953. I was just a man across a crowded room. Man lives in anticipation, but never certain of fucking."

"I see you haven't lost a bit of romanticism. There must be other outcomes. Beautiful men don't have this problem. The Marlon Brandos and so on."

"I've met Brando and I know he doesn't decide. This holds true not just for men and women but for animals. Unless we're talking about rape. But I'm not. I'm talking about consensual fucking. The female decides. Now I can plead my case to you. I can try everything to convince you. But my precision can only take me so far. You already decided before you walked into the room. That's your innate, God-given power. The incredible weight of the cunt."

"I didn't know you had so many ideas about pussy, Alan. The orgasm, I knew."

"What else do you remember? From that night. Don't you remember you could have me and it took little convincing."

"I remember I called in sick in order to stay in bed."

"How did I make you feel?"

"Dirty."

"Magnificent. I wonder if I can still make you feel dirty."

"Oh, I'm dirtier, Alan. I'm filthy. That's what age and a little bit of confidence do to you. But you'll never know."

"You have a delicious cunt."

"Alan, please." Meredith looked away.

"Meredith, can I make another confession?"

"I don't see how I can stop you."

"This talk is giving me a raging hard-on."

"Oh, dear. I'm so sorry for you."

"Don't be."

He slid over in the booth until their knees touched under the table; it was electric for him, the contact. Meredith began to laugh. "What are you doing!" she said.

"Is that your foot?"

"No."

"Then it's the leg of the table. How about that?"

"Yes, that's my foot."

"I thought we could talk a little closer."

"I'm married, Alan."

"I know you have a husband. Where is he? I don't see him. You remember what you said to me back then about being married? Not tonight you're not."

She took her napkin from her lap and dabbed the corners of her mouth. She stared at him with a smile that made him feel ten years younger.

"What's your room number?" he said.

"It's 6-2-60," she said. "That's the month and the day I was married. June second, 1960."

"I want to taste your cunt."

Her hand went beneath the table and found him stiff through his pants. "You're not kidding," she said.

"I want you out of this dress," he said. "What's your room number?"

"You don't need it," she said. "We'll go to yours."

And this is how it went. Meeting in a foreign city. Dinner. Then to bed. Entire weekends, never more than a handful of times a year. He had cheated on his first wife with Meredith, and so in some significant way this was a kind of revenge for Eastman. He was now the mistress. It was exciting and without guilt. Unlike him, Meredith didn't seem to experience guilt from their relationship, at least she didn't show it when they were together. She had probably had many lovers during the course of her marriage. But how she was when she returned to New York was something that didn't concern him and so he tried not to wonder. That was the beauty of their affair. Nights together were pleasurable and without hassle, a weekend in Germany or France or Italy, and when they returned, they went their separate ways, different flights and days, back to their normal lives.

But when he met Penny in the winter of 1962 after a war protest in Washington Square, he put the brakes on relations with Meredith. He knew with Penny he'd found a woman he could give himself over to. Meredith had sent a postcard to him within his first month of dating Penny—*Paris on 22nd the Ritz—M.* He didn't know how to reply. He made an excuse involving his daughter, Helen—she would be visiting—and sent a short letter to Meredith's office. This seemed to save him for a time. A few months later a letter, typed, came to his home. *Rome, Hotel Giacomo on the 11th. Riviera possible on 13th. Would be nice to see you.—M.* He tore up the letter before Penny returned home.

They ran into each other at the ballet at Lincoln Center shortly after Meredith's last correspondence. Meredith was arm in arm with her husband, David Lazlo, soon to be his publisher, and when she saw Penny cradled in Eastman's arm, looking up admiringly at whatever he was saying, very much in love, Meredith treated him like a stranger in passing, a stranger whose behavior had severely offended her. She gave an angered look that burned with true hurt. Eastman was embarrassed and couldn't explain any of it to Penny.

Shortly after the run-in at Lincoln Center, he couldn't get Meredith off his mind. He felt like shit, cutting out on their affair without explanation. It was cowardly. He could have just lived his life, onward with Penny. But he wasn't able to, not with Meredith hating him. In a way, he needed her blessing, an idea he found absolutely ridiculous but altogether necessary. When the mind wants what it wants, who's to reason with it? He was not in love with Meredith, no, he would never let those feelings overtake him. But she let him do whatever he wanted with her body. She had ownership over him. He didn't want to lose her, to lose his respect for her. So he tried to make it right somehow.

When he tried to contact her by phone at her office all he got was silence. She wasn't there. She was away on business, she was out to lunch, she was in a meeting. What could he do? He was acting like a jealous boyfriend.

The following spring, a few months into his engagement to Penny, they had a fight so incredible he began to doubt his choice to remarry. Things were thrown—an ashtray, a glass of water, his mother's pottery, all smashed around the house. The screaming and tears filled his mind long after the fight had passed. For a week he hardly spoke to Penny. She would leave in the mornings to teach her classes at NYU, and when she was back, he would be at the corner bar, smoking and drinking with cops, elevator mechanics, and doormen just off work. On one of these drunken nights at the bar, feeling it wouldn't work out with Penny, he wrote a letter to Meredith in which he stated, *I'm sorry about Paris.* He followed the letter with the dates of an upcoming conference in Madrid and the address of the hotel where he would be staying. Perhaps it was premeditated, because he happened to have his address book with all the details on him. On his way home, swaying in the streets, he dropped it into a mailbox and then threw up on the street corner.

By the time he left for Madrid, he had nearly forgotten that he had written Meredith. It was a letter composed in a drunken state, not one that he would expect a response to. Penny was still acting stale toward him and he left with the engagement in question. What of it? He didn't care. The troubles in their relationship were sapping his energy, stopping him from focusing on anything, which only angered him more. When he arrived in Madrid it was springtime, and he had a day to rest before meeting with his hosts at the university.

On the second night, he gave a mediocre lecture and felt like he had cheated the university of what they were paying him. They took him out to a quiet dinner with academics. One of the faculty members, a Spaniard with a goatee, mentioned Eastman's relationship with Norman Heimish, and this left Eastman disgruntled. He returned to his hotel in a rancid mood, just wanting to take a hot bath and sulk. But as he made his way through the lobby, the desk man informed him that Mrs. Eastman had arrived and had been shown to his room.

"Excuse me?"

"Mrs. Eastman has arrived, señor."

He had had the fight with Penny, and for a second he thought there was the possibility that she was sorry and had flown all the way to Spain to apologize. But then there was the letter to Meredith; he suddenly remembered composing it on the bar. Eastman, now conjuring a cold sweat, thanked the desk man and went up to his room. Darkness, but for the slither of light coming from under the bathroom door. Short of breath, he approached the bathroom. The shower was running and he did not know who he would find. He hoped, prayed that it was Penny, come to forgive him. He knew then he did not want to get back into it with Meredith. He stood outside the door for a short while before he pressed on it. In the doorway he let the steam fill his nostrils. Her tall figure through the shower curtain. Soap ran down her body and over her breasts. He pulled back the curtain and stared into her mouse-colored bush. Meredith screamed.

They had to make up. And why not, she had flown all this way. His disappointment was impossible to hide.

He arrived late and unannounced at the Lazlos'. Meredith came to the door and when she saw Eastman standing there in the hall, a look of dire surprise spread across her face. Her husband had invited him and

it was mutually understood that Eastman would not come. The cocktail portion of the dinner party was already under way. In the foyer was
Lazlo's billiard table, where some of the partygoers were gathered
around in casual conversation. Eastman stepped inside past Meredith.
At first he tried to act as if they hadn't seen each other in years, but it
had only been six months since they were both in San Francisco lying
naked together. Meredith understood the pretense and carried on as
best she could. He had appeared out of context, his mass of curly hair
combed down with grease. He wore a navy wool suit on a warm evening, a mackintosh over that. He looked like he was running for mayor
of Cincinnati. She decided to treat him as she would any guest. She
transformed herself into a stranger and he knew not to take offense
and responded accordingly. He was Eastman the author, just a casual
acquaintance, nothing more. Her coldness, in fact, helped Eastman
keep himself together. He hadn't the necessary strength for a party
after these past few days of trauma and heartache.

"It's good to see you again, Alan," she called, sounding false. "I
didn't know you were coming."

"Is that Alan Eastman?" called Lazlo from the living room.

"Yes, it is, darling," she said. "He's just arrived."

"Well, bring him in!"

"Hello, Meredith. Where can I put my coat?"

The Lazlos' coat girl came to the door and Eastman took off his
mackintosh.

"You need a tip?"

"That's not necessary, Alan," said Mrs. Lazlo, as the girl took the
coat from him. "Why don't you follow me to the kitchen and I'll fetch
you a drink?" She put on a smile for him. Eastman looked around
the apartment at the other guests. Bookish types, socialites, the same
bunch of bloodsuckers from 1953.

Eastman followed her into the kitchen, where hired caterers prepped hors d'oeuvres.

"I think you should go home," she said. "You're not looking well."

"What is that smell? It's like a Bombay whorehouse."

"It's curry."

"Christ, you're serving Indian."

"It's delicious, Alan. There's meat and potatoes. You'll love it."

Eastman suddenly thought of the prospect that Penny had renewed her relationship with Vaz, the yogi who took them to India. Was he the phantom whose number he had on the matchbook? The one who dined her at the Waverly Inn? It was impossible for him to imagine that Penny would have gone back to Vaz. He would cross-check the phone number with his address book once he got home. Why hadn't he thought of it before?

"I've been to India, Meredith. I caught dysentery. When I wasn't shitting I was up all night with fever and heartburn."

"Well, perhaps you'll want to slip out before dinner."

He didn't like her suggestion; her forwardness was now working against him. "I'll eat bread," he said.

She took him by the arm and moved him into a more secluded corner of the kitchen, where there was less commotion.

"What's going on, Alan?"

"I don't know where else to turn. Penny left me a few days ago. She took the boys. I don't know what to do."

"Oh no. I'm sorry."

"You're the first person I've told."

"I wish I could say I'm honored. This is tragic. What did she say?"

"It was like talking to someone I no longer knew. Suddenly everything was weighted on happiness. Was this as happy as she could be? Could she be happier with someone else? Could someone else love her more than me?"

"Is there someone else?"

"There's always someone else."

Meredith hesitated. Was she embarrassed by him? No, she'd derived as much pleasure from their rendezvous over the years as he had. It could have simply been his presence in her home with her husband.

"Do you know who it is?" she asked.

"That's what I'm trying to find out. I have a matchbook from the Waverly Inn. Inside there's a number and I suspect it's his. I found it in her nightstand."

"What about your kids, Alan? When are you supposed to see them?"

"I haven't even thought about them. Jesus. You see what this is turning me into? But you're right. I need to see them. She can't do this to them. She's dragging them into some affair she's having with this scumbag. And the worst part is she's *lying*. She's lying to me! She's lying to herself! Our two boys caught in the middle. You don't just break up a family like that. You want to fuck someone, go fuck someone. Don't break up a family. Am I wrong?"

"You're not. I'm very sorry to hear this, Alan. This is very distressing. Excuse me, I have to play host. Here, take a drink." She removed a bottle of bourbon from the cabinet and poured two glasses.

For the first time in days he had the healthy desire to have a drink. It was a party, after all, and from the looks of it, a bad one. He'd need the social lubricant if he was going to get through tonight. Meredith shot down her glass right away, composed herself, and left the kitchen. Eastman stood in contemplation of the drink. As a young man, he had had trouble with controlled substances, though he loved to party. He knew not to mix depression with alcohol. But what was he celebrating now? He hated turning to substance in times of depression. Substance he reserved for mind-altering experiences and whenever he needed extreme courage. Perhaps it was just one of those times. He sucked back the whiskey and poured himself another. On his way out of the kitchen he stopped to look over a cook's shoulder at meat simmering in a lavalike sauce and said, "Easy on the spice, chief. We have Caucasians in the mix."

The party was not massive, nevertheless the apartment was filled to capacity. And this was not a small two-bedroom tenement, it was a godlike apartment on the Upper West Side. Casa de Lazlo. It was filled with people Eastman despised and those he half-heartedly cared for. Some young women were in attendance, possibly editorial assistants of Lazlo's—early twenties, oiled and rosy cheeked. He always treated the assistants kindly and flirted with them when he found the opportunity. It helped his case whenever his name was in question, say in an editorial room, if some asshole bad-mouthed him one of these young eager assistants could stand up for him. He wondered if that's what occurred when Jay Husskler mentioned his name for the Vietnam piece.

Within a few minutes in the living room he had finished his second drink and began to feel tipsy. He thought he should have a drink of water, but a waiter came over with a tray of gin cocktails and Eastman, in poor form, took one and began sipping. Weaving through an underwhelming crowd, he found himself in conversation with Lillian Krassner, the critic who often wrote for *Commentary, Dissent,* et cetera. Lillian had a stern, high forehead, which made her look as if she'd had a facelift, the skin stretched so tight around her face. There wasn't enough skin to go around. He had always liked jousting with the old broad; she was cold to the touch.

"You're looking well, Alan," said Lillian.

"I'm drinking gin," he said. "Ghastly."

"I quite prefer it, actually. Especially in the summer months."

"You would. What's shakin', sister? I feel like I haven't seen you since Ali was Cassius Clay."

"I'm not your sister, Alan. Excuse yourself."

"I'm being amiable, Lillian. That was some blow job you gave Heimish in *Commentary* last month."

"I won't justify that comment. Not everyone writes with a score to settle. At your age, you should know this. Criticism doesn't work that way, it never has, although I know it seems like it does through your eyes. Even so, don't tell me you've never whored yourself. I think everyone has read quite a bit of your whoring."

"I am a whore. And I come cheap. That's why I can cast the first stone."

"I don't write to please, either. I assessed Heimish's latest book on its own merits."

"You assessed his dick after you sniffed his crotch."

"Speaking of whores, how's that lovely wife of yours?"

"Good old Lillian. You're right on the money."

"Are you staying for dinner or will you be making one of your famous exits?"

"If I'm still standing, I'll be staying for dinner."

"Alan, may I talk seriously for a moment? I'm concerned about a rumor I heard regarding you, and I want to express that no matter how much your very being can offend me at times, I certainly don't want any harm brought upon you. I hope I'm not talking out of turn,

Alan, but I am just very concerned for you. Have I ever told you about my friend Alvin?"

"Why, whatever do you mean, Lillian? I don't understand."

"Oh please, Alan, are you going to make me say it? Your safety. Your life. None of us want that for you, no matter how many people in this room you've offended. My friend Alvin was a great journalist, he went over in sixty-six for the *Times*. He was most certainly eager to go—"

"Lillian, I still don't know what you mean. You must be clear, otherwise I just don't know what we're talking about. What about my safety?"

Lillian lowered her voice. "Vietnam, Alan. When I heard I was immediately afraid for you. Not just because of your age, but for anyone to go at this point in the war seems very dangerous."

For Eastman, it felt as if a fantasy had suddenly come true. Had Broadwater talked? Had Jay Husskler, the paper's owner? The only answer he had given the *Herald* was a definite no. And the only person he had told otherwise was his wife, Penny. The room began to take on a lifeless effect. Conversations seemed to slow down and Eastman knew he was having a bout of anxiety. He felt as if he had been caught in a gigantic lie, but he had not lied to anyone except Penny. And that was his own private plan to get his wife back. Vietnam and Penny were now intimately connected.

"Lillian, where'd you hear this? Baxter Broadwater?"

"I think it was Leslie Feldman who told me. Who told him I have no idea. Is it not true?"

"No. No, it's not true."

"Oh, thank God, Alan. I'm glad it was just a rumor. In that case, enough serious talk. I hope you choke on a chicken bone at dinner."

He wasn't in the mood any longer to spar with Lillian. His mind was working, connecting several dots. He looked across the room and found Meredith, who was talking to Lazlo. Lazlo looked at him with a type of suspicion as he whispered something to his wife. Was everyone at this dinner party talking about his reporting from Vietnam? A tough rumor like this was fine—it did something for his reputation—but the implication meant something different to Eastman. If he told Penny, then it was likely that Penny had told her lover. It was therefore a lucky break. His phantom would know just what kind of crazy bastard he was dealing with. Just as likely, it could backfire, and his phantom could conclude that with Eastman out of the picture, Penny was for the taking. With these possibilities in the air, Eastman deduced that it may have been his phantom who let the cat out of the bag, spreading the rumor at a bad literary party. *Was she fucking someone in this room?* He began suspecting the men in the living room. The phantom loomed in a crowd of publishers. He began to grit his teeth. It made him furious that someone, another writer perhaps, or worse, an editor, was fucking his wife and then rubbing it in his face by talking about Eastman's private plan (or private lie, rather, as it truly was too early in the game to tell). The situation was like a spy novel in which a mole had infiltrated an intelligence agency. And by pouring some false information down the pipeline, he could track his phantom and flush him out.

Meredith called for the guests to begin heading into the dining room, where the couple had a two-tone red Mark Rothko. She loved this painting. She'd talked about it when they first acquired it. A painter friend of his from 1954, Jean de Franco, had once owned a similar canvas, and he wondered if the Lazlos had bought it off old Jean. Eastman had once taken Barbara to de Franco's apartment to show it to her. It was the largest painting he had ever seen outside of a museum or gallery. He contemplated the transfer of ownership, how de Franco could have parted with it. If it was the same painting, de Franco must have gotten himself in a bad way and used the Rothko to buy himself out. When life falls apart, use what you have to stay idle.

Just then, Lazlo put his arm around Eastman, giving him a little scare. "Why, Alan," he said, "I hope you haven't thought I've been ignoring you."

"Nothing of the sort, Lazlo."

"Why don't you come sit by me at dinner. We have much to talk about."

The two men walked into the dining room, Lazlo's arm still around his shoulders. Meredith, who was standing at the far end of the table, took notice of them. Both men were hers, she had a right to be nervous, though she hid it well. Lazlo assumed his position at one head of the table, Meredith at the other, and Eastman, guided by Lazlo's grip, sat to his right.

Out of the twenty or so dinner guests, Eastman narrowed down his prime suspects. There was Peter Kaminsky, usually the funniest man in the room but hard to imagine as Penny's lover. Kaminsky seemed incapable of stealing her. He was here with his wife, Rose. Kaminsky would usually make a dirty joke or two with Eastman, but he hadn't tried Eastman this evening. It was out of the ordinary, and therefore Eastman still held him as a suspect no matter how unlikely. There was George Willington, a handsome WASP who was single and always came dressed to the nines. Penny could find him attractive, sure, but Eastman had always suspected George to be homosexual. Forty and single, with never a date on his arm. Eastman watched Willington unfold his dinner napkin and very delicately place it on his lap. He was a prep-school boy, very proper and wet behind the ears. But he had youth. He was closer to Penny's age. Willington took out a cigarette and began to fumble for a lighter he could not find. Eastman stood up and took the matchbook from the Waverly Inn out of his jacket. He reached over to Willington, offering it faceup. "Allow me, George."

"Why, thank you, Alan." Willington took the matchbook. There was no hesitation as he opened it and struck his match. He either did not see the phone number inside, or was too polite to bother. He returned the matchbook without any suspicion. Eastman sat back down. There was a look of ridiculousness on Meredith's face.

Next to Willington were Virgil and Sylvia Arnold. The Arnolds were both writers he had known since the fifties. Virgil wouldn't fuck a seventeen-year-old whore if you paid him, and had he done so, Sylvia would have had his prick taken off for good. But Virgil had some sour feelings about Eastman. The two had appeared on a talk show together in 1970 and Eastman had stepped all over Virgil's chances to express himself. Virgil, the quiet type, wasn't made for TV, with his smug nose and harsh skin. But being talked over on TV wasn't a good motive to conduct an affair with Eastman's wife.

There was bad blood between him and almost everyone in that room of publishers and publishing allies. At some point, he had either put down one of their books or asserted himself over them in public, to steal the spotlight or to turn the topic in his favor. It was merely about keeping hold of the reins. The reins kept him relevant.

To look at Virgil, getting old, next to his Sylvia, his white nose hair popping out of his nostrils, Eastman felt embarrassed for suspecting him. Virgil wasn't one for gossip; it wasn't in his nature.

Lazlo began some meaningless conversation. Far from Eastman's mind was the book he hadn't delivered and that Lazlo was waiting for patiently. When Lazlo asked him what he was working on, Eastman suspected that Lazlo, too, had heard the rumor his phantom was spreading.

"I'm working on a piece about Vietnam," he said.

This seemed to bring Lazlo immense pleasure. His reaction was normally hard to gauge. But this time there was no mistaking Lazlo's enthusiasm.

"Your bravery precedes you," Lazlo said.

"What does that mean?"

"It means I know. I know. There's no need to say any more. I'm your publisher, I ought to know, shouldn't I? This is very good news, Alan. Very good news, indeed. I won't ask you about the book. I know what grand plans you're capable of were you to get the goods everyone wants. Leave the man be, is what I keep telling them."

"Who told you? And who is them?" Eastman was careful here and didn't want to suggest Broadwater or Jay Husskler at the *Herald*.

Lazlo gave him a wink. "It's hard to keep news this good under the rug."

Meredith was talking with Frances Faye, one of her authors, but she had one eye on the conversation between her husband and her lover.

It seems Eastman's phantom had filled Lazlo's head with dreams, too. Or could it be that Lazlo himself was his phantom? Lazlo had good enough reason to fuck Penny out of jealousy and retribution. He had more reason than Willington or Kaminsky. He asked Lazlo, "Could you meet next week to talk about the book?"

"Sure. Call the office, we'll have my girl set it up."

"No, let's not go to the office."

"Nicholson's?"

"Somewhere downtown. Waverly Inn."

Eastman wasn't sure about the connection between the phantom and the Waverly Inn. They were two disparate elements that he'd grouped together. And there was no discernible sign from Lazlo that he had ever been there. Lazlo willingly agreed to meet Eastman wherever it suited his author. Eastman suddenly felt certain that Lazlo could come off the list, though he was still intrigued as to who had tipped him off. He pressed him for a name. "Where'd you hear, David? This is all very hushed at the moment."

"I didn't hear. I suspected. I suspected what you were working on and I was right. With the end of a war now in sight, all the best war journalists are in demand. Young reporters have been making their careers over there and garnering Pulitzers. Halberstam, for example. You can't put one over on me, Alan. I know you too well."

Meredith got up from the table and excused herself. Eastman wondered if he should get up and follow her, but he felt it would be too suspicious.

"It's an illegal war in the first place," Willington was saying to the table. "We've never declared war on anyone. We've been pouring in troops, but there has never been a declaration of war. Therefore it's illegal. And now we're leaving. Training the South Vietnamese army, which is what we were told we were doing there in the first place. Yet they won't be able to hold their own once we leave. The country will remain divided, as I see it, until the North takes over the whole damn thing. In which case you'll have one country, united under communism."

"What's so bad about that? What do we care?" said Sylvia Arnold.

"Of course *we* don't care," said Willington. "But *we* aren't the heartland of the country. *We're* New York. The fact remains, though, there is a war. Vietnam's greatest hope is that the North wins after we withdraw and they end the violence of a civil war. Once we're out of the way, Americans will cease to be harmed, and we can move on."

Meredith returned with a full glass of wine and joined the conversation. "Does anyone truly believe the domino theory? That communism will make its way to the West if it gains the whole of Vietnam? I know that I never heard of the place until Kennedy said the words. I still don't quite know where it is! Cuba, I know. Vietnam?"

"It's near Thailand," Eastman said. "Bordering Laos and Cambodia."

"She knows where it is," said Lillian. "And not all of us have spent time in Southeast Asia, Alan."

Meredith finished her point. "Curious, the only time we hear about foreign countries is when they go to war, or we invade them."

"History is made on the brink of war," said Eastman. "The idea of history. Recall what you were taught in school. The Napoleonic Wars. The Crusades. The Revolutionary War. The Civil War. We study conflict from a very early age. Why? Because we must justify to ourselves, to our young, that this is the natural course of events. Nations war with each other, we are taught. We've always assumed it's been that way. Freedom is only a concept after it is won on the battlefield. There will always be someone encroaching on another's freedom, and the encroached will always have to go to war to win that which they didn't have a word for."

"Who said that?" asked Willington.

"I did. Just now," said Eastman.

"It sounds rather eloquent, but it is a pessimist's view of life," said Willington.

"Alan Eastman, a pessimist?" said Lillian. The table began to laugh. Eastman politely smiled.

"It's a pacifist's view," he said. "Not a pessimist. I consider myself a pacifist, having been to war myself."

"I was in the war, too," said Virgil Arnold. "And I never wanted us to fight one again. That was the promise when we freed Europe from Hitler. At least, it was our hope. And that one only lasted four years. Already it's 1973 and we've been in this damn Vietnam too long. And what for?"

"What we need is for someone to tell us what for," said Lazlo. "That's the book I know I'm waiting for. It still hasn't come across my desk. But maybe it's about time."

Although Lazlo made the comment in Virgil's direction, Eastman took it as a direct challenge and a vote of confidence. Lazlo was excited by the prospect of a book Eastman had no intention of writing.

"Oh my, can we change the subject before we begin eating?" said Meredith. "I just can't imagine working up an appetite over war."

Willington agreed. "Of course! What would you like to talk about, Alan?"

"Genitalism," said Eastman.

"He's always been the provocateur," said Lillian.

"I don't know if that's a word?" said Willington. "Genitalism. Hmm."

"It refers to genital excitation," he said. "And who's been exciting you in that general area lately?"

This seemed to pull the air out of the room. He was approaching his phantom all wrong. An open declaration against his enemy would not bring him any answers. Meredith seemed appalled by his behavior. Luckily, Lazlo interrupted and quickly made a joke out of it. "I'd like to propose a toast," said Lazlo. "To genitalism. And to all of you for bringing yourselves uptown on such a hot and humid night."

"Hear! Hear!" said Willington. The dining table raised their glasses.

Worse than being a joke, Eastman thought, was not being worthy of one. Therefore he accepted his defeat in this joust, knowing he had gone about it all wrong. Lazlo had saved him from embarrassment, that was a publisher's job, and they weren't always there when he was about to make a fool of himself. He took a sip of his wine as the scents of cumin and coriander made their way into the dining room. The staff brought in platters and placed them before the guests. He was quite drunk, and his drunkenness gave way to hunger. So much so that he decided he might even try whatever braised and boneless meat was simmering in baths of curried tomato.

"Dinner is served," said Meredith with quick relief. "The war is over. Genitalism prevails."

"Shall we talk of publishing?" asked Lillian.

"No!" the group exclaimed.

6

The amount of food he had consumed at the Lazlos' was impressive. He hadn't eaten as much in a week and had lost some needed pounds off his waist. Only his waist now seemed to fill back up. The cuisine was too spicy for his palate, but the oblongs of warm bread took care of his tongue when it felt on fire. Others noticed his appetite, too. He had requested seconds from the waiter. Perhaps this snobbed-up group thought he was a pig, not merely pig-headed. Penny wasn't there to stop him from overdoing it. Hunched over, feeling his belt buckle with the tip of his belly—his shirt had come untucked—he thought of her cautions whenever they used to dine out. "Please, Alan. All I need is you passing out on the sofa from overeating."

After dinner he excused himself. The far reaches of the apartment were now quiet and empty. He found the master bedroom and snuck into the Lazlos' private bathroom. He had to urinate from all the liquor, and rather than lift up the toilet seat he pissed into the bidet. Maybe he was feeling a little jealous of Lazlo's setup here. He washed his hands in one of the double sinks and toweled off. The towel he neatly placed back on the rack. In the bedroom he gravitated to their bureau. He opened a few drawers and found the one containing Meredith's underwear. He riffled through her panties. The one he liked most, a black lace, he pressed up to his face and inhaled. Even though it was clean, there was a scent of her on it. He closed the drawer and placed the underwear in his jacket pocket, then went over to the bed, which was made up professionally. Knowing she always slept on the left side, Eastman sat down near the head of the king bed and opened the nightstand. There was a small, Oriental box, and inside he found a number of condoms. He had never used a condom with Meredith. Did she use condoms to fuck her husband? Beneath the condoms was a small vibrator. He twisted its base, which made it shudder in his hand. It fell on the bed and Eastman scrambled to shut it off and place it back in the small box with the condoms. Next, he took the phone on Meredith's nightstand and brought it onto the bed next to him. He dialed his mother-in-law's house.

"Hello," Cathy answered.

"Cathy, it's Alan."

"She's not here, Alan."

Bingo, he thought. Friday evening. Penny was acting like a teenager. She was out on the town with this phantom fuck and it hadn't even been a week since their separation.

"That's not why I'm calling. Put the boys on the phone."

Cathy called Lee, his oldest.

"Dad?" said Lee.

"How you hanging in there, champ?"

"Grandma has us watching *The Girl with Something Extra* instead of *The Six Million Dollar Man*."

"Where's your mother?"

"She's out."

"With who?"

"She didn't say."

"Well, what did she say?"

"She said she was going out."

"And you didn't ask her where? Don't you think that's a little odd?"

"Not lately."

"Did she say what time she'd be back?"

"Grandma said she'd be back late."

"Has she been out often?"

Lee didn't answer, because either he didn't know or he didn't know how to respond. Eastman realized he was putting his son in an awkward position and let it go.

"All right, never mind," he said. "How's your brother?"

"He's here. Toby! Pop's on the phone!"

Lee dropped the phone and Toby came running to the line.

"Hi, Pop." Toby's voice was solemn. The boy had real empathy, whereas Lee, the oldest, was more physical, an athletic type. Lee was like Penny, independent, hardened. Toby, however, he needed to be mindful about. Like Eastman, he often got depressed.

"Toby, how you doing, kiddo?"

"Not so good, Dad. I wanna come home. Where you been?"

"I've been home, waiting for your mother to decide what she's doing."

"We've been calling the house. No one was there."

"Well, now I'm out at dinner. I had meetings in the city all day. Listen, I just called to tell you I love you and I'll see you tomorrow for sure. You need anything from the house? I'll bring it on over."

"Nah, I guess not."

"What about your favorite pillow, you want that?"

"Nah, I guess not."

"I'll bring your pillow anyway. Listen, Toby, I want you to know that this stuff between your mother and me isn't about you guys. We're gonna figure this one out. Most likely you'll be home in a few days and this will just be a distant memory. In two weeks you won't even remember it. We'll be going to see the ball games at Shea just like always."

"What if we don't come home?"

"What do you mean if you don't come home? Listen to what I'm telling you. Am I ever wrong? You worry too much about the what-ifs. You're like me. Lee, he's like Mommy, but you . . . you're different." Eastman could hear Toby begin to sniffle, on the verge of tears. "When I was your age your granddad pulled the same thing your mom's done. Granddad left home and I was left alone with your grandma. I felt really sorry and uncertain like it was my fault. Like it was something I had done. But your granddad, see, he just had a lot of problems. I told you about the gambling. The man couldn't stay out of debt and we had bookies coming by the house even when he was out. You know what bookies are, right, Toby?"

"Creditors."

"That's right, only they don't send you a notice of payment in the mail. They come to your house and break your legs. Only Granddad wasn't there, the coward, so we got the brunt of it. As I said, I was scared out of my wits, so I know what you're going through. And your situation isn't half as bad as how I had it. At least you know where your daddy is. I'm right here, waitin' for you to come home to me. In the end . . . you know what happened? Granddad came back. My uncle Leo lent him the money and he made the payments. It wasn't the last time, but he came home. That's exactly what your mother's gonna do once she comes to her senses."

He heard Toby begin to cry on the other end, and the sound of his boy losing all composure broke his heart.

"C'mon, now. Be strong, Toby. Don't let your brother see you crying. Go to the washroom and clean up, then go back in there like nothing happened, okay?"

"*Eff-uh, eff-uh, eff-uh.*" The poor kid was in full tears, sounded like he was speaking another language.

"Put your grandma on."

"*I-uh phuh-phuh. I luv-uh yuh, Pop.*"

"I love you, too. Now go clean yourself up. Don't let them see you like this."

"Grandma!" Toby put the phone down and ran off. Cathy came back on the line. "Alan, we're in the middle of a program," she said.

"Cathy, where is she?"

"She went out. I told you. And I don't think it's right, your trying to get information out of your boys."

"I can't talk to my boys? I'm their father. I'll call there six times a day if I want to and what we talk about is none of your business. Who's she out with? Did you meet him yet?"

"No, she's being very secretive. I don't know what's going on with her. I'm trying to stay out of it."

"Lee said you know what time she'd be home. But she isn't coming home, is she? She's staying at his place. How does that make you feel, because I know it makes me feel like shit."

"Alan."

"Cathy, you're very much in it, because your daughter chose to bring our children there. I'm only asking you these things because you may be called upon in court, so I want you to be honest to yourself about her behavior."

"What court?"

"If we split up, she'd be an unfit mother while carrying on an affair with another man. She won't get custody. I want you to be honest with yourself now, Cathy. Do your part to help me here. I'm trying to keep this family together and she's out on the town, whoring around. And it isn't as if we're divorced yet. She's still my wife. This is unfit behavior for a mother. If you weren't there would she just leave the two boys home alone while she went out? Help me, Cathy. Help me now, and it won't come to calling on your testimony."

"Alan, I won't get involved. And from what she's been saying, you haven't been such a saint yourself."

"Those are justifications, Cathy. She's trying to justify her own behavior to herself and to you, most of all. You're her mother. She looks to you for approval. Don't give it to her. I can't even think what they're doing together, but I assume the worst. She's a smart girl, Cathy. She has a PhD. She's just lost it, and I need help to get her back here. Look at what she's doing to Toby. He's in the bathroom crying."

"Why, what did you say to him?"

"Nothing. He's upset."

"I better go check on him."

"Have her call me if she comes home. But I won't wait up. Also, I'm coming over tomorrow to see the boys. Toby needs his favorite pillow. Whether she wants to be there or not, that's her decision. You tell her."

Cathy sighed into the receiver. He was running her down. If he could generate enough sympathy from her, she would take his side. That's what being the abandoned one has over the one who flees. Everyone feels sorry for the orphan. He could come out looking like the forlorn hero.

Eastman returned to the dinner party just as dessert wrapped. Willington, Kaminsky, the Arnolds, and the rest of the guests were already lounging in the living room with aperitifs and coffee. He thought he could slip out now and no one would notice, but he hadn't come any closer to finding out who his phantom was.

Meredith found him in the hall. "Where have you been? I was worried, but I couldn't possibly come looking for you."

"I had to phone Lee and Toby at my mother-in-law's. Penny's out on some date. That bitch."

"Boy, does she move fast. I can't say that I feel sorry for you, Alan. The way she's acting I'm beginning to think you're better off."

"Let's not talk like that yet."

He was feeling a bit tired from a pause in drinking. He wanted to do something out of the ordinary. A waiter came by with a tray full of brandy. Eastman took a glass and began to swirl it in his hand, thinking of his next move. Come tomorrow he would see Penny. It would frustrate him terribly to have to ask her about where she was when he called. He thought again of his phantom. Perhaps the man wasn't here at the dinner party as he had initially suspected. If Penny was out, then he was most certainly with her.

"He isn't here," said Eastman.

"Who?"

"Him. The man she's seeing—*him*."

"What on earth would make you think he would be here?"

"Something was said over cocktails by Lillian Krassner that led me to believe he was here spreading vicious rumors about me."

"You're being paranoid. No one is spreading rumors about you except yourself. David told me you plan to go to Vietnam. Are you out of your mind?"

"I'll tell you the truth if you keep it between us."

"It's not true, then?"

Eastman hesitated for a moment, not knowing what to say. He recalled what he had said to Penny that morning about Vietnam. He generated a good bit of sympathy from it. "The truth is," he said to his mistress, "I'm going on a very dangerous mission. I didn't say anything because I didn't think you would understand."

Meredith looked at him as if he were a stranger. "My God, you're serious. But why, Alan? Is it because of Penny? I must say, you're acting quite out of character. And don't think I'll be meeting you in some Saigon hotel."

"I didn't want to tell you this way. It's that damn bastard she's seeing. He leaked it to someone here."

"Will you stop."

"I happened to come across special knowledge that led me to believe the man I'm looking for was here or intimate with someone here."

"But he isn't, as you say."

"No, he isn't."

"Unless he's some type of phantom and can be in two places at once," Meredith said.

Had Eastman communicated his inner thoughts to her? Was he going crazy?

He ran a hand through his hair, confused as to what was real and what was just a figment of his imagination. He patted his breast pocket to make sure he still had the matchbook, and when he felt it there, he knew that this nightmare was real.

"I know this may all sound amusing to you, but this is the reality I've been living with the past few days."

Eastman swigged his brandy and felt a new jolt of energy, a compulsion to act, to do something of bold consequence.

"Meredith, I want to make an announcement."

"Please don't embarrass me."

"I'm here on my own accord. If I embarrass anyone it would only be myself. An announcement would only turn this drip of a party into something memorable."

"Lay off our party. May I remind you you're not even supposed to be here."

They joined the others in the living room. Eastman spotted a dessert fork resting on a half-eaten piece of white cake. Before Meredith could stop him, he began to clink the fork against his glass.

"Ladies and gentlemen," he said. "Would you please bring your attention this way? Ladies and gentlemen, I have an announcement to make of major national importance."

All eyes were now on him. Willington, the Arnolds and Kaminskys. Lillian Krassner. Meredith had skirted out of the hall and back around through the dining room, joining Lazlo by the baby grand piano.

"What is it, Alan?" asked Willington.

"I want to first thank our gracious hosts, David and Meredith, for such an ethnic meal. I've been to India, as some of you have, I'm sure. And I think we can all say that the food was not only better here, it was elevated to a level equal to such company."

"He ate enough of it!" said Peter Kaminsky, to an eruption of laughter.

"I had my fill, Peter. But I'm not up here to talk samosas and curry. That's not what I have to say. I have an announcement of great historical consequence. Listen, friends. As of recently I have proposed to the *Herald* that I will travel to the far reaches of Vietnam in order to report on the feeling on the ground. The who, what, when, and where. The why, too. I will be reporting front-page dispatches from Saigon, Da Nang, Nha Trang, maybe even Hanoi. Straight from the lion's den. On the front page of the *Herald*, when you awake, you'll read and see photographs of what I have been seeing. Transmitting my impressions across the wire in order for you to stay abreast of the situation. They have agreed to send me into what is still very dangerous ground. I, Eastman, will walk that ground." He took a pause to see how the crowd was taking it all in. Meredith had her head down. Her straight, shoulder-length hair covered her face, which seemed to be flushed. If he wasn't crazy, he would say that she was on the verge of tears. Next to her was Lazlo, who seemed completely riveted. So he continued: "When I return, David and I will work together to turn this journey into a major book. And if I were not to return, God forbid—although I don't often believe he's watching over us, especially in Southeast Asia—I want you all to know that the people in this room tonight, faces I've known for the last twenty years or so . . . you are some of my most cherished friends and colleagues. You are. And we've established something close to love, haven't we?"

"We sure have, Alan," said Peter.

"However, to think of drastic consequences will only hinder the prospect of our success. Ladies and gentlemen, I shall return."

"When are you leaving?" asked Virgil Arnold.

"In a matter of days and weeks."

"What does that mean?" asked Sylvia Arnold.

"I'm waiting for visas and some rather tedious paperwork to come through. Once I have that in order I'll be off and may not see most of you until I return. So I bid thee well. Ideally, I'd like to have a minute or two with each of you to say good-bye. Time permitting."

There was a silence in the room. Had his speech sucked the air out of the party? He was running on adrenaline, and had thought what he had to say would take much longer. It took all of two minutes to deliver, one of his shortest speeches. He wasn't sure if it had the historical importance he had promised. Meredith had now turned completely away from him and the rest of the room. She was still by the piano, but all he could see was the back of her head. Lazlo seemed to be oblivious to his wife's disposition. It was hard for him to see her like this. He hadn't thought Meredith would take it so personally. And why wouldn't she—they had been together for so many years, nearly as many as he had with Penny. He wanted to go over and put a hand on her shoulder but realized it would seem uncouth.

In the living room there was Lillian, seated on the sofa, who looked completely perplexed by Eastman's about-face. He had denied the rumors at the beginning of the party, and now he had flip-flopped into going. He noted an apology would be in order; however, it wasn't at the top of his priorities.

Then, as sudden as a fart in the air, the party resumed. Each person turned back to a drinking companion, the Arnolds and the Kaminskys, Willington and Lazlo. Only Meredith had disappeared from where she'd stood by the piano.

It was as if nothing had happened.

7

For once, Eastman managed to sleep a solid seven hours and when he woke in the morning in his bed, alone, he had the energy of a spry gazelle hurtling through Hemingway's Africa. A lion could come at him and he would be slick enough to skirt its teeth. Something had shifted, altered the atmosphere, and what that was could only be attributed to his announcement the night before. The announcement was action, it was purposeful, reasonable. Whether it was a move in the right direction only time would tell. The forces of his life were always pressed up against the other, tectonic plates of urges. A balance of order was what he craved, whether or not it was a mere illusion. All that purposefulness that had been provided by his marriage made him lazy and eventually put the marriage in peril. He sat at the edge of his bed, still in the shirt and tie from the night before, and was jolted by the feeling of movement, by rapid thinking on a positive plane.

He dressed in sweats and a pair of old white tennis sneakers and went downstairs, avoiding the back kitchen, where on most mornings he would have found his wife and boys eating breakfast. He went to his study in order to phone Broadwater. There was already some paperwork on his desk that Broadwater had left behind. He looked through it for the first time. There were visa applications for both South and North Vietnam. Beneath the visa applications was a contract with the *Herald* for three dispatches. The payment was on the low side of mediocre. Ten years ago this would have been an insult, but he wasn't taking this job for the money. He'd make the money back on the other end, when he turned this into a book. Was it his damn career that always interfered with his love life? Certainly, his first marriage succumbed to his literary affairs. Back then the two always seemed to be competing. Now he felt one was going to solve the other. The problem of love could be resolved if his actions showed Penny that he had passion. Passion in his work. Passion by the fistful. Eastman made a tight fist and slammed it into the stack of Broadwater's papers. He picked up the phone and got through to the newsroom's secretary. She was quite clear that if he were to hold on for a moment he could be transferred and speak to Broadwater himself, but Eastman grew impatient and decided he hadn't wanted to talk to the putz at so early an hour. He needed to keep the upper hand in this whole matter. It was hard for him to accept that he would be working again for Broadwater. It made him feel like the two were back at Harvard. Broadwater on his Pegasus high horse at the *Advocate*. So Eastman left instructions with the secretary. Times Square, the Tic Tac. It was the only strip club he could think of that was convenient to the offices of the *Herald*.

After a bit of breakfast he drove his Saab over the Manhattan Bridge, overlooking the tenements of his ancestors. There were Eastmans who had made it out of the Lower East Side. His grandfather Aaron came from Vienna to start a sporting goods company on Orchard Street, which he then sold to the Herman family of Herman's World of Sporting Goods. His great-aunt Frieda had worked in a garment factory on East Broadway and then went on to become a schoolteacher. His mother was born in a railroad apartment on Cherry Street and then moved to Long Branch, New Jersey, once Grandpa

Aaron sold the business. It took a single generation to rise out of the bottom rungs of Manhattan, and then Alan Eastman himself, the family's pride and joy, the golden son of Crown Heights, attended Harvard. Driving over the bridge, he couldn't help reliving his college days. For Grandpa Aaron, Aunt Frieda, his mother, Fran, his father, Bert, the gambler, Alan's academic success was the peak of American progress. He entered Harvard with a partial scholarship, and Grandpa Aaron paid the rest of his tuition plus room and board, which his grandfather was more than happy to do. A grandson at Harvard, for him, what luck! Alan entered as an engineering student. He had been a whip in biology, chemistry, physics, and mathematics. Those tall, elegant structures that connected his part of Brooklyn to Manhattan— the bridges—had fascinated both him and his grandfather: the intricacies of the wire and steel, the massive phallus of iron rising out of the East River. Who built those? Engineers! Therefore it sounded to him like a respectable service. When he told his grandfather what his intentions would be at Harvard, they shared a moment of pride. "I was a no one in Europe," his grandfather had said. "Look at where we are going!"

Hidden from his grandfather were Eastman's aspirations as a writer. During his first semester at Harvard he slipped a battered copy of *The Sun Also Rises* inside his mechanical engineering textbook, and it held his attention much more than the equation of bridge building. He dropped the engineering program, hid his literary dreams from his mother and grandfather, and began to write poems and stories for himself, his friends, and the *Advocate*. He had gotten little excitement out of girls when he spoke of his big engineering dreams, but when he spoke of literature he became attractive in their eyes, he knew, at the mere mention of Dos Passos or Maugham or Hemingway. These were writers, celebrities, thinkers, stars.

Eastman drove crosstown on Canal Street, hit the gas at a yellow light, and blew it as it went red. The speed had some ability to take him out of his own head.

In the passenger seat was his son's squashy pillow, and he grazed it with his hand then squeezed it as if the object would relieve his stress. Driving past the Village made him think of the matchbook in his left pocket and the Waverly Inn. A younger man would be disappointing, but what if his phantom was someone his age? He could kill her. He took his son's pillow and began hitting the dashboard of his Saab, punching the upholstery, feeling nothing. His blood was running hot by the time he hit the tunnel.

Pequannock, to see his boys.

Eastman was reminded of his daughter, Helen. Her twentieth birthday was approaching. If he went to Vietnam he would have to telephone her from Saigon. She was a student up at Vassar, a choice Eastman was happy to pay for, thinking he would see so much more of her now that she was in New York, but he saw about as much of her as he did when she was growing up in Mexico. While he was away he would need to write to the boys. If he could phone, that would be better. He didn't want them to get too used to his absence. He needed to keep a fatherly presence, otherwise Penny would get the best of them. They would favor their mother simply because she was the one around.

The house in Pequannock was a white two-story colonial with black shutters. Cathy had had the yard and bushes landscaped professionally. Outside, an American flag. The fact that Cathy still hung it after her husband passed away made him feel a bit sorry for her. With his son's squashy pillow in hand, he made his way across the Kentucky bluegrass and up to the front door and knocked hard with the brass handle.

A neighbor's dog barked and Eastman waited, the early sun already too warm on his back. It was just about eight. It would be one of the first hot summer days.

Cathy came to the door in her terry-cloth robe.

"Alan, you're here early."

"I brought Toby's pillow."

Cathy looked past him at the street and seemed somewhat unsteady.

"Come in, Alan."

"Are the boys up?"

"Not yet. They stayed up watching the late movie."

He hesitated to ask about Penny as he entered the living room, having a look around. Green sofa, coffee table, a big standing television. The coffee table was clean, which meant Cathy had stayed up with the boys and cleaned up whatever they snacked on during the movie. If his wife had been there, Cathy would have gone to bed at a normal hour and Penny would have left whatever mess the boys had made for the next morning. It was safe to assume that she hadn't made it back. She had stayed out late on her date.

Cathy went to the kitchen to put on some coffee. He sat on the sofa and looked at his reflection in the grayness of the TV screen. He was a stocky figure bound in sweats.

While Cathy made the coffee, he went upstairs to look in on Lee and Toby. They were asleep in the guest room, together in a brass bed. It made him uneasy to see them like that, sharing the bed, their suitcases spread out on the floor. Toy soldiers were set up in some kind of battle on the circular rug. The green versus the black. A small pocket of red invaders. Indians on horses that didn't quite match the time period. Little men with bayonets pointed at each other, flags raised. What kind of war were his boys waging? The Alamo or the taking of Hamburger Hill? It was more innocent than that, it had to be. They were children. They didn't yet know about American conflict, unless he told them. And he told them enough of his days in the Pacific. Though Lee was of that age when he would be taking American history, he wondered if they taught boys Lee's age at that Quaker school about the bombing of Pearl Harbor and Nagasaki? He made his way through the battlefield on the rug. One little soldier—a red!—caught him underfoot and he swiped at the toys with his tennis shoe. By Toby's bedside, he watched his son sleeping, the slim sheets bundled together in his arms. Eastman carefully lifted the boy's limp hand and brought the favorite pillow into his son's embrace. Then, without wanting to wake his sleeping angel, he pressed the pillow as deep against Toby's body as he could. He lifted his son's arm again to gather more of an arm's length. When he would awake he would have everything he once had, minus his mother and father and his home, but Eastman was here to fix all that.

Toby's right eye opened for a moment. Eastman winked at him and the boy went back to sleep, moving a bit, bringing his leg over his favorite pillow as if it had been there all along. Sitting there, watching his son drift between sleep and dream, Eastman felt a deep connection to the half-asleep boy—his son!—a connection that surprised him with its intensity and filled him with joy.

Eastman remembered his own childhood, which could be called troubled by today's standards. His father, Bert, would come home around this very same hour, not from a night of philandering, at least not known philandering, but from a card table somewhere in Flatbush or Canarsie. The sun would just be breaking the sky, and little

Eastman would rouse himself at the sound of Bert's Model A Ford rattling into a space in front of their building, and he would lie awake listening to his father's keys rattle along the sidewalk and then through their front door and onto the hook in the foyer. He'd listen to the squeak of the floorboards as Bert approached to take a peek into Eastman's room. The smell of smoke from his father's overcoat would overtake him and Eastman would have his eyelids partially open but still visibly shut to his father. Bert would just take that peek at his sleeping son and then quietly close the door and sneak off to the living room, where he would sleep an hour or two before he had to be off to work.

The song of Bert's car coming home, rattling, shifting, steering through his son's sleep. (The car would disappear from their lives for some months, held for collateral with a loan shark, only to reappear without explanation. It finally went to Mr. Landau on Eastern Parkway, who bought it when Bert was in an irredeemable hole.) No other idiot species on earth can make those sounds. No other idiot animal sneaks home in a machine, the loudest of machines.

Toby's eyes opened and settled on Eastman hovering next to the bed, and this is when Eastman knew his wife was home. Those sounds weren't only in his head, he wasn't the only one hearing them.

Not so quietly, a car door slammed. And Eastman was down the stairs and at the front screen door before he could hear the click of any heel walking toward the house.

His phantom drove a Lincoln, a very unhip automobile, and he saw it pulled over to the curb in front of the house, unable to fit into the driveway because of the two cars already in it. Cathy's hunk of junk and his Saab.

For Penny it had been an all-nighter. She was stuffing a cardigan sweater into her oversized purse, peering over at his car in the driveway.

She was tired and maybe a bit anxious, because she didn't yet notice him through the screen door. The Lincoln idled, waiting for her to enter the house. So he was a gentleman. The least he could do.

Eastman went outside, descended the brick porch, and walked across the damp lawn toward her, his tennis shoes wet at the toes, sweat stains already under his armpits.

She looked at him nonplussed, as if she couldn't believe he still existed. He continued in her direction and held a judgmental eye. Was he overdoing it? Sure. He was trying to work up enough judgment in one foul look without having to say anything. Making Penny feel awful inside. As awful as he felt.

"Alan," she said, but he walked past her almost with a clever smirk, not even stopping to give her the word she deserved. He would deal with her later. He walked past her and out to the curb toward the idling car.

"Alan, stop," she called after him.

But he didn't stop. Eastman gathered all he had and stepped out into the street on such a perfectly wet summer morning. He got in front of the car, the oversized Lincoln, and the same judgmental gaze he used on his wife he now applied to the windshield and whoever was behind the windshield. Most of this was a tough-guy act. He wasn't really a tough guy. He had known some tough guys in his life, boys in Crown Heights, marines in the Pacific. He wasn't one of them, even though he would never back down from the chance to prove that he was. Intimidation, fear, a touch of the imbalanced, these were the intimations Eastman wanted his phantom to grasp as he stood there in the street. He placed his arms on his hips. He must have looked kind of ridiculous in his gray sweat suit, like an overweight prizefighter. Funny how he cared so much about his appearance at a time like this.

From his vantage point he was incapable of making out his phantom. There was a case to be made for him not entirely wanting to know. The top portion of the man's windshield had that tacky blue tint that came down four, five inches, which shielded his phantom's eyes. Eastman could only make out his mustache, a small mouth and a chin, strong and prominent by any standard. Eastman tried to channel a message. What are you gonna do now, shit stick? Go ahead, throw it into gear. I want you to run away. Show her who you really are. Run away. Eastman tilted his head down in order to make out the man's face, but he remained a phantom. When Eastman crouched a little, the man raised his bold chin slightly so that his eyes remained behind the tinted portion of the stupid windshield. He looked like a Harlem pimp and it was hard for Eastman to get a grasp on the type of man he was dealing with. He could have been ethnic. Spanish, Indian. Hell, he could have been anything, Eastman couldn't see him clearly.

All this time Penny had been calling him back from the curb, but Eastman ignored her.

"Get out of the car," he said. He was being calm, which he hoped would make the man sweat a little. "Get out of the car or I'll take you out of the car." Eastman was pointing now, and his rage was true, it was taking over.

"Alan, you're acting like an idiot. Please get out of the road."

"I'll get out of the road when he gets out of the car. I'll even be polite." He returned to speaking to the man behind the tinted glass. "Get out of the fucking car, *please*. Let's discuss this like men do. And by *this*, I mean my wife. You knew she was my wife?"

Still nothing. He stepped to the car and the car came forward and abruptly stopped. "Are you nuts? Get out!" The wheels steered left toward the center of the road, and Eastman pivoted, at the ready were the man to hit the gas and make a run for it. The car idled forward a bit and then drifted into the road, and Eastman shortened the distance between them and put his hands on the hood. The man stopped the car once again, and to Eastman it was clear that he had put the fear of God into this man, his phantom, and he wasn't getting out. Eastman had him; this standoff was a show of wits and he was nearly victorious. There would be no punches thrown, thank heavens. He had won without the need for it. Still, there was the matter of him in front of the Lincoln holding on to the hood as if the vehicle were the horns of a bull. The car started again, slowly, and Eastman walked it backward, like a matador taming a bull, until they were in the center of the road. He planted his feet on the ground when he thought the man had enough, but the car kept creeping forward, and soon his entire body was on the hood. A sit-in! You remember, Penny. The shit you pulled as a graduate student. The car stopped. If the car moved any further he would have to jump onto the hood. Eastman, on his stomach, looked up once again into his phantom's shielded face and told him to get out.

The car door opened and the interior lights came on, which didn't help him see the man any better. My, he was getting out. Eastman had misjudged the situation and wasn't ready to throw any punches. It was too late to back down now. Eastman got off the hood and made his way to the open door in order to attack, but the man shut the door and made a left maneuver forward. Eastman caught his profile for a brief second and banged on the driver's window, then he ran to the front of the car to block it from passing once more. Ha! Bastard. The car was going nowhere until the man, with a stroke of ingenuity, threw it in reverse and took off backward down the block. Eastman found himself out of breath and watched the Lincoln navigate wearily to the end of the block, hook a backward left, and then hightail it out of there.

Neighbors were out on their front stoops and manicured lawns. Had Penny been screaming for him to stop this whole time? It woke the entire block, including his boys, who were now by the front screen door behind Cathy. Penny had her head in her hands, weeping.

Everyone was watching the tomfoolery in the street. He was fighting for her honor, couldn't she see? Wasn't that heroic enough? The thing he knew about being the hero is that it never had the effect he thought it should. What was heroic in his mind was shortsighted and self-serving in hers, and he could see that this was the case presently. Wasn't what had just happened the sign of a passionate lover and someone who cared?

He walked back to the house and a neighbor called out, "Are you Alan Eastman?"

Eastman waved a dismissive hand and the neighbor called out to him, "Asshole!"

Penny walked ahead into the house and he followed her into the living room. Cathy must have taken the boys back upstairs in order for him to straighten things out.

"I'm not going to apologize," he said. "I had no intention to hurt anybody, Penny, but that coward would not get out of his car to talk to me. I don't know who he is. What kind of a man is he? And then he tries to run me over. You saw it. He tried to kill me in the street."

"You embarrassed me."

"I embarrassed you? Penny, you embarrassed yourself. Coming home at this hour. Out all night. What kind of a mother goes out on a date while she's still married to her husband? When did you turn into this superb cunt?"

"Are you kidding me, you hypocrite? You're going to scrutinize my behavior? I'm not going to let you judge me, Alan."

"What other behavior is there to scrutinize. I've been home, Penny. I've been falling apart without my family. I need to know what is happening to us."

"We had this talk, Alan. I've left you. What I do now is my own business. Now let go of my arm."

He had been gripping her forearm tightly and hadn't realized it. She brought this out in him. Would it be the last time he touched her? His wife, the mother of his children.

"Just answer me this," he said. "Who is he? I just want to know who he is. It's driving me nuts. He wouldn't get out of the damn car. He tried to run me down. I may press charges. I have witnesses."

"You are something else."

"I just want to know what I'm up against. What's his name?"

She wouldn't answer him. Instead, she put her hand on his temple and pushed it with hatred. "Get out of here."

"Penny." He tried to plead with her.

"Get out of here." She struck him on the ear and he raised his hands to defend himself. He grabbed her hands before she could take another swing at him and maneuvered her onto the couch.

"I didn't mean for any of this to happen. I didn't want to see you coming home like this."

"Fuck you, you hypocrite. You know what I mean."

"I don't know what you mean. But I didn't want to put myself in this position. I came to see our boys and talk to you. And say good-bye. And see you one more time, because I am leaving and I don't know if I will be back."

Penny's eyes were still fuming with rage and he could see he wasn't going to get through to her in this state. Sympathy is what he needed from her if his plan was going to work. Perhaps it would have been better if he had just let the john drop her off and drive away. Had he done that, they could have had a more civilized talk. What could he do now to save his marriage? He didn't need to ask her what she wanted because he knew she needed time alone. Time with his absence, and only then would she see that she couldn't live without him. Eastman tried to produce some tears. He cringed his eyes together until his face turned purple but he was too angry to cry.

He looked at her shaking her head in disgust. So he let go of her hands.

The two of them just sat there in the living room of Penny's childhood, the house still, motionless.

He broke the silence by informing her that he was to leave in a few days' time, as he had already said under pretense, but now it was very much the truth. He said she should move the boys back into the house a few days before his departure. He would like to spend time with them before he was off. She said, of course, they were his children. And the "of course" seemed to generate a little bit of sympathy. The morning's fiasco was receding.

He knew now that he wanted to go to Vietnam. There was still the matter of meeting Broadwater to fine-tune the details for the trip. As a correspondent, he would need to be in some sort of physical shape. That was why he was wearing sweats this morning. At some point he planned to go into his basement, where he still had a punching bag, a pull-up bar, some barbells. He had installed all this equipment years ago, when he was under the spell of boxing. Frustrated with his lack of progress on a piece of writing, he would venture into the basement and hit the bag around barefisted. The resulting swelling

knuckles, the twisting of his left wrist, made him abandon the punching bag. It then collected dust, grew mold, and maybe saw a little
action when the boys were feeling up to it. Eastman's body further
receded into old age. If you didn't use those limbs, they would abuse
you. It was more than likely, were he to shadow some soldiers in
Vietnam, he would be injured on a routine hike. An ankle sprain, a
dislocated something. Were he to witness combat, Lord have mercy.
He would perish. It was a dangerous mission, indeed, and he was
willing to risk his life, all of it, to get Penny back.

Her lover, his phantom. Had he scared the bastard off? For now.
But Penny was probably already on the phone with him explaining
that it was over with her husband and that he shouldn't worry. Well,
it just so happened that Eastman had an excellent memory when it
came to minute details, and he had been able to commit to memory
the license plate of his phantom as he drove off backward. New York
plates. He figured Upper West Side or the Village. There was just
something bohemian about him, apart from the mustache. He wore
the brown coat of an assistant professor. Of course, he could have
pushed Penny for the man's name, but he didn't want to go deeper
into the hole with her. He knew she didn't think it important that he
know the identity of her new dick, and Eastman would keep her
thinking that way. He had other means of getting the information.

Back in the city, Eastman parked the Saab on a safe-looking corner on Seventh Avenue and ran into a phone booth with a pocketful
of change. He put in a call to his friend Eddie Sheenan at the 120th
Precinct. They had been together at Boys High, and while Eastman
went off into his literary endeavors, Eddie worked his way up the
New York ranks to police captain.

"Well, you're either in trouble or you want something from me," Eddie
guessed. Penny had disliked Eddie. He was a rough-around-the-edges

friend from Brooklyn without sophistication or culture, all that stuff Eastman had developed, but Eddie was a reliable friend with tact and smarts, and he could certainly outthink any intellectual.

"It's a little bit of both, actually," said Eastman. "I got troubles and I need a favor."

"You don't write, you don't call, not even a Christmas card at Christmastime."

"I'm a Jew."

"Then Hanukkah. Your tribe doesn't send the occasional greeting card? I'm kidding, you son of a bitch. It's great to hear from you. What's shakin'?"

"My wife."

"Barbara," Eddie said.

"Penny. Barbara was my first wife."

"My mistake. I had the order reversed. Penny, go on."

"She's seeing another man. I can't seem to get it out of her—who the guy is—but I'm curious."

"Sure you're curious. That's elemental."

"I got a look at him in his car this morning. He's a real jackass. Knows all about me, but still, that didn't stop him."

"Messing with another man's wife. Unforgivable. I'm very sorry to hear about this, Al. I figured you especially would have it all together. Not that you don't. You can't control how other people act? It's not your fault. What do you want done?"

"I got his plates. I just want to know who the guy is so I know what I'm up against."

"Easy. Say no more. I can have a couple boys in blue put the fear of God in him if you want."

"I don't want anything more than the man's name. Maybe a few details. What he does, et cetera. I want to know the score, so I know how I fare."

"I can have that for you later today. Gimme the plates and call me back in a while. It's done. And if you want him to back off, I'll take care of it personally."

"I don't need anything like that." Eastman thought about it and was flattered by Eddie's offer. After all these years of not speaking, things resumed like they were still just kids in the schoolyard, with Eddie watching Eastman's back. "I'd like to take care of this myself. If I need more I'll call you."

"All you have to do is say the word. I can make this man's life a living hell. Mess with another man's wife. Piece a shit. That's all I have to say."

Eastman gave Eddie the plate number and felt the slightest bit of relief. His friendship with Eddie was from a time before Penny, and this reminded him that he had a life once in which she didn't yet exist. And if nothing else, was he willing to go back to it? He didn't know. All he could do was wait and see.

So he waited. Eastman had an hour to kill before his meeting with Baxter Broadwater, and he strolled up along Seventh Avenue into the land of peep shows and go-go clubs and hot dogs and fast fried food. The district named after the paper that never hired him—the *Times*—was like the part of his brain that he hid from everyone, a circus of desperation. He was feeling a little desperate these days, so why not visit the part of town he often neglected. The Times Square of his youth was mostly a parade of ticker tape and Broadway theater. He could have been an actor, he thought, had he not chosen Heming-way and Dos Passos and Maugham as models in his youth. He loved the movies as a kid, and he was certainly born in the right place to become an actor. As he walked on, he caught a reflection of himself in the window of a peep show, his bulb of gray hair, his face a mug shot of his former self on a very drunk evening. Was he too old? Nonsense! He almost shouted it out loud. He had the will to do anything, hadn't he? If he needed to he could summon the energy of a nineteen-year-old and get a hard-on just as quickly. He could prove it by walking into any one of these theaters. He passed some dirty-movie marquees, *The Filthy 5, The Pig Keeper's Daughter, Is There Sex After Marriage?*

There was plenty of sex after marriage if you knew what you were doing. A strong couple could make their way through anything. Especially extramarital relations, when they happened. Sure, when Penny had her infidelities, they were incredibly painful to discover. But it didn't cancel out their love; in fact, it had only made it stronger. Only now could he put it into words: I am hurting because of her claim. That he had fallen out of love with her, wasn't that how she put it? But that was only a way of saying that she had fallen out of love with him. It was her way of placing the blame on Eastman. That was the true betrayal. How could she bring herself to blame him, to hide from her feelings, to declare it as truth to his face? She was a mixed-up woman, like Anna Karenina, like Emma Bovary, like Molly Bloom. He had been through it before with Barbara, and to throw in the towel, be a quitter, would only set them back years. And he didn't have years, did he? He didn't have years to spend in loneliness. He wanted his life *now*. He wasn't about to let her take his life away. And he would keep trying to have it, their life together, till he was victorious. Eastman walked into the Tic Tac, a strip club he had frequented in the long-ago past. He took a seat at the horseshoe bar in front of the pole dancers and looked up into the thinly veiled crotch of one of the girls. If Penny had been manipulated by this phantom to leave him, then Eastman, her husband of ten years, the father of her two children, should be more than capable of moving her to stay. He placed a twenty-dollar bill on the bar to be changed. The dancer whose crotch he'd stared into so longingly saw the singles being counted out on the bar, and so she centered herself in front of him. She turned around and danced for him to the tune of a country-and-western song. She moved her hips with rehearsed sensuality, an inelegance as she bent over for him and lowered her ass seconds from his face. Penny the liar, he thought, as he took two bills from his stack and placed it under the band of her string panties.

It was too early in the day to have a drink. And last night's drunken party at Lazlo's hadn't helped him with his wild emotions. He wanted to be straight and narrow for his meeting, so he ordered a club soda with lime and watched the dancer stand up and bend over and repeat.

Baxter Broadwater entered the Tic Tac at a quarter to three. He was early, and Eastman was happy about it because he didn't want to sit there alone for very much longer appearing desperate. His twenty singles were running low and he didn't feel like spending more. These girls made him melancholic. He wasn't able to give in to fantasy at the moment when reality seemed too demanding of him. Broadwater saw him right away, took a big gulp of the damp air, and hesitated to take a seat next to him at the bar.

"You come here, Alan?"

"If ever I'm in the neighborhood. It keeps you in touch with your limits, and if you can get a hard-on, I see no shame in it. Sit down, Baxter."

Broadwater followed suit reluctantly, as if the barstool had been contaminated with bodily fluids. He wiped it down with a handker-chief and then discarded it on the floor. "This is awful."

"You hungry, Broadwater? They have a full menu. The fried oys-ters aren't bad. Maybe not what you're used to out on the Vineyard or wherever the fuck it is you go."

"No, I'd rather not eat anything here."

"Would you have a bite of her?" said Eastman. A young topless chick with a collared bow tie made her way over to Broadwater from the back rooms.

"Don't be disgusting, Alan."

"Here's what you do," said Eastman. "Give me twenty dollars."

"What for?"

"Give me a twenty. You can't just sit here without tipping the girls."

Broadwater got out his wallet with a fuss and handed over a crisp twenty-dollar bill. Eastman put it down on the bar and the bartender changed it into singles.

"They're here for your entertainment, therefore you toss them a tip every now and again. Haven't you been to the Playboy Club?"

Broadwater continued his skepticism and Eastman was glad for it.

"Are you telling me you've held an office this close to Times Square for the past I don't know how long and you haven't been to a nudie bar? You ever relieve yourself in a peep show? Jack off a bit on your lunch hour?"

"I only go to the *Herald* from the subway. And return. It's a short distance. This isn't for me."

The girl with the bow tie moved in on Broadwater from behind, petting his shoulder.

"It's for everybody. Now look, be nice to her. What's your name, sweetheart?"

"Brandy," she said.

"Brandy, that's a lovely name. This is my good friend Baxter. He's feeling a little uncomfortable."

"Baxter," she said, "you should have a drink. I'll have what you're having."

"She's very charming," said Eastman. "Now be nice and show her some appreciation."

Broadwater turned to the girl, who couldn't have been more than nineteen, and got a face full of her cone-shaped tits.

"You're very beautiful," said Broadwater.

"You're sweet. You want a dance? A titty shake? You can look at my pussy in one of the back rooms."

"You see, Broadwater, isn't she friendly? There are virtues in places like this. The Tic Tac is an institution."

Broadwater held up his small bankroll and turned to Eastman. "How much do I have to tip?"

"Whatever you think is justified. That's the beauty in it."

Once Eastman felt Broadwater was unsettled enough to hear what he had to say, he sent Brandy to fetch them a couple of drinks and told her to keep the change. Meeting Broadwater here, in the smoky lounge with girls dancing on the bar top, made Eastman feel at ease. Brandy brought them Scotch and water. A jolt of whiskey would loosen Broadwater up a bit. Eastman pretended to sip his but wasn't really drinking.

"Have you given any thought to what I proposed?" asked Broadwater.

"I have looked over the proposal. Why do you want me again?"

"Is this another test? Am I going to be humiliated?"

"This is business. I'm going. Not for you or Jay Husskler or for the goddamn shitty money you're paying, but because there is a story here that should be told; there is a perspective that has not yet been taken and which I think I can provide. It could really put some punctuation on the end of the war. *If* it's done properly."

"The war is ending. Men are coming home. This is what we know. But what do the people who remain know? We need a human piece, to tell us what the people are saying. Those in Saigon—civilians, contractors, villagers. Whatever you can get. How about those in Hanoi, how are they handling the cease-fire? Has there been an end to fighting altogether? Like you say, put things in perspective."

"You really want me. You and Husskler and the *Herald*?"

"Yes. Do you have the contract? We can get this under way and have things move along quickly. The North Vietnamese visa will be the hardest, but we'll be able to take care of all that. How's your back, by the way?"

"It's fine. I have chronic pain because I fuck too much." A pained look crossed Broadwater's face, making Eastman think he should ease up. "Thank you, by the way. For coming out with the doctor."

"He gave you your vaccines."

"That's why my arm still hurts. I can barely remember."

"You're all set medically speaking. How's your family? Will they be able to manage?"

"My family is on hiatus. I feel this will fix things if I get away for a while."

"I ask because I care about your welfare, Alan. You'll be working with us, and we want every precaution taken. If things are not well at home, and I suspected this much, a month in Vietnam may be hard on you. And your family, particularly. Some of our correspondents get divorced and end up staying out there, jumping around from paper to paper. But you have things going on here at home. So I trust you'll have enough sense to be safe and make it back."

"I'm not planning on throwing everything away, Broadwater. Not on this salary."

Eastman got out the contract and slipped it over on the bar. "I've made my adjustments. I'm not doing three dispatches, but two longer ones. Six to eight thousand words apiece. For the same money, or if you can better it—better it. One dispatch from Saigon, wherever I get around in the South, and the other from Hanoi, in the North. I'm going two places so three dispatches makes no sense and I wouldn't know how to divvy up the story. And I want final approval on everything. I want book-length rights and movie rights and any old rights . . . I retain."

"That's standard. So we have a deal?"

"Why do I feel like I'm bending over like this broad on the bar and you're about to mount me from behind?"

"You're not getting fucked, Alan. This is great news. You're doing a remarkable thing for the paper. Something good. A return to form, some might say. Husskler is going to be pleased. I'll run everything back to the office now and we'll get moving on the visas."

"Buy me a lap dance."

"Whatever you want, Alan." Broadwater was pleased. "Who would you like to dance on your lap? Pick a girl. It's on the *Herald*."

"Do me a favor. Get me on a flight to Saigon as soon as possible."

Broadwater seemed relieved to make his exit, and Eastman felt a little sorry for him. The guy was an office man, unhip, a square, everything Eastman fought against becoming. Did a man like Broadwater have regrets that he hadn't performed to the best of his abilities? Eastman could have done better, it occurred to him. That morning in Pequan-nock, he hadn't apologized to Penny for allowing things to fall apart, hell, he hadn't even proposed the possibility of changing himself for her. He had too much to lose and too much pride to let up on her, so he continued to make demands. Move home, Penny. Now this plan of go-ing to Vietnam in order to appear heroic. He wasn't a celebrity author anymore, so he may as well be a hero.

In the back of the Tic Tac, past private booths with red velvet curtains, he found a phone where it was quiet but for a few debauched whispers. He put some change in and dialed Eddie Sheenan to see about the matter of his phantom. Eastman was a bit fearful in mak-ing the call. Would this be the piece of information that brought his mental state to collapse? He could still choose to live in igno-rance, and maybe that would be preferable. But he couldn't stand the uncertainty.

"Eddie, it's Al," he said. "Were you able to make any headway with those plates?"

"Yeah, I told you I would, didn't I? Where are you?"

"The Tic Tac. I had some business I had to take care of with an editor up here."

"The Tic Tac? They were shut down a bit ago. Some girls were caught turning tricks in the back rooms. Not that I see anything wrong with that, this is a democracy. But one was a captain's doped-up daughter, got picked up in there for soliciting a blow job from one of ours. And the captain, he had to put the hammer down on the place."

"Well, it's open now. And it's just as seedy as I remember it."

"All right, here's the guy's name, you got a pen?"

Eastman had another matchbook, which he'd taken off the bar. He opened the flap and readied himself to write.

"Arnaud Fleishman. Four Twenty-seven West Twenty-eighth Street, the Chelsea neighborhood."

"What's his name?"

"Ar-nod. Ar-node. Pernod. I don't know how to say it, he sounds like a French pastry."

"He's some kind of French Jew? Fleishman?"

"And that's the address. It's a house."

"How do you know that?"

"I had a car drive by. He's not home."

"I didn't want you to do that."

"I just had somebody ring the bell to verify the information, see if the title of the car matched the owner of the house. You never know, the car could have been a loaner registered under Fleishman, who turns out to be a grandfather. There was no funny stuff, Al. Unless you give me the go. Mess with another man's wife. We've all had our temptations. I'm no saint either. But hey, this ain't right."

"You're damn right this ain't right. He's fucking my wife."

"That's what I'm saying. So I wanted to make sure. Just in case we got it wrong."

"What kind of car is it?"

"Lincoln Continental. Color black."

"That's him. That's the one. He's fucking my wife."

"What more can I say, Al? Again, I don't mind applying a little pressure if it's gonna alleviate matters. But the best thing to do now is to talk to her. Talk to her, show her who you are. You're a man, plain as day. You step to this Fleishman, who knows how it's going to look to her."

"Bad. It'll look bad. I gotta take the high road on this one, Eddie. I gotta be the bigger man. I have been talking to her and I have a plan. I just had to know who he was. To hear it from someone else so that I knew he was real."

"What can I tell ya," said Eddie. "He's Arnaud Fleishman of Four Twenty-seven West Twenty-eighth. Good luck to you, okay? If you're going to do anything stupid, don't. Call me instead."

Good old Eddie hung up and Eastman lingered a bit with the receiver in his ear, staring at the name, Fleishman, which he had written on the Tic Tac matchbook. Another clue, another matchbook. A curtain opened up on the nearest booth and a Midtown man walked out, straightening himself. He said to Eastman, "Could you talk a little louder? We couldn't get the whole conversation."

"Fuck you, pervert," Eastman snapped. He hung up the phone. The man left, just wanting to tell someone off for the heck of it. In the booth was a girl about Helen's age, putting on her bra, arms pinned behind her back. Her makeup was heavy, especially around the eyes, and the dark eye shadow made her look tired. Her lips, however, painted pink, inspired some excitement. "Man, what do *you* want?" she said.

Eastman put the phone down. "I don't know what I want, hon."

"Well, if you want a dance, ask for Tillary. That's me. Tillary."

"Tillary, let me ask you something. If a man wanted a date tonight where would he go?"

"That depends. You a cop?"

"No, I'm not a cop."

"Because you kind of look like a cop, man."

Eastman considered the way he was dressed. He still had on the sweatshirt and sweatpants from that morning, which sort of made him look like a police cadet in training.

"Man, I guess if you weren't a cop or anything and you needed a date, I guess you could maybe see about something like that here."

"I need a date for a few hours, not just a back-room exchange. I need someone to take a ride with me downtown." He was considering taking a woman home. He hadn't been with a prostitute since his days in the marines. He had visited a Filipino brothel while his ship was docked in Manila. She was just a girl, maybe sixteen years old, he didn't know, and he felt guilty about it after. The challenge was in wooing someone. He wasn't after just empty sex, there were no stakes in it.

"Man, that's a little harder, to be honest," the girl said. "Lot of these girls are working their shifts to real late, man. I dunno."

He desired this Tillary when he saw her dressing as that asshole came out of the booth and decided to shit all over him. Maybe it was because he had been insulted and wanted to go a step further than the dumb shit who paid her for a dance. He pictured Penny fucking another man. It was evil, the whole mess of it. He looked at Tillary. It didn't feel right. As she stood there in the booth under the pink light bulb above, fake name, fake desire, he regretted the whole thing.

"Listen, forget it. I changed my mind."

He glanced out to the front of the Tic Tac, past the red velvet curtains that hid the lap dancers, past the horseshoe bar with poles and strippers and dollar bills. Middle-aged men drank beer from cans and stared up at tits that stared down. He was in the pit of his mind with Arnaud Fleishman and Penny.

Eastman left, and when he hit the street he passed more prostitutes and pimps. What was he doing thinking about paying a woman to take home? What if Penny decided to return, how would that look? She still had this incredible hold on him, it was proof; he couldn't do what he desired on a whim because he was still a married man, however hypocritical it seemed, considering his own affair with Meredith. He stared at the matchbook from the Tic Tac where he had written down Fleishman's name and address. He struck a match and set the whole thing aflame.

Get me to Vietnam.

8.

Penny agreed, without much fuss, to let him spend a weekend with the boys before his departure for Saigon. He picked them up in Pequannock and brought them back to Brooklyn. Penny stayed on the front stoop when he arrived. He got out of the car and waved and it was clear she wasn't going to come down and say hello. The boys, with their suitcases and backpacks, gave their mother a kiss and came running to their father. He met them on the curb and gave them a communal hug, packed them in, and he fought the urge to look back at her. It seemed like all he was doing lately was driving back and forth to New Jersey. The plan, as they had discussed on the phone, was that the boys would move back home first for a long weekend to spend with their father. His daughter, Helen, down from Vassar, would join them, and at the end of the weekend, when Eastman got on a flight departing for Saigon, Helen would watch the boys for a night before Penny moved back. As he drove away from Pequannock, he breathed a sigh of relief. The worst was over. He knew he was acting every bit the angry, abandoned, deserted husband, and hated himself for not being able to control it. Forget it, he told himself, the weekend was about the children, not the mess their parents had made.

Once home, Toby and Lee made a beeline for their rooms upstairs and began unpacking. Eastman occupied himself by making them lunch, tuna sandwiches, his mother's recipe. Celery, carrot, chopped almonds, relish, garlic salt, mayo, on rye toast with lettuce and tomato. He had bought the wrong tuna, the kind that came in water and not oil. And this made the tuna salad taste too dry. They were out of olive oil, so he melted some butter in a pan and poured that into the bowl of tuna. It had the right consistency, only now it tasted like buttered fish. He compensated with more mayo, and when the dish seemed beyond saving, he began to lose his temper, slamming things on the kitchen counter. He toasted the bread and cut the tomato while he waited, slicing his finger in the process. When the toaster popped, the bread was still soft. The toaster had been unplugged. He'd about had it with cooking and didn't want to spend another minute making sandwiches. So he gathered everything on plates with his good hand, spread the tuna and then topped it with lettuce and tomato, and cut each sandwich in half with the wrong knife, forcing tuna out the back end. "Boys! Come and get it!" Toby and Lee came down and took their seats around the kitchen table. Eastman put their lunch in front of them, managing to put on a happy face, and he sat down, staring across at the empty chair where Penny used to sit. Soggy tuna salad without their mother. Toby and Lee, it seemed, were doing their best to keep his spirits up and he appreciated that.

"Real good, Dad," said Lee. Toby was a little more picky. Like Eastman the kid wanted things done his way than his older brother. So Toby nibbled at his sandwich in a manner that exhibited his displeasure.

"What's the matter?"

Toby looked inside his sandwich then looked at his brother.

"He doesn't like tomato," said Lee.

"Since when?"

"He never eats tomatoes."

"So take it off." Eastman reached over to Toby's plate and took the tomato out and put it on the side. But Toby barely touched the sandwich, a few nibbles, that was all. The boy ate mostly pickles from the jar, his little hand able to slip into the jar and fish around for the smallest spears. Eastman wasn't going to force him to eat more. The sandwich was shit. He'd fucked up a very simple family recipe and didn't know how he would take care of the little things were the family to separate. Would he get the boys every weekend? How would he manage? The shopping and cooking and cleaning. It occurred to him how much Penny contributed while also working regular hours.

And then Toby and Lee in two different homes, the back-and-forth. He couldn't redo what happened with Helen when she went to Mexico with Barbara and her new husband—missing out on all those birthdays, not seeing her grow into a young woman, milestones lost in time. He knew he'd failed Helen. But he hadn't been able to see his mistakes then. Now he could almost see them happening. His love for Penny and the kids felt like a second chance. The thought that it could all go away if he didn't convince Penny to stay terrified him.

"So how's your mother really doing?" he asked.

Toby looked at his older brother for the answer. Lee took the reins. "She cries a lot. I think she misses home."

"I told her she can move back anytime, but she didn't want to be with us for the weekend." *Don't be too harsh.* "She wanted me to get time alone with you guys before my big mission. She knew I needed your help to prepare."

"For Vietnam?" asked Toby.

"That's right. Eat your sandwich."

"I'm not hungry."

Eastman let the boy be. "What has she been up to?" he asked.

"She goes out a lot," said Lee.

"I know all about that. Has she introduced you to her new friend?"

No answer. Again, Toby looked to Lee for guidance.

"His name, I heard, is Arnaud. Did she introduce you to this character, Arnaud?"

"Nah," said Lee. "We haven't met anyone new."

"So she hasn't brought anyone around?"

This scared the boy off a bit, and Eastman regretted being so aggressive.

"She's being very secretive," Eastman said. "Look, I don't want you boys to feel like you can't tell me anything. If there's something you think I should know, just tell me and we'll decide whether we should keep it between us or not. We can't dance around this. You guys are old enough to sense what's going on. Your mother is seeing somebody else, somebody she thinks she's fallen in love with. And she also thinks that I don't love her anymore, which just isn't true. It's the furthest thing from the truth. I want her to come back. I love her. I love our family. And I love the way things are. So I need your help. Remind her how I love her. I'm going to let things run their course, allow her to see this son of a bitch—excuse the expression—and my hope is she'll see that me, I'm better. I'm more suited to her than anyone else. You understand?"

"Yeah," said Lee.

It was as if Penny had coached them with silence, because he could sense they knew not to say anything that would upset him. He hated what this was doing to them. Toby looked like he was on the verge of tears. And Lee was nervous with his answers for the rest of lunch.

"Anyway, this weekend isn't about me and your mother. It's about us. The three men." Lee continued to devour his sandwich. Toby took a bite of a new pickle and left it on his plate.

When Helen arrived late Saturday afternoon, the boys were happy and almost relieved to see their half sister. She had gained some weight up at college and it suited her. Helen had Barbara's flare, a prominent nose like her mother, a wisp of excitement and energy to make things lively around the house. She had turned into a hippie at Vassar, wearing faded jeans and a loose blouse and smelling of patchouli oil. Her energy is what he needed, since his was flagging a bit with the boys after lunch. Helen still called him Daddy, even though he'd been absent from her life except for the few birthdays she spent in New York, and their phone conversations, monthly at first, and then less frequent as time went on. Barbara's husband, Castle Martinez, was a decent, handsome man who came from a wealthy Mexican family. Eastman knew Castle was true from the very beginning, and trusted him to do a fine job with Barbara raising Helen. It took a certain kind of man to embrace a woman with a young child, a man who could give himself over to someone else's life without objection. This is why Eastman thought well of Castle. He wasn't so sure he could have remarried someone who came with a family. In fact, he got along better with Castle than with Barbara.

Helen brought the boys candied apples from upstate and gave Lee a kiss. Toby she picked up off the floor and ran him through the house saying, "Faster than a speeding bullet. More powerful than a locomotive. Able to leap tall buildings in a single bound. Look! Up in the sky! It's a bird. It's a plane. It's Su-per-maaaan. Yes, it's Superman. Strange visitor from another planet who came to Earth with abilities far beyond those of mortal men."

Mortal men. That was something that rang out to him. He was a mortal man past the prime of his life, which meant that he didn't have as much time as he felt he deserved. Would this marriage split for good and Toby and Lee go to Penny and the Frenchman? He would be miserable. Although what would he do if they were to remain in his care? He'd have to hire help, a full-time maid who cooked and took care of the children. What those uptown snobs called au pairs. He'd have to go on dates, meet women, find a new wife who didn't mind inheriting two young boys and an estranged teenage daughter. Assuming he won a custody battle, like the one he was anticipating in his imagination.

He knew if Penny didn't change her mind and work things out, he would have to give up primary custody of the boys. It irritated him to know that he was too selfish with his own time to care for his children. Maybe this is what he inherited from his own father.

Helen settled in the spare bedroom they kept for her. It was still done up as a teenage girl's room, with white lace curtains, a pink credenza and vanity mirror, four decorative Beatles pillows on the day bed. John, Paul, George, and Ringo. It was Penny's idea to keep the room like this so Helen would feel right at home whenever she visited. He watched from the doorway as she unpacked her bags.

"It's really good to have you home," he said. "I'm glad you could come down and help me out for the weekend. I needed to see you before I'm off."

"Dad, it's fine. Finals are over and summer session hasn't started. Are you going to fill me in on what's going on? Are you guys separated? I can sense the tension in Lee's face. He stiffens his jaw whenever he's nervous."

Helen was majoring in behavioral psychology, a subject she seemed quite suited for, in his opinion. She was an avid observer of human behavior. Not all children were like that. Some ignored the world, or if they knew the score they shut down. As a girl she could sense what was wrong in a situation even when the adults couldn't quite grasp it. Helen was one of those children who would speak up when things were not quite right. He remembered her constantly begging him to apologize whenever he acted erratic with Barbara. Lee and Toby knew all about what their mother was up to, her behavior was evident, they were living with it, but it was in their nature to remain silent.

"It's some kind of unspoken separation," he told Helen. "We haven't worked out the details because she's impossible to talk to right now. Penny's seeing somebody, and she moved out a few days before that affair commenced. Though I have to believe they were fooling around behind my back already. For how long I'm not certain."

"Oh my God. I am floored, Dad. She was cheating on you?"

"Not was," he corrected. "Is."

"And the boys, to think what they must be going through. No wonder Lee is so tense. He's stressed out." Helen moved to the doorway and put her arms around him, resting her head on his shoulder. "I'm sorry, Daddy. I don't know what to say."

Right then he was sorry he hadn't spent more time with Helen over the years. He had made a perfect human being with Barbara. The whole thing had been worth it just to see her now, comforting him when he felt so alone. Helen was warm and worldly—he owed that to Castle, for sending her to Europe with her mother at a young age. Not to mention Helen's big heart. She had the face of a child on the verge of womanhood. And how selfless—she would drop everything, put herself aside and hop on the southbound train for hours to be with him. She was already twice the person he could ever be. And he had been such a lousy father to her. He wasn't so sure he'd done anything so nice for anyone in his life without thinking what an inconvenience it was.

"Who is this new someone she's seeing," said Helen. "Has she told you?"

"No, but I know who it is. I have my ways of getting the information. That's the reporter in me."

"You haven't done anything illegal, have you?"

"No, not at all. In fact, it was a detective friend, Eddie Sheenan, who found the bastard on my behalf."

"Who is he?"

"An old friend. You met him when you were a baby."

"I remember Eddie. I mean the guy Penny's seeing."

"His name is Arnaud Fleishman. The name's not important. And what he does, I don't know. I'm trying not to fixate on him. I'm trying to file it under none of my business." They were interrupted. Toby shot past Eastman and into Helen's room yelling "Help!" Lee came after, chasing him from behind.

"This is so unlike her," Helen said.

"Help! He's trying to kill me," said Toby. "Stop him." The boy hid behind his sister.

"But you're Superman," she said. "He can't kill you. There's only one thing that can kill you and you can't come by it on this planet, Superman."

"Kryptonite!" yelled Lee as he went storming out of the room. Toby cringed with worry. Lee went along, stomping down the stairs, searching the house for anything that could be used as Kryptonite in their game.

He wanted to know her whole take on Penny, from the beginning. He trusted her, was interested to know what she had read about affairs, divorces, anything that could give him some comfort. He'd be damned if he turned to some self-help book. He still felt he could handle his problems on his own terms.

"If you want the Freudian treatment on what divorce can mean in the development of young boys, I can probably give you that," said

Helen. "Sure, splitting up is bad, it's going to devastate them. Re-member, I went through it. As far as predicting what this will mean for you and her, who knows? You have to give me more details. Here's where we should probably be careful, because after all I'll have to see her come Monday."

"Don't use that word. Divorce. I can't stomach it. No one's talking about divorce yet."

"Well, Dad, are you going to live in some open marriage?"

"I'm not against it, if it means staying together. As long as this place doesn't turn into some progressive commune."

"In as limited but clear detail as you can, what did she say?"

"She said . . . she said that it was over. She claims I've fallen out of love! Me. Can you believe that? The reverse psychology that she's putting on herself. She's fallen for someone and she's denying her feelings for me while also placing the blame on me. That I . . . I no longer love her. She had her suitcases already packed before we even talked. She had made up her mind before it even hit me what was going on. So there was nothing I could say or do, the argument was stacked against me. When I think of it now, I realize the work she put into this decision without me. If there wasn't another man, then maybe I could have had a chance to convince her to stay. But no such luck. I drove her to New Jersey, that was that."

Helen was sympathetic. "Why didn't you call me right away?" She sat down on the bed with a look of confusion and slight abandon. People were cruel to each other, he had taught her this when he cheated on her mother. All Helen could do now was shake her head.

"I'm never getting married," Helen said. "I'm sorry to bring it up but this whole ordeal sounds too familiar. People do this again and again to each other and where does it end? I wish I were a lesbian."

"That wouldn't solve anything. Besides, ours is a family that believes in procreation. It could have all ended for us in Europe. Your job, young lady, besides being a crack psychologist, should be to think about continuing the lineage."

"Are you kidding me? I'm not bringing children into this world. So they can be sent off to some war and die? Or if they're lucky enough to be girls, wait home with babies while their men fulfill themselves by other means. Nuh-uh, none of it sounds appealing in the least."

"Don't turn this into a women's lib argument."

"Dad, I'm here on this earth because of you and Mom, I'm aware of that. And I'm grateful. But life in this country is the worst it's ever been. How can I even think about procreating? I should be thinking about fixing the country first."

"You can't fix the world, it isn't an automobile. And it's been in worse shape than it is. You're up at Vassar getting a great education, one that you couldn't get anywhere else, and you can be whoever you want. Freedom. Choice. This is the greatest goddamn country in the world and there are things you can do to ensure a better life for your children."

"Yeah, like not have any. And become a lesbian."

"I've had it!" He stormed out.

"Dad!" Helen called after him.

He felt bad, instantly. She was developing her own philosophies, outlooks, opinions on the way to live her life. God bless her. The boys were making a racket downstairs and he went to quiet them.

For dinner they grilled fish and corn and foil-wrapped potatoes in the backyard. Helen was a vegetarian but ate fish, and he had sense enough to defrost two red snappers that Penny had left in the freezer. The boys were unhappy having fish two meals in a row. After dinner, while his children adjourned to the living room to watch television, he went into his study in the next room and closed the door, settling into his reading chair, where he had spent so much time rehashing his final days with Penny.

His own happiness was not something he constantly took gauge of, and this was the difference between Penny and himself. She was convinced that she was unhappy and that this state must be brought on by him, and that another man could bring her a higher level of happiness, and that this transition to another person, once undertaken, would bring those levels of happiness up. It was utter nonsense.

Perhaps it was his upbringing. The Eastmans were not happy people and they were not concerned with happiness. Success was paramount, and happiness was the outcome of that success. His grandfather Aaron building his own sporting goods company and then selling it to the Hermans, moving the family to Long Branch, New Jersey. From there his mother was able to go to a good high school and have a true American life. If you plummeted, you were unhappy; when you rose and stayed aloft, you were happy.

There were exceptions to the way he thought about happiness, but for the most part the feeling was in tune with life's successes. But concerning women's lives, in particular, this was no longer the case. Women commanded their own destiny, unlike in his mother's time. In fact, this is what he most admired about the women in his life. All of his past lovers had some big, commanding presence, an outward destiny, that made him feel the need to attach himself, for maybe that's what made him happy. To be with a woman who was going places even if his own life felt stagnant. Yes, being with such a woman provided him happiness.

He decided to compose a letter to Penny, a love letter, of the kind he hadn't written to her since they first met. He would leave it for her in the house. It seemed an excellent way to get his feelings across. Her in the home among their things, his absence looming.

Dear Penny, it is awful how much I am hurting for you and I know how you must be hurting too. We are connected, the two of us, and I know that when I feel something you have the same ache in your heart, the same pain and longing that I feel. First I must apologize for my behavior the other morning in the street outside your mother's house. No—*home.* He wanted the language of the letter to be subliminal. A home is what she has thrown away. *I acted irrationally. I was in the wrong and I admit it. I came to bring Toby his favorite pillow and yes, I confess, I wanted to see you too so that we might speak to each other like man and woman.* No—*husband and wife. The boys were still asleep and I did not want to wake them. I also did not expect to catch you coming home at that moment looking like a complete whore.* He struck that last part. He would rewrite the letter in a final draft before sealing it for her. He might as well get it all out now. *You looked so beautiful, I thought to myself when I saw you coming across the lawn. You had been fucked thirteen different ways from Sunday by Arnaud Fleishman and still, barely able to walk, the hair on the top of your head in a permanent nest from being on your back while he laid you . . .* This letter was going to utter shit, he couldn't be honest, there was too much anger. *Did you still have his cum inside you that morning as you walked to me? Could you feel the wetness between your legs as you looked your husband in the eye and scolded him? And for what? For what did I do but love you and come to see you and get our family put back TOGETHER?* The all capital letters was a sign of madness and would have to come out. *Why was I scolded and you important enough to do what you want? Whatever you want. Why when I was there to salvage what is left while it is still salvageable? I will make an agreement. Fuck as much as you want while I'm away in Vietnam, reporting on a very important mission of NATIONAL IMPORTANCE. Fuck him good,*

suck his cock, get it, let him eat your cunt. I will assume you are do-
ing it all unless you tell me otherwise in a detailed letter of your own.
Let him open up your asshole with oiled fingers and then jam his cock
inside. I hope he comes in your swollen ass. Swallow every load he
gives you while I'm away. I will allow it, Penny. I will allow all of
it—anal, coitus, bondage, masochism . . . anything that suits you. I
will allow you to jack him off in a porno theater. I will allow him to
choke you, as you like. I hope he chokes you till you turn purple, then
I won't have to. Get as much of his dick as you can swallow, take ev-
ery inch till you gag, because when the time comes, it's over. It's over
when I return, and we will not speak of it any longer. And this little
affair will be behind us and maybe we can get on with our lives as
two adults who made a promise to each other long ago. Happiness is
a concept that is not real, but a word for a momentary feeling that we
have experienced time and time again. Your concept of happiness has
been clouded, baby. Happiness could just as easily be called satisfac-
tion. Get satisfied. Get your cunt satisfied. And when you are sore
from his limp prick, once you have used it for every one of your pur-
poses, in every hole you could take pleasure from, then we will hear
no more of it. I will accept you as you are. Fuck you, rancid bitch.
Love, Alan.

The letter he crumpled up into a ball.

On Sunday night he said good-bye to Lee and Toby and Helen. The
weekend had passed easily, and by Sunday afternoon he was stirring
with anticipation and impatience. He wasn't yet ready to get used to
the feeling of sitting put and watching his children. And there was
nothing real about Vietnam yet. Nothing tangible until he got there.
He spoke to Broadwater on the phone before he left, and all the necessary papers, a visa for the Republic of South Vietnam, were in his

possession, except for a visa to the North, which Broadwater said they were still working on and that he shouldn't worry, they would get it to him in Saigon. With a few bags and some clean clothes, he parted ways with his children. He didn't leave a letter for Penny. He couldn't bring himself to write anything dishonest and besides, he didn't know how a letter would be taken, but he knew how his absence would. He had been wallowing in her absence for days on end; it was a prison sentence.

By the time he got to the airport he already missed his children. Knowing he wouldn't be seeing them at least for a couple weeks affected him greatly. If he called them before he left he could say good-bye one more time and he might even catch Penny as she came home.

He rang them from a pay phone at the terminal and Helen answered.

"It's me," he said. "We're waiting to board. Normally I would call Penny if I was flying somewhere. You know. In case anything happened. I love you, darling. I don't know what I would have done without you this weekend. Will you think about coming down from school more often?"

"Daddy," Helen said. "Don't say 'in case anything happens.' It's bad karma."

"I'm sorry I won't be around for your birthday," he said.

"I'll be spending it up at school anyway."

"I'll try to call you."

"Only if you can. After all, you will be in Vietnam."

He asked about Lee and Toby, and Helen called the boys to the phone. Hearing the three of his children in the house together was humbling. He said good-bye and sent his love once again. He told Lee to watch over his little brother and not to let Mom go out too much. "And tell me if she has any guests over."

"Who, like Grandma?" said Lee.

"Yeah, Grandma Cathy. A girlfriend. Or anyone else. Keep a mental record if you can. The address of the hotel is on the kitchen counter if you want to write me." Leaving the address was more for Penny's benefit. He hoped if she saw it she would be compelled to write him. And just as he was thinking this he heard Toby in the background call, "Mom's home! Mom's home!" At the same time, an announcement was made that his flight to Bangkok was now boarding. From there he would catch a connecting flight to Saigon.

Helen got back on the line. "Penny's here. You want to talk to her?"

"Okay."

He stood by and listened to the household without him. It was crushing to hear. The children and their mother reuniting. Helen holding out the phone to Penny. A feeling welled up inside of him, one of bitterness and affection. Why did it have to happen this way? She wanted passion? She wanted him to act? Action was getting on a plane and leaving for a dangerous place where no one was waiting for him. He could get some perspective in the Far East instead of remaining in New York on the edge of losing control.

Penny took the call. And as he heard her voice say his name in a concerned tone, much gentler than when they last spoke, he hung up on her without saying a word.

II
Bao Chi

9

The Saigon bureau of the paper was on the second floor of the Continental, room 32. When Channing wasn't there, she was in her room on the same floor. In the mornings she woke up with the stale taste of tobacco and the impending heartache of anxiety, even when she didn't need to be out in the field. She took her breakfast outside in the courtyard at the same table under the banyan trees, in the shade, where she could be left alone until David Wheeler came down to join. That morning, Wheeler came down at the leisurely hour of eight, reeking of whiskey and prostitutes. He didn't eat or say anything, he just sat there and looked up through the tree branches. It was an understanding they had. If he was going to sit at her table in the courtyard he wasn't going to say shit. If he were to say shit, she would carefully remove herself and take the remainder of her coffee in her room. At which point Wheeler would usually apologize and ask her to return.

Then he would just sit and shut up, listen to some bird chirp in the branches above, that was it.

Channing was in the middle of composing a letter to her father, who lived in Oakland. It took concentration to write her family. She spent most of her time writing dispatches, where you looked outside yourself, at others, at what was happening around you. To focus on herself, this was a hard thing. She hadn't written her father in six months. In her last letter she had described to him a walk through Saigon along Tu Do Street, and what a day was like at the Continental, in and out of the bureau, the people she met, the soldiers she spoke to. At the beginning of her term here it had been all American boys. Then what was left of the MACV. Now it was the South Vietnamese ARVN. She neglected to tell her father about the combat and dead bodies she had seen in villages as close as thirty kilometers from Saigon. Anyway, she knew he kept up with the paper and got hold of whatever she wrote at the local library.

Wheeler grew restless in his chair and made motions that he was going to break the silence. "I have something that you may just want to hear at this ungodly hour," he said. "It's about someone who may interest you."

"Sounds like a lead you're too hungover to follow and want to pass off to me."

"No, I'm just making small talk. But it can wait. I know you have your routine. I have a routine, too. A regimen I like to stick to. I'm practically religious about it." He squinted into the sky. "I like to sit here in silence. Let the morning overtake me. Let the sun shine on. Breathe the air."

Wheeler couldn't seem to shut up this morning, which meant he was excited about something. "He's a celebrity of sorts," Wheeler said.

"So it's a he," she said.

"Take a guess."

"Walter Cronkite."

"Not of that caliber."

"Marlon Brando."

"Not as famous."

"Marcello Mastroianni."

"Now you're just naming men you want to sleep with."

"I'm naming men I've already slept with," she said.

"David Wheeler," he said.

"Full of shit."

"Alan Eastman," said Wheeler. "Come to collect his Pulitzer Prize." Wheeler sank low in his seat and raised his eyebrows in a type of mock amazement.

"I never read him," she said, not knowing why she lied. She had read Eastman in college, and then reread him in journalism school. Maybe she just wanted to end this conversation with Wheeler and get back to her letter home. But it was too late, she had already lost her train of thought, so the letter would have to wait. Eastman wasn't one of her favorite writers by any means, but he was a celebrity writer, shooting his mouth off about feminism and race on television, and yet he retained a sort of dignity that followed men like Eastman around. It was unfair, really, when she thought about the man and his reputation. How a man could say so many stupid things and be exonerated after a short commercial break. But why was she thinking about him now? The young photo of him on a book jacket. The wild, unhinged prime-time talk-show guest who babbled incoherently. She was daydreaming about him though she couldn't even remember the last book he wrote.

It was time for her to go. She didn't have a second coffee as usual. She gathered her things and left Wheeler, who suddenly looked as if he were asleep with his eyes open.

"Stay, Channing," said Wheeler. He wasn't good at being alone. He spoke of his wife in Philadelphia often, not by name. Every morning he woke up well before he needed to in order to sit with Channing at breakfast. He was often in the bureau, just lounging around, smoking. He hardly went out into the field these days but seemed to linger around Saigon more and more. He'd be on the terrace in the evenings, drinking "33," if not with other newsmen then with a prostitute on his lap and a vial of cocaine in his jean pocket. He was still of some value to the paper, having shown he could weather the culminating years of this war in unsavory places.

Back in her room she turned on the rattling air conditioner and took off her sandals, placed her feet on the cold tile. She sat in her green lounge chair next to which was the pile of ten books she had flown here with. Joseph Mitchell, A. J. Liebling, Tolstoy, a copy of Lenny Bruce's autobiography. Resting on top of that was an ashtray. She called a room boy to bring up another cup of coffee, and when he did, she smoked in the chair, her thoughts returning to the celebrity.

She took a shower, and there was still a minute of hot water left so she was able to wash her hair. She got out and toweled off. She had her hair cut short to keep soldiers from daydreaming, to not get her caught up anywhere, to keep it out of her face when she was in a dustoff helicopter.

She had landed in the country with long black hair and not only was it a discomfort in the heat but she was asked once by a soldier in Da Nang if he could touch it. He was being sincere and didn't mean any harm, she knew, and when she had said no she felt guilty, like it was a gesture she should have permitted because who knew what would happen to him. The soldier told her she was beautiful and she thanked him. When she got back to Saigon she cut it all off. That was more than a year ago, the soldier in Da Nang, and her hair had now grown to the length of her chin. She'd become unrecognizable, she thought, at least to anyone who knew her back home.

She stayed in her towel awhile and finished her coffee before getting dressed, in no hurry to get anywhere. She turned on the radio and listened to some rock and roll, then went by the window, where she smoked her last cigarette of the morning and watched Lam Son Square begin to liven. The French windows were crossed with masking tape to keep them from shattering in case of shelling. She had moved the bed and desk away from the windows to the farthest corner of the room, closest to the door and the bath, so that her room looked particularly empty except for the lounge chair, the pile of books, and the cassette player with a stack of tapes. Country Joe and the Fish, CCR, Neil Young.

From her room overlooking the square she could see the park, the National Assembly, the roof of the Caravelle, where she would sometimes end up. Prostitutes with their boyfriends or handlers crossed the square back and forth at night, but right now it was sparse with cyclos and bicycles, a few men in green fatigues lounging around the National Assembly, looking playful.

She was supposed to meet a man named Lin this morning in the lobby and she didn't know what he looked like. She still had some time, and from her window she saw an ARVN soldier leaning up against the stone balustrade bordering the park. He could have been part of the National Assembly detail, the men who guarded the old Opera House in the square. But since he stood at some distance from the other men, she decided he wasn't. He was taking a break, smoking, no rifle. She could see the top of his head and his sunglasses, his hair cut like so many of the other Vietnamese men, cropped short from the neckline and jutting out at the ears, so that the top formed a mushroom of black hair. She watched him for a moment and thought that there was always somebody watching something happen, especially in the war. There were no fallen trees in the woods that no one heard. No bombings that went unwitnessed. Everything was getting reported, everything was getting seen. Even this man, were he to be Lin or not. She was watching him as he looked at the Hondas and cyclos go. He was watching over the square, the passersby, the women and children, the stray dogs. He was taking it all in while she watched his head turn side to side, smoking.

Her mornings were like this; it took some time to get out into the world. There was a lot of waiting, waiting like you wouldn't believe.

When the ARVN man put out his cigarette and looked at his wristwatch, she had a hunch he was the man she was waiting for, so she stubbed out her butt and readied herself. She dressed and put on a sun hat and sunglasses. She was downstairs in a minute flat, taking the stairs to the lobby.

Mrs. Nguyen, who worked the desk in the mornings, tried to stop her as she walked by. "Ms. *Chain*-ning, you have message." And Channing signaled her—never mind.

She stepped out onto the sidewalk and saw the ARVN man walking toward the Continental. He was slow, walking with a limp. She didn't want to greet him out in the street, so she went back into the hotel, past the lobby boy on the stool, and went over to the desk by Mrs. Nguyen.

"I'll take my message," she said.

"Very well, Ms. *Chain*-ning."

She had two messages, in fact. The first was a note from the news bureau in New York alerting her to the fact that the celebrity would be arriving today at the Continental, and if she didn't mind would she so kindly set him up on his feet. *Kindly* had been underlined in the telex. The second message was handwritten on hotel stationery from Bob H., the bureau chief, and the message was the same. *Alan Eastman coming to the Continental. Do what you can for him or do nothing. Up to you.*

The man came inside after a word with the lobby boy and stood as a shadow in the open doorway. He took off his sunglasses and looked around. When he saw her, she approached him with her hand out. Like so many Vietnamese he was hesitant to touch her.

"Are you Lin?" she asked. "I'm meeting Lin."

The soldier nodded, speaking politely. Yes, he was Lin, here to meet Anne Channing. His command of English was strong, and his eyes had a certain intelligence. She brought him over to the sitting area in the lobby and they were seated. She got out her pad and pen. A waiter came over and brought them some iced tea.

"If you don't mind me asking, how old are you?" she said.

Lin seemed a little uneasy in the lobby, looking around at the staff. Mrs. Nguyen was nosy and watched the both of them out of the corner of her eye. Channing didn't want to bring Lin up to her room, because she knew Mrs. Nguyen would tell somebody she had a Vietnamese up there. It was better for her if they spoke in the lobby, but she could see that this was going to be difficult.

Lin said he was twenty-one but he looked younger. She was put in touch with him through a friend named Davis, who worked for the embassy. Channing had put the word out that she wanted to interview North Viets who were in Saigon, and Davis had recommended Lin, an ARVN soldier who would know about such things. Channing wanted to talk to anyone who was in Saigon from up North, former prisoners who were reeducated and released, politicians, even spies. Davis had suggested by the embassy pool one evening that spies were easier to come by. And now that the majority of American troops had left, she might find one or two intent on speaking to journalists, anonymously, of course. They probably would speak to her under a pretense of sorts, hoping to spread propaganda into the American press.

"Davis tells me you may know someone," Channing said. "Someone from the North who is in Saigon who'd be willing to talk to me."

Once again Lin looked around.

"It's okay," she said. "We can talk here. It is safe."

"There's a cook in Cholon that you want to meet. He also wants to talk with you."

"He wants to talk to me?"

"Yes. To American press. He's willing to talk to you but you cannot use his name."

"If that's what he wants, of course."

"He's the cook, they call this man."

"Why do they call him that?"

"He cooks at a restaurant in Cholon. I will take you. First we meet him at restaurant, and if he likes the looks of you then he will meet you another time. A second time."

"Why can't we just talk at the restaurant? If he works there he'll feel safe."

"It is not the case. Lots of American are eating there."

"When can we go?"

"I can take you this afternoon. We eat lunch." Lin adjusted his bum leg so that it looked straighter as he sat forward.

"What happened to your leg?" Channing asked.

"It was near the border near Cambodia. I was hit in two places. Here in my hip and here in back of the leg." He pointed to just above his calf muscle.

"You were lucky, then," she said.

"I am lucky."

Lin seemed embarrassed, so Channing smiled as an attempt to put him at ease.

"Lin, I would also like to hear your story very much. I have time to talk more now, before lunch. And then you can take me to Cholon."

Lin shook his head. "I don't think I have anything to talk about."

"You can start with what happened to your leg."

"I'll come back to the hotel to pick you up for lunch."

She took that as a polite no and they set a time for when Lin would return. They shook hands and Lin straightened his leg as he got up. He walked out of the lobby, again moving slowly, dragging his foot behind him. Channing sat there finishing her tea and took some notes in her pad. She considered the book she was writing, in addition to her work for the bureau. The interview with the cook was something she hoped she could use were it to go well. She had been absorbing people, sites, and stories for the last eighteen months. She didn't want to explain Vietnam, there were enough newsmen doing that. She wanted to single out a feeling in time, using those she met and spoke to. A moment in time was a simple way to wrap one's head around a book about war.

To do this work took a certain degree of arrogance. The other newsmen displayed this arrogance and mistook it for bravery. Channing tried desperately to mask her arrogance from her subjects, particularly men in combat.

These were the issues she often struggled with up in her room, whenever there was stillness and nothing to do but wait. She was sitting, noting this down on a pad in the lobby of the Continental, when the celebrity entered, with more luggage than anyone else she'd seen in Vietnam. How he got through Tan Son Nhut Air Base with a matching set of suitcases and a portable typewriter was unimaginable to her. The men who received him must have had a chuckle at his expense. He was much smaller than he looked on television, here in his safari shirt with pens and pads and passport sticking out of each pocket. He seemed to disrupt even the breeze that was passing through the open wooden doors. A lobby boy came to his assistance and relieved him of some of the luggage. His typewriter case he kept on him.

When Mrs. Nguyen recognized him she came out from behind the front desk to welcome him. Bob H. must have shown her a photo on his way out and left instructions.

The celebrity could have been nicer to Mrs. Nguyen. She didn't come out from behind her station for just anyone. "I need my room," he said. "Can someone show me to my room?"

"Welcome, we are so pleased to have you with us," said Mrs. Nguyen. "Yes, your room."

"Is it up this way? I haven't slept. I need my room."

"Of course, you've been on a long journey. Did you have an escort?"

"From the plane? Yes. That all went fine. Does the room have an air conditioner?"

"Indeed, sir. You are staying at the Continental Palace."

"Then the room, please, check me in."

It was like watching a mental patient being processed into a psych ward. The celebrity ranted, shuffled, scratched at himself. He could have been on amphetamines.

Channing didn't want to have to introduce herself while he was in this state. But she had lingered a bit too long in the lounge area of the lobby and couldn't possibly slip away without being seen. Then Mrs. Nguyen brought him over to the waiting area, where Channing was seated. He was to wait here, Mrs. Nguyen instructed, and someone would bring him his welcome drink and the room deposit form.

Channing could have left then, gone back up to her room, but it was all too pitiful to abandon now.

He sat down across from her, not directly, but adjacent. Mrs. Nguyen returned to the front desk. Out of his chest pocket he pulled a handkerchief and dabbed the sweat on his forehead. His head looked enormous. His face was handsome but appeared pink and bothered. His temples immediately dampened again with humidity.

A waiter came with a tall glass of sweetened milk tea on ice. The celebrity took it with no thank you and proceeded to stir the tea with the spoon, clinking the glass disruptively. She had once read a column he had in the *Village Voice,* in which he referred to his height as five foot ten. But he was a good deal shorter than that, maybe by four inches, which would make them the same height.

Resting the tea on the side table, he produced a little pill tin out of his pocket and took two of whatever was in there, washing it down with the milk tea. He didn't cease drinking until he had finished the glass, choking a bit at the end. A line of milk trailed down the side of his mouth and under the chin. He gasped after swallowing. An annoying habit, Channing thought. Must drive his wife mad.

For someone so attuned to detail in his books, he didn't seem to notice her sitting there across from him.

Only when he turned to look out the window did he finally see her. Channing had her sunglasses on, and had placed her hat on, too, in order to disguise herself. Her lenses were dark and so he couldn't see her eyes. With her black hair and pale features, he probably didn't know if she was Vietnamese or American, though from her clothes—jeans and blouse—he should have known that she was American.

She had the request from her boss on her lap. The note on a 3 x 5 index card. *Do what you can for him or do nothing.* And at this moment she was very much of the mind to do nothing.

But he did notice her now and he wasn't the kind of man to turn away or play coy or polite. He was invasive, and she'd sensed this as soon as he had stepped foot into the Continental. As a challenge, she didn't turn away from him, although with her shades, she had on a kind of shield, a way to view without being too self-conscious. However old or loud or pigheaded the celebrity seemed to be, his gaze on her was thrilling. It felt as if they were on a New York subway car and he had been staring at her, trying to communicate something deeper. She hadn't come across his type in Vietnam before, this mixture of naiveté and hubris, not from another correspondent.

It took some willpower to hold his stare. Before she knew it she was playing a game with him. He really wasn't going to turn away. She grew tired of this, and when she saw that Mrs. Nguyen was returning, Channing nonchalantly turned away from him as if it were nothing. Which it was. She caught herself being as egotistical as he was, defending her line of sight, her own airspace. She should have just ignored him to begin with. In fact, had she ignored him and left the lobby before he sat down, she thought, she might have been able to save herself.

10

The eight districts of Saigon were clustered together like the arrondissements of Paris, an illogical urban spiral of shanty-towns and French quarters and low-lying apartments, and on the outskirts of town it was green, green, green. Inside it stank of colonialism, giving him intimations of New Orleans. Still, Saigon was a beautiful mess of a city, and at the center of it was the square in front of the National Assembly, with the two hotels facing off across the bustling plaza—the Continental Palace and the Caravelle—both seemed to be competing for journalists. Stringers, correspondents, newscasters, novelists. The Continental, of course, had its famous terrasse, where newsmen as far back as one can recall came to drink away their nerves. But the Caravelle, the more modern of the two, was a tower in comparison and had its rooftop bar, where everyone ended up at some point in the night. There was a curfew going, but the nights were still long, and if you were caught staring into your ice when the lights came on, one could still find the way to one's room at the Continental, zip across the square if need be, say hello to the night boy, and fall into the coolness of one's feather pillow.

The journey from New York to Saigon had been tolerable. Eastman cried a bit on the plane with a sleep mask over his eyes, thinking of Penny and the boys. It had been harder to leave them this time, more so than any other trip. Going away meant that Toby and Lee would be left in their mother's care. They would get used to his absence as their lives returned to a kind of normalcy. There would be bright days of summer without him, Penny airing out his soul from the house. He would mean nothing to them by the time he got back.

Somehow he needed to be present while he was away, so during the flight he took out a pen and paper and began composing a letter to the children. *My Dear Boys, I'm calling on you from thirty-nine thousand feet, moving at five hundred knots or close to it. Ask your teachers about knots. A commercial airliner like the one I'm on cruises somewhere in the area of 450–500 knots, which if you learn the conversion is somewhere near six hundred mph (miles per hour). Fact-check that for me. . . . I'm thinking of you guys, remembering the time the four of us flew to San Francisco when I was to cover the Democratic National Convention. We took both of you when you were quite young and your mother and I were nervous for Toby, especially, who was only three and had never been on a plane. Lee must have been seven. Your mother was sick with a yeast infection and I was struggling to hold it together by the strength of my fingernails. And not a peep out of Toby, no airsickness even through turbulent winds. He slept over the entire Midwest. It must have been the first time you both sat eye level with the clouds. I remember because I told you that clouds were just masses of condensed water vapor, no more. The same matter that flows out of your mother's humidifier in the winter, the one by her side of the bed.* He remembered the four of them on that particular plane, seated in two rows, Toby and Penny together. He and Lee behind them. He had been explaining the cloud condensation to Lee. Penny turned around and said, "Way to be a killjoy, Alan. Let him enjoy the view. Can't clouds just be clouds?" "Yeah, Dad," said Lee. Eastman enjoyed being their stick-in-the-mud. "Sure," he said, "clouds can be clouds. What do you both see out there? What does that one look like to you?" He pointed to a cluster of white clouds in the distance, far enough away to appear unmoving. Lee looked out and said he saw a person's face, sad, like it had been crying. "You see," Eastman said to Penny. "He has so much empathy. He could be a shrink when he grows up."

"Don't patronize him," she said. Penny looked out her window over little Toby, who was fast asleep. "And you, what are you seeing?" he asked her, a little miffed.

"I see several horses. They're crossing a bay so I can only see their heads." She counted out three of them. Eastman looked out at the clouds and he was desperate to find what Penny was imagining. He wanted to be inside her head so often, to see what she saw, to feel what she felt. He wanted to get as close to her as possible. And she, he felt, wanted the same. She had the ability to guess what he was thinking by the look on his face. The right person, he believed, tended to know every variation of you. "Did you find it?" Penny asked. He couldn't find the horses she saw in the clouds but said yes anyway. "I see them, sure."

As he finished the letter to his boys on the plastic meal tray, his voice began to sound false to him. He was now aware that Penny would be reading over the boys' shoulders and so he began to take advantage of the situation. *I still love your mother, unconditionally, and it was on that trip just a few years ago, which I am reminded of now, when I discovered my true potential as a man, and it had much to do with family. A man has reached only half of his potential if he hasn't felt a true love. Love of a woman. Love of his children. I could have climbed a redwood the day we went to Muir Woods with the strength I had drawn from the three of you. My attitude toward your mother has not changed since that day even if she thinks otherwise. I only wish she could believe that. Boys, how shall I convince her?*

I want her to have what she wants. That's always been my wish for her. I won't give up the fight, men, and I will do everything in my power to keep us together. I'm hopeful that when I return from Vietnam I can

win her back and prove that I am the one for her. I look forward to more
deliberations on the matter.

He ended his letter with a recollection from that same trip to California, when the Eastmans drove south along Highway 1 toward Big Sur. What he remembered, vaguely, as a happy time, he colored in with scenery he couldn't actually remember. An unworldly sunset, a few cliffs above a chilly California beach, the children playing in the sand, and two parents in the distance, watching them. The mother takes the father's hand. The father holds it for a long time. It made him tear up all over again.

When he touched down in Vietnam, Eastman was met at Tan Son Nhut Air Base by an ARVN officer, who drove him to the Continental Palace Hotel. He was interested in the officer and pushed for more of a tour of the city, but found it difficult as the man's English was limited. So he checked in and met Mrs. Nguyen, who seemed pleasant and accommodating. She could be useful, and he even thought to interview her at some point, as this was the famous Continental where newsmen had stayed for the duration of the entire war. His room was sufficient. A double with two beds, a desk where he could work, a set of lounge chairs, a ceiling fan, and a window-unit air conditioner that rattled ceaselessly. He was a floor above the *Herald*'s Saigon bureau, which he avoided for now. He set up his typewriter on the desk and organized his papers. The letter to his boys he signed *Daddy* and sealed it in an envelope to give to Mrs. Nguyen in the outgoing mail.

His reluctance to check in with the bureau was due to the phony pretenses of his trip, a trip that began as a lie, a fib, although it was a lie so convincing that it spread itself around New York publishing circles. And the last person to take him seriously wasn't any of those

publishing bloodsuckers he called friends, or his wife, but Eastman
himself. He would have to be truthful now if he was going to write the
kind of stuff Broadwater and the *Herald* wanted. A record of history.

He loaded a piece of carbon-backed paper into the typewriter
and began:

<u>THE UNLIKELY CORRESPONDENT,</u>

<u>A.K.A. THE UGLY CORRESPONDENT</u>

Our title recalls how our hero was
feeling when he first stepped out onto the
tarmac at Tan Son Nhut Air Base without any
love in his heart. U.C. was heartbroken, you
see? He was a palindrome of sorrow, front
to back. Wait a minute . . . U.C. backward
was C.U. <u>See you</u> as in <u>so long.</u> So it wasn't
a palindrome, but it resonated with him
nevertheless. His marriage was falling
apart just when the <u>Herald</u> was making
arrangements to bring him to Vietnam. They
wanted from him a series of hard-won
dispatches to get you readers wiping the
sweat from your brows each Sunday morning.
U.C. in a foxhole with grunts. Hard
conditions. But he was in no shape for this
kind of work. Partly because of the
aforementioned marriage. Partly because he
had sent himself to a bombed-out country
ill equipped and with no one to blame but
himself.

He lost interest in what he was doing and wandered over to the bed to lie down. In the time between that surge of inspiration and the end of a single paragraph he grew depressed. There was no getting around it, and this deflation of all feeling was causing fatigue. He would have liked to talk to Penny at such a time, to even have her here with him. He could send her a letter and an express ticket to Saigon. Wouldn't it prove to her that he was the passionate man?

He needed to talk to her.

Eastman reached for the phone on the bedside table, knocking over an ashtray. If he was going to overthink this he thought it best to just talk it out. He dialed the front desk and asked for an outside line to the U.S. As he began to dial he hesitated, then dialed, then failed, redialed. It took a few minutes to finally get something resembling a ring, a *rat-a-tat-tat* that made him sit up. He didn't know what to expect. He was sweating. My God, will she still respect me?

A man picked up at the other end. "Hallo," he said.

"This is Alan Eastman calling for Penny. Who is this?"

"Alan eats what? No, I don't understand at all."

"Excuse me. Am I calling New York?"

"I don't know, are you?"

"Don't play around. Is this Arnaud Fleishman? Are you in my house, you son of a bitch?"

"I'm waiting for the car at my house. I've been waiting for thirty minutes. Where are you?"

"Where am I? Who is this?"

"Where is the car? The car to take us to the airport. It's been thirty minutes and I'm still waiting. Are you coming?"

"No, listen. This is a mistake," Eastman said. "I think our lines got crossed. I'm not taking anyone to the airport."

"I don't understand."

"I'm trying to reach my wife, Mac. Her name's Penny. I think the lines got crossed. This is her husband. I'm calling from Vietnam."

"Oh my God. Is everything okay?" The man sounded genuinely concerned.

"I don't know how to answer that."

"Well, are you in any sort of danger?"

"Not really, no. Listen, are you in New York? Maybe you can get a message to her for me."

"Paris. I'm in Paris."

"Oh, for Chrissake. I have to go."

He was losing patience. All the energy Eastman worked up to call her had tired him out, and for what? Wasted on a wrong number. He again dialed the front desk to complain. Had they given him proper instructions? Yes, yes, the man apologized for the inconvenience and asked him to try it again. He ordered a pitcher of cold water. "I'll try again," he said. This time he didn't get a *rat-a-tat-tat* but more tones of signals and circuits gone haywire.

He reconsidered calling Penny at this hour (New York was twelve hours behind) and concluded it would be detrimental to his health. So he gave up.

A room boy knocked on his door and Eastman yelled for him to come in. The boy placed the pitcher of water down on the nightstand. He handed over a few crumpled piastres as a tip. How was he going to manage in this country, he asked himself?

Eastman drank a big glass of water and then lay down, placing a cold-water compress on his forehead. He needed to rest, to nap, only he couldn't fall asleep. He watched the ceiling fan circulate the musty air until finally he dozed off.

The water he drank and that soaked the facecloth on his forehead didn't agree with him. Not yet anyway. He woke in the early evening to a stomachache deep in his intestines, and for the next two days he lived in the bathroom of his hotel room. Next to the toilet he kept a copy of *Cosmopolitan*, which he had bought at JFK because of a headline that read HOW TO GET OVER HIM, and he thought, or hoped, rather, that Penny would be reading the same thing. Healing a wounded heart, it said, was all about changing one's way of thinking. If your husband or gentleman has left, you had to form new paths for yourself, both mentally and physically. Create new memories, it said, with those you didn't have time for in your now defunct relationship. Take a different route to work and begin frequenting a different market. Eat dinner with a girlfriend at a restaurant you have never been to. Take a trip (you deserve it!).

He had to admit, even the rhetoric in *Cosmo* seemed a bit patronizing. An article on locating the G-spot he found much more compelling.

He didn't leave his room at all and he hardly ate, except for some fruit and portions of a single croissant when he could keep it down. He took water that he was told was purified. The room boy came twice daily with fresh fruit in the mornings—bananas, mangoes, dragon fruit, kiwis—then a second pitcher of water in the afternoon and a fresh wet facecloth to take down Eastman's fever. When the fruit on the coffee table began to shrivel, the room boy replaced it.

11

He didn't head straight to the news bureau on the second floor of the Continental, and this, he would later learn, was a mistake. It made the *Herald*'s staff in Saigon feel insignificant. Instead, he followed a lead set up by Broadwater, and set out to an early lunch to meet General Burke, a man who had been sending him messages since he arrived.

Eastman crossed Tu Do Street and took a short walk down Le Loi. He moved past the bookstalls, the paperbacks and newspapers in Vietnamese. Many of the books looked flimsy, as if they had been photocopied. Still, they were a literate culture and words seemed to carry some magnitude here. It was like that in oppressed societies. One could be imprisoned for writing a book, and not only because it was obscene—that was American puritanism—but because the book's ideas were provocative and feared. The right book here could start a revolution, and so in the North words were policed, just as in the Soviet Union and China and North Korea. When a government censored words, censored its people, that was fascism. That was Hitler and the Nazis and mounds of burning books. It pleased him to see the people of Saigon stopping midday to step into a bookstall out of the heat. A lovely thing it was for a writer to witness. No, no, having a series of bookstalls didn't justify an occupation or killing. That was the writer and historian in him talking, not the humanitarian. He was a humanitarian, wasn't he? *I am a type of humanitarian on a mission, am I not? If that wasn't true, why would I be here? The historian is in part humanitarian and pacifist. Sure, I have my own selfish reasons, but does anybody have to know that? I could do something good for these people, couldn't I? And not just by recording history, hence keeping a choir of Americans updated on just how bad we've ripped apart this little country. I could report ideas, the very ones people on both sides of this are afraid of. It is my privilege to do so. To be two things at once. The two H's. H. H. Humanitarian and Historian.* And for a revolution to start it took a literate culture. America's literacy and literary totem pole seemed to have toppled over by the end of the fifties, in the wake of television. Even he read less than he once had.

Saigon was a meditation. It excited him.

He had once been to Moscow on a trip for the State Department in the early sixties on a cultural exchange. There he found Moscow's sleek political surface majestic, its representatives both kind and disciplined. He thought not of totalitarianism but of human beings getting on, a normalcy to life, a thrill behind the iron curtain. Of course he was wrong about Moscow and the whole of the Soviet Union. He saw only what they wanted him to see, shuffled around from palace to palace, meeting dignitaries and other writers who swore to the Soviet Union's wide berth for tolerance. It turned out to be all baloney.

Saigon would take time. Its layered surface cautioned him to be careful not to rush to any conclusions.

Eastman didn't know his way around yet. He had no perspective, he had done no research prior to coming, hoping that his impressions would be enough for his dispatches. But from the little map he had been given at the Continental, he was on the right path. Down Le Loi and on to the Rex Hotel, where he was to meet General Burke. Eastman learned from the notes the general left at the Continental that they had both served in the 112th Cavalry out of San Antonio. They must have been in the Philippines at the same time, but it was a big outfit and Eastman wasn't betting on recognizing someone from thirty years ago. Burke's notes were written on Military Assistance Command, Vietnam stationery, MACV, and they had an intimidating look, as if Burke were trying to impress Eastman with his long-term status here.

When he arrived at the Rex he didn't go in right away. He stood outside on the corner, looking up and around the open city. Women and children, commerce and traffic. The park with its tall trees and a row of neatly parked bicycles. Across Le Loi, a corner café serving hot soup under an awning. It seemed he could get a decent sandwich from one of the many street vendors for a nickel or whatever the equivalent of a nickel was. The air, despite being full of exhaust and tasting of smoke, felt warming.

He was spending too much time on the corner, because a slow-moving rickshaw pulled up to the corner. "Hallo! Give you ride."

"No. No ride. I'm here," said Eastman.

"Hallo. How're you? Give you ride."

"No, dammit, I don't need a ride. I said I'm here. I've reached my destination. I'm not going anywhere."

"Get you girl. Grass, get you high."

"Not interested, little man."

"Boom boom. Meet you nice girl."

Eastman had his hanky in his hand, toweling off the sweat on his forehead, and waved it at the rickshaw driver to shoo him off. When the man persisted, he thought he'd have to speak in a language this cyclist would understand. "You're a pimp." Eastman spit on the ground. "Shoo!"

The man didn't move. He still wanted Eastman to get into his little carriage. "I'm going inside. You better not be here when I come out, you understand me?" Obviously he did not. The man stood there on his bicycle, gratified, and something in his stillness told Eastman that the bastard would be there when Eastman came out. He waved the man away with his hanky once again and entered the Rex.

The situation in the Rex wasn't all that bad, but he still liked where he was at the Continental better. When he arrived at the restaurant on the roof, he saw the general at once at a table closest to the bar. The general was in civilian clothing, khakis and a tight undershirt that showed off a powerful physique. He kept his sunglasses on until he saw Eastman enter the restaurant, then took them off and placed the glasses neatly on the table. Burke stood and quickly waved him over.

"You're a hard man to track down," said Burke. "I left a message at your hotel every day since you got in."

"I was stomach sick. Something I ate. Two days on the commode, it *wudn't purtty*." He started to use a Texas accent, a parody of the general, but a note below Burke's twang to be safe.

"You're drinking plenty of fluids I take it?" said the general.

"Yup."

"Because you've lost a lot of water and you're dehydrated. You need to stay hydrated in this climate. It takes some getting used to, but you've been to the Far East before so I don't have to tell you."

"Gen'ral, that was a lifetime ago. I barely remember it. It was hot, wudn't it?"

"Hot as the inside of an asshole."

"Humid, too, as I recall."

"It's the humidity that builds stamina. Sweat it out a couple days and you'll be used to it. Sit, have you eaten?"

"I could eat a long-horned bull."

"You can get a steak here. It's the best in Saigon. Me, I get the filet *min-yone*, bloody."

Eastman sat down at the table, and from his position he could see the Saigon skyline, gray and bright. Burke sat across from him in what seemed like the safest location in the room. From that vantage point he could see whoever came in and out of the restaurant and his eyes were on the door often. He was a safe man, he didn't seem to take chances, and this made Eastman a bit paranoid. He looked over the menu, pretending really, because he was having what the general was having. They ordered. Two filet mignons, bloody, no potatoes. A side salad.

"I've seen you on television several times," said Burke. "Is it an act? I wonder. You like to run your mouth off about matters concerning this war. Hell, I don't take offense. Listen, I called you here because I like you. I'm a fan. I'm one of your biggest fans. I thought *American War* was the best damn book written about our conflict in the Pacific and not that Jew's, Norman Heimish. He didn't get on the ground like you did. He took on a bigger picture, perhaps. But yours was about the boots on the ground. The voices heard and not heard. It made me proud. Not only because it was about the 112th. But the war stories it told were true to the reality of war."

Eastman noted Burke's anti-Semitism and didn't take offense. He was used to it and he was used to blending in. He had cultivated himself that way, this was why he was using this Texas accent on and off again. He could change himself, mask his identity, so that people would say things to him that they wouldn't say to ordinary reporters.

"Why thank you, general, that's kind. Heimish won the Pulitzer that year. I thought I wrote the better book, too."

"What have you written since?"

"Not anything that's come close to my first book yet. I wrote two novels, the most famous of which was called *A Heaven Among the Stars*. Then I wrote a book of essays called *To Each His Own*. Have you read them?"

"No, I don't read novels."

"Well, they were just unfairly panned by the critics. Scoundrels, every last one of them. And I'm one of them. Unfortunately, where I hail from, not Texas, but New *Yawk*, people take a critic's word literally when it should be taken for shit. Anyway, I began work on another novel about veterans, men like you and me who had been to war, only this time in Europe—Italy. Naples, to be exact. They pass through Italy on their way to a trip hunting boar in Sweden. It's twenty years later and—"

"Let me cut you off there, Alan. May I call you Alan? I don't want to know your whole life story. I just wanted a brief summary, maybe talk about some books that I could get my hands on. History, conflict. Real matters. That's what I read."

"Then *To Each His Own* is the book for you. You know, I'm the one who should be asking you some questions. I'm interested in what's been going on here and your part in all this. I take it you're a man who knows how this country works. Where could I get the scoop? Where should I stay out of? That's probably where I should start."

"I can help with that. There's fighting, if that's what you're looking for—ARVN forces up North."

"Yes, that's where I want to go."

"First I need to know something. Are you capable of writing a true war story? The kind you once wrote before? The kind that spoke to me, and spoke to others? Because your track record tells me different. You don't like this war, do you? And you haven't shut up about it too often."

"No, I don't like this war and I don't understand it. That's why I'm here. Of course, I know the reasons given, but the reasons don't make any sense to me. There's a gap in my comprehension, you see.

That's why I've spoken out against it time and again. But now that's all over, we're past it. America was here, came, fought, and went. I'm not against the military, General. I'm of the military."

"Discharged, wasn't it?"

"Honorably. Not the other way around. I threw my hat in because there was an injustice."

"Man of principle."

"Principle, yes."

"You see, Alan, I need assurances you're not going to throw gasoline on a fire were I to stick my neck out. Are you capable of writing a war story and not the kind of anti-shitshow that is published every damn day in the *New York Times*?"

"I don't write for the *Times*. And assurances—no—I won't give those. I won't tell you what I will and won't write because I don't know yet. But you know who I am, what I've written. Where I served. Maybe we differ on some matters. But I'm the same man who wrote that book all those years ago. The one that brought me here to meet you."

Burke sat back in his chair and watched the door. He glanced at Eastman, pleased with himself. The general's eye began to twitch as if he had something in it. It was a tick, Eastman noticed. Burke put his sunglasses back on and said, "I heard you were a hard son of a bitch. It's good to finally meet you."

"It's good to meet you, Gen'ral," said Eastman, returning to his Texan talk.

"You can call me Don. All my friends do."

The waiter brought them their steaks and Burke cut his into equal, bite-sized pieces, not even trying the meat until the whole thing was divided. Eastman waited patiently, and drank his water until Burke was done, and they started their lunch. Burke spoke with his mouth full.

"Dak Pek, does that mean anything to you?" asked Burke.

"I don't know it."

"It's northwest of Kon Tum near the Laos border. I think you should go there. There's fighting up in Dak Pek, and I have good contacts up there."

Eastman wrote down Dak Pek and Kon Tum.

"The VC had our base up there seized for a few months, then cleared out, and ARVN took it back over. Also, I'll fix you up with the new ARVN press officer so you can get into some of these press conferences that go on each week and just stink to high hell."

"I won't be reporting anything as newsmen do. I'll be writing my impressions of this country as it is now. But I will sit in on some press conferences for a start."

"Well, your ID says Bao Chi, doesn't it? As far as transport to Dak Pek and wherever else you want to go, you let me know first and I'll see what I can do. But remember, even if you won't give me any assurances on what you write, I'm counting on you. I'm not sitting here with Norman Heimish, am I?"

Eastman considered the comment, the anti-Semitic remarks made earlier. He said, "Why would you be sitting here with him?"

"Cuz he's in Saigon, that's why."

"Heimish?"

"I'm surprised you haven't run into him. All you boys seem to know each other."

"He's writing a book, too. If he's here, that's what he's doing. Heimish is going to scoop me."

"I thought you said you wouldn't be reporting anything. It was just . . . impressions."

"I know what I said. But this changes things drastically. Do you know where he's staying?"

"Why would I know that? I'm not his babysitter. He's either at the Continental where you are or he's at the Caravelle. That's where I would start."

Eastman felt stifled. He began to get those heavy feelings in his chest again, the kind that weighed on him so deeply for the past two days. He felt the oncoming nausea, the hot and cold sweat on his temple. He began to scratch at his knuckles. Then to breathe in and out through his nostrils. He could use a Valium; he had them in his room, only he was too proud to bring them along, thinking all of his anxiety was behind him.

"Your steak's getting cold," said Burke.

"Goddamn Heimish," said Eastman. He steadied himself and tried to mask his irritation. The general seemed to be having fun watching Eastman fume. Maybe they were alike, and the general enjoyed seeing others suffer just as Eastman did. Then this was just what he had coming. But no, he was able to steady himself in the presence of others, the distraction of talk took him out of his head.

"Oh, I wonder before our lunch is over," said Burke, "would you mind autographing a book for me?" Burke called over the waiter and Eastman's *American War* was produced on a tray. "I want you to address it: *To General Donald Burke, a true friend from the 112th, San Antone. And to his wife, Kitty. In warm admiration, Alan Eastman.* Something like that."

Eastman hated it when people instructed him what to write and it almost always set him off. He took the book and wrote quickly, *To Gen. Don Burke, thanks for your vote, you mensch. L'chaim!* et cetera. And he got up and excused himself to the toilet.

Eastman had written Adrien McClure, his editor at Rhinehart, in November of 1963, while on his honeymoon with Penny in San Sebastian. The subject: adventures and travails with Norman Heimish.

The honeymoon was a happy time for both Penny and Eastman; in fact, it was a reunion for the two newlyweds. That summer, shortly before they married, they had split up for a month. Eastman had somehow forgotten this, apropos of his current situation. Why had he suppressed the fact that this had happened to them before? It was Penny back then who made them take a "pause" before the wedding, a pause needed to warm her cold feet.

Penny had been exchanging letters with a friend in London, a man she swore was "as gay as they come." (In truth, back then Eastman used to go through her mail whenever he saw a man's name on the return address, usually in a handwriting he didn't like. So he was already familiar with a man named Eric Nagel.) Eastman knew by Nagel's hand that he wasn't opposed to Penny's affections. The two had exchanged letters, several lengthy letters, and planned to meet when she would be visiting the London School of Economics for an academic conference. Eastman knew something was up by the tone in their correspondence. There were innuendos he didn't quite understand, pages from the letters missing here and there, and so he was unable to track what exactly was being implied. All of it was strange behavior for Penny, and upon discovery he accused her of foul, unfaithful intentions, things he couldn't take back nor had he really wanted to put forth. She denied it with fervor, took off to London, stayed with Nagel under the pretense that he was gay, and as they fought over the phone, she extended her stay from what was to be a long weekend in August to another three and a half weeks. Penny needed some time to breathe before the wedding and no, she didn't want him there.

He would have flown to London and brought her back had he not been strapped down making edits on *To Each His Own,* a collection of previously published essays. He was correcting the proofs and suddenly adding extensive changes. His attentions were needed on his work, and he figured let her have her time. He could certainly use the three weeks to complete the book. In between writing, Eastman still had a good amount of time to rummage through her things upstairs, her closets and her desk. He was looking for evidence, proof of what he knew but didn't want to admit. Then, in the top corner of her closet he found a pink shoebox with white lace tied tightly around it, Penny's precious secrets waiting for him to unravel. What he found inside were old photographs of her ex-boyfriends from high school, college, graduate school, old love letters, and most important, the missing pages of her correspondence with Nagel. To his horror the pages were from very recently, and in their exchange were feelings and intentions that proved Nagel was not "as gay as they come"; in fact he was far from it. In one of the more filthy pages Eastman had come across, Nagel graphically described what he intended to do with Penny's cunt once he got his mouth around it (transcribed here verbatim). Nagel had also detailed a kiss they had in New York when the English rat was visiting. Eastman looked for the evidence— that Nagel had fucked her—but where was it? All he could determine from Nagel's pages was that they had shared a kiss, a long, drawn-out, poorly rendered peck. And that these dreams of defiling Penny's cunt were Nagel's dreams alone. He couldn't find proof of Penny reciprocating Nagel's wet dreams (of course, her responses he didn't have, they were on the other side of the Atlantic). Though he couldn't prove they hadn't slept together when Nagel was in New York, he somehow knew Penny had refrained from going to bed with him.

But the truth of the matter wasn't found in the letters, it was discovered through her actions. She was in England with Nagel, and would be for three more weeks through to September. And it was only a few months before they were to be married. In his heart he wanted to strangle her, Nagel too, and die himself, alone. But his head was still quite level and told him to leave it be. If she wanted to be with someone else, how could he stop her? There was no sense in forcing her to be by his side when it wouldn't be true and of her own volition.

While Penny stayed on in London, Eastman, tired, betrayed, horrified, vengeful, flew not to London but drove himself to Norman Heimish's sixty-acre ranch in Illinois. He had met Heimish in the fifties as a correspondent. Norman Heimish of the *Chicago Tribune*, who had expanded his reporting into a beautiful book called *In the Shadow of Eden*. It was more of an autobiographical novel than a work of nonfiction, and had it been published as such, Eastman would have taken the Pulitzer instead of Heimish. Eastman wrote to Heimish via his publisher, stating that it was Eastman's honest opinion that they were the two best writers in America. This sort of competitive camaraderie was endearing to Heimish. So they met one night in New York City, where they went from the bar in Heimish's hotel on the Upper East Side and drank themselves down to the bottom of the Bowery. Eastman felt Heimish was someone he could sincerely relate to. Of course, once Heimish indeed won the Pulitzer, Eastman couldn't stand the fact that he was now the lesser writer in the eyes of the Pulitzer committee and quite possibly the American public. Eastman's huge success had been diminished, especially when in the presence of Norman Heimish. Because of this, Eastman chose to keep his distance, and that competitive camaraderie began to decay.

Heimish had set up a type of writers' commune on a working farm, and these early hippies took to the fields naked, strung out, doing each other bodily harm night after night. It was, indeed, a place to get off the map and to begin living however you wanted.

When Eastman arrived he sensed underneath the farm's bucolic se-
renity a sourness, as if all the crops were about to rot. There were
nudists, communists, Marxists, polygamists. Open love was encouraged. Everyone was either bisexual or open to it. It seemed the kind
of place where the voyeur in Eastman could stretch his arms and
legs, howl at the moon, and forget Penny for a few days.

Heimish's circumstances were the strangest of this crazy lot. He was
sharing a woman, Sylvie Dietrich, who was married to Gerd Dietrich.
The Dietrichs lived in a small house on the far north side of the sixty
acres. The couple co-owned the land along with Heimish. Eastman
thought Heimish might have also been bedding Gerd Dietrich, for the
whole setup was beyond his understanding. At the same time, seeing
Heimish and Sylvie and Gerd entangled in this open love triangle made
Eastman wonder whether he was being too hard on Penny for wanting
sex outside their relationship. If the times were changing, the people
would go with it, and where would that leave him? If Heimish's artists'
colony was a model for the second half of the century, then maybe Eastman needed to get his hands dirty and open his mind to experiences he
had often rejected. Man and wife, that was what he always thought was
decent. Looking around the farm in Marshall, with Sylvie's head resting on Heimish's shoulder and Gerd Dietrich on the other side, holding
her hand . . . Was this what we were all heading for? And should a man
adapt to the change in order to be with the woman he wanted?

Eastman had once thought of himself as bisexual, back in the
days when he was experimenting with marijuana and Seconal. His
first sexual experiences were with other boys, and where he grew up,
that wasn't so unusual. He learned to masturbate with a high school
friend on the wrestling team, and they had once masturbated each
other while looking at a nude magazine. He grew out of it, and as a
young man and an adult his sexual appetite was solely for women.

He stayed on the farm for a few days and was reintroduced to marijuana, which relaxed him. Heimish gave him a room in the main house, where Heimish lived along with a cute teenage couple, the girl a painter, and the boy a poet who built Heimish bookshelves and whatever else was needed. She couldn't have been more than eighteen, and the boy looked even younger, especially the way he went around the compound, shirtless at all hours, his skinny, frail torso, ribs and all. They had matching haircuts and wore dirty jeans.

He woke the second morning to the sound of gunfire. He rushed to look out the window (perhaps Dietrich wasn't so hip with sharing his wife after all), but it was just Heimish out in the field. He was walking to the house with a rabbit by the ears and a hunting rifle slung over his shoulder.

These were eccentrics living at the edge of the world.

Late nights he spoke with Penny on the phone in the kitchen and pleaded with her to return to New York. He tried to get her to tell him what was going on. A few more days was all she wanted now. A few more days alone and then she would come back and they would be married. He brought up the letters and how she had lied about Nagel being gay and this only seemed to make matters worse. Penny did not like being put in her place. She scolded him for going through her things and swore that there was nothing going on between her and Nagel. It was a lie told in order not to worry him. He tried to believe her. He tried to look around him at this shitty colony and trick himself into thinking this is how his life would be. Rabbit for dinner. Teenage couple fucking in an adjacent room. Shared relations. Forced friendships.

One night after a long phone conversation, Heimish was up and came into the kitchen in a bathrobe. In his hand was a coffee mug of bourbon. He poured Eastman a splash into the only clean jar and laid it down on the country table.

"Tell me brother," said Heimish. "What's with these late-night sessions?"

"I'm getting remarried."

"To your ex-wife?"

"Barbara? No."

"I'm always confused by the term 'remarried.' You're getting *married*. Is it to this little Penny in your pocket? I'm listening to you plead: *Penny, listen. Penny, wait.* It's none of my business. But it is my phone."

"I'll pay the bill for the month. You've been kind enough."

"That's not what I'm getting at. I got ears you can chew on."

"I think there's someone else. She's fucking someone when we're to be married in a few months. It's not an open thing, her and me. We're . . . committed."

"I'm not against it. Obviously there's someone else. You've been accusing her of it for four nights. Instincts are usually right in this kind of thing, if you're levelheaded and an observer of human beings, like we are."

Heimish brought over the bottle and the two sat at the shabby table under the dim kitchen light.

"Your choice now," said Heimish, "knowing what you know, is to accept this third party or react. Your reaction could work against what you saw as your future. Or your reaction could prove beneficial to the relationship as a whole. You want control, I get it. Don't we all? But you live in the here and now, where things fluctuate, sometimes beautifully, to no end."

"To no end?" Eastman thought Heimish's ideas were spiritual nonsense. "I've flirted with existentialism for many years. Who wants to live a life to no end? Yes, I want control. But no, not complete control, I'm not a maniac. I want control of my own life. I know I can't control a person, that's why I'm here and not on a plane to Heathrow. I'm accepting the situation and I'm leaving it up to her. Ultimately it's her decision. I'll plead my case every night because she's the only thing that matters to me. She's everything, Norman."

"You're accepting of her, that's good, Alan. Acceptance is what we practice here."

"Then I accept your offer to get drunk on your whiskey."

They stayed up into the night talking, and Heimish told the story of how he fixed up with the Dietrichs. He had run into a substantial sum from the sale of the movie rights for *In the Shadow of Eden* and put most of it into the Dietrich farm. Heimish believed in the colony life, having finished *Eden* there after he quit the *Chicago Tribune*, and as he spoke of Sylvie, Eastman really believed he loved her.

That didn't help Eastman get on with the Dietrichs. As the week went on, the colonists met in the Dietrich house every evening for a communal dinner. Each member of the colony took on a job, either peeling carrots and potatoes, chopping garlic, onion, greens, stirring sauce to thicken, or worse, doing dishes. Now, Eastman had done his share of cooking in the marines and believed he knew his way around the kitchen. He had wanted to help the first night, feeling grateful for Heimish hosting him. But Sylvie, who assigned the duties like a sergeant with a pearl oyster up her ass, stuck Eastman on dish duty every night. Once, he said to her, "Let me get my hands dirty, Sylvia. Toss me that peeler."

"It's Sylvie, and you can get your hands dirty after dinner by washing the dishes with Cameron. We pitch in here and things run smoothly."

Eastman, a little drunk by the five o'clock hour, imitated her in front of the other colonists, and didn't win any laughs or favors with his sordid imitation. Even Cameron, a novelist from Michigan who'd been on dish duty for weeks, didn't find the impression the least bit humorous. "What's a matter with you?" Eastman asked him. "You wanna do dishes forever?"

"Well, I can't cook, so I don't mind," said Cameron.

"You don't seem to mind anything. Do you mind licking my nuts?"

The young Cameron shook his head in disgust.

Eastman began to wonder what else had been lodged up Sylvie's ass that made her such a dominatrix. What had he done to cross her? He had been a pleasant enough guest with the exception of the late night phone calls with Penny, he tried not to eat too much and to take an equal share of the meat and potatoes and greens. Since he was Heimish's guest, he didn't think it necessary that he help with anything around the farm. Mostly he stayed in his room and read through his proofs, made corrections, wrote additions and footnotes for *To Each His Own*. He had made this clear to Heimish, that he was coming to the country to work, to get out of the city for a few days. What was Sylvie's issue with him? Every evening he chose to sit across from her in order to loosen her up, but there was always tension. And after dinner the tension only grew, as Eastman dunked dishes into the soapy water as he'd been instructed, then passed them to his fellow dishwasher, Cameron. After a few minutes of washing he'd usually excuse himself to the toilet, where he would take pleasure in a bowel movement for the good part of a half hour, reading a copy of *Commentary* that had been left on top of the toilet seat.

Therefore, she was giving him guilt for his trips to the toilet. So was that pushover Cameron. One evening Eastman decided he would do the dishes with complete vigor. His bowel movement would wait until after the stupid chore. A number of items slipped out of his hands, glasses broke in the sink, some plates cracked. He was no longer complaining or huffing by the sink when Sylvie walked by. Still, she treated him as if he had defiled her youngest daughter.

First, he approached Heimish about the Sylvie situation and Heimish told him to leave it alone. "Just do your work. We all want you here, Alan."

On one of his afternoon walks, chewing on a tumbleweed, he saw Sylvie out by the grazing cows in the far meadow. He went out to see if he could remedy whatever was ailing her.

He shouted her name from a good distance and she gave him a startled look, then turned away from him, continuing to fiddle with a cow.

"Can I help you with that?" he said.

She ignored him, as if he were an invisible man. He felt quite foolish, wearing a pair of shorts with no shirt on, a piece of tumbleweed in his mouth. Sylvie continued about her business, checking the cow for something as the fine animal grazed.

"Sylvie, it's come to my attention that you don't like me very much."

"Whatever made you come to such a conclusion?"

"The way you walk past me like I'm invisible. The way you scowl and roll your eyes anytime I say something at dinner. And just now, ignoring me when I was calling you."

"You think a woman should come when you call her?"

"I think someone should respond when their name is called, yes."

"You think a woman should be doing dishes, is that a woman's place? While you get fat and drunk with Norman, eat our food, fuck our women, take what you want."

"You see, this is the kind of thing I'm talking about. You're doing it again."

"What is it that you think is wrong with me?" she asked.

"Your attitude, for one. But I'm here to make amends if I've wronged you in some way, because you're my friend's girl. And I'm your guest."

"I'm no one's girl, you pig shit. I'm a woman of forty, is that a girl in your stupid head?"

"C'mon, don't be such a cunt. I'm trying to appease the situation."

"How dare you."

"You called me stupid first. You wanted to get nasty, let's get nasty."

"I've seen you on television. We all have. I've been utterly offended by your remarks, particularly those made on the subject of sex and the woman's role in society. You do not consider women writers to be of any worth, do you? Of no value whatsoever. To you they are all girls, aren't they? Waiting for a man like yourself, a pig of a man."

"Is that what this is about? A fucking TV show? I've said a lot of stupid things, some of it I've said on national television, but that's entertainment, Sylvie. That's why they have me on. Half the time I'm spouting out things because of nerves, stepping over my own words from having cameras on me. I say what I say at the moment, and yes, sometimes that ends up biting my ass. So drop the wounded bird act."

"You are unchangeable, you see. It is built into your point of view, your speech. You can't be changed because you think you have ultimate authority. We're all cunts to you."

A rage bubbled up inside of him. He spit out the tumbleweed and his hands tensed as blood rushed to them. He choked the air in front of him. "I ought to come over there and give you a good smack," he said.

"I dare you to try" was Sylvie's reply.

The woman had ruined a perfectly good attempt at redemption, as well as a perfectly good afternoon. Though she had a point, and that's what got to him. She had pegged his behavior square on the nose. He went back to the farmhouse in total disrepair to put on a shirt. The teenage artist was home in the kitchen frying bacon in a cast-iron pan. "Where do you people get off?" he said, simply because she was the only person around to take his rage.

"Fuck you, square," she said.

He would be gone by dinner and not by choice. Complaints had been piling up since the day he arrived, and Sylvie had just put the case against him over the top. Eastman took a walk along a dirt path that took him through the brush forest behind Heimish's house. At the end of the path was a small clearing of green where, by late afternoon, the sun came through the trees and warmed a cold patch of grass. When he got to the clearing he was already beginning to feel a sense of calm. The cicadas and the gnats, the tall grass, all those summer elements he was now attuned to. He found the patch of grass, the same one he had found a few days before, just as the sun was beginning to sprinkle through the branches of the pitch pines and American larches. Soon, the sun would be on his body and all would be forgiven. And just as he was about to rid his mind of Sylvie, queen bitch of the manor, Heimish came barreling down the dirt path like a battering ram, all two hundred pounds of him, and he tackled Eastman into the ground. Heimish had played football in high school, offensive tackle, and what he may have lost in athleticism he had gained in size. Looking back at it now, Eastman knew what was coming. A man like Heimish was too similar to him in temperament. He knew Heimish wouldn't allow his lover to be slandered. He knew Heimish wouldn't allow him to linger on the property, picking berries in the Illinois brush. And he knew, sensed even, as he picked out that little patch of grass, that something was coming at him from the side and there was nothing he could do. Once on the ground there was a quiet struggle as if the two men were wrestling underwater. How could he come up on top when Heimish had flanked him? It ended with Eastman's head pressed into the earth, his face stained with green moss, while Heimish said into his ear that he wanted him off the property by nightfall.

Eastman detailed all of this in his letter to Adrien McClure, exaggerating the actual fight in his favor. Eastman might have placed Heimish's rifle into the scene he described for McClure, in order to illustrate that he hadn't a choice in the matter. It was leave and take his life with him, or stay and take a bullet.

He drove back to New York, sucked up his hurt pride, finished his proofs and sent them back over to McClure. Penny returned from London in mid-September, flew in one evening just past eleven. He was hurt and playing it up, so he didn't offer to pick her up at the airport. She took the subway home. They were both exhausted from their travels. He didn't want to talk much more about what she did or didn't do in London, as long as she was back and it was over. He could understand her wanting to get something out from under her skin; if she'd had to know something, whether there was some type of future with someone else, and she saw nothing, that would satisfy him. He didn't question whether this behavior of Penny's was some-thing that would recur biennially. How does one judge somebody for things they haven't done yet? And how could he anticipate behavior that would be more akin to his nature than hers? When she returned from London he was trying his best not to be judgmental. From their talks on the phone, she made it clear that she would not be judged by him, she would not come home to be shamed, and if that was what he wanted she'd rather not come home at all. Then fine, he had said. Fine, fine, fine, fine, fine. In November, they were married.

As for Heimish, they never met in person again. They had exchanged a few letters after Heimish left Sylvie. Eastman apologized but added that he thought Heimish the most idiotic and brilliant man he had ever met, and if those two agencies weren't at work within his soul, Heimish wouldn't be as good a writer as he was. The artists' colony in Marshall folded. Sylvie left her husband, Gerd Dietrich, and the writers were replaced with ostriches. Ostriches Gerd raised all by himself.

Now that he knew Heimish was in Saigon, Eastman began to feel the riptide of competition pulling away at him. He had never backed down from a fight, especially a fair fight. It seemed as if his whole life was up in the air in Saigon, and as he walked home from the Rex Hotel, up Le Loi and through the square toward the Continental, he couldn't help but sense a kind of fear. He saw it in every odd and foreign face he passed, the faces of people he didn't understand. He had lied to himself getting here. The size of the job was beyond his capabilities. Yet he was a product of the protest era, he knew the issues, what was at stake. How could he, and quickly, devote himself to this country and dig in deep? He would have to, to get the story he wanted. And to square off with Heimish. Now he had to get out and talk to people. Find a translator and hit the city. That's where he would start. The various pockets where the people gathered. He thought, yes, that's a start. But first a translator. Maybe he could get one at the bureau.

In the lobby of the Continental he went up to Mrs. Nguyen. He wondered if she could find an "old friend" of his staying at the hotel. "Norman Heimish. He might be with *Rolling Stone* magazine."

"Oh, yes," said Mrs. Nguyen. "I know Mr. Heimish verrry well. He's a very handsome man. He's staying here many times. Eat on the terrasse, drink, talk to everyone. But I have bad news for you."

He anticipated the gruesome details of Heimish's death and began to feel bad about how he had left things years ago. He even felt guilty about his intent to scoop Heimish.

"Oh, dear, what is it?" said Eastman with great concern.

"You must not have heard from your friend," said Mrs. Nguyen.

"What happened to him?"

"I hate to tell you this, Mr. Eastman, but Mr. Heimish . . . he left. He's not staying here."

"Oh, Jesus, you nearly gave me a heart attack."

"I'm very sorry. He was here many days before you arrived."

"Did he leave a forwarding address?"

"No."

"Did he say where he was going?"

"No. It is not my place to inquire about where he goes."

"What can you tell me of his whereabouts?"

"You may try the *New York Times* foreign office."

"Of course."

"Have I offended you, Mr. Eastman?"

"No, darling. Careful with the term 'bad news.' When you throw it around like that you're gonna kill a few people yourself. If I get any messages, ring me immediately."

Eastman went up to his room. He tried to nap under the loud air conditioner, but sleep evaded him. He was still slightly jet-lagged and knew he should try to stay up through it so he wouldn't have a repeat of sleeping most of the day, worrying at night. Maybe this news of Heimish was good for him. He was having trouble getting his ass moving. He still needed a translator, a fixer, a lead. He gave up on the nap and went down to the second floor to check out the news bureau for the first time and meet some of the staff of the *Herald*. He dreaded asking the bureau for help. He wasn't staff and didn't want to be humiliated, the way stringers and freelancers were. While he was down there, he thought he would call New York and check in with Broadwater as well. Let him know that he had made it over.

He walked to the end of the hallway, past a few other foreign offices operating out of hotel rooms. A little makeshift news machine. This was where all the stories were being dispatched. Gulf of Tonkin, Tet Offensive, My Lai. Those stories were filed in these halls, sent back over the wire to America. Stories that made reporters. He passed a plaque for *Rolling Stone* and thought of Heimish. Heimish had covered the Republican National Convention for the magazine. It was great reporting, Eastman had to admit. Though on a sentence-to-sentence level he felt he had Heimish beat. But what did that matter when he hadn't been writing about anything worth a damn lately? You were only as good as your latest work. And Eastman's had been a soft piece of fluff on Mayor Lindsay for *Parade* magazine, and the article stank to high heaven.

When he entered the bureau he noted their silence. No one said anything to him. They were defending their territory; he was trespassing. He knew it was a waste of time and that he wouldn't get anything through here. He turned to a man who was typing at the closest desk.

"Hey, young fella," he said. "You the bureau chief? I'm looking for Bob H."

The man kept on, ignoring Eastman.

"Maybe you didn't hear. Said I'm looking for a Bob H., he's the bureau chief here, young fella, and I just rolled into town."

Either the little twerp was deaf or he was playing games and

Eastman hadn't the time. He reached for the paper in the man's typewriter and tore it out. The man shouted, "What the fuck? I'm not the bureau chief. The bureau chief ain't here!" When Eastman glanced at the paper in his hand, the man told him not to read it. Suddenly he had everybody's attention. Work stopped, all eyes were on him. He gently dropped the paper on the man's desk.

"As I asked my friend here, I'm looking for Bob H. Where can I find him?"

"Alan Eastman?" a man in the far back said. "You were expected days ago."

He was a zombie of a man and he got up from a desk by the window. This was David Wheeler, a man who had spent more sleepless nights in Vietnam than anyone he would meet while in Saigon. Wheeler informed him that Bob H. was in Manila and wouldn't be back for another week, but he could show him around and get him anything he needed, within reason. Wheeler was impressed that Eastman had met with General Burke, the former head of MACV. Said the general had been after him since he got to town and had been calling the office, looking for him. The bureau had never gotten so much interest from MACV or a general of Burke's stature in the entire time they'd been in Vietnam. Everyone at the bureau assumed Eastman was connected up the chain of command and didn't need any help from around here, so this was one of the reasons he was just treated like a pile of shit. Wheeler cooled off the hothead Eastman had fucked with, a reporter by the name of Sykes, and Wheeler and Eastman stepped outside into the hallway for some fresh air. The upper floors of the Continental were open in the French Colonial style, with little rooftop courtyards opposite the rooms. Wheeler lit a cigarette and asked Eastman about his situation. He offered some resources and said he'd call a friend over at *Newsweek* who had to lay off a good translator recently, and thought he could get him over to the Continental. Where did Eastman plan on going? He didn't know. Eastman wasn't sure if he would be following the general's advice, hopping transport somewhere deep to see some fighting, or whether he would hang about town for a little and talk to some locals. Besides, fighting was covered by the real newsmen, and he hadn't felt like one of those in a long time. Wheeler brought him up to speed by saying that Eastman wouldn't get how this bureau worked because everything was so dysfunctional, so he shouldn't bother figuring things out. Things couldn't be understood around here because they didn't make sense. The only reason Wheeler was in the office was that he was asked to stand in for Bob H. while Bob was in Manila. Otherwise Wheeler felt the place could burn. Get what you need and get the hell out, he said.

Eastman thought Wheeler was honest enough, and though his way was off-putting, Eastman wasn't getting anywhere with anyone else inside the bureau. Wheeler told him about the press briefings, every day at 4:15 P.M., what the correspondents called "the follies," and invited him for a drink on the terrasse later in the evening.

The only other thing Eastman wanted to know from Wheeler was whether he knew the whereabouts of Norman Heimish.

"The other famous writer in our midst," said Wheeler. "If you don't bump into him on the terrasse I'd be surprised. Better yet ask Monsieur Francinni, the owner of the Continental. They're friends."

"Mrs. Nguyen said he was staying here on and off."

"I wouldn't trust a single word that anyone here tells you. Including me."

Wheeler went back into the bureau and Eastman no longer saw any reason to follow him. Knowing that everyone was aware Eastman had been up in his room and meeting with Burke just this afternoon made him feel confident. It also told him that Saigon was a loose-lipped hooker who swore you had just popped her cherry, meanwhile everyone behind your back knew you'd been the sixty-seventh man inside her. Eastman was proud of that metaphor and made a note of it in his pad.

12.

If you walked along Tu Do Street from the Continental in the year 1973, you would pass the *New York Times* bureau and dead-end into Notre-Dame Basilica. A left on Duong Nguyen Du would take you past Independence Palace, then the American Embassy, bicycle-repair shops, rickshaws and noodle stands, street kitchens and soup stalls. There was the steamy smell of something good in the air. Bones and broth, prawns, shrimp paste and fish sauce. Pot of soup burning over a wood fire. A bar and restaurant here and there that catered to Americans. He didn't eat what the locals ate, he was afraid of it. So he stuck to heavy Italian food, pasta, burgers. American food was ubiquitous. To say that the city wasn't thrilling would be dishonest. You could get everything around the corner from the Continental, including grass, hash, heroin, acid, and young women. He found himself on another street named Nguyen, Nguyen Thai or Nguyen Tri, and he walked past the open-air parlors with eleven beautiful women sitting cross-legged, done up in a way that enticed the senses. He had half a mind to visit one of them one night, but he wasn't about to go there yet. How could he? You're here to get your wife back, not drive her further away. So he swore off prostitutes, women, sex of any kind. He wouldn't be having it. Not while he was here. He was still a married man, even if Penny was acting the divorcée. He fingered his wedding band each time he passed one of the parlors. Women waved at him politely.

He took this walk many times while in Saigon, venturing a little farther each time. He got about a radius of a mile and a half out from the hotel, and then circled the Continental for days. To the east was the Saigon River, a busy waterway with boats like cargo trains. It was not a pleasant place to be at night. There were water lilies or some type of shrub growing on the water's surface along the banks, a few houseboats scattered in between, that rocked all day from the brown river's traffic.

The day he met Wheeler he had taken such a walk, and when he returned to the hotel in the early evening there was already a crowd of newsmen drinking on the terrasse. He went in and saw Wheeler at a table with a woman of indiscernible age. Neither young nor middle-aged, she was attractive in a mysterious way, her posture alert and yet distanced as she sat and smoked. Wheeler was chain-smoking, talking very fast. The amphetamines he was taking made him sweat more than they all were in this heat.

Wheeler waved him over and he made his way to the table and sat down. They had all come from a press briefing that Wheeler said lasted but ten minutes with not enough bullshit to report.

As Wheeler jabbered on, Eastman's eyes kept shifting to Channing. He was interested in her and he couldn't tell why. It wasn't just raw attraction, it was more arresting than that. He felt as if he couldn't get close to her. He was ready to dismiss her after a drink, but suddenly she turned to him and began asking questions about his brief time in Vietnam and they began to talk.

"I'm curious," he said. "You seem to know so much about this place. How long have you been in Saigon?"

"Eighteen months total, but with brief trips out of the country. Otherwise I've been here since the cease-fire and the Paris treaty. While it was still an American war. I mean, it still is."

"Talked to a General Burke this afternoon and he seemed to imply it was over. Just the fellas at the embassy were the only troops left."

"Sure. Only he's still here walking around under the guise of a civilian. So are two hundred other guys. What's happening right now is that they're trying to fix their unfixable problem. A political problem. But all of this doesn't matter. It's soon going to come down on their heads. Personally, I don't think we have much time left."

"You think the city will fall to the North."

"The city and the whole country."

"Is that what everybody's saying?"

"That's what I'm saying. Everyone's still here because they want to see how it will end. They need to see how it will end."

"Have you been up to Hanoi?" he asked.

"No," she said. "I haven't."

"Would you know how one would get there? I've had trouble acquiring a visa. The *Herald* was supposed to have it squared away and that didn't happen."

"The American Embassy will say you are on your own. But there are ways. You'd have to move through Cambodia or China. It wouldn't be impossible, but it would be a major pain in the ass. If that's what you're looking for."

"I haven't figured it out yet."

She sat back and picked up another cigarette. Channing liked to drink and it was exciting (that word, again) to share a round with somebody who liked to drink as much as he did. The women in his life didn't behave like this, not anymore.

Circling them were young Saigonese men with sunglasses and sparse mustaches. They were pimps, he assumed, because there were a hell of a lot of bar girls working the room. Wheeler seemed to know most of them.

He wanted to ask her more questions. She was much more interesting than Wheeler.

"What paper are you with?" he asked.

"She's with us," said Wheeler.

He did remember now seeing Channing's name in the *Herald* once or twice before and he was impressed with her writing, as he was with most of the war reporting from Vietnam. The writing was different from the stuff he did back in his youth, the articles were frank and honest with respect to the truth, they redefined patriotism and America's meaning. Yes, the dispatches of this war were some of the best goddamn reporting he had ever read, and Channing could be counted among the best.

"I went by the office today," said Eastman. "I've met our friend David here but I've yet to meet Bob H."

"He's in the Philippines," said Channing.

"Manila, I heard," said Eastman. "You've been with the *Herald* here for a whole eighteen months! You might have some advice for someone who just arrived."

"Try not to walk alone at night. The square outside is pickpocket central, so watch your camera, your watch, any jewelry." She looked at his hand.

Eastman became conscious of his wedding ring and he wished he hadn't worn it. She must have seen it, which meant what? That she was interested in him? He was talking rather quickly, rapid-fire questions. He was acting nervous. He couldn't help seeing her as someone he could go to bed with. This used to invigorate his pride. Now he knew he had no control over going to bed with anyone. He knew he was being flirtatious—it should have been the last thing on his mind at a time like this. He was an old man getting caught up in an old man's daydream and it made him uncomfortable in his own skin, to have at his age the self-consciousness of youth.

She seemed to be enjoying sitting there talking with him. Her eyes frequently broke into a warm smile, telling him not to be nervous, not to leave.

Wheeler said to Eastman, "I found you a translator. Someone good and he'll be coming round tomorrow."

"That's great, I have to thank you."

"You can buy me a drink," said Wheeler.

They ordered another round.

He asked both Wheeler and Channing what went on at the press conference earlier in the day and Channing said, "Reports of miscalculated deaths and overestimated progress."

"Our daily horseshit briefing," said Wheeler. "Complete and utter horseshit."

"Anything to report as news?" he asked.

"If you need to keep your name in the paper," she said. "If not we can skip it and look for something real. I don't know how much of the city you've seen, but it's a horrible place."

Eastman disagreed. He was falling in love with Saigon. The street smells, the garbage, the stink—bad stuff, like the cigarettes burning in the ashtray, like the whiskey in his glass. It was all vice.

"It doesn't seem so bad," he said.

"You've been here four days. Nothing's blown up in your face yet. No one's ripped off your wallet or broken into your room. You haven't gone out there and come back to this."

"I guess I'm a rube. I don't know my way around yet, and I've just been eating pizza and burgers."

"You'll get sick of it," said Wheeler. "We all do. Try a Vietnamese sandwich. Try a noodle soup."

"Soup? It's too hot for soup."

"Not here, it ain't. Me, I don't eat much. Ask her."

"I don't think about his dietary habits," she said.

"You think about a lot more. You have something in the works, Channing. She's writing a book."

Channing shook her head. Their playful banter made Eastman a little jealous.

"What's it about?"

"It's about the war. The people I've met in the war. What they do when they arrive home, if I can track them down. I shouldn't be talking about it because I haven't written a word."

"I find that the more you talk about it the more real it becomes. You've told people about it now. Therefore you'll have to write it if you want to be someone who keeps her word. There's no backing out once you've made it public. The stakes are too high."

"Are you a man of your word?" said Channing.

"Most definitely."

"Have you told people about the book you're writing now?"

"You're familiar with my work?"

"Very," she said. "Everyone's read that one book in particular. What was it called?" She smiled and he knew she was kidding.

"I have told people about the book I'm writing now. I'm under contract for it. It makes the book quite real, although I haven't written it yet either. We're in a similar bind."

"No, we're not. No one's waiting for a book by me."

"So you get to take your time."

"I'm writing a book I haven't written, too," said Wheeler. "I've been not writing it for five or six years now. Ask me about it."

Eastman was about to when Wheeler gave him the finger.

He was having a good time until the conversation seemed to get away from him, away from him being the center of attention. It was his nature to take over an evening or a conversation, and he grew bored whenever people moved out of his orbit. That's probably why he used his accents. Texas, Irish, British. He remembered a time at a party in New York in the sixties. It was a boring party, thrown by Adrien McClure, his then editor. He fought off boredom whenever he could because the boredom made him feel self-conscious, which led to a type of anxiety he found hard to control, even with alcohol. And so he went full Texan at that party and though the night ended in disaster, he was able to keep himself entertained for the rest of the evening. He needed things to go his way. When they didn't he was miserable.

Wheeler and Channing spoke more and more about things that didn't interest him. But because he was intrigued by Channing, he thought he would relax, not take over. Allow the evening to go where it may. He needed things from these people, more than he needed to be entertained.

He wondered if Wheeler and Channing had slept together or were doing so currently.

Around the time of their fifth drink, after a cool breeze came in through the open arches on the terrasse, the conversation turned to insurgents and terrorists and spies. This was a topic that interested him.

"Saigon is a city of spies," said Channing. "They pay the people who work in the hotel to report on things. There are American spies pretending to be contractors. There are Northern spies pretending to be cooks and room boys."

"Why is it that you're so paranoid, Channing?" said Wheeler. "Where does this mistrust in the good Vietnamese people come from?"

"I'm paranoid?" she said. "You're being a hypocrite."

"Maybe *I'm* paranoid, but it's not for the reasons you think. I don't think people are conspiring against journalists." He looked at Eastman to back him up but he didn't take the bait.

"You came from the same news briefing I did," she said. "There is what we know and what they don't tell us. So we work to find out. And there are the people who don't want us to find out."

"But we always find out," said Wheeler. "This is the most transparent war in history. You covered World War II, didn't you?" he asked Eastman. "You only just got here, but I bet you know the fucking difference between this war and those others just from reading about it."

Eastman was following now and was able to formulate his own questions. "When you say it's a city of spies, I'm interested in how you know. I believe you. I do. How do you get to them? How do you penetrate these people?"

"Why, you want to write a spy novel?" Wheeler asked.

Eastman ignored Wheeler. He was concentrating on Channing, working on some kind of trust.

She smiled because she either knew something he didn't or was too careful not to share what she didn't know. Journalists were protective of their stories, he remembered now. This is why everyone acted the way they did in the bureau. An outsider was a threat, someone who would scoop you if you weren't careful.

She said to Eastman, "The only way into Saigon is to be here for eighteen months. Misery brings clarity. If you're here long enough."

"I've been here since sixty-eight," said Wheeler.

"Five years," Eastman said.

"Five fucking years, man. Do I look happy to you?"

"Maybe you guys are the story I'll write," Eastman said. "The men and women reporting the war, living the war. Someone somewhere is going to have to write about you. They did about us in my day."

"We wouldn't give you access," said Channing. She was joking, but there was always truth in humor. Especially with someone who had her brand of intelligence.

It was about time to change the subject so he wouldn't seem too eager.

That night he went back to his room thinking about her, the woman with the cigarettes and the mysterious posture. He wondered if he would ever see the inside of her room. What she looked like underneath, what she felt like, how she slept. He imagined himself sharing a cigarette with her after, talking about absolutely nothing. She would be a great mistake, but for the first time since he arrived here he wasn't thinking about his wife, he wasn't bedridden and emanating sorrow. Saigon was a city of spies. He was a little drunk at this hour but he couldn't sleep because he couldn't stop thinking about Anne Channing.

Saigon was a city of spies.

He was lying on his back under the ceiling fan when he got the idea. Someone in this hotel knew something about her. It was late but he was feeling giddy; he got up and peeked outside, down the dark hallway. The light from his cracked door woke the room boy sleeping on a mat on the tiled floor. The room boy was on his side and his eyes were open. Eastman waved him over with two fingers and the boy jumped up and ran hurriedly on the balls of his feet. He was hesitant to enter a guest's room, so Eastman left the door open and they stood in the inside corridor by the closets under the light, letting the heat in.

"Listen, kiddo." Eastman got out a few piastres and held it out between them. "There's a woman staying here in the hotel, you understand?" He didn't. "There's a woman with dark hair, shoulder length. She was downstairs with me on the terrasse. We were talking. You know who I mean?" The room boy didn't. "Channing. Anne Channing. You know that name?" The room boy nodded yes. "What can you tell me about her?" The room boy was silent. "I want to find out where in the hotel she's staying. Find out what you can about the woman Anne Channing. Find out her room. When you come back to me with the information I'll pay you more."

The room boy had no issues understanding commerce. He was eager to be paid. Eastman, still a bit drunk, was too exhausted to push the boy any further on whether what was being communicated was understood. To his relief, the room boy said, "The woman."

"The woman. Yes. You come back when you find her. The woman Channing."

The room boy took the money and Eastman was satisfied. At the very least he was glad to have somebody on his side in Saigon, helping him get information. A little spy of his own, under the employ of the *Herald*.

Eastman went back inside, undressed to his underwear, and aired himself in front of the window unit. He looked out at the Caravelle, whose rooftop bar still seemed to be going. The square was quiet, just a jeep parked in front of the National Assembly, the old Opera House, with two ARVN troops keeping watch. He went to the other window and opened the French doors that led out to his two-foot terrace. Chatter from the Caravelle could be heard. He felt the need to listen to some music. Jazz would be appropriate, that was his sound. Mingus or Monk. But that didn't play over the airwaves here, at least not at this hour.

Below, there was a boy defying curfew, walking fast across the square along Tu Do. The ARVN men shouted to the boy and he stopped in his tracks. They waved him over and the poor son of a bitch had to comply. "Leave the kid alone," Eastman said.

He pondered the sky and then the Caravelle. Nothing doing. When he looked back down at the jeep, the boy had a gun drawn on the two soldiers and fired on them, emptying out a round into the jeep.

Eastman dropped to the floor of the terrace and got his head down. He peeked out over the flower box and saw the kid, running away in the direction of the Caravelle. The chatter from the roof was now silent. People on the ledge looked down while more people came to their windows.

Soldiers ran out of the National Assembly and into the square. They took a knee and aimed at the boy, who was still running, and quickly put him down in the middle of Tu Do Street.

Eastman's hand was covering his mouth. Still on his knees he cowered behind the flower box on the terrace.

He'd never before witnessed a murder. Not when he was in the war. Not anywhere. He'd never seen a kid transform into a gunman, either.

There was some shouting below in Vietnamese, echoing in the square. *Bao chi! Bao chi!*

It was Channing, running across Lam Son Square to the cluster of ARVN soldiers surrounding the body. She ran toward the men with guns. She was snapping photos.

13

Had he been transformed, Eastman reflected, metamorphosed into a man of action, fully restored to his long-lost self, no longer a pathetic being? The trip to Vietnam, as promised in his head, was supposed to incite the change he sought for Penny's sake. He thought of all the people he had written about over the years, starting with the marines of his first book, to the profiles of actors and politicians and all the imagined faces in his failed novels. These characters followed a simple formula. They are in peril when we meet them and by will or stamina or chance they have a transformative experience. By the end, if they are still alive, they are changed, altered, enlivened, sentimental, gloomy, up, down. Within a book, life was molded, shaped into something that made sense. There was a morality in the act of storytelling. Reporting fact, or creating fiction, they weren't so different. He was not the author of his own life. He was the author of his own books. Books imitated life but told of life cleanly, in a manner of comprehension. His life was not a book, his purpose in Vietnam was not adding up to a book, and his own story felt backed up like a constipated shit.

A knock on the door and it was the room boy returning. Eastman was no longer in the jovial state he was in when he contracted the room boy to spy on Channing. Things had changed drastically after the murders in the square.

However, the kid had earned his pay. Anne Channing was in room 53. He asked for the room boy's name. It was Ngài, but he would never remember that name nor would he remember how to pronounce it. So Eastman just called him Nestor because he had remembered a bellhop in the Philippines by the name of Nestor, whom he liked very much. He considered the knowledge of Channing's room and he told Nestor to come back in an hour. He'd have a letter for him to deliver. Then gave Nestor an extra twenty piastres.

Eastman had his portable Olivetti set up on the desk by the window. Only some of the window panes were crossed with masking tape, meaning some could shatter while he was working, but he wasn't working, so he didn't see the sense in moving the desk away from the window. Already the typewriter had accumulated a layer of dust. Had he been there that long? He had the windows open last night during the horrible assassination in the square. The air could have brought the dust in. From his position on the bed he stared at the typewriter. Words needed to be produced. Broadwater would be asking soon enough.

He got to the edge of the bed and stared at it. The typewriter. There it was. He sat at the desk and did have the nerve to bang out a few words. A description of Lam Son Square. When he got stuck he heard the rapping of another typist, working away at high speed. Someone had something to say and it seemed as if they were rubbing it in his face. He couldn't tune out the sound of someone else typing and it put him off from the few sentences he had started.

He stood up and pressed his head against the wall. It was coming from the next room. Someone working on an IBM Selectric, he knew the sound. He had one at home in his study. Sounded like the person in the next room had the Selectric pressed up against the wall so Eastman banged on the wall with a few raps.

Eastman tore out the page and loaded a fresh sheet. This one a letter to Channing.

Dear Anne,

   I saw what you did last night and I
thought it was brave as hell. Braver than
anything I've seen in a long damn time—in
or out of a war zone. It's becoming clearer
to me that you're the real deal and that a
story follows you, somewhere, trailing
behind in your dust. I'd love to have a tete
a tete with you over lunch, possibly include
you in my next dispatch, because bravery
like that doesn't come around very often. I
watched it all from my room where I was
cowering behind the flowerpot, down to my
skivvies. But you were running full force
toward the thing. Permit me an interview. I
know we're at the same paper and that might
be a conflict of interest. This may be
something I use for my book and not for the
Herald. Not sure what the book will be yet
so I'd like to get as many sides of this as
I can. The first real bravery I've seen
since I've been in Saigon and it didn't come
from a foot soldier or lieutenant, it was a
correspondent running toward a story. I'm
in room 73, because Graham Greene's room was
taken by Rolling Stone (joke). Give me a
ring whenever you get this or have time
within the next few days. I'll be in Saigon
till Friday I'm assuming, unless something
comes up, in which case I'd like to catch up

```
with you when I get back. From here I'm not
sure where I'll be catching a lift to, but
maybe you can advise on some prospects when
we meet. I will get back to you if things
change.
                        With admiration,
```

The room boy came back, then delivered Eastman's letter to Channing's room. He didn't receive a phone call within the next few hours, so he assumed she was out. He checked the bureau late morning to see if she was there. She wasn't.

A little runt of a clerk said to Eastman, "New York sent you a telex." He handed Eastman a slip of paper. It was from Baxter Broadwater.

```
    NO GO ON HANOI VISA. CALL ME AS SOON
AS POSSIBLE. HOW'S PROGRESS?
```

"Can I use this phone?" asked Eastman.

"There's the time difference," said the clerk.

"I'll be sure to call his home phone. He didn't say not to."

The clerk gave him instructions on how to patch a call through out of the office. It took several tries, bouncing around with MARS operators, but eventually he was able to hear the familiar ring of a United States telephone.

"Broadwater, it's Alan Eastman. Hope I'm not calling too late."

"No, I'm still up." He heard Broadwater muffle the receiver and mumble something to his wife.

"Is that Elaine? Tell her I'm sorry. She'll know what I mean."

"Quit it. How's it going out there, Alan? I haven't heard from you."

"It's been a slow start. The great staff of the *Herald* here isn't the least bit helpful, so I've sort of been on my own. Also, why can't your numb nut office get my damn visa north squared away? I don't know how in the heavens I'm going to get up to Hanoi without it."

"We're still working on that, Alan. It's been rather hard to do it from here. We're checking to see if we can get it expedited through our bureau in Paris, so that's where we are now. What do you have going? Husskler wants an update."

"He'll get an update when I'm good and ready. No one said anything about you hounding me."

"We're paying you, Alan. As well as your expenses."

"So far I haven't received a dime and what you're paying me isn't good enough to stress over. You'll get updates on a need-to-know basis. But here's a little something for you that I'm considering, only I can't speak freely at the moment." Eastman looked at the clerk whose desk he made sure he was sitting on. "Fear of getting scooped. But I'll keep this short," Eastman said in a low tone and cuffed over the receiver. "Anyone writing up the assassinations that took place last night outside the Continental? I saw the whole thing from my window. Two ARVN soldiers killed in cold blood by a young man, a teenager. Couldn't have been older than sixteen. That's not the story I'm bringing in. That's only the backdrop."

"You're better off asking the Saigon bureau."

"Then what can you tell me about Anne Channing?" said Eastman.

"She's ours," said Broadwater. "Good correspondent. Reliable. Precise."

"She's a hell of a brave woman. Saw her put herself into certain danger last night, a situation I wouldn't get close to. Heroic stuff. I can't say any more as you probably want her story, not mine, but

I've been thinking about the correspondents out here as a possible story. The press has been getting killed constantly. You should hear what they're up against still. What if I get to know what it's like to cover this war through the eyes of not me, but another correspondent. Plus Saigon. Plus the feelings on the ground. What do think about that?"

"Can I make a suggestion?" asked Broadwater.

"Please."

"How many women have been covering the war and how many are out there presently? Could you slant it toward gender politics, since I know you have some thoughts on the subject. Women and the war. I think people would want to read that from you."

"I'm not going to turn it into feminist propaganda, Broadwater."

"Wouldn't it be easy, though. I could cull together all the names of major women correspondents from over here and send them to you. Let me do that at least, and you think on it."

"There's nothing to think on, I'm not a damned sociologist writing a pro-woman bra burner."

"Just think on it, Alan. I'll cull something together."

"You can cull all you want, I'm not writing any such thing. You made your suggestion, just be happy that you made it and that I listened. I'm going to get together with Anne Channing and see if she'll have the time."

"When can we expect copy?"

"Broadwater, I just got here. I don't even have a translator yet, though I'm supposed to secure one today or tomorrow. I'll get on this story and get back to you in a few days. But I can't promise anything for another two weeks."

"Two weeks? You're kidding. Let's do better than that."

"You do better. I'm going to hand you the best thing you've ever read on the war, and I'm working as fast as I can. What more can I promise beyond that?"

"Just try to keep me up to date on your progress. Send me an update end of the week."

"Fine. And Broadwater, one more thing. Did you know that Norman Heimish is here in Saigon?"

"It doesn't surprise me. Aren't you two friends?"

"It's a fraught relationship. But that's the kind of thing I need to know from you. Who is he working for? Find out for me."

"I don't see how it affects us, but I'll ask around."

"Please do."

Eastman hung up and turned to the clerk whose desk he was sitting on. "Did you get all that?"

"How could I miss it? You're using my phone."

"Do you know where Norman Heimish is?"

The clerk looked at him incredulously. "*New York Times* would be my best guess."

"Mine too. That's what I'd be doing if I were him. Instead, here I am stuck with you."

With nothing much to do for the day except wait for Wheeler on word of a translator, Eastman went down to the terrasse for a cold beer. They brought it to him with a glass of ice. He took a seat in the front, looking out onto Lam Son Square. The day's traffic proceeded as normal. Bicycles, rickshaws, Hondas. There were more ARVN guards out today. A cleanup team was scrubbing the blood out of the street in front of the National Assembly, where the two soldiers were killed. Across the way a portion of Tu Do Street, where the boy had been shot, was sectioned off. Otherwise everything seemed to go on as usual. Maybe this was usual.

He left his beer and told the waiter to hold his table. He would be back. The waiter brought him a pack of cigarettes instead. Miscommunication, it seemed, was part of getting on in Saigon, and so Eastman took the cigarettes rather than argue and put them on the table next to his glass. He went out through the lobby and crossed the street. He got close to the men cleaning the pavement from the steps of the National Assembly. But it would take more than soap and water to get the blood out. Eastman recorded some of the details in his notepad, then crossed the square toward the Caravelle, retracing the steps the assassin took before he was shot. He walked the killer's path. Although the boy's body had been removed early in the morning, the blood remained on the pavement, dry and sticky. People went by, students and regular hardworking people, not recognizing what had happened less than twelve hours before. Pickpockets were out; he saw a young boy patting the pockets of passerby. With nothing left for him to observe, Eastman went back to the terrasse.

No sign of Channing.

Early afternoon Wheeler found him still sitting by himself. Eastman was on his third or fourth beer already and he had a pretty good buzz going. He was writing in his notepad a sad letter to Penny on the subject of trust. *Trust is an entity that must be guarded in our marriage. I trust that you agree with me. I am willing to overlook the boundaries we've crossed and to slowly rebuild that wall of devotion. Only it can't be done alone. It is also true that even if we were to split we would need to reestablish our trust, because we are attached for the rest of our lives, with Lee and Toby, our boys. You didn't grow up in a broken household and neither did I, Penny. Think about what you want for them, because they, too, need to know that they can trust us.*

Wheeler sat down and said, "May I? I have some people I want you to meet." He called over a young woman and a man following behind her. "Eastman, this is my new girlfriend, Lieu. And this is her brother, Tang."

Eastman stood up to shake Tang's hand and knocked over an empty beer can in the process. He was appearing drunk, though that wasn't really the case. He was just feeling out of sorts, being taken away from writing a personal letter. The two joined them at the table and ordered water. Wheeler, a "33." He put his arm around Lieu. The poor girl looked so uncomfortable that Eastman didn't know if they were really together or if Wheeler was just kidding about her being his girlfriend. Perhaps he had a different one every night, judging by the number of pimps he seemed to keep employed at the Continental. "Tang here is quite an accomplished translator," said Wheeler. "You should use him."

"I will," he said. "I may be putting together a trip to Dak Pek. Are you familiar with Dak Pek?" he asked Tang. "It's possible that I'll get a chance to go there, but that wouldn't be for a few days. If I go, maybe you want to come with me?"

Tang said he couldn't leave Saigon.

"I'll pay you well," said Eastman. But Tang shook his head.

"You'd have to get a lift to Pleiku, first," said Wheeler.

"General Burke said he could help with that."

Wheeler looked at Lieu and said something that made her laugh. Then he snuggled himself into the crevice of her neck and put his hands on her bare stomach, feeling her up. She was Helen's age, and Tang looked not much older. Eastman was certain now that Lieu was a prostitute and he felt sorry for the brother who had to witness his sister making out on the lap of an American. That is, if he was, indeed, her brother.

Wheeler took out a vial of white powder and a tiny spoon and snorted a little under the cover of Lieu's neck. He shoveled out a little for her and she snorted it. "It's a partay," she said.

"That's right, baby, it's a party," said Wheeler. "You want some speed?" he asked Eastman.

He declined. For the boy's sake, Eastman thought he should distance himself from Wheeler. Tang just sipped his water and pretended not to care about anything.

"Relax," Wheeler said. "He's not really her brother."

The fallout of a war wasn't pretty. Isn't this what Broadwater wanted? It made him uncomfortable and he thought this was good. This was something he could write. In Saigon he saw a place that had been disfigured, a mangled history, people living beyond repair. He lost interest in the general's proposition to take a trip out to the boonies to see fighting in Dak Pek. Hell, he heard he could see bombings galore from the roof of the Caravelle. He was more interested in the city. It had it all. Refugees, prostitutes, assassinations, death. Plus he wasn't made for the field anymore. He wasn't half the correspondent Anne Channing was. Even drugged out Wheeler was more capable than him. He saw no reason to leave now.

It was now evening, and in his mind he thought Channing would have gotten back in touch with him, perhaps they could have had dinner. He wanted to ask her about what she saw up close last night, what she knew about the situation, and if she had any thoughts on his proposal to follow her around for a few days. He knew he had to be careful, because he was attracted to Channing and he could be flirtatious. Penny knew how flirtatious he could be when he met a woman he liked at a dinner or party. She never seemed to mind, or she would ignore it and only mention it in passing as a joke later in the evening. Besides, he never let it get out of hand, at least not in front of her. In fact, sometimes he didn't even realize what he was doing. People were drawn to other people. He was even attracted to some men, not in completely sexual terms, and the only difference was he would joust with them instead of flirt.

He was in his room for a while, finishing his letter to Penny as his buzz receded.

He mentioned the events of the previous evening in the square and he was trying to get her sympathy. *Not to worry. I'm fine and what I've learned is that all is relatively safe. One can't really prepare for random acts of violence. And this one seemed to be planned, a planned assassination and I just happened to be witnessing it. The hotel reminds me of a place we stayed together in Bangkok.* Eastman and Penny had been to Bangkok for a few days en route to Manila. It was the ten-year anniversary of *American War* and it was being celebrated at a literary festival. This was during their first year of marriage, and Eastman took Penny along to show her that it would be exciting to be with him. *I wonder if you remember those few days we chartered a boat to a near island. Ko Samet? Maybe it was only a day or two, we were on a pretty strict schedule. But I think of those days now. Swimming out as far as we could, our toes unable to feel the bottom. You were in love with me then. Swimming transported you into childhood. I remember you took off your top in the water and wrapped yourself around me, which gave me the best hard-on of my life. We made love in the ocean. When was the last time we did something like that? Thailand? How could I let us get far away from that kind of excitement? That passion?* He might have forced the word and the memory here to directly impact Penny's concern about his being impassionate. *I can't change the way things have gone recently, it has happened because it was bound to happen. I want to know where things went bad for you, exactly where, and if I could adjust them now, I'd do everything in my power.*

There was a knock on the door and a note slid quickly underneath across the tiled floor. Eastman got up from the desk and picked up the envelope. It was from Channing. She would meet him tonight at the Jerome and Juliette, the rooftop bar of the Caravelle. The good news provoked a jolt of panic, electric and terrifying at the same time. He put Penny's letter away in a journal to be finished later. He had to get dressed. Wear something comfortable and cooling. He went to take a cold shower first, quickly dried himself and shaved. He laid out an outfit on the bed and then switched the top several times. For some reason he couldn't decide on a proper shirt, the brown or the light blue. He tried the light blue on and then took it off. It wasn't a dignified blue, but a circus blue. Then he tried the brown and back again to the first shirt. Soon he was sweating profusely and would have to take another shower in order to cool down. What was happening to him? Why was he so nervous? Of course, he was meeting a woman at a set time, and he was separated from his wife. It wasn't a date, it was a professional meeting, but his body was reacting as if it were a date. Channing hadn't specified a time on her invitation so he didn't know when he should go over there. He could check to see if she was downstairs first before he left.

Outside his room he found Nestor, his spy, and explained that Nestor was to keep watch on Channing's room to see if she's still there. "If yes, notify me as soon as she leaves."

Eastman finally settled on an outfit, the brown shirt and khaki pants with brown leather shoes. The room boy came back soon and told him the lights were off and she wasn't there. Eastman didn't want to get there too early and seem overly eager, so he took one of his short walks, up to the American Embassy and then down to the basilica. Back to Lam Son Square and on to the Caravelle. He entered the hotel, which was air-conditioned and comfortable, and made his way up to the Jerome and Juliette.

There was no sign of Channing yet, but the bar was reasonably full of newsmen.

He found an empty table and ordered a drink to calm his nerves. Alone, he thought back to his letter to Penny. When he was away from home, abroad, he mainly thought of Penny when they were traveling together, which they used to do a lot before the boys were born. A few years into the marriage the traveling seemed to stop, and they took their respective trips separately—Penny's psychology conferences, his literary festivals, television appearances in California, book events. They started this routine before Penny was pregnant with Lee, and then once the boys came around one of them tended to stay behind and their trips together ended. In fact, they hadn't traveled together much in the last few years. That must have been his fault. He looked forward to seeing Meredith when he went away for a weekend. Spending time with his mistress was more exciting than spending time with his wife, simply for the novelty of it. What Meredith had over Penny was the fact that she was married to someone else. He wouldn't see her for months, sometimes a year or more—especially when Penny was pregnant. Meredith understood and Eastman didn't have to make excuses. A year would go by and then they would rendezvous somewhere they had never been. It was like stepping out of his life. He no longer wished Penny could be with him wherever he was—London, Berlin, Montenegro—he only felt regret when Meredith couldn't make it. And if his mistress was detained by her marital duties to her husband, David Lazlo (lest we forget), then he would venture alone and enjoy the little bit of freedom he had to do whatever he pleased. To act like a buffoon, to ogle young women, to make advances, to drink and smoke and live like the young literary king he still thought he was.

Did Penny know about Meredith? She had reason to believe that Eastman had a mistress. This came up rather recently, when Eastman brought Penny to a Black and White gala at the Met. It was a publishing event, which meant they would have to interact with David and Meredith Lazlo. He knew once his mistress and Penny were in the same room that he would be found out. Women always knew, not by confession, but by the actions of their husbands. The tells, the strange behavior, the pressure under fire, the need for improvisation, the quick thinking on one's feet, the backstories. He was guilty as soon as he saw Meredith across the room while he was holding Penny's hand. "Who is that woman?" Penny had asked right away. "Which? Who? What woman? Be more specific, there are a lot of them here." "You know the one. Standing with your publisher. Introduce me." "Oh, that woman! Of course! That's David's wife. What's her name . . . ? Meredith, I think. Yes, Meredith." "And you know her from where?" "Through David, of course." "You're using the phrase 'of course' a lot, as if you're having multiple revelations because your memory has failed you so often. But your memory never fails you. But of course I shouldn't know her because I'm only meeting these people for the first time. Now introduce me to her and we'll discuss who she is after you do that properly." And like that she had him pegged. His face had gone through iterations of embarrassment— pink, orange, red, purple. He was able to get it under control once they made their way around to Lazlo and Meredith. Penny was civil but unfriendly. In the limo home he scolded her for embarrassing him in front of his publisher. It was a defensive tactic, to throw her off his scent. "If there was one couple in the room I needed you to be nice to, Penny. If there was one couple. It was the Lazlos."

"You have some explaining to do," she said.

"I have some explaining to do? Oh, I think it's the opposite."

"When were you last inside that woman?"

"Oh wow. Wow. Meredith Lazlo? My publisher's wife. My *employer's* wife. When was I inside of her? You're nuts. You know that?"

"That wasn't the question. I already know you were inside her. When were you *last* inside her?"

He was nonplussed. He needed something. Something quick, fast, appropriate. He needed the best lie he could think of. This affair he would take to his grave. He wouldn't allow it to ruin his life because, after all, it wasn't as important as his marriage. Then he did it why? "Okay, I slept with her in the fifties. When I was with Barbara. She was an editor working for my first publisher and we had a little fling. It was so many years ago so I didn't think it important to tell you. As you can see, it's also embarrassing, because at that time she was Meredith Chase. Now she happens to be Meredith Lazlo, married to my publisher. It makes me nervous to be around her because I'm unsure whether Lazlo knows that I have slept with her and he's just being the adult about it, or if he doesn't know and I have a secret I'm keeping from him. I just want the whole thing out in the open already! What am I supposed to do? Yes, I've been inside his wife. A few times, a long time ago. This was before we even met, Penny. People as old as me come with histories. I'm a decade older than you, which means a decade more active. Sexually. I'm sure we've been to parties with dicks you've had in your mouth! Only I'm not curious enough to inquire. Why would I do that to you? The fact is there were several women there tonight who I've had relations with in the past. I was promiscuous in publishing circles when I was younger—fame came early to me and I dealt with it badly. I see that now. It's the reason my marriage to Barbara failed."

It wasn't a great job and Penny didn't believe everything. He was playing the victim in all of this, a victim of circumstance. She didn't forgive him or excuse her behavior at the gala. She simply turned to look out the window at the buildings along the East River as they rolled down the FDR Drive toward home in Brooklyn. It didn't come up again. Either she didn't believe an affair was going on currently or she did and didn't care to press him.

Perhaps she was looking for a way out even back then? Or was this another strike against his character, being tallied in her mind for that inevitable day when she would leave?

Ungrateful evenings with his wife. These were not the memories he wanted to be thinking while he was waiting for Channing at the Jerome and Juliette. How could he help himself? He had heard that only a small percentage of animals were monogamous, which is perhaps why he kept a mistress. He needed more than the average man to keep himself sane, and he didn't trust himself in monogamy. Perhaps he would have sabotaged the relationship himself had Meredith not been in the picture.

The bar was filling up by the minute. He recognized some of the newsmen from television.

Channing entered through the double doors. She saw him right away and smiled, but she was stopped by someone near the bar and forced to say hello. He could tell from the way she kept glancing over to him that she didn't want to keep him waiting. She ended the conversation before it began and hurried to Eastman's table.

He got up and pulled out her chair for her. She gave him a surprised look; the formal gesture had made her feel awkward. Perhaps she was reconsidering their meeting. He should have just sat in his place and waited.

They ordered drinks. The waiter brought them quickly, with a bowl of cocktail nuts.

"Thank you for meeting me," he said. He could feel that there were many eyes on their table. A stringer at the bar who was, perhaps, attracted to her.

"Do you know what the others refer to you as?" she asked.

"They don't refer to me by my name?"

"I mean before you arrived. What they call you."

"An asshole?"

She shook her head no.

"Scumbag?"

"No."

"Male chauvinist pig," he said.

She laughed. "That has been said about you, hasn't it?"

"Yes, it has. Many times over. Each of these things I've been called before and not just in private. So what is it they call me?"

"'The celebrity."

"Because I'm on television."

"Because you're a famous writer. And yes, a famous writer who appears on television."

"You want to hear a confession apropos of celebrity? Many in my position would say to you that they didn't plan it. They didn't ask for it. All of this just happened. But I have the hindsight of almost twenty-five years in this business. Not the news, but in literature. And I did ask for all this success. I made it happen because that's what I wanted and I wouldn't settle unless I was considered one of the best writers in America. I know that sounds brash, egotistical, competitive, narcissistic, even pompous. But to be called any name you have to be somebody first. I needed to be a little of all of those things. If you have ideas that are controversial people remember them."

"I just thought I'd let you know. Is it nice for everyone to know who you are when you walk into a room?"

"A room like this, no one is batting an eye. It doesn't matter. Here I'm a tourist. I feel like a tourist. That's why I want to talk to you. You got my note."

"I did. I considered it." She lit a cigarette and made him wait. "I'm afraid the answer is no."

"Why the hell not?"

"I don't mind talking to you. I just don't want to be a character in your book."

"Have I said something wrong?"

"No, absolutely not. I'm flattered, I am. But I simply don't have the time to be someone's subject. I have too many stories of my own, and who else is going to write them?"

Eastman didn't handle rejection well, and it is at this point that he might have gone into one of his special accents to offset the balance of power in the conversation. But he was okay with Channing's answer. She let him down nicely. And maybe, he thought, if he spent a little more time with her he could convince her otherwise.

"I accept," he said. "No harm done. I'll find something. I'm perfectly happy just to be friends. Colleagues, rather," he corrected himself.

"I'm working on something now that's a little delicate," she said. "I'm grateful that you understand." He was curious but decided not to press her.

"How are you?" he said. "Considering what happened last night in the square. I saw everything from my terrace."

"Did you see the shooting?" she asked.

"Yes. The square was empty and I saw the boy first. I thought he was cutting curfew, I suppose. He seemed normal. Walking maybe a hundred yards away from the two guards in the jeep. He might have gone on about his business had they not called him over. But they called him over. I thought, just leave the kid alone. I turned away and when I looked back he had a pistol drawn on them. He killed them while they fumbled for their rifles. Then he fled."

"Then what happened?"

"More guards came out of the Opera House and fired till he was down. It was incredible. I mean, I have never seen anything like it unfold before my eyes. Then I see you. You're running across the square."

"I didn't see what happened," she said. "I only heard the shots and I got my camera and went out."

"He was there to kill them."

"Sure."

"Had he kept walking."

"He knew they would have come over. It was past curfew. Any Vietnamese knows to avoid crossing in front of the National Assembly."

"How often does this happen around here?"

"More often than not. I wouldn't say that your life is in any more danger than it was the day before yesterday."

"Do you know anything about an investigation? Who was the boy? The assassin. Where did he come from? Did he have a name?"

"I haven't gotten ahold of it yet."

"Are you pursuing this?"

"No."

"What about the photos you took?"

"There weren't any Americans involved. Therefore it's not deemed American news."

"It could have a greater meaning. Would you mind if I took a crack at it? Maybe I could see your photos, too. I have some special privileges and might be able to get information. You see, I'm here because the *Herald* wants my impressions of what it's like on the ground. At the same time, I don't want to scoop you."

"You saw what you saw, I can't tell you not to."

"If you come across any names, I'd be grateful. And again, if I can see those photos."

She was being generous with her time and expertise, but he had to be careful not to ask for too much. He had already exhausted the favor before the relationship had even begun. It wasn't smart to send that note about wanting to place her in a story. He was definitely out of practice. He should have gotten to know her, to talk first, find out what she knew, cultivate the relationship, not ask up front, tell her that he wanted her to be the story. Even he would have said no. Reporters weren't in it to become the news. It was the mistake of a novice, and hopefully Channing didn't overthink it too much. He liked talking to her and wanted the evening to continue. She had a way about her, how she did things, like tapping into the ashtray. Her face was long and gaunt and she was a lot younger than her appearance let on. Her hair was shoulder length, silver and gray and black. Her figure could be described as lanky. She was tall, however. Taller than him. He placed her in her midthirties. He watched her light another cigarette, a habit he had given up when he was about her age.

"May I have one of those?" he asked.

She slid the pack of Marlboros over to him. It had been many years and he had forgotten how to hold one. He felt awkward when he lit up. He coughed an old man's cough, which he could only suppress with a sip of beer. He put the cigarette out quickly.

"You don't smoke."

"I gave it up." Once he felt composed, he said, "Where are you from, Channing?"

"I'm from the Bay Area."

"I lived in California briefly. In late fifty-nine. I wrote screenplays for MGM. One was an adaptation of a book I wrote, which was rewritten by different hacks until it became unrecognizable. I wrote one gangster picture called *To High Heaven*. Damn good. Never made. But that was in LA a lifetime ago."

"I've never even been to LA, believe it or not. I moved east for college and ended up in New York."

"I'm not surprised. I grew up in New York and never went anywhere until college. I have no idea what the rest of the state contains. Albany, Binghamton, Rochester—these are places I've never seen. I have no idea what they're like."

"Wheeler is from upstate New York."

"Let me ask you," said Eastman. "What's the story with Wheeler? He seems off his rocker a little. Nice guy, don't get me wrong."

His inquiry was loaded; he specifically wanted to know if Channing and Wheeler were together.

"He's a good reporter when he's sober. Unfortunately that's become a rare occasion."

"He strikes me as somebody who has had a psychological break."

"None that I know of."

"Do you think he should be taking something?"

"A bath," she said and they both laughed.

They stayed much later than he wanted to. It was past curfew when they realized that they were drunk. He had been having a good time talking with her and she was helpful when it came to answering questions about Saigon. He had wondered where he should get his translator to take him and where he could get a sense of how the Saigonese were feeling about their future. He had quite a week ahead of him. There were places, sections of the city that he wanted to see for himself. He thought he would follow through and see the things that Channing recommended, this way he would have something to thank her for when he saw her next.

Together they decided to leave the Jerome and Juliette and walk back across the square past curfew. They waited inside the lobby of the Caravelle until they thought there were fewer ARVN patrolling. He felt bigger and more courageous with all the beer he had drunk and so he went through the double doors first and Channing trailed behind him. Confident enough, he took her hand instinctually, and when she didn't pull away he sped up his pace. They crossed in front of the old Opera House and the many ARVN guards out in front just watched them and paid them no mind. Being white, even here, got you certain privileges. They hurried and made it to the steps of the Continental when the lobby boy opened the wood doors. It wasn't until they were inside the hotel that Channing let go of his hand. They rode the elevator together. Inside, he pressed his floor and said to her, "I'll walk you to your room."

"It's not necessary," she said.

"Of course it is, it's late. This is what colleagues do."

She was thinking about something, the way she chewed on her bottom lip. She had missed her floor, he knew that, but didn't say anything. She hadn't pressed the button. He was willing to take her up to his room but the thought of it made him nervous. Once they were in the room he didn't know what he would do. Maybe they could talk some more and have another drink. He had a fifth of rum in the nightstand. He'd leave it to her.

The elevator door opened to the third floor and he got out. Channing remained in the small elevator. She was going back down.

"I missed my floor," she said. "I'm on two."

"I'll walk you."

"No, that makes no sense. I'll see you tomorrow or the next day."

"Goodnight, Channing."

He walked over to the banister of the central staircase and listened as she got off the elevator on the floor below. She walked to her room. He heard her fumble with her keys, enter the room, and then close the door for the night.

She hadn't pressed her floor's button on purpose when they were in the elevator because she was entertaining going to bed with him. And when he got out on his floor she changed her mind and took the elevator back down.

She was attracted to him in a sad kind of way. He had a riveting presence, and she felt they had arrived at a moment. She didn't need anyone to protect her, she had done just fine on her own, though she liked holding his hand when they crossed the square. She was reminded of an old boyfriend in New York, one who was prone to holding hands. She had broken up with him before she left for Vietnam. Their relationship had been touch and go, and she was surprised when he cried as she told him it wouldn't work out.

She went about her breakfast in the courtyard. Up early, coffee, soup. The same table at the same time. Today was the day she was going to meet the cook, this time for an interview. He was willing to talk to her but only with Lin present to translate. The cook, she had learned, was indeed a spy for the North Vietnamese. He was something of a courier. As she understood it, he put people in touch with other people. She didn't know for sure if that meant rebels or weapons. This is what she wanted to find out.

She was thinking of the assassin in the square the other night. There were other incidents, bombings of American establishments, Vietnamese owned. There were real threats in the city and this is what she wanted to focus on in a larger work—the reporter and the city of Saigon.

The day she met Lin they had gone for lunch at the cook's restaurant in Cholon. She had a noodle soup and ate very little. Lin was less shy and encouraged her to eat while they waited. If she didn't eat, Lin said she would make the cook nervous and that this wouldn't be good for her chances. So she ate as much as she could and tried to take her mind off meeting a spy.

There were so many Americans dining at the restaurant. The clientele appeared to be nonmilitary. The cook was right under their noses.

It was only when the restaurant began emptying that the cook came out from the kitchen and joined them at their table. He said a few words to Lin that she couldn't understand and Lin was able to get him to sit for a minute. The man didn't address her, only Lin. They talked about arrangements, and she found out that he would allow her to interview him because he needed help getting his family out of the country. He had relatives who had worked for the Americans and could not stay here much longer if Saigon were to fall. This was a lucky sign, that he needed something. Channing could not make promises, but she said she would share their names with her contact at the embassy. Once things were settled, the cook turned to Channing and nodded in agreement.

He would talk with her at the Continental. Lin would arrange their meetings. He gave her little information to go on, no details about what he did. It gave him power, she realized, to leave her in a state of speculation. This is how things were: you accepted it; a good story demanded it.

She had been practically celibate in her eighteen months in Vietnam. She was afraid of the stigma, afraid of the hotel staff and the other correspondents talking about her, which was strange because she had never cared about such things in the States. A few months ago she learned of a friend, Elaine, who had slept with a CBS

newsman. When Elaine tried to keep it casual she developed a reputation. The men Channing's age were not discreet, they got together
to drink and gossip every night at the Caravelle. If you were a woman
among them you sensed their intentions. She witnessed how they
went after their female counterparts. She'd seen asses grabbed and
had notes passed to her in press conferences. *I love you, Channing.*
Let's fuck. They made passes at you even when you were shaken up
from a firefight, it didn't matter. These boys were relentless. Many
lied about not having wives and children back home. She stayed on
the safe side of things, not sure how long she'd remain in Saigon. She
worked, filed her stories, kept notes for her book.

The only affair she had in Vietnam was with an older man, Davis,
her friend at the embassy. When she met Davis she felt she deserved
a break from her routine. He was handsome and a good listener. He
knew the city and took her to places different from the American
restaurants along Tu Do Street. He introduced her to his many Vietnamese friends, who in turn became her friends. He had a patience
the younger men didn't have and that she found attractive. With him
she felt like a better version of herself.

Davis had an apartment just west of the city center, which he kept
up year-round. She stayed with him for a week once. He had good
books and a turntable with some jazz records. The kitchen was small,
but he had cookware, spices, olive oil, onions hanging from a basket
over the sink, pasta and canned tomatoes in the cupboard. They made
spaghetti, tomato sauce with fresh basil, drank wine, and listened to
the stereo. It felt comfortably domestic to be with such an able person, even for just a short period. Davis would return to the States frequently to visit his wife and kids, and he usually rented the apartment
out to other correspondents. She wasn't expecting too much to come of
it, not of any of her relationships out here, and she didn't feel guilty

about having an affair with a married man. She was always on the move, everyone was, including Davis, and so this wasn't a time for attachments. When it ended, she was as relieved as he was.

Since then, she had been careful, overly cautious. She thought of Eastman again and applauded her decision not to go to bed with him.

The cook was to arrive at six in the evening and she waited in the lobby for him. He would be coming with Lin and they would go up to her room together for the interview.

She had to assume the cook had contacts inside the Continental— everyone was working for somebody else. It's the only reason he would agree to meet here. She was probably being watched by the staff, the room boys, or the waiters at breakfast. He knew more about her than she did about him. He was a spy, after all. They took precautions that reporters did not.

Lin she trusted and she didn't quite know why.

He arrived first, limping his way into the lobby. The cook followed behind. She greeted them and shook their hands.

They went up to her room on the second floor. The cook sat down in the green lounge chair and Lin pulled up a desk chair to sit beside him to translate. Channing sat across from them and asked if it was okay that she record the meeting. She said it would be confidential and no one but her would hear the tape. Of course, this was untrue, because she would have a translator at the bureau make a transcript for her. The truth needed to be fudged, part of the correspondent's arrogance. Get everything you can by any means necessary. But be careful not to promise anything. Be vague when you can, regarding all forms of repayment.

The cook said no to the taping and Channing agreed to just take notes. He spoke English extremely well. She was taken aback. They hadn't conversed in English at the restaurant, Lin had translated for them. She supposed this was a great advantage for a spy, to understand what was being said while you were invisible to the Americans. He went by the name of Pham, which was probably not his real name, but this is what she could call him for ease of conversation.

"You have contacts at the American Embassy?" he asked.

"I have some and I will do what I can to help your family. I can't make any promises, because it's not within my power. After we finish you can write down the names and phone numbers of those in question."

The cook pulled a list of five names out of his pants pocket and handed it to Channing. She looked over it carefully and then placed it beneath her pad. That seemed to settle the matter and he was ready.

"To begin, can you tell me about what you do," she asked.

"I handle information," he said. "Information that would be considered time sensitive. This can be anything. Knowing where people are and where they will be. Who is in Saigon at this time and who needs to know. Information of all kinds. This goes direct to North Command."

"How long have you been doing this work?"

"Many years. That's not important. Right now is an important time."

"How so?"

"Saigon will soon come under attack, beyond what happened during Tet. There will be an invasion and I won't know about it until it happens. I am never handed information, I gather it. I will be left alone, on my own. Some of my family will be captured. I cannot help the ones on the list because they have been employed by the Americans."

It wasn't new information—the South falling to the North. The sentiment had been going around for some time now. It was speculation and it didn't seem likely that Pham knew more than anyone else.

"What about the Paris peace treaty? The cease-fire?" she asked.

"The North will not settle until this country is united as one. Now that America has retreated under the conditions set by the treaty, the South is weak. What we want, even in the South, is one united Vietnam. Not like Korea, divided. This is simple, something you already know."

"America is hoping for the treaty to work and to hold."

"To divide the country is to leave it fractured. This is not a solution for Vietnam. It will take time and the Vietnamese people are very patient. They will wait years. And when the time is right they will take what is rightfully theirs. It will not stop until this solution is reached. Both sides want the same thing. Unified as one."

"Is this the opinion of your countrymen as well?"

"The peace treaty is for the Americans. So that they may go. And Vietnam wants very much for them to do so. So we will agree, what choice do we have? When America goes home, nothing gets resolved in Vietnam. Still the same problem exists. There may be quiet time, but each side will try to liberate the other. Nothing's changed by the American war. Think of your Civil War. Would not fighting continue if America remained divided, North and South? There would be another war, an inevitable war, to unite all. We are behind you in history but we are not so different."

"Many people in America sympathize with you on that point. It has been in our interest for years to withdraw from Vietnam and only now is it becoming a reality. Is there no sense of relief on your side?"

"Yes. Now we have to deal with ourselves only. No longer involvement from foreigners. And once we are united quickly, then we can defend our way of life against the next imperialist."

"I understand that you have permission to talk about these things with me."

"It is the desire of my superiors to express this to the American press so they will understand."

He seemed as if he could go on and on, but she wasn't interested in his opinion of what would happen. She wanted to know the things that she could not see when she walked around each district of Saigon. She led him to the recent bombings of American bars and restaurants. It was causing a flurry of closings and Western civilians were staying in. There were shootings targeting ARVN units, like the two soldiers killed in the square.

The cook shook his head no, and he looked at Lin. He would not be made to comment on rebel activity.

"There was a shooting in front of this hotel two nights ago," she said to Lin. "Ask him if he knows about it."

Lin complied. The cook sat back in his chair and said nothing.

"Ask him if he knows who the boy was who killed the two soldiers."

The cook shook his head no.

"No he didn't know him or no, no comment?"

"Both," said Lin.

"This does not matter," said the cook. "I'll tell you a story. A close relative of mine, my cousin, was captured by the Americans and imprisoned. Near Tan Son Nhut. He was North army, captured near the Laos border. In prison they were treated like dogs, pestered and beaten. But soon, he was set free to live his life in Saigon. This meant one thing. That he had cooperated. What information he could have given them, I don't know. He may have only told lies. When I was informed by my eyes and ears in Saigon what my dear relative had done, I was put in a position. I would need to inform on him to my superiors and then await an order from them. Would he live or would he die? I would be the one to relay the order. I would be his executioner. Should anyone ever be in this position? As long as a divide exists, we will be made to ask such questions of life and death for generations to come. The war goes on until we are unified."

"What did you do?"

"I did my duty."

"And what happened to your relative?"

"This is why I give you the list of my family."

They seemed to talk in circles about the same thing. Unification. And when she asked something that diverted from this topic he sat in silence then spoke in Vietnamese to Lin, a displeased look on his face. Lin was apologetic to him. All the while on her lap was a list of names given to her by the cook. What was she to do with this? She couldn't write her book collecting lists of names from Vietnamese, it would be impossible to negotiate. Her willingness to accept such a list became a promise in itself, and she would have to carry this around. Sure, she would get the material for her book, but at what cost? Channing didn't know if she should continue with it—interviews with dark characters in her hotel room. Should she scrap the book and just do her job? Attend the four o'clock follies and write mediocre stories? She could go into Cambodia, it had been calling to her for some time, it would fit in at the end of the war narrative.

The meeting ended, the cook left first, alone, and she thanked him. A few minutes later she walked with Lin downstairs into the lobby and watched as he slowly exited the hotel.

Back upstairs, Channing consulted her notes and quickly began typing them, expanding on what she remembered from the interview. When describing the cook's physicality—the way he sat in the green chair and the way he was silent when he was asked a question he did not like—she realized that she was writing in loose imitation of Alan Eastman's style. She usually wrote in the plain voice of the *Herald*, a straight report without any style of her own. Now when faced with the blank page of a book, she had no other language in which to tell it. She had yet to discover how to portray this war in her own words.

She spent an hour writing out details from the meeting and then decided to break. She lit a cigarette and thought of the shooting outside the hotel. She remembered she'd dropped off her roll of film at the bureau this morning. So she got up and walked down the hall to see if the pictures were ready.

Bob H. was back from Manila. He was drinking coffee at his desk by the window. "Anne," he said. "Have you met our celebrity writer?"

"Yeah, we had a drink last night." Already she didn't like the way that sounded. Too casual. So she added, "He was at the Jerome and Juliette. I wanted to hear about *The American War* and the old days of publishing. He's full of stories about himself."

"Oh is he? Watch out for him. He's got a reputation."

"What do you mean, Bob?" Bob was protective of her, he was of all of his correspondents, but he had never been so forward about who she should see. "You're the one who told me to help him. Now what are you telling me?"

Bob looked concerned and turned a little red. "Just that he has a reputation of being an antagonist," he said. "Forget it."

Now she felt she was being overly sensitive and perhaps misread Bob's tone. Eastman did have a reputation, Bob was right. He didn't mean any harm. She apologized, blamed it on a lack of sleep. She told him about the shooting in the square.

"I heard. Damn shame."

"Want me to file it? I got photos."

"Not really. I know it's close to the hotel, but there were no Americans killed and I don't want to panic three hundred press corps families." He had a point. She suspected it would be a no. "Has he asked for much help?" said Bob.

"He seems to be getting along," she said. "He had a meeting with General Burke of MACV."

"That I heard. Everyone's kind of pissed. It's funny that Burke is still here when MACV disbanded months ago. What is he up to, I wonder?" Bob had that New York cynicism that she missed from home. Everything seemed to cause him distress. He was an ace worrier, highly caffeinated and combustible. She liked how he ran the bureau.

She walked to the bathroom and knocked on the door before entering to make sure no one was developing film. She was called in. Inside was An, one of their Vietnamese photographers. He was hanging photos in the bathtub under the red light. Many of the photos were hers.

"This happened the other night," she said. There were photos slightly out of focus, taken as she ran to the body of the boy assassin. Then the soldiers getting her to stand back, hands in her lens. She was able to get low and shoot the boy on the ground between their legs. He was still bleeding in these. The clearer photos were of the soldiers in the jeep. Young, green, and forever lifeless. An told her that her photos were quite good and that it was a shame this had to happen so close to the Continental. "And during the cease-fire," he added.

"Do you recognize anyone?" she asked. She pulled down a shot of the assassin's face, half covered in shadow. "Maybe the boy?"

"Never seen him," said An.

She thought about whether she would share these photos with Eastman. He had asked for them. She wasn't pursuing the story so there didn't seem harm in it. Only now, as she studied the face of the assassin, did she find the event compelling. She would follow up. At least find out his name. And if and when she saw Eastman again she would just tell him that the film was still being developed. Be protective of your leads, that's what Bob H. told her when she first arrived. All newsmen, even the ones close to you, will scoop you if they get half a chance. Eastman didn't look like the sort who would. He wrote literature, not news. Perhaps she should try to get to know him a little better.

15

He no longer wanted to write about Channing and he was unsure if he ever really did in the first place. His request for an interview was partly a ploy to see her again, perhaps to develop a relationship. He craved companionship; without it he felt unsure of himself. The thought of a new love could creep up on you without realizing it, and you could begin to change your behavior without knowing why. His attraction to Channing, the slow burn of it, made him think of Penny. Not the sexual thrills that consumed him of late, but Penny at the beginning, when they were first making a life together. After the marriage and a few months at home in Brooklyn, once life resumed to normal, there were moments of complete stillness. Penny had the summers off so they would be home together in the house for the entire day. Eastman in his study, thinking, writing, brooding. Penny in her office upstairs, before it was the boys' room, quietly doing the same. An equilibrium was found, hours would go by like this. At night, they would walk through their neighborhood, and when the weather was warm and he was feeling up to it, they might jog together in the middle of the street where the road was well lit. In the late evenings they actually said very little to each other. They went about their nightly routines of brushing teeth and washing their faces, then got into bed to read before shutting out the lights.

It took time for two people to find the rhythm of their lives, a rhythm that could sustain them for years to come.

Eastman was at the desk in his hotel room, trying to picture this same life with Channing. She wasn't as elegant or pretty as Penny. She didn't dress the same, and her clothes seemed to be those of a graduate student, jeans and collared blouses, things collected on the cheap. Of course, Channing was covering a war and was smart not to wear anything too dressy. She wasn't here to meet men, damn it, she was here to work. Still, she had charisma and fearlessness. She was smarter than he was. Somehow this was a common theme among all the women he chose to be with. They were all much more intelligent. He felt it to be true. Eastman was drawn to intelligence. Who wasn't? He was lucky to have been in all those stimulating conversations with women who showed him more than he knew, who introduced him to concepts he had previously ignored.

He got up from the desk and pulled open the curtains. The sky was filled with smog. In the square below, motorbikes and cars drove along Tu Do Street spewing exhaust. He lay down on the bed and again he tried to picture himself together with Channing. Sharing a house in stillness. Doing the things he did with Penny. Only he was troubled. And the more he tried to visualize a different life, his thoughts returned to Penny, to the reality of his situation. He thought back to Penny's strange behavior in the last few weeks, when she'd asked him to choke her to the point of her turning purple. What had that been about? Was she trying to rekindle some sort of sexual attraction toward him, knowing she was falling in love with another man?

Eastman tried to imagine how she met Arnaud Fleishman. He auditioned the scenes. In a supermarket aisle. At a faculty Christmas party. At a dinner he had declined to attend. On the street near Fleishman's Chelsea apartment. At that academic conference in Boston, the weekend before the choking incident. Yes, he decided it was the conference; that was when her behavior changed. Perhaps they met in the carpeted halls of one of those old Boston

hotels along Commonwealth Avenue. She noticed him, the phantom
Fleishman, in the audience at her panel discussion and he followed
after her. They spoke of psychology, colleagues they had in common,
overlapping areas of research. She was captivated by the fact that he
was taking an interest in her work when her own husband showed
little spark for it; in fact, she said to Fleishman, her husband had just
recently called the field of psychology a load of crap one step beneath common sense and sociology. They shared a laugh at his expense. During one of their awkward pauses, Fleishman suggested
that they have a drink at the hotel bar for further discussion of her
paper. Flattered and maybe a little bit excited, Penny said yes. This
was followed by a short dinner, which she allowed him to pay for
upon his insistence. What a change of pace for Penny, or Penelope,
as Fleishman was calling her. She wasn't home in Brooklyn, exhausting herself over her two children. She wasn't tending to every
mood of her husband—his envy, malaise, rage, his erratic complaining. She was her own woman when she was away, full of personality
and humor. And here she was, dining with a handsome gentleman
who was charming the panties off her with every brush of his mustache. So what if Fleishman drank from his wineglass like a woman
and sipped his after-dinner tea with his pinky pointing north. She
was having the time of her life and he realized she wasn't talking
about her husband very much. Fleishman found it not strange, but
fortunate. Maybe, just maybe, he could steal her from the sad louse.
But Fleishman wasn't thinking that far ahead yet—that would be
giving him too much credit. He was handsome but aloof (a kind word
for his brand of idiot). Penelope didn't talk of her husband lovingly
the few times she mentioned him, if at all, and this invited Fleishman to entertain the notion that there was no longer any love between her and her husband. He was more of a life partner than a

husband, she might have said. The check was paid. Fleishman had a bottle of cognac in his room, just sitting there, he said. Just sitting there next to two glasses. But it wasn't just sitting there, was it? It was placed there earlier, along with a stack of condoms and silk scarves and blindfolds. Yes, this Fleishman had a little rapist in him. Penelope wanted to go to his room, but she had a responsibility to her marriage, she might have said, and to her children. She felt confused and so she said no, but only at first. They parted, a lovely parting. Kiss on the cheek, a glance back over the shoulder. She couldn't stop thinking about him when she got to her room, and knew now that not having that drink was a mistake. Fleishman, clever bastard, had planted his room number in her head at the end of dinner. "If you change your mind." "The offer still stands." "I'm in room such and such."

And she did change her mind. Penny never had it in her to have just an affair. With her, everything was absolute. She could handle the guilt of an affair, but what she couldn't handle was the abnormal, the in-between. So this affair would be her walking out on the whole marriage. She made her choice in a glance over dinner.

Once they were inside room such and such, Eastman couldn't quite figure out how it began. Who touched whom? Eastman was too scared to picture her going down on him, even though he assumed it happened, knowing very well how Penny operated. He couldn't picture how the choking was introduced. Was it a fantasy of hers to begin with? Some kind of rape fantasy that she was only willing to share with a stranger? Or was it Fleishman's fetish? Was it he who wanted this degradation put upon himself? Eastman saw it clearly now. She tied Fleishman to the headboard with her stockings while he nibbled her tits. Fleishman wanted to be dominated, decimated, strangled beneath her. Perhaps it just slipped out, like a foul word one blurts during sex. He asked to be choked the closer he came to coming. Penny was not shy in bed, especially not the first time she took a lover. She gave it her all, and if it was in her mind that this would be a onetime affair, she would give it more than her all. "Choke me," Fleishman begged. "Choke me while I come." Not being the least bit bashful, and close to orgasm herself, she did as he asked.

Lying in his bed at the Continental, Eastman had a hard-on from the thought of his wife's affair. Strange, though, he was also feeling a slight physical pain. Pain in his lower side near the liver and along his lower back. His longing for her was still real, even now, halfway around the world.

He got up and walked around the room in his underpants, feeling himself through the cotton fabric. It took him a moment to devise the experiment, but when it struck him—like many bad ideas he'd had in the past several weeks—it seemed as reasonable and sound as any of his decisions. The only way to know Penny was to become her on some psychological level. Maybe her discipline wasn't bullshit after all.

With a belt and buckle, Eastman decided he would cut off the oxygen to his brain while he jerked himself off to the thought of Penny and Fleishman. And he had to move quickly if he was going to maintain his solid erection. Looking around the room, belt in hand, he noticed the bed didn't have a headboard that would work. So Eastman thought the closet might be an ample place to conduct such an experiment. He put the chain lock on the hotel door first, then began to clear the closet by the bathroom. He hung all of his weight onto the closet's rod to test that it would hold him while the hangers jangled. Good old French construction. The bar would hold his weight for the experiment.

Looping the belt through the buckle, he formed the noose and placed it around his neck. The other end of the belt, where the creases across the belt notches told of his widening waist, he tied around the hanger pole of the closet. He made the knots tight and tested them, but he had only a few inches of slack. The prospect of success in the experiment began to turn him on; he felt like a kid back at Boys High, and the receding lump in his underwear began to rise again into a proper erection. Tied to the horizontal pole, he closed his eyes, bent his knees, and eased into it. He returned to the fantasy of his wife fucking Fleishman, hands tied to the headboard, and Penny pouncing on his large pink penis. She was cutting the oxygen off from Fleishman's head, officially choking him out. With barely any breath left, he wanted *more . . . more . . . more.*

Eastman, in the closet, noose tightened around his neck, underwear now about his ankles, was experiencing the same painful pleasure Fleishman was getting from Penny's ravenous cunt. Eastman tugged at himself, leaning forward more and more. The grip of the belt tightened around his neck as he shifted the weight away from the balls of his feet. His face blew up red, blood rushed to his center. He kept his eyes closed and mind focused on blasting inside Penny. She would have let Fleishman finish inside of her and that was both repelling and exciting to Eastman.

The experiment had already gone on for a few minutes and he didn't seem nearly there. Was it working? Was he really embodying the passion or was he faking? Was the fantasy alone exciting him or was it the asphyxiation? These questions caused him to let go of his body a little more, to lean forward, away from the pole, tippy-toeing into the light of the room like a ballet dancer, both toes in pirouette. And yes, he was spinning. He began to feel weightless, euphoric, nearly there. He couldn't breathe but sensed Penny a breath away from him. And had he not disregarded his recent back difficulties—psychosomatic or not—he would have completed his experiment. Instead, Eastman experienced a sudden failing of the body—back, legs, and all gave out on him until he was just an old fool hanging by his belt in the closet. He had hung himself, my God! He had truly hung himself and he couldn't stand up to save his life. He felt something beyond pain, the quick snap down upon his larynx wasn't strangulation but a hanging. He was desperate to get his stance, to pick himself up by his legs, but when he tried, the pain in his back pinched at him, returning him again to his self-fashioned noose.

His hands and arms, gripping for the belt and pole, held him aloft for a few seconds, alleviating the pressure on his neck, allowing him to breathe. How badly the experiment had gone and so quickly, a slight pleasure into a fatal slip. Pain everywhere. Mind and body. He could just let it all go, and in a few minutes the pain would recede along with all of his worries. No, no. He was stronger than that. He came up for air once again, pulled through the pain, his biceps taut, and as he regained some of his breath, Eastman called for help.

It took some time and several hoarse shouts. Meanwhile he was able to spread out his legs so that no pressure was placed against his back. Still, he was seesawing back and forth between back pain and asphyxiation, and when he screamed for help, which took the use of his core muscles, it sent him right back into choking.

Help!

There was a light tap on the door. Nestor! His room boy was just outside. He knew that polite, Vietnamese tap. "*Nestor!*" he screamed.

"Mr. Easyman?" said Nestor.

"*Nestor, help! Open the door. Quickly, son!*"

"Mr. Easyman, but it is locked."

"*Use a key, goddamnit!*"

Nothing happened.

That was his last attempt to speak. Eastman was now out of breath and his arms were getting tired of hanging on.

The room boy unlocked the door but was stopped by the chain that Eastman had fastened before he tied himself in the closet. Nestor could just barely squeeze his small face beside the doorjamb in order to see the spectacle, a dangling man flailing back and forth as if he was wrestling with an octopus.

"*Break it!*" Eastman was gritting his teeth, his mouth plastered into a wide grin.

Nestor disappeared. He didn't know if the boy was coming back. For Eastman, hanging by his throat, swaying back and forth in pain, ten precious seconds were ten whole minutes. But the boy returned with someone strong enough to break through the chain, a passerby on the floor who Nestor was able to convince with his poor English, and the door burst open.

In came the two people destined to save his life. Nestor, the room boy, and David Wheeler, the weary correspondent.

Wheeler grabbed him around the waist and held the poor fool up while small Nestor unfastened him. They brought him over to the bed and laid him out. He could breathe clearly now, and deeply. His belly rose up, blocking sight of his genitals, a sight he didn't ever want to see again. What had they done lately but cause him more pain and suffering? Someone should neuter him, get it over with, maybe then he'd have the wherewithal to concentrate on something other than himself.

Wheeler sat down in the lounge chair and lit a joint. Nestor stayed too, standing at the foot of the bed.

"You all right?" asked Wheeler.

He was, in that he was alive.

"You tried to kill yourself." Was Wheeler stating this fact in order to spare Eastman the embarrassment of what he was actually doing?

"*It was . . .*" said Eastman, but his throat was too painful, his voice too hoarse.

"Don't talk."

"*An experiment,*" he said out of the corner of his mouth.

"Ain't that what suicide is. A great experiment."

Eastman pointed to Wheeler and said, "*I wasn't . . .*"

"Relax. I don't judge, man. I know where you're coming from. Whatever you want to call it."

Wheeler took a few drags and then brought the joint close to Eastman's mouth, like he was to feed him. Eastman had quit marijuana, hadn't had so much as a puff in a decade. But here he was, naked and alive in a Saigon hotel room with the two people who saved his life. He took the joint and puffed it with the desire to alleviate all of his pain quickly and without effort.

"Man, I tried to kill myself once," said Wheeler. "A girl had left me. She was a great chick. Great in the sack, great talker, knew how to treat a guy right. You know what I mean, man? Kinda girl just the thought of her gets you goin'. I was obsessed with her, man. When she was with me I felt like I could do anything. She was like a drug. Great tits, too. Real good in the sack. I don't know what happened, but this chick just lost interest and I couldn't do anything about it. I used to drive around at night. Thinkin' about just turning that wheel and running off the road, barreling into a fat tree. Fast and in the dark was how I'd do it. I thought about killing myself day and night. It was scary, man. This chick really fucked with me.

"I think it was six months later. Bought a gun, some bullets, got drunk and high. Loaded one bullet and played Russian roulette until I would be dead. Three pulls, man. I took three pulls. Pissed myself, crying. I couldn't pull it one more time if I tried."

"Mr. Easyman," said Nestor, trying to get his attention. Eastman handed Nestor the joint, and the boy took it and held it for him. Nestor, not knowing what to do with it, passed it back to Wheeler.

"So what did I do?" continued Wheeler. "Came here. I thought if I'm over here long enough it's bound to happen anyway. Now it's been five years in the service of the great *Herald Tribune*."

"That's a moving story," said Eastman. "But if you please, I'd like to be left alone."

"I don't think that's a good idea, man," said Wheeler.

"No?"

"No. Not like this. I think I'm gonna stay. Burrow into this chair here and take a nap for a while. Let you recover."

"That's not necessary."

Wheeler had already closed his eyes. "You can thank me later." He got comfortable in the chair and seemed to doze off with the joint still in his mouth. He was breathing small inhales of smoke. Once Wheeler passed out, the roach fell onto his shirt. Nestor delicately removed it and put it out in a nearby ashtray.

"Mr. Easyman," said Nestor.

"You want your tip. Take some piastres out of the desk. This stays between you and me and the man in the chair. Understood?"

"Mr. Easyman, a note for you. See?" Nestor produced the note from his pocket.

"Who's it from?"

"The woman. Channing."

"Well, give it here. And take some money, I mean it."

Nestor went over to the desk for his tip, but the boy hesitated. He

opened the drawer and shut it, not taking anything. Even he understood he had a human duty. Eastman was touched by the boy. Nestor
ran out of the room.

Channing's note was curious, a reversal of what he understood as
her rejection, declining to come to his room the other night. Had the
note only arrived sooner he might have avoided this afternoon's
fiasco. Written in very beautiful hand, it said:

*Still interested in seeing what Saigon is all about? I'm free tomor-
row afternoon if you are.*

He knew how love could enter his life at any moment, how it could
renew his mind and body. In the past he had used love as a healing
method, and sex could always help him regain his footing.

Channing was perhaps only showing an interest in him as a colleague, he wasn't sure. He woke up the following morning eagerly
looking forward to touring the city with her. Maybe he'd also fall
upon something to add to his first dispatch. Staying in his hotel room
wasn't getting him anywhere and the thought of failing Broadwater,
of all people, was beginning to eat at him.

In his room, he tied a blue bandanna around his neck to cover
some of the bruises he'd sustained. And in the afternoon he met
Channing in the hotel lobby and from there they took a taxi together
along the Saigon River, south, toward Cholon.

She wanted to show him civilian life of all kinds, the absolute
poor, the refugees, monks and temples. They continued along the
outskirts of the city, to view the shantytowns that collected and grew
and expanded the city limits. A city of scrap metal and huts, refugees living under tin and tarp. Naked children playing in muddy
alleyways. Old men sitting on stools, smoking. Women selling all
types of edibles from street kitchens. In some of the huts he could

see the glow of television. They had wired electricity throughout the shanty villages, stripped it off the main lines, one of the reasons for the frequent power outages—twenty thousand people siphoning off power from the rest of the city. They drove past mounds of garbage, clusters of ARVN roadblocks, foul-smelling canals. In one of the worst alleys, Channing stopped the taxi and they got out.

"Where are we?" he asked.

"You wanted to see the real Saigon," she said.

They started out on foot and Eastman felt the eyes on him at the intersection, where men gathered around a soup stand run by two hunched-over women.

He welcomed the stares. It made him feel uncomfortable and rightfully so. To go where you didn't belong—wasn't that the correspondent's duty?

They walked for a long time in the middle of narrow streets, from the shanty villages to Cholon. Channing called out restaurants she had eaten in, landmarks and temples.

Eastman was thirsty and tired but talkative. He liked listening to her as they passed the places she knew, the boulevards she liked to walk late in the day. They passed a two-story, yellow apartment building at a triangular intersection, and Channing pointed to the second floor. It was the apartment of an embassy man she knew. "There used to be great parties up there," she said. "Long, drunken nights where people stayed up into the morning hours talking and laughing, waiting out the curfew."

The way she referred to this time, with immense nostalgia, made Eastman suspect that she had once had a relationship with the man who lived there. She spoke of it as a place she would no longer return to. So he didn't press her on the subject.

"I thought about moving there once," she said. "He rents it out from time to time when he's back in the States. I missed having a kitchen. Things like boiling water. How I'd love to have a kettle. But I decided it wasn't worth giving up my room at the Continental."

"You're so close to the bureau."

"That's right."

They ended up at a quiet corner café, drinking water and coffee on ice. Channing spoke a little elemental Vietnamese to the proprietor. Eastman toweled the sweat off his neck and forehead. The humidity seemed to suck it all out of him.

"Wheeler told me you haven't been feeling well," she said.

"Is that what he said."

"He said you had taken ill in your room."

"I had a little accident. My back went out. I don't know what he indicated, but he's most likely exaggerating. Anyway, I was wrong about him. Wheeler's all right. He was a great help to me. Happened to be passing by when I was in need." Eastman desperately wanted to change the subject from yesterday's events. The mere thought of it embarrassed him. He was blushing. "Can I be honest with you? It may seem like I'm not in the greatest mood lately. You might have picked up on it. You've met me at a strange time in my life. My marriage is breaking up, and it was a good marriage, but before I came here it all sort of went to shit."

"What happened, if you don't mind me asking."

"She left me for another man." He was careful not to use Penny's name. "That's the short version. We have two boys together, so that's where it gets complicated. It's hard to keep myself from imagining how it happened. Her meeting him. I thought coming to Vietnam would help get my mind right."

"You thought coming here would do that for you?"

"The work. The clarity. Staying busy, that's what they tell you."

"I'm sorry to hear about your marriage. That's really quite sad."

"Ever married, Channing?"

"No. Never."

"Ever thought about it?"

"I'm a single woman past the better part of her thirties; of course I've thought about it. I think I've moved past it."

"You don't seem like the type to rely on other people."

"Don't you find that other people always let you down?"

"I suppose I do. I've been reliant on too many people for too long. Especially the women in my life, I've always felt closer to them than men. My mother over my father. My sister. And now my daughter, Helen, who I'm just getting to know. She grew up in Mexico with my first wife and attends Vassar now. In Helen's case, I suppose I'm the one who has let her down. Come to think of it, I've let all of them down at some point."

"I wouldn't be so hard on yourself. You can't possibly blame yourself for what's happening in your marriage."

"No. I don't blame myself. Right now I blame her. I blame him."

"It's not his fault, is it? Maybe he didn't know."

"He knew. They always do. Ever have an affair, Channing? Bodies don't lie that well. Even if you've been misled, the truth comes out. Especially as things progress." He was making her uncomfortable, he could see it. She looked down at her feet. He shouldn't have asked if she had ever had an affair. There was the possibility that she wasn't as advanced sexually as her years let on. She could never have been in love, possibly why she was liberated from the idea of marriage.

"I met him," he said. "Outside my home. In the middle of the street. The man my wife is fucking. We came face-to-face." A little lie.

"My God, what happened?"

"I don't normally do things like this, I have to say. But he was dropping my soon-to-be former wife off from a date at eight o'clock in the morning. I was at home taking care of the children." There he was, bending the truth. Though it could have happened this way. "They had just slept together, it was apparent. I could smell her on him. I looked into his eyes. We were at a standoff in the street. Asked him if he knew who I was. He said he did. And then I asked him if he knew what he was doing. No. He admitted he had no idea. He was out of his depth. 'Are you prepared to take this all the way?' I asked him. I don't know what I meant, I was losing my mind. I could have knocked him in the teeth. I was a boxer, you know. Not bad, either. Good left hook. I could have clocked him. I could have done a multitude of bad things. But I didn't. I backed off. I wouldn't give them the satisfaction of demonizing me."

As he lied to her he began to see his mistakes. The more he lied, the worse he felt. He was trying too hard and it humiliated him. He was trying to entertain her, or worse, to win her pity.

"So what happened?" Channing said.

"Nothing. I frightened him. He got back in his car, scared. He put the car in reverse and drove backward the entire way down our street."

"Remarkable. I don't think I could restrain myself in that way."

"Years of practice."

They finished their coffee, paid the bill, and started walking again, turning onto a main boulevard.

"So now you know something personal about me," he said. "It's your turn. I don't know anything about you."

She smiled and shook her head. "The man I told you about, with the apartment we passed. The embassy officer. I guess you could say we were together for a bit. He was much older. He had a wife. I didn't feel terrible about it, either. Is that wrong? Being here things are different. It's as if what's back home doesn't matter."

He wished he could feel the same, but it all mattered to him—Penny, her affair, his children, his life and career. He couldn't think of anything else as important, and he supposed that he hadn't really been present in Vietnam at all. His mind and moods were dependent on what happened back in New York.

As they continued to walk, he got the lowdown on Channing. She came from a long line of Quakers who had settled in California. Vallejo, Petaluma, Santa Rosa. She had a father still out there and an older sister somewhere in Seattle. College, she went out east to Vassar, and then journalism school followed at Columbia. That was the midsixties, and Eastman wondered if they had ever passed each other on campus when he was participating in Vietnam protests. He had spoken in Morningside Park the day students took over Hamilton Hall on the Columbia campus. "I remember," she said. Channing was there, but documenting the whole thing as part of her journalism classes. She felt as if she'd missed the sixties because already she was reporting, churning out copy.

He was curious as to why she had been in Vietnam for so long. He'd been here for a short time and knew he wouldn't be staying. He'd sit and wait out his marriage until things cooled down. "What is it about Saigon that's kept you here?"

"I like it," she said. "I have good friends, and I'm so accustomed to the pace of things. That thing they say about adrenaline is true. You probably know that."

"I'm no journalist. I write books, long ones, and it takes years. There's no rush in what I do. I may have started out as a correspondent, but having seen what you and the others do, I'm not that. Never was. When I was covering the war in the Philippines it was already over. I was there collecting details for my book. I never had any investment in reporting."

"The Philippines must have been similar. You write the larger picture. I've read your work, remember."

"Not like here," he said.

He was gratified. There was no quicker way to Eastman's heart than to flatter him over his work. His stance began to perk up, he grew confident, and he was now playing the great writer, the famous documenter of war who had left his mark on the world. He wanted to say that he had read her work, too, and admired it. But he found himself reluctant, hesitant.

"Tell me more about this book you're writing," he asked her.

"God, I'm ashamed to talk about it. I've been spending half my time here collecting tape." Channing had been interviewing soldiers and civilians since before the American withdrawal, compiling interview after interview. She wanted to write about the people she met, the individuals. A book that would work as a collage. "Not anyone's story in particular," she said, "but a compilation of all of those lives, a collection of personalities."

Eastman thought it was a fine project. "It could put you on the fast track," he said.

"Hah," she said, smiling, obviously pleased.

"I have to tell you," he said. "I don't read many books by women. I find that they don't understand my perspective and so I shy away from their work. I'm ashamed of this. It just so happens that's the way I read. I find women's prose distracting. I say this because this is what you'll be up against. People will see you, a woman, writing the war, and they'll not want to listen. They'll dismiss it and think there will be too much sentiment, too much eye shadow where there should be blood and guts."

"You don't read women because you find them too sentimental? I have taken my share of crap for being a woman here, believe me."

"Overly sentimental. I'm just being honest with you. As a woman, though, you're more in touch with emotion. Something men lack. That's where your book can be major. Where others are writing about power and the struggle for power—the larger picture, as you say— you can concentrate on the power of the people, their thoughts, their feelings, who they are. Woman is our child bearer, our seductress, our priestess, the mother who cares for us, gives us life. If you can match those instincts with prose that's not too sentimental, or too feminine, you may just have something."

She was offended, shaking her head, and rightfully so. Eastman realized he had made a faux pas, letting his mouth run like that. What was he thinking? Just when they were making a connection. As soon as she had complimented him, he suppressed his weaknesses and allowed his massive navigator to take over and direct him. She was so taken aback that she needed to stop in the street for a moment and assess what was being said.

"Do you really believe the bullshit you're spouting?" she said.

"I know it's hard to swallow, but this is how you'll be read. Many readers won't take you seriously, and not just men. Women, too."

"You really do believe this, don't you? I am shocked that a writer like you can be so blinded by his own convoluted hype. I have been here for eighteen months, in and out of combat. I have seen what men have seen, and I don't think when I write it there is a single difference."

"That's short reporting, so maybe not. But in book length. The kind of book you want to write. Listen, I'm only trying to help."

"You've helped by pointing out the kind of reader I won't be writing for."

"I've pointed out the majority of readers. I'm trying to explain the way it is."

"The majority of readers? Eastman, this isn't 1953. There is no basis for your thinking. Not all women are protectors and mothers for you. Not all women write sentimental romance."

"Forget I said anything. It was a mistake."

"I will not forget you said anything. I think you are grossly misinformed and the fact that you think this way leads me to believe that you don't understand the world at all. When you look inside yourself, you must feel completely alone."

Eastman couldn't help thinking that Channing was right. Inside he was alone. The need to enlighten the world with Eastmanisms was exhausting and erroneous. Where did this habit of enforcing his ideas come from? And when did he stop believing that he could be mistaken? His urges were totalitarian. He knew it came from a dissatisfaction within himself. It was dangerous not to have humility, and Eastman knew that if he continued he would certainly end up on the wrong side of history. But Channing had no right to say such things. He had to attack her, to knock her off her high horse and bring her back down to earth.

"I'm not going to debate women's lib with you," said Eastman, "because that'd be a fool's errand. This is the book business, honey, and I've been in it for twenty years. I've made my living."

"Writing is a man's job to you, isn't it? I'm well acquainted with the notion. It's been rubbed in my face all my life."

"Oh, forget it. I'm sorry I said anything at all."

"I hope you are. And I hope you reconsider your position."

"You got it, sister." He walked on ahead of her. Easier than to say it to her face.

"You're patronizing me?"

"If I did you would know. You'd be in hysterics."

"Hysterics. Listen to you. The classic hysterical woman, isn't that what would prove everything for you?"

"Right on, sister."

Channing quickened her pace, overtaking him and leaving him behind her. She walked purposefully up the boulevard, past the markets and soup stalls. Eastman increased his pace in order to keep up with her and it caused him to become winded.

"Will you wait, Channing," he shouted.

She stopped, reluctantly, and allowed him to catch up. They continued their walk along the boulevard back toward the city center. They said nothing. Channing had been offended and he wasn't up for apologizing. *For what*? he now thought. He had been offering his advice to help harden her. To protect her from how people would likely read her work. Oh, forget it, why should he help anyone? Besides, there was a major chance that he'd never hear from her again once he left Vietnam and that there would be no major book on the war by Anne Channing. How many aspiring novices were plotting the exact same thing? Sure, she was a good correspondent, showed no fear the other night in the square. But he saw her now as insignificant, just one of many. He began to feel better as he maliciously predicted her failure.

From the boulevard they found their way to Tu Do Street and then on back to the Continental.

But he felt absolutely terrible. Once he was alone in his room he thought things through. Channing had been kind enough to take him around the city, to spend her Saturday afternoon with him. He realized that this was probably her only day off and she was spending it with him because, in some sense—romantic or not—she liked him, as he did her. What a fool, what a stupid prick, talking about her readership. And what had he done lately that was so special? He had written several critical failures, good efforts but not his best. His game was undoubtedly off. He thought he was playing to his strengths, offering what he knew, but she wasn't interested. She was right, this wasn't 1953. Twenty years had gone by. Rock and roll, the Kennedys, Vietnam, Watergate, even the damn feminists were more relevant. He had become clouded, irreverent and irrelevant both. He didn't know how the American public would read her; he only knew about his own select tastes.

He went out into the hall to find Nestor, who was carrying a load of towels.

"Nestor, drop what you're doing. This is important."

Nestor immediately placed his towels down on a cart and came running over to Eastman, who waited by his door.

"I need you to find me some flowers. Roses or whatever they have. Get two dozen, as many as you can carry. We gotta repair some damage I've done with Channing. Send them to her room." Eastman wrote an apology on the back of one of his business cards.

> *Forgive me, I've acted out of line.*
> *Foolishly,*
> *Eastman*

He handed the card and a handful of piastres to the boy and sent him off.

When Nestor left, Eastman went back into his room. He thought it strange that it hadn't occurred to him to send flowers to Penny after the breakup. Not after she left, none in the past few years. He could have sent a bouquet to her mother's house, a gesture that there was still love to be salvaged. Even when Eastman was miserable, desperate, there was too much pride in him to admit he was down. He wouldn't come crawling to Penny. He had to keep up the impression that if this was what Penny wanted, then he would be able to live with it. A man without respect wasn't what women wanted to love, at least that's what he had always assumed.

It occurred to him that Channing was right and that he didn't understand the world at all. Or he didn't understand her world. *His* world he understood meticulously, and it was full of people he could relate to, people who listened. His children, for one. His beloved Helen, the boys, Toby and Lee. They looked up to him. There was his mother, Fran, still alive and strong like her father was before her. And for a decade there was Penny, his life, his soul, his unicorn! The center of it all. She had understood his ways and ambitions and took his advice from time to time. She admired who he was, or she had once. The shellac had worn.

He passed the rest of the day writing and rewriting another letter to Penny, expressing the bit about the flowers, how he should have sent a bouquet, how he realized that she was right about outward signs of passion. He had grown too comfortable, took her for granted, all the nonsense he could come up with until he realized it was far too dramatic. Remember, he was going to win her back not with pity, but heroism. That's what she'd admired in him before. That's what will get her to turn.

In the evening there was a knock on his door. It was Channing.

"Don't send any more flowers," she said. "I don't need anyone thinking I'm being wooed. It's hard enough being taken seriously as it is. Even by you, as you made clear this afternoon."

"That's what I mean to apologize for. Will you come in?"

"I don't see why I should."

"So that I may apologize. Allow me to apologize. Please."

She looked around, and seeing that no one was in the hall watching her, she went into his room and quickly shut the door.

"I got your note," she said. "There's no need to apologize again."

"Look, I spoke out of turn. I don't know why I said those things to you. This is my own fault. I've always seen women writers differently for many years and I see how closed off I've been. It's shortsighted. If a woman can do a correspondent's job, such as you've been doing, there really is no difference. I think you're solid, Channing."

"You haven't read my work."

"Yes, I have. I remember now. I think you're very, very good. You're someone who has the chops. Anyone can see that." He was relieved, getting all of that out in the open. "I haven't changed my mind about profiling you. Think about it. It could be a win for women everywhere."

Eastman could see that he was getting through to her. She was beginning to relax and she finally sat down on the edge of the bed.

"Can I get you something to drink?" he said.

"I'm still not interested in being in your book and you don't have my permission. And yes, a whiskey and water if you have it."

"I do." Eastman went to the minibar. There were little bottles of scotch and gin inside and he went about pouring two bottles into glasses with a splash of water.

"Thank you." She drank the whiskey quickly. "Have you really read any of my work?"

"I have," he said, though he couldn't remember an exact story. He did read the *Times* and the *Herald* back home, daily. "What did you write about last?"

"The withdrawal. The last GIs to leave South Vietnam. After that probably the marine guards at the embassy. They're the last ones."

"Then I've read your work without a doubt. But it's my sense of you. That and what I saw the other night. I know you're good. I don't need to read much to see that."

Channing was adjusting into this rather well. She took out her cigarette pack and began to smoke. "You're looking for something to write about?" she asked.

"Something good, something Norman Heimish and the rest of the *Times* won't have."

"I'm going to Cambodia, to Phnom Penh. That's where I'm going next. A reporter can get a Pulitzer for what's happening over there now. Nixon has a covert war going on and it's getting heavy."

"Sounds dangerous."

"Some of it, maybe. I'm asking you if you want to come along and do some real reporting. The kind of reporting you ought to be doing."

He hadn't thought of Cambodia at all. He didn't know much about Vietnam and he knew even less about Cambodia. He didn't see a prospect of a story there. She would know better than him, of course. Still it's not what he was hired to do. He was hired to write the situation in Vietnam, not America's pivot into Cambodia.

"What about Dak Pek?" he said. "I can get us transport to Dak Pek near the Laos border. I hear from General Burke things are going on there. The *Herald* wants impressions on Vietnam from me, not on Cambodia. Covert war or not."

"Dak Pek is too far north. That's nowhere near where I need to be."

The prospect of traveling and working with Channing was enticing. He could certainly learn something from her. But Eastman didn't want to be following anyone around. He wanted to be the leader, the one who gets the scoop, the star correspondent. That's what this trip was supposed to be about. For his wife to open the front page and see his dispatch from Vietnam, the biggest story on the longest war. He'd still need to write his first dispatch from Saigon, but he could have his second piece be from Cambodia as he worked his way up to Hanoi. Still, there was no possibility of securing a North Vietnam visa and he didn't know what the consequences would be if he were to go direct from Phnom Penh without it. He could get stuck following her around, and would that grow tiresome?

"Let me consider it," he said. "I'd very much like to go with you, but I may need to rearrange some of my plans."

"Think about it," she said. "You can send me one of your famous notes." Channing put out her cigarette in the bedside ashtray and got up to leave.

"I have the feeling there's a lot of risk," he said. "Going to Cambodia."

"Really?" She cocked her head at him. "And you—what have you risked by coming here?"

Everything, he thought. But nothing that mattered to anyone else but him.

16

A few days passed and Eastman neither saw nor heard from Channing. He was hoping they might run into each other on the terrasse or in the hotel lobby. He appreciated her company and he had enjoyed sparring with her. Yet his mind was made up on the subject of Cambodia, probably as soon as she had left his room the other night. He wouldn't be going. He wasn't moving a muscle in the direction of that civil war, not even with her. He delayed telling her, and the more he delayed, the more absurd it felt to send her a note: "I can't go to Cambodia, but what do you say to dinner for two?" The idea of seducing her began to seem far-fetched as he began playing and replaying rejection scenarios in his head. For she would reject him, he felt sure; yet, like a dog with a bone, he couldn't let go, couldn't stop himself from wanting it.

He was spending most of his time in the room, ordering room service. Steaks and fries, club sandwiches, beef noodle soup, eggs over easy. He billed it to the bureau, tipped generously. Nestor was beginning to know Eastman's quirks and gave instructions to the bellhop bringing up the carted meals, "Put by bed."

He listened to the radio, only got an hour of jazz per day. The rest was rock and roll, a genre that bugged him. He couldn't think while listening to rock music, the lyrics were too boundless, they didn't sit well in the background and took over portions of his mind he needed to concentrate. Other stations played Vietnamese music, which he preferred because he couldn't understand what was being said, and the language, although sharp and tedious, allowed him the mental space to compose his letters.

He wrote Helen at Vassar, and then his mother-in-law, Cathy, explaining his intentions to save his marriage. To Helen he wrote: *You've needed me at times and it seems we find ourselves in a role reversal. It's now me needing you. What a burden I'm placing on you when you should be hammering out schoolwork, allowing boys to take you out, everything but caring for an emotionally crippled father. When I'm back I want to make it up to you. I'll come up to Poughkeepsie for a few days, bring you some supplies, whatever you need.* Cathy he pressed with guilt: *You may allow Penny to do whatever she wants. I know, Cath, I know. You can't stand in her way and you can't tell her how to live her life. We're in the same lifeboat. But please just watch out for my boys and make sure they aren't exposed to too much of her nonsense affair with the Frenchman. I'm afraid they won't know what to think of their mother and why she's banished me (figuratively—I went to Southeast Asia of my own accord). Nor do we want them exposed to the shitheel (excuse my French) who is sleeping with their mother—what corrupted morals he must have. It takes a bitter man, a sick, envious man, to steal another man's wife. Harold would have never approved of what Penny's doing to me, God rest his beautiful soul.* Good, reference the dead husband, Cathy's beloved—that should get her steaming.

He wrote Meredith, his mistress, a kind thanks for the dinner party and an apology for ruining it with his announcement. *I've done worse, much, much worse, and you've been lucky enough not to have witnessed it over the years, only to hear about it after. Now you see what kind of attitude I'm up against and the altitude I'll plummet from, professionally, personally, romantically. Lately I feel as if I have a black hole deep in the pit of my stomach, blooming inside me, enveloping me in sadness from the inside.* He didn't mention Lazlo, because there was still the book looming over his head.

Most of his time went into his letters to Penny. He scrawled on hotel stationery updates of things he only half believed, impressions of the country he had not even explored yet. *There's another reporter here, a young woman named Channing who writes for the* Herald *(look her up, dear, she's quite good), and she's invited me to tag along to Phnom Penh, Cambodia. It took some convincing, but part of this vile Vietnam narrative has spilled over the border into Cambodia, where we (U.S.) are bombing the North Vietnamese, Viet Cong, and the Cambodian communists. With the war slowed down here except for a few terrorist attacks on Americans in Saigon (extreme caution has been recommended), I've decided to follow Channing into Cambodia to see what the situation there is on the ground. My safety isn't guaranteed, but when is it ever? And what do I have to return to there but the mess we've made, my darling? I'm being pulled by larger forces over the border, a prodigal man, magnetized, drawn into Phnom Penh, the center of this magnetic field*—his letters to Penny were some of the best writing he'd done in years. They were written with passion and persuasion and at least partial honesty. Through them, he began to sense the core of his purpose in Asia, which inspired thoughts about his book, the elusive book he owed Lazlo and that now began to take shape. It would be in a new style—less analytical, more emotional—different from his previous works. He would be the central character, Eastman. He would eviscerate himself to write the book. With Vietnam as the backdrop, he would tell his personal story and interweave it with the story of a country under siege. The political and the personal would come together and reflect off each other, becoming both a journey to the heart of a war-torn country and to the soul of a man who'd lost everything he had believed in. Loss would be its theme, loss and the regaining of value in the world. It would take his original invention (history in a novelistic style) as executed in *The American War*, but he would be the book's protagonist, its hero. It would be about Penny and the phantom, and the state she left him in. Broadwater, gutless and manipulative, would be in the book, too. So would Channing. Meredith he would leave out, same with Lazlo; he wasn't absolutely mad. He still planned to rescue his marriage, not ruin his life and those around him. It would be a major book, ahead of any of his contemporaries.

The draft of his letter to Penny had the voice he wanted, it presented him the way he would appear at the start . . . a wounded man, a marriage on the outs, yes, yes, this was brilliant stuff. I've done it, I've cracked the bastard! he thought. This could be major.

Eastman went down to the bureau to send off a telex to Broadwater and mail his letters to Helen and Meredith. He held back the letters to Penny and her mother. He would place those with the outgoing mail at the front desk, not wanting to send a letter to his wife and mistress in the same bundle. The bureau had news of his visa to Hanoi. Denied. It wouldn't be happening. The North had rejected his application on the basis of his reputation and Broadwater couldn't grease the wheels enough. With the cease-fire in effect, it seemed unlikely that he would have had a problem. If he still wanted to go up to Hanoi to see what it was like, he'd have to find other means. He told Broadwater he needed more time and that he would file a dispatch within a week. "Scratch the Hanoi part of the story," he instructed him. "I'm not about to hang my neck out while there are good things right here in Saigon."

Downstairs he dropped the letters to Penny and her mother with Mrs. Nguyen to be sent at once.

He went shopping that afternoon, thinking he would be making a

move somewhere into the countryside soon. He found a tailor, recommended by the bureau, who was able to provide him with the
proper military garb he needed to report in the field. The combat
boots he already had. In a few days' time his clothes would be ready.
While he waited he felt he would have to start making some tough
calls. Either get busy making plans to move out or do nothing. If he
were to do nothing, he had the feeling that this would weigh on him
and that it might force him into an uncomfortable situation—like
following Channing into Cambodia.

He went back to the hotel with the intention of going straight to
Channing's room to tell her he wasn't going to Cambodia and to invite her to have dinner with him. He strolled through the lobby,
imagining the surprise on Channing's face. "Oh, Mr. Eastman!"
called Mrs. Nguyen, getting his attention. "Mr. Eastman, we have
wonderful news for you. I hope you will be most delighted."

"Go on."

She came out from behind the front desk and stood in front of his
path to the elevator. "How has your stay been with us? Is there anything we can accommodate you with?"

"My stay has been just fine. More than adequate."

"Then I am proud to hear it, Mr. Eastman. Again, if there is anything at all that you will be needing, I'm sure you will not hesitate
to ask."

"You had something to tell me."

"Yes, a wonderful surprise for you. Your wife has arrived. We
went ahead and let her into your room and provided her with her
own key."

"My wife?" Of all the things that could have come out of this
woman's mouth. He was confused and looked around the lobby, trying to get his bearings on where he was, the day, the hour. How long

had he been asleep? Could his letters have already arrived in New York? Impossible, he had just brought them down to send off. "You said my wife. My wife is here?"

"Yes, she arrived this afternoon." Mrs. Nguyen was smiling.

"I wasn't expecting my wife. What did she look like?"

"Your wife? She was white. American. Very beautiful. You are a very lucky man, Mr. Eastman."

He had a deep impression of déjà vu. This had happened to him before. He remembered walking into a hotel on a boulevard in Madrid, blindsided by Meredith. Was it her, once again? Impossible, the very thought of Vietnam scared her. Besides, he wasn't on good terms with Penny, and with things so up in the air Meredith would know better than to come all this way to surprise him. It was understood that when there was real turmoil in their marriages, the affair was put on hold.

Eastman ran up the steps, not even bothering to wait for the elevator. Three flights up and he was out of breath. He fumbled for his damn keys. There had to be some sort of mistake. They let a stranger into his room, someone posing as his wife. A thief, a good one. He was being robbed. In Madrid, Meredith had been taking a shower when he walked into his room. He had hoped it was Penny. What if it really was Penny now? Come to reconcile. She was the only one who knew his exact whereabouts. She had all of his contact details, even his room number. Had she broken it off with Fleishman and come immediately to repair the damage? If that was the case, all of his troubles would have been worth it. He put the key into the keyhole and turned the knob. No one in the bathroom. Empty. No shower was running. He took a breath and then he went into the bedroom. All of his praying and pleading for Penny, and wouldn't this be a merciful ending to a horrible journey.

There she was, seated in the green lounge chair by the window. His mistress, not his wife. Meredith Lazlo, in the flesh, had played a gullible hotel staff once again.

Why was she in Vietnam?

"Meredith," he said her name, somewhere between a question and an answer.

"Alan. I know. I should have written ahead."

"Meredith, what are you doing here? In God's name."

"Well, I'm glad you're happy to see me."

"It's just such a surprise. We're in a war zone. It's dangerous."

"Actually, it doesn't seem that dangerous. Of course I've only seen the airport and came directly here to the hotel. I'm starving. Have you eaten?"

"What are you doing here?"

"I came to see you."

"I can see that. It's just so unexpected."

"Alan, I've left David."

"No." This frightened him.

"Yes. I've left him and that is all there is to that. It wasn't because of what's happening to your marriage. This is completely separate. I just want you to know that first. But it has occurred to me that I have not been happy for quite a long time. And then when you left for here, I was devastated. I couldn't allow anything to happen to you. You were in such a state. I mean, my God, and we couldn't even embrace. I'm tired, you see, Alan. I'm tired of this double life. Of course, I've adored meeting with you over the years, I look forward to it. We've seen the world together. We've grown old together. So when I left David, I came here because I didn't know where else to go."

"That's crazy, Meredith. Are you crazy? Does David know about us?"

"Of course not. I didn't tell him. I'm not a complete idiot."

"Are you sure he doesn't know? What did you tell him when you left?"

"He thinks I've gone to Australia. There's a book fair. I made something up. It doesn't matter. He doesn't know I'm here."

"Well, he wouldn't think to guess, I can say that. Nobody in their right mind would be so foolish as to come to Saigon in the middle of a war."

"You're here," she said.

"I'm here working, Meredith. I'm working on a story. On a book that I plan to publish with your husband. How on earth would I be able to do that if he finds out we're together? Do you suddenly want us to be out in the open? That's not an option, it never was. That's why we've worked so well all these years."

"I've never been ashamed of being your mistress. I quite enjoy the time we spend together. Like I said, I wasn't thinking clearly and I had nowhere else to go. You know how New York is. All of our friends are David's friends, too. That or they work with him. Publishing is so incestuous."

"Meredith, my God." He paced the room, back and forth, trying to think of a solution. His head was swimming and sweat was accumulating on his forehead and under his arms. Was it so bad that she had come all this way to see him? Was it so bad that she had missed him and wanted to comfort him during this time? But that's exactly why he wanted distance, not just from Penny, but from her, too. Their relationship would cloud his attempts to get Penny back. It would sap his mojo, his strength, his will. And then there was Meredith's safety to think about. The shooting in the square just outside the hotel. The bombings he could hear at night. They didn't sound like they were only on the outskirts of the city, like he'd been told. They sounded quite close.

"This is a very dangerous place. The other night I looked out the window and *BAM! BAM! BAM!* Three people. Murdered! An assassin right outside the hotel. The situation is volatile, Meredith. We need to get you out of here."

"Now, Alan." She came closer to him and put her hands on his chest. "Is it really so bad? Is it really so bad that I came here to be with you?"

"Meredith, please." He was trying to get out of it. "You don't understand. It's for your own good. We need to get you on a plane."

"But Alan, I missed you." She was pouting her lips and moving closer.

"I know you have. I missed you, too."

"Have you been thinking about me?"

"Yes, I thought about you." He didn't tell her about the letter he had written to her because meeting her here mainly canceled out his feelings.

"What did you think about?" Her hands moved down his chest and onto his stomach. She was caressing him and he hadn't the power to stop her. Meredith's sensuality was addictive and it certainly worked its power over him. "Go on," she said. Her hands moved to his thighs and then slowly crept onto his crotch. "You can tell me, darling." She was whispering, goddamnit. And he wasn't stopping her.

"I thought about you plenty," he said.

"Did you think about this?" She was rubbing the outside of his pants and his penis responded into a full hard-on. "Alan, my God. You must be very pent up. All by yourself with no one."

"I am, dear. I am very pent up. I'm sorry, my love."

She undid his belt and zipper. Meredith could seduce the life out of him, there was no way out of it.

"Please, Meredith," he was pleading with her, only it was a very poor attempt. So he tried to talk himself out of it. Stop. Get out. Lock yourself in the bathroom and take a cold shower like the champs.

"Please what, Alan?" Seductress! She had one hand down his pants, the other was unbuttoning his shirt.

"Please," he said.

"But Alan . . . Do you know what I think?"

"I have no idea." She pulled him out and massaged him in her hand.

"I think you ought to fuck me."

What a coward, our Eastman. What a hypocritical coward. Succumbing to his mistress, no longer thinking about what was important. He really did want her now. Before, perhaps, he hadn't, and wanted to rid himself of her, but she convinced him with her enchanted caresses, the anticipation of her glorious mouth and the sex that would follow. He could do nothing but kiss her now. And he kissed her hard, like he wanted to swallow her whole. He kissed her until they were both on the bed, kicking at the air on their backs, squirming out of their clothes. Pant leg, underwear, brassiere strap, hairpin. Off it all went.

Meredith came out of the bathroom with a towel wrapped around her head and smelling of soap and skin cream, her own, not the hotel's. She slipped back into bed next to him and twirled the hair on his chest with her manicured fingers.

"Let's talk about something," she said. "Tell me about your trip so far. What have I missed?"

"Nothing. I've been making decent contacts. Staying here in the hotel . . . meeting with generals and other newsmen."

"What have you seen of the country?"

"Poverty. Great poverty is all around us. Outside this square you won't have to go far to see a man with no legs, pleading for piastres. I ought to write that down. 'Pleading for piastres.' It's usable."

"Can I read something?"

"I haven't written much. A paragraph here and there. Notes, I have notes. Nothing else."

They both stared ahead at the dark reflection of themselves in the television. She might have liked the way they looked together. And what he saw was the same, only it made him sad. It was as if he couldn't cheat unless he was really cheating. With both of them broken off from their spouses, the affair should have felt right. Only it didn't.

"While I'm here I might as well meet some of the reporters. Maybe someone is working on a book."

"I don't think you should be staying very long. We should get you to safety."

"I've already seen plenty of well-dressed women walking around outside the hotel."

"That doesn't mean anything."

"Alan, I'm staying. At least for a few days. The flight to get here was incredibly long. I am not getting back on another plane. I would just die if I had to."

"You don't know how serious this is, do you? You could die here. What am I supposed to do? Watch over you every second of every day? I have to work."

"No, you don't have to watch over me. I can handle myself."

"I have plans, Meredith."

"Well, don't let me interrupt. I only want you for your body." She pinched his ass. He pulled away.

"For instance, I'm supposed to travel to Cambodia."

"What's in Cambodia?"

"A war. A civil war. The Cambodia thing is serious. I'm going with another reporter. Anne Channing. She's very good. Have you heard of her?"

"I don't think so."

"She's a crackerjack reporter and she's my ticket over there. You see that I have obligations already set up." He was changing his mind about Cambodia as he had done about Vietnam when Broadwater first proposed the idea.

"You really want me to leave. You want to put me back on a plane and shoo me off. Alan, I need a holiday. I've just separated from David and have been under a lot of stress. Knowing that your wife just left you, I'd expect you to understand."

"Wait, you and David are separated? I thought you left him."

"Separated, left him, what's the difference!? If you must know—I didn't think you cared—we're separated."

"So it was mutual."

She leaned back on the headboard, not wanting to talk about it. "I suppose I left him, but yes, we came to an understanding that we would separate. For now."

"So there's still a chance you and David might get back together. This isn't a permanent thing."

"I don't know. It happened so recently, I told you. I needed to see you."

"I thought you wanted to . . ." he trailed off, unable to complete his thought.

"You thought what?"

"I thought you were here because you expected that we would be together. I thought you were coming after me."

"Well, you are my lover. You are who I come to when I need to be loved. I'm sorry, Alan, I take offense at that. You seem so sure that we could never be together."

"Let's not get into that. There's nothing wrong with you, you're a perfect, beautiful woman. Looks, intelligence, money. I just haven't thrown in the towel on my marriage. I'm trying to work on things with Penny, I thought I made that clear before I left."

"But she left you, Alan. For another man."

"So?"

"She's cheated you, moved out, and you still want her back? How can you trust someone like that? She's moved on."

"Will you shut up?"

"Don't tell me to shut up. You shut up."

Eastman got out of bed and picked up his underwear, his pants, and began to get dressed. He paced around the room looking for a missing sock.

"I'm not moving on," he said. "The facts are not yet clear. I have two children with her. There are my boys to think about."

"For your information, Alan, I'm not here to win you over and wait to ask you to marry me. I'm here because I'm also in pain. I have also experienced a loss. And I wanted to see you."

"Well, it's just a hell of a time right now."

"I'm sorry. If you want, I'll get my own room."

"No, I don't want you to do that."

"I don't need you to take care of me. I can take care of myself. Jesus, you're being a prick."

"This is what happens when you surprise me, Meredith. I'm sorry if I'm being a prick. But I've seen some things out here that I wouldn't care to share right now. You know what happens to men who come over here. They return forever changed."

"Oh, you've been here what? Two weeks?"

"I need some air."

"Then get some!"

Eastman put his shirt on and left. Once he was out in the hall, he felt as if he had exited a bad dream. Meredith was one of the factors that had contributed to the dissolution of his first marriage. She was the start of his philandering. Not that Meredith could be faulted for anything. Her attraction to him was real, and was once without attachment. There was love between them. Now it seemed as if Meredith wanted to turn his unfaithfulness, his dirty little secret, on its head. To come out with their love. Although a monogamous life was simpler, it wasn't exactly what he wanted. Eastman wanted his life to remain as it was before the falling out with Penny. And if he could have her back, would he still continue his sporadic affair with his mistress? No. He'd have to end it.

Meredith was rarely demanding of him. They'd hit a rough patch in 1967 when Meredith became pregnant with what she believed to be Eastman's child. She was already forty-six years old and they weren't taking precautions. To him, the situation was an absolute crisis. But Meredith, always a voice of reason, remained calm, collected, and made all the hard choices for him. His would have been the principled, dignified way. When she told him about the pregnancy, Eastman was already calculating the cost—what he would need to allot each month for child support. He would never have left Meredith holding the bag. And that she was Lazlo's wife was another factor that weighed heavily on Eastman. A secret affair was one thing, but a secret child, duping another man into thinking it was his own? His publisher, no less, a rising star at the company. Beyond being scandalous, the thought was beginning to sicken him.

They spoke over the course of a week, Meredith from her closed office in Midtown and Eastman either from his study when Penny was out or from a pay phone at his boxing gym. It was Meredith who suggested the abortion. "I don't want children. I never have. I know of a doctor in New Jersey who can safely have the whole thing taken care of. At my age, if I was to have the child it would be a danger." "Maybe we should give it a few more days and think of another way." "This is the only way, Alan. You would have me ruin my marriage over this?" "It's a baby, Meredith." "It's my life, and my decision." "Then I'll come with you. I want to be there." "Too suspicious. Don't get emotional, Alan. This is just something that happened and this is the way I have to take care of it." "At least let me pay for it. I feel guilty as hell here. Getting off scot-free." "We've done nothing wrong and I don't blame you for anything. You'll make it up to me." "I will, darling."

That's the kind of woman Meredith was at her core. He suddenly felt selfish for wanting to get away from her now.

Eastman went down to the terrasse and ordered some food to have brought up to the room. Noodles and soup, Caesar salad, French bread, a bottle of champagne. There was no sign of Channing at any of the tables. He was hoping to run into her. He could have just gone to her room, but it now seemed inconsequential.

He went through the lobby and checked his messages with Mrs. Nguyen. A telex from Broadwater asking what the fuck was going on. More of interest to him was an invitation to the presidential palace for a "celebration of peace" that very evening. Perhaps General Burke had something to do with getting him on the list of attendees.

This was the perfect opportunity to open up a dispatch from Saigon. A presidential party, a glimpse of President Nguyen Van Thieu and other dignitaries, there was potential in this. He went back upstairs to the room and told Meredith to pick out something nice to wear because tonight they were going out.

17

The only visible sign at the new palace that there had been a war on were the spirals of barbed wire, waist high, bordering the palace gates. Eastman and Meredith walked alongside these barriers for a few blocks, under the canopy of trees and beneath the squeal of bats. They came to the front of the palace. Security seemed tight and excessive, which demonstrated his point that Saigon was still too dangerous for Meredith to act recklessly. *See,* he seemed to say to her with his eyebrows as they walked through the security outpost. Meredith, however, disregarded him. Instead, she looked ahead in anticipation of a proper Saigon party. They continued up the driveway around the great lawn. The night air was humid and they could smell the flowers along the path. Eastman admired the palace at night, the way it took to the light. It was a modern construction, three stories high, with a presidential balcony and columns that resembled bones, perhaps double the size of the White House.

"It's not very French, now is it," said Meredith.

"This palace is new, I'm told," he said.

"What happened to the old one?"

"They blew it up."

Once inside, they were led through the main hall to a large assembly room, where the reception was already in progress. He scanned the room. Mostly Vietnamese men in suits exhibiting political importance. Sprinkled in between were tall Westerners, contractors and diplomats, newsmen from the bars around the Continental. Some of these men he imagined were CIA or former MACV. The who's who of Saigon. And at the center of the room, a mountain of prawns and exotic fruit, mangoes, pineapple, papayas and jackfruit, little spiky nubs called chom choms.

Eastman took Meredith by the arm and they moved to the bar, where they secured some champagne.

"Did you know I've been to the White House?" he said.

"Johnson or Nixon?" she asked. They clinked glasses.

"No, it was before that." He wanted to let her believe it had been with Jack Kennedy, that perhaps he'd been invited to dine with him and Jackie, to whisper into the president's ear something about the state of the nation. Only Meredith was too intelligent to let anything slip by her, even for a second.

"Kennedy didn't invite you the White House," she said, as if it was unheard of.

"Eisenhower," he admitted. It had been a lame press dinner in 1956, and it wasn't even attended by Eisenhower or his crony Nixon, who was vice president at the time.

"My God, we are getting old."

"It's just a number." He didn't believe that and he didn't know why he said it. He was intensely aware of getting older, especially at this impasse in his marriage.

"I'm bored," she said. "Let's talk to someone. Introduce me around."

"I'm afraid I don't know many people here. I suspect there are a lot of agency men. CIA. We're in the belly of the beast."

"What about him?" It was General Burke, moving toward them fast with his hand out, ready to shake. "You must know him."

"Eastman," Burke called. "You got the invitation. I'm glad you came."

"Meredith, meet General Donald Burke. General, this is Meredith."

"Call me Don, please. Where have you been hiding?"

"My calendar has just been full of interviews," said Eastman.

"I didn't mean you," said Burke. "I know about you. I mean this lovely woman."

"Meredith's just in from New York."

"It's a pleasure, Don," Meredith said and Burke took her hand.

"Come to see the last of Saigon, huh? Well, this is it. I'm glad you could both make it to the party. President Thieu is here. He'll be saying a few words about the so-called 'peace' we've been hearing so much about. Personally, I don't think he knows his right hand from his asshole. I know, I shouldn't be talking like this. But what do I care? I'm going home in a few days."

"And where is home, Don?" asked Meredith.

"Anywhere but here. Forgive my sarcasm, dear. West Virginia. You're not a correspondent, are you? You have an aura of mystery about you."

"You're very charming," she said. "I'm a publisher. I worked on Alan's first book."

"You're kidding. *The American War* is my favorite book of all time. *In the Shadow of Eden* comes in a close second. Have you read it?"

"I have," she said, referring to Heimish's war book published that same year.

Eastman scoffed.

"You're a tastemaker then," said Burke. "You didn't take me for a reader, did you?"

"I would never think that of you. I'm completely thrilled that you admire Alan's work."

"How's the writing?" he asked Eastman.

"Gestating. I never talk about a piece of writing until it's finished. I do, however, want to talk to you about Dak Pek."

Eastman looked at Meredith to gauge her reaction. Dak Pek sounded dangerous, like he had plans to act on. The sound of the name was pressing.

"Not here," Burke said. He looked around. "Let's go over by the shrimp."

"My, you two are secretive," she said. "I'll let you go. I'll be here."

Eastman and Burke walked through the crowd and over to the shrimp station, where the general gathered an obscene number of crustaceans onto his plate. His method was to devour. Tear the heads off, chew them up, spit out the inedible. Eastman stuck with the fruit because he would be drinking tonight and didn't want to risk another upset stomach by mixing alcohol and seafood.

"I'm sorry I've been out of touch," Eastman said. "I'm dealing with a lot of factors. Also I've had an unexpected surprise. Meredith arrived this afternoon."

"I don't give a rat's dick. Just keep that lovely lady safe. That's your first priority. Now Dak Pek."

"Can you still get me up there? If you can, I want to check it out, even if it's just from the air."

"Situation is hairy. Cease-fire is out the window near Dak Pek. Fighting continues, but you won't hear that at the four o'clock follies. I believe that is what you in your business call a scoop."

"Yes, indeed. So it's possible?"

"It can be arranged. You'll have to drop into Pleiku first and get a dustoff to Dak Pek. I'll call you in the afternoon. What about your wife?"

"Meredith's not my wife. She's just a good friend. She stopped here en route to Sydney to look in on me."

"When you leave for Pleiku I can see after her if you'd like."

"She'll be fine."

"They don't make 'em like that anymore."

"How's that?"

"Women with backbone. A head on her shoulders. I bet she holds her own in a room full of grunts. Does she cook?"

"I believe she has someone for that, Don."

"Now I'll have to determine whether we can get you up there," the general continued, "if not tomorrow then in the coming days. You should have called me sooner. I thought you would be in touch. Answer your damn phone when I call. I'll leave it to the discretion of the pilot whether you can touch down or not."

"I'd be happy just seeing it from the air."

"The ground war, isn't that what you said? Talk to the men on the ground."

Eastman found himself backing out of the trip already, just as the general was proposing the plan. He was trying to get away from Meredith, but why? He wasn't so sure. It may have been his interest in Channing, and not wishing to appear attached. They had something, he was sure of it, at least before he shit the bed. Rather than suffer any more embarrassment, he left his plans with Burke intact for the time being.

"However you can help get me there is much appreciated," Eastman said.

"Did you ever track down Norman Heimish?" asked Burke.

"No. He left town, I think."

"He's back."

"You've seen him?"

"He's standing right over there. Talking to your Meredith."

Eastman swallowed his champagne whole and dropped the glass

on the table of prawns. It *was* Heimish. Conversing with Meredith among a swarm of Saigon's elite.

"Why Gen'ral, what have we got ourselves here?" Eastman said, using his Texas accent. He placed his thumbs into his belt as if beneath his dinner jacket were two quick-draw revolvers. Of course, he felt nothing but two extra inches of belly flap. "I believe we have ourselves a Mexican standoff."

"I sensed there must be some bad blood between you two boys," said Burke.

"He robbed me of something once."

"A woman?"

"A Pulitzer Prize." Eastman dropped the Texas twang. "Don, if you would excuse me now, I have some business to attend to."

The general turned to refill his plate. "That's fine. Better get some more shrimp while the gettin's good. We'll be in touch about tomorrow."

Eastman walked toward Heimish and Meredith as if in a trance. He was thinking of ways to skewer his old friend in front of his mistress. He downed another champagne quickly while the waiter stood by. Then he took two more flutes, one for himself, the other for Meredith.

She had probably welcomed Heimish over, as they knew each other from New York. She was well aware of their falling out but she wasn't going to be impolite to anyone on his account, especially to an author of Heimish's caliber.

The years had been kind to Heimish. Eastman sized him up from the profile. He may have lost a good amount of hair but it suited him. He was not very tall, but he was broad, as broad as they came, with thick shoulders and arms, one of those men who looked uncomfortable in tailored clothing.

When was the last time they'd seen each other? Was it all those years ago at Heimish's polygamy farm in Illinois? They hadn't been completely incommunicado for the last decade. Besides the few times they'd spoken on the phone after the Illinois incident, Eastman sent letters to Heimish, concise paragraphs of backhanded praise written after Eastman found a particularly bad review of one of Heimish's books and could hence quote the worst parts in his letter.

Heimish turned around and smiled at Eastman as he approached. His face was still handsome in that boyish way, with his square jaw.

"Alan!" Heimish said. "What in God's name has brought you to Vietnam? And you've gotten Meredith all mixed up in your fiasco. I look up, I see her, I swear I think I'm at a New York publishing party. God, it's good to see you, brother." Heimish put his hands around Eastman's arms.

"Norman, what has it been? Seven, eight years?"

"Too long. And God, I feel old just looking at you, which means I'm old, too. Meredith, do you know I met this man nearly twenty years ago?"

"So did I," she said.

"And you're just as in love with me as you were then," Eastman said to her. "More so."

"Flatter yourself if it makes you feel better," she said.

"I heard you were in town," Eastman said. "But I didn't know how to get ahold of you."

"I was in town. And then I wasn't. You should have called the *Times* bureau. They usually know where I am. I just got back from Cambodia."

"You're kidding," said Meredith. "Alan was just about to go there. Weren't you, Alan?"

"Meredith, please," Eastman said.

"I thought you said you were going to Cambodia?" Meredith said.

"I said I might go to Cambodia. But now you're here. So maybe I won't."

"I don't think the situation in Cambodia is getting any better," Heimish said. "The war will be there when you get there."

"I know that. I just don't want to announce my plans to a roomful of newsmen."

"Alan," Heimish said, "that's not the way it is out here. There are no scoops to be had. There's just a shit situation and a bunch of brave individuals bearing witness to it. It's a calling, you know that."

He didn't know that, actually. All these years Eastman didn't think of writing and reporting as a calling or vocation, but as a job. A job where he'd done well, not having to work for anyone. A job where he could exist as he was and not have to change for anyone. He wanted to say something equally impressive about the work, but he didn't have anything in reserve. So when he opened his mouth, he found himself saying, "Chasing the war is like chasing a fine woman. Once you lay her she can never be enough."

Meredith was appalled. "That's a hideous analogy," she said. "Absolutely hideous." She shifted slightly in Heimish's direction and shook her head as if to apologize on Eastman's behalf.

"That's the old guard talking," said Heimish. "You see, Meredith, old guys like us feel threatened by women in charge. We'll die out soon enough." Heimish was being courteous. Eastman knew his statement was hideous and he was sorry he'd made the remark. Still, there was a time when Heimish would have joined in and had a quip or two to add. The remark had made Meredith uncomfortable, and she was now so visibly disappointed in Eastman that all he could do was deflect her rage by keeping a smile on his face, as if he didn't care about her feelings. But he did care about her feelings. Why couldn't he just apologize? It was Heimish's presence. It put him off his game and he was resorting to animalistic modes of survival at a cocktail party. Whenever he did so, the night was sure to end in disaster.

A change of subject was desperately needed to save him from himself, and when he looked to Meredith she continued to scold him with her eyes. Only she could absolve him and remedy his evening.

"Norman," Meredith said, "I think your new book is just wonderful, I had meant to write you."

"Thank you. You're opinion means everything."

"I haven't read it," said Eastman. "What's it called?"

Heimish appeared burdened to have to recall the title of his new book for him, which meant two things. The book wasn't living up to its expectations or Eastman was finally getting to him.

"It's called *A Winter in May*," Meredith said. "Such a brilliant title, don't you think? You must read it, Alan. It's profound."

"Thank you," Heimish said. "I'll send you a copy, Alan."

"Don't bother. She has a copy."

"I'll send you a book anyway. You can give it to someone. You're at the Continental, right?"

"That's right. Where are you?"

"I'm staying in town, a private residence. The amount I've been coming and going, it's better than trying to book a room in Lam Son Square."

There was an awkward pause filled with aggression and it was mostly coming from Eastman's body language, the way he stood in a fighter's stance, still holding in his fists two flutes of champagne. He offered the extra glass to Meredith as a peace offering. She took it from him in exchange for her empty glass, so right away his hands were once again full. This discomfort made him feel the pangs of anxiety. He was having trouble finding his footing in the room.

"You have an apartment, you say," Eastman replied. "I'd love to stop by and see it." It occurred to him that Heimish no longer lived in Illinois but had moved to Rhode Island with his wife and two daughters.

"I'm renting from a friend at the embassy," said Heimish.

Eastman thought the profile fit Channing's former lover. He got the feeling he had whenever he figured out the ending to a book he was writing, when all the players began to align neatly and the erroneous details fit like pieces in a cardboard puzzle. He felt clarity of mind. As if suddenly the walls of the palace had turned to glass and he was allowed a glimpse at the truth. It wasn't spiritual; it was a truth experience. He thought of Channing and looked around the room for her. He wanted to share the news with her (perhaps because he felt left out) that Heimish was renting the special apartment she mentioned.

Meredith, sensing a shift in the atmosphere, tried to change the subject yet again. She asked Heimish questions about Saigon. She asked about safety in the city, and that only irritated Eastman more. Was she trying to upend his authority? Heimish recognized the motivation behind Meredith's questions, and he was happy to oblige. He told her just how unpredictable things really were and that she should be taking extreme caution.

"That's why invitations for tonight arrived so late," Eastman informed Meredith. "They probably didn't want too many to know that there would be a gathering with the president. Too dangerous."

"No, I knew about it for a few days," said Heimish. "Speaking of which, have you met the president?"

"I've met several presidents. But no, I haven't met this one."

"I interviewed him," said Heimish. "A few times, although I can't recall just how many."

"What's he like?" asked Meredith.

"He's like all politicians. Short on time and answers questions that weren't asked while dodging the ones that were. Then time's up and you're shuffled off."

"Is that what you're working on?" said Eastman. "The political angle? Is it a book?"

"An article for the *Times* magazine. But there's always a book, isn't there? And don't worry. There are plenty of Vietnam stories to go around. Tragedy is dynamic."

"Now he's going to tell us about tragedy," Eastman said.

Heimish didn't take the bait and politely smiled.

"It's good to see you back at it, Alan. These are tough times, what with this Vietnamization baloney. We need writers like you to dispel the lies and the bullshit."

"That's why I'm here. To do the good work." Eastman looked around the room at the faces he didn't recognize. A commotion started up on the other side of the banquet hall, near the stage. Some armed men had entered the room, presidential guards. They were clearing a path rather aggressively, which was becoming a theme for the evening. Once a suitable path was cleared of partygoers, President Nguyen Van Thieu entered to a round of applause and made his way onto the stage to the center podium.

Heimish explained that they should get a little closer and led them, with his wide frame, into the crowd toward the stage.

Eastman got out his pad and began to take notes. He knew Thieu hated journalists, much like the infamous Madame Nhú, who, in the early sixties, had wanted them all thrown out of the country.

Thieu made some lame duck introduction, the same stuff any politician back home would start out with, only his way of speaking was guileless. Even when he spoke of peace he seemed angered. He

briefly complimented the success of the Paris agreement and as-
sured everyone that South Vietnam's relations with the U.S. were
intact. It was only when Thieu began to speak of history that Eastman became interested.

"History has proved," said Thieu, "that the world cannot have
solid peace without stability in the Pacific region. Our brothers and
sisters with interests in our region know this to be true, and that is
why they have worked tirelessly to repair what has been broken. Disruption in the Pacific has always led to a fractured world and a broken economy for all. History has also shown that for the Pacific
Ocean to deserve its own peaceful name we must have the courage
and determination to push for lasting peace."

"Pacify" was the word that came to Eastman then. America was
trying to pacify South Vietnam as it removed itself under the guise of
Vietnamization. Train, support, aid, disappear. The messy business
of removing itself from a lost war.

As Thieu concluded a rather short speech, it felt like everyone
needed a time-out before the party could resume. The words were
uplifting, but his delivery sucked some of the air out of the room.

"What do you think?" Eastman asked Heimish.

"I think he's in for a rude awakening when the checks from Uncle
Sam slow down."

Meredith excused herself to go to the powder room and Eastman
and Heimish stood alone together for the first time in a long while.

"I'm looking for a friend who's supposed to be here tonight," said
Eastman.

"Who?"

"Anne Channing. Do you know her?"

"Yes, I believe I do," said Heimish.

There was no reaction in Heimish's response, not even the least bit of interest. He couldn't tell if they were friends, couldn't confirm whether Heimish's embassy man was the same as Channing's.

"Let me know if you see her," said Eastman.

"Sure thing. What else is new? Are you and Meredith . . . ?"

"We're just friends. Why?"

"I was only wondering how long you two would be traveling together."

"You old dog."

"Not in the way you mean."

"How's Jenny, is it?"

"Yes, she's wonderful. Thank you. And your wife?"

"Not so good. In fact, do you remember that time you had me out to your farm?"

"We had a bit much, hadn't we? As I remember you two were on the outs about something."

"It was before Penny and I were to be married. She got cold feet and ran off to London. That was why I came out to see you, I was lonely. Anyway, I've been thinking about back then and it was foolish of me to try to get her to change. You gave me some sound advice, something I never forgot. And even though my trip to see you didn't end too well—in fact, it ended about as bad as it could have—I never thanked you for your help back then. So I guess that's what I'm doing now."

Heimish rubbed his temple as if he were having trouble remembering those days. Eastman let him have his memory lapse. He was being far too sentimental with Heimish anyway. That's what a broken marriage did to a person.

"Don't mention it," said Heimish. "It was in the past."

As the night went on and his consumption of champagne increased, he left Meredith and Heimish for a breath of fresh air and had a look around the palace. Outside the banquet hall were rows of rooms, many of them locked, some open for dignitaries to wander through. A wing of the palace had been blocked off, and this seemed to be the residential quarters, no doubt where President Thieu had retreated. He walked back to the banquet hall. The party was getting rowdier and he didn't feel like reentering it just yet, so he slipped out through a row of French doors that led to a balcony. The hot air outside was like a smack in the face. The feel of Asia, of faint smoke, was rousing.

At the edge of the balcony under the open sky was Channing, smoking.

He went toward her eagerly. When she saw him she asked, "Have you been avoiding me?"

"I thought it was you avoiding me," he said.

She turned away and looked out at the palace grounds. He approached her slowly, his hands in his pockets.

"Your invitation," he said. "I'm sorry I haven't gotten back to you about Cambodia. I've been indisposed. I have a friend in town and her visit was unexpected. I'm eager to get her on one of the first flights out of here."

Channing was distant. She continued to smoke, leaning against the balustrade.

"Are you okay, Channing?" he asked.

"Well, about Cambodia. You can forget it. I'm leaving tomorrow."

"Look, I can't be everywhere at once."

"I'm not asking anything of you. I only extended an invitation because you showed an interest. Frankly, I don't know why I thought it would be a good idea."

He looked behind him to see if there was anyone else on the balcony and then he moved in closer to face her. He hadn't seen her in a dress before, with makeup on. He wanted to offer a compliment, but he sensed it wouldn't be welcome.

"I like you, Channing. I didn't give you an answer yet because I'm not sure if I'd be stepping into a dangerous situation because I'm attracted to you, or if I would be doing it because I'm interested in the story."

"And what have you concluded?"

"I'm not interested in the story."

She put out her cigarette underfoot, blew the smoke over his shoulder.

"And your friend, the woman you've been with all night. Aren't you involved?"

"What does that have to do with it?"

"Everything," she said. "You're unavailable. Too unavailable to send me a note, yes or no, that's all I needed. Even while you stand here you're being dishonest to me. And to her."

"You want to talk about dishonesty. You didn't tell me you knew Norman Heimish."

"What are you talking about?"

"Your ex-boyfriend with the embassy and the fancy apartment. Isn't he renting it to Norman Heimish? I assume you're all friends having a laugh at me behind my back." Eastman had been almost certain that the three knew each other, but as the words came out of his mouth, he couldn't be more uncertain.

"I don't know Norman Heimish any more than I know who you are at this moment."

"He seems to know you."

"What are you insinuating? You want to call me a whore? Call me a whore."

"That's not what I'm saying," he claimed. Although it was. He was accusing her of sleeping with her own lover (which she had every right to do), and he was vilifying the act because of an association with Norman Heimish (which he couldn't prove), imagining this all took place at a location he knew not where at a time when he was not present. It all seemed so clear when he was in the banquet room. But his proof was insubstantial because he didn't know who her lover was. Why would he? What was he doing to this woman?

"You are crazy," she said. "Everyone is right."

"Forget it."

"I confided in you about something very personal."

"I want you, Channing."

The confession was so ill timed and landed so off the mark that Channing seemed astounded.

"You're tied up in something that seems to be very messy," she said.

"I'm not tied up in a thing. I'm free. I do whatever I want."

"You're kidding yourself." She cringed as she said this and he thought this made her look rather ugly. "And you're behaving like a jerk."

"Shut up," he said.

"Don't tell me to shut up."

He grabbed her from behind and kissed her. He pressed her against the balustrade, hard. She struggled to get his lips off her and she managed to push free. He'd smeared her lipstick and this gave her the quality of a victim. Channing looked horrified. Would she scream? She looked down and got a pocket mirror out of her purse.

"You know, I thought we may have had a chance. Had you not done that." She began fixing the smear.

He reached out and handed her a handkerchief, but Channing

recoiled and turned her back to him. The kiss had been a violation. He felt absolutely terrible about it. Of all the bad decisions he'd made in the past few weeks, this one brought him the most shame.

She walked to the other side of the balcony. A man and woman came outside for fresh air. They were no longer alone. He remembered Meredith inside and he didn't want to leave her much longer with Heimish. So Eastman wiped his mouth clean of Channing's lipstick with his handkerchief. He folded it, put it back into his pocket, picked his head up, and went back inside, leaving Channing on the balcony.

18

There was no one in the bureau office at that late hour, even though one of the ashtrays was still steaming with smoke. Eastman sat down at the cleanest desk and spread out his notes— scraps of paper and a notepad. He arranged the notes into some chronology—arrival, paranoia, faces around Saigon, assassination, delays, indisposed, the presidential palace. He had enough for a story, an impression at least. Whether it was newsworthy, that was another matter. He told himself it was newsworthy because he was writing it. That was the story. Himself in Saigon, and his impressions didn't need to be historically accurate, they just had to be true and somewhat informed. This was a dispatch, a narrative. What he sees, the reader sees.

Eastman wrote it out by hand in lead pencil. He took intermittent sips of water, got up every now and again to stretch his legs, played with the air conditioner, then sat back down. He set the scenes with himself as the guide, the narrator and protagonist. He stuck to the beginning of his trip, Tan Son Nhut, the scenes at the Continental and the Caravelle, leading up to the assassination of the two guards in the square. Then he wrote about her, running out into the square in the middle of the night without trepidation, while he cowered upstairs behind a potted plant. There was a crowd of armed soldiers who were still jumpy, and Channing took great strides to get there in time, snapping photos as she went. As he wrote about her, she became a character of great integrity, and he began to fall in love with this character. She didn't need anyone. Got along on her own terms. He began a flashback to earlier in the evening, during drinks at the Jerome and Juliette, when he was telling her about his failing marriage and trying to generate a good amount of pity. She listened, that was the reporter's greatest gift, to hear everything and retain what was important. Channing reminded him of this. She listened intently, and it was satisfying to be heard. He wasn't being heard back in New York, not by his wife (before or after the breakup), that's what was so aggravating about his situation. He allowed his character to have this revelation just as he experienced it in the act of writing it down.

Then back to Channing in the square after the assassinations, doing the job he had forgotten how to do. There were no American deaths, and so it was not news until he placed her in the scene. Then it became an American story that he could see readers caring about.

He got some paper into a word processor and went on to draft it up. He poured out some six thousand words, most of them decent and clear for this time of night. He searched for a title, something appropriate. "Eastman on Saigon." It didn't matter, Broadwater would figure out a way to better it.

The sun was coming up and the roosters in the alleys off of Tu Do Street were restless. A man came into the bureau and Eastman recognized him as the guy who sat by the window and filed the stories with New York. Eastman pulled his copy and put it on the man's desk. He didn't need to say anything because the man knew what to do and it was too early in the morning to talk anyway.

He collected his notes and went upstairs to bed. In his room, he found Meredith under the sheets, breathing rhythmically.

He woke up briefly, once the morning was a little brighter, and he saw Meredith getting dressed in front of the window, her image hazy, as if she were a dream. In that space between sleeping and waking he thought he could have imagined her this whole time. Her arrival in Saigon, the two of them together at the presidential party. It almost made more sense than finding her in Vietnam.

"I'm jet-lagged," she said. "I woke up at four and couldn't get back to sleep till six. Where were you?"

"I was filing a story."

"What time did you finish?"

"No idea. You were asleep when I came in."

"You want me to wake you up?"

"No, let me sleep."

"I'll be downstairs for breakfast."

He closed his eyes and listened to her leave the room, click the door shut.

She took her table in the courtyard as usual, under the banyan tree. It took some time for her to get up this morning. The party had gone late and she had a bit to drink. All those correspondents in one place, all those famous faces of previous wars. She had to overdo it in order to feel relaxed. And then being accosted out on the balcony by that pigheaded shit Eastman. She felt used, violated. Perhaps she imagined kissing him once, but last night, in public no less, a kiss was unwelcome. To be unable to move him, that was the ultimate violation. He'd used his strength to establish dominance over her. He was out to prove something. That he was free and could do what he wanted. Take what he wanted. It wasn't about her, and this made her feel used. After the incident she had three or four more drinks, who was keeping count? Then she went back to the Continental and passed out atop the covers.

The waiter brought her coffee and croissants, a plate of fresh fruit. She had no appetite, so instead she drank the coffee and smoked. She was nervous about the day's journey. In a few hours she was due across town, where a guide would take her all the way into Cambodia and on to Phnom Penh.

No ashtray, so she flicked her ash on the floor.

It was a bad idea to begin with, letting Alan Eastman tag along with her to Cambodia on a story. Why had she invited him? She never extended herself to anyone else. Was it the pity she felt for him? He seemed so lost and clueless and eager to learn from her. Was it his celebrity, the way his presence interrupted a room? Was it to teach him something? He had the ability to disappoint, to ruin a moment, and she had the urge to correct him. Eastman's stupidity could be so transparent, so infuriating, and yet she couldn't dismiss him. He infected everyone around him. He had changed her priorities. Did she really want what Eastman had? She wanted to write like him once, in graduate school, this was true. She wanted the visceral quality of his writing. Her work for the *Herald* was cookie-cutter reporting.

That son of a bitch, taking advantage of her. Now she wanted to beat him, pummel him to the ground. She wanted to write circles around him. He would never write a book on Vietnam that could come close to what she was capable of. He was too slick, too superficial for it. She had been here longer, she understood the culture, the people, the way of life, had done hundreds of interviews. Civilians, soldiers, spies. She had visions in green. She slept and dreamed Vietnam. She would go to Cambodia today, stay for a while, but when she returned to Saigon she would start writing her book.

A hand appeared in her line of sight, a woman's hand. Red nail polish, wrinkled knuckles, taut veins. The hand reached out and offered her an ashtray.

"You can use it," the stranger said. Channing recognized her as the woman Eastman had brought to the party last night. She was sitting at a table in the sun, behind Channing.

"Thank you," Channing said, and took the ashtray. She was wondering if this was Eastman's wife. She recalled him telling her that his marriage was not doing well. Was that a lie in order to get her into bed? Channing noticed the woman's long fingers and a gold wedding band. So this could be Mrs. Eastman coming to his rescue. He was like a big child who needed pampering. How pathetic. Perhaps he begged her to come all the way to Saigon for help.

"I'm Meredith," the woman said. "I saw you at the palace last night. We didn't get to meet."

Channing smiled politely and tried to return to her breakfast.

"Are you a reporter?"

"Yes," she said.

"Fabulous. What's your name? I must have read your work."

Channing introduced herself.

They talked about the weather, the heat, and then moved on to meaningless chitchat about the service at the hotel. Meredith mentioned how it was remarkably decent for wartime. Channing attributed this to Asian hospitality, quickly realizing she'd just made an unfounded generalization. They were looking for common ground. When Meredith showed Channing part of a manuscript she had open on her table, they soon got to talking about what constituted good writing.

"I'm much older than you are," said Meredith, playing with a green pencil. "Yet I find what I'm doing isn't any clearer than when I was your age. You see, I'm at a turning point in my career. I'm breaking ties with the publishing house I've worked for, oh God, for I don't know how many years. I'm going off on my own. Well, technically I'll still be working for the same company, but I'll be starting my own imprint, specializing in new women writers. I'll be the publisher and will have a good amount of independence over what I want to print. Meredith Lazlo Books. New women's writing. What do you think?"

"New women writers," asked Channing. "What does that mean exactly?"

"Of course, there is no real difference between the writing of men and women. Think of it as new writing by leading female thinkers and undiscovered female talent. We'll have feminists, essayists, academics, poets, novelists, all writing about women's issues or tackling the female perspective. And if I'm lucky, war reporting, too. Have you ever thought of writing a book?"

"I am writing a book."

"Then just my luck! Tell me. But only if you care to talk about it. I respect what you do so much and I know how unsettling the process can be."

Channing was beginning to like Meredith. They were two people who would never speak back home, but finding each other in Saigon provided an immediate familiarity.

"It's about my time here," said Channing. "I've been cataloging people. Their experiences. Interviewing them, getting them to tell me their stories. The personal stories, not just war stories. I want to know where they came from and maybe how we arrived here together. I have a story of a man's special pair of boots, or one about how someone lost feeling in their leg. I have an interview with a woman, a socialite, on where she gets her clothes made. A young girl who disappeared from her village and resurfaced in a brothel in Saigon. The commentary about the war will be in each story, but it won't be the focus of the stories themselves. It will be a chronicle of the people in the war, not of the war and its people."

"Fascinating. A chronicle of stories telling one story."

"I want it to be personal. I want it to move you on the human level."

"I want to read this book," Meredith said. "I would publish such a book."

"You're too kind," said Channing.

"I have a sense about you. You're intelligent and you know what you're doing. We'll have to exchange information." Meredith went into her purse, a black leather hip bag, and produced a business card, which she gave to Channing. "Do you live in New York?" Meredith asked.

"I do." Channing hesitated. "Well, I did. I haven't been back in over a year."

"When you're back in New York I want to take you to lunch."

"I don't know how much writing I will have done by then."

"It doesn't matter. I'll take you to lunch anyway."

Meredith handed her a pen and Channing wrote down her information on Meredith's manuscript. "You can reach me through the *Herald* when I'm back," Channing said. "I don't have a phone or even an address anymore. I've let all of that expire."

"Oh, the *Herald*! You must know Alan. In fact, I think he mentioned you yesterday. He said wonderful things."

Channing pretended not to recognize his name right away.

"Alan Eastman," Meredith clarified.

"Oh, yes," said Channing. "Of course. I've met Alan."

She wanted to ask about their relationship and it was her hesitation that gave her interest away.

"You're wondering why on earth I'm here," said Meredith. "I've come to visit my dear friend. But I can't seem to stop working. Why not meet a few swell reporters while in Saigon and maybe find a book to publish?"

"I didn't mean to pry," Channing said.

"Darling, please. I'm not so secretive. Alan and I are old friends."

"I'm not interested in him in the way you mean. I'm sorry if I'm giving you that impression."

"I didn't take it that way and it would be an insult to you had I assumed it. He's so old! When he was younger, though . . . my, he was fun. And not too bad on the eyes. Always married to someone else, of course. Men like him will do anything to be near you and when you start to want something they suddenly have too much going on to give you attention. You know the type. Great flirts with poor timing."

Channing politely smiled. "If only I'd met you sooner," she said. "You see, I'm off this morning and won't be back for several days."

"Well, then we'll see each other in New York, won't we."

Meredith was warm and Channing decided that she did indeed like this out-of-place woman from New York. She would give her a call when she returned home. Eventually, once she had a little more of a book to speak of.

After breakfast Channing exited the courtyard, leaving Meredith to return to her manuscript. From the hotel she walked into Lam Son Square to the steps of the National Assembly, where the two ARVN men had been killed. There were still faint spots where the blood had settled. A guard outside regarded her with contempt. She was so used to this she barely gave it any thought and continued to think about the night of the shoot-out. She went from one kill scene to the next, across the square, through the parked cars to where the boy assassin had been taken down. Here the blood on the ground came through the sand that had been poured over it. You couldn't seem to get the blood out, no matter how many days passed. And she wondered about this place, what it would be like when all the men and women in the hotels were gone.

When she arrived at the American Embassy, there were crowds of Vietnamese waiting in a long line outside along the embassy walls. She was able to bypass the line; the MPs had her name on a list and let her through the gates. She walked along the shaded path to the main building and went inside. She gave her name to one of the receptionists and waited in the cool air. When Davis came out to meet her he was in a hurry and waved her over, then started down the hallway that led out to the grounds.

"I need to talk to you," she said.

He turned around and put his finger over his mouth. Then he suggested they go outside.

She hated being silenced more than anything, but she needed a favor from him. She followed him outside into the heat and they walked across the lawn in the direction of the embassy pool.

"What is it you need?" he said.

"Nice to see you, too."

"Look, I'm sorry to be curt with you but I'm having a hell of a week. I'm not even supposed to be here. I was supposed to be home with my kids this month."

"Thank you for giving me Lin. It was a good lead."

"Is that what you came here about? To thank me? Send me a thank-you note."

"It was you who told me not to put anything in writing."

"Not anything that we discuss."

"I'm off to Cambodia in a few hours," she said. "I don't have much time either."

They walked around the tall hedges and reached the pool, where they could be out of sight of anyone inside the embassy. Davis began to pace. He was nervous about something that didn't involve her. Not wanting to waste any time, she took a paper out of her purse and unfolded it and handed it to him.

"I need another favor."

He regarded it with little interest then handed it back to her. "What the hell am I supposed to do with this?" he said.

"I thought I could give it to you. It's a list of names."

"I can see that."

"They're Vietnamese who've either worked for the press or were employed by Americans. I had them checked out. Can you do anything for them?"

"Who are they to you?"

Channing hesitated. She knew what a long shot this was, to get Davis to use his connections at the embassy to secure visas for these strangers. The cook hadn't done anything for the Americans except talk to her, the press. But it had been weighing on her since she accepted the list of names. She shouldn't have, it was a mistake. But she'd wanted the interview. She had them vetted by the bureau and learned they were mostly secretaries and translators, young men and women.

"I got them from a source I met through Lin. I don't know his name," she said, "but he's a spook. He talked to me on the basis that I would pass along this list of names to anyone I knew who could help. I said I would."

"You should never have taken it. I can't do anything for these people. You know what kind of trouble I'd get into?" he said. "You don't know them, what do you care?"

"I don't, but I said I'd do something and so I'm asking you if you can help or if you know anyone here who could take a look into it." She handed the list back to Davis. "Just a look."

"So you can have it off your conscience? When the shit hits the fan here it's every man, woman, and child for himself. We have people who've gotten married here. They have families in Saigon. They've inherited relatives. We're talking thousands of people. This is what happens in an occupation. And when we leave we have to take a hell of a lot more people with us than we brought here. There's no room for cousins of some North Viet spy who gave you a story." Davis handed the list back to Channing. "And you shouldn't feel bad about it either, Anne."

Davis was right. She shouldn't have taken anything from the cook and she was letting her conscience get the best of her.

"Think of it this way," said Davis. "You made a mistake. You don't know these people. You had them vetted? Bullshit, they get around that. We have a line of Vietnamese outside who've been vetted. What if we do take all these refugees? Put them on a plane to Manila and then where? San Diego? What if they are spies? Spies are made to deflect suspicion. There's no way of knowing." Davis turned around to check if anyone was listening in. "Look, I understand how you feel. I have my own list of friends. We all do. You're just trying to do something that feels right. Something you think will matter. And if it makes you feel any better I'll take the list. Get it off your conscience." Davis put his hand out. "Here. Give it to me."

Channing handed it over to him, knowing that Davis would do absolutely nothing.

"I'll take a look," he said, for her sake. "Be careful."

Not knowing if it had been ten minutes or ten hours he woke up. In his dream he was already on a plane somewhere out of Saigon.

Eastman got himself together, put on a hotel robe, shook his hair out of its mussed helmet, and went out into the hall. There he found

Nestor, wheeling a cart full of toiletries. He called for the boy, told
him to keep an eye out for Meredith were she to return while Eastman was out. Then he hurried down the stairs to the second floor and
ran to Channing's door. He'd made a mistake last night that he was
sorry for. He knew that kissing her the way he did was completely ill
timed and the thought of it was burdensome. He needed her to know
that he wasn't a complete bastard. He wanted to tell her the things he
realized about her when he was writing his dispatch. He wanted to
make it clear to Channing that he thought she was the real deal. A
major talent. The bravest he'd seen. He knocked on her door. No one
came. Was he too late? He knocked harder, again and again. He
pressed his ear to the wood and heard shuffling in the room. "Channing," he called. "It's me, Alan. Open the door."

But it wasn't Channing who came to the door. It was a young man,
a Vietnamese with no shirt on, just a pair of blue jeans.

"Who the hell are you?" Eastman asked.

The young man didn't answer, just rubbed the sleep out of his eyes.

"Where's Channing? You speak English? Français?"

"English."

"Where's the woman whose room this is?"

He didn't have the time to waste, so Eastman pushed past him,
rushing into the bedroom expecting to find her there under the
sheets. It would pain him to see this, but when he reached the bedroom there was no one. And the young man had been taking a nap
on top of a made bed. There was the impression of his body on the
comforter. Eastman looked around and was a touch relieved. All of
her things were still in place. The stack of paperbacks by the green
chair. The ashtray balanced on top of Thomas Mann. Little bottles of
feminine products on the bureau. Silk scarves, a carton of cigarettes.

"Channing?" he called.

He went into the bathroom to see if she was in there and came up empty. She was gone. He went back over to the bed and sat down.

The young man joined Eastman by the bed, dragging his leg behind him. He had to adjust it in order to stand up straight. He came close to where Eastman was standing, reached for his cane beside the bed.

"She went away," the young man said. "I am her friend Lin. She is allowing me to stay in her room while she's gone."

"Well damn, why didn't you say so?" He was angry that Channing wasn't here, that he was too late. "I didn't mean to pry into whatever it is you got going. What happens between you two is none of my business. You hear me? It's neither here nor there."

The young man put on a shirt and moved around the bed to sit in the green chair by the window. He looked down at his feet. He was telling the truth. Channing had let him stay in her room while she was away in Phnom Penh and Eastman had come barreling in like a jealous ex-boyfriend.

Eastman had talked to so few Vietnamese that he found it hard to talk to Lin. In the corner on another chair were some uniform greens neatly folded. Beneath that a pair of standard-issue boots, next to what looked like a bag of groceries. He figured Lin for a soldier in the ARVN.

"What happened to your leg?" Eastman asked. "Were you hurt in the war?"

Lin nodded.

"Is it permanent?"

Lin shrugged, not wanting to answer.

"Stupid question," Eastman said. "Forget I asked. I'm a writer, like her. Only not like her. I wouldn't go to Cambodia. I have kids, you know. You married?"

"No."

"That's good, you're young. Where you from?"

"Hoi An."

"Which battalion?"

"Fifth Division. Quang Tri."

"Infantry?"

"Yes. But I'm stationed now in Saigon."

Eastman recalled reading about the Fifth as a hard-hitting division of the South Vietnamese Army. They'd been punished in some offensive battle the previous Easter.

"Were you in that battle at Quang Tri last year?"

Lin indicated that he was.

"Is that where this happened to you?" Eastman looked at Lin's leg.

"No. Near Pleiku."

"I can't imagine. Being stationed in Saigon must be a hell of a lot better than Quang Tri."

"It is."

"Did you know any of those boys who were killed out here in the square?"

"No."

Eastman felt as if he'd taken too much from the young man already and moved to excuse himself from the room.

"Can I ask you one more thing?" Eastman said. "What do you think she wants? You think she's happy out there, risking her life?"

"It's not my place to say. She has been very generous to me. It wouldn't be right to speak about her like this."

"You guys are all so polite." Eastman walked to the door, then turned back to face Lin once more. "Look, I'm sorry," he said to Lin. "I didn't know who you were. I don't know what I thought. I'm sorry. Would you tell her that?"

Lin looked down at his feet again.

"Tell her I'm sorry."

III
The Phantom

19

For history to be made it must be witnessed. And the correspondent's duty is to witness and record history so that sense may be made of the historical. Eastman saw himself as a type of historian, as someone who could chart the importance of an event within the course of the American narrative and the collective memory. This recent history, the history of America in Vietnam, was composed of so many poor decisions and miscalculations that they made for tragedies. *Vietnam was the whore who had been smacked around by a succession of pimps—Chinese, French, American. Now she was out on the street, a woman divided on the inside, not knowing which way to turn. She was a casualty of modern stupidity and of outsized delusions.*

By the time he was getting these thoughts down into his second dispatch, apropos the party at the presidential palace, Eastman was far gone. There were rumors that the city would soon fall and it was only a matter of time. He was too fearful for Meredith's well-being, and too guilty to just put her on a plane to somewhere, so he got on a plane with her. They took a Pan Am flight to Honolulu, where the *Herald* had a satellite office and where Eastman could finish up his work while Meredith browned by the pool and healed from her split with Lazlo. It was a fifteen-hour flight, and when they got in they slept for what felt like a day and a half.

All of this, of course, was given the green light by Baxter Broadwater, who reluctantly agreed to Eastman's demands for an extension on his deadline and some R&R in Hawaii. "We're not paying for the room," said Broadwater over the phone to Honolulu. "We'll pay for the flight home to New York. But this wasn't a part of our initial deal."

"Let's make it contingent on how large a spike in papers you get when my dispatch hits the stands," Eastman said.

"It doesn't work that way, Alan. We have a contract, which you signed."

"I know I signed it, it's with my lawyer right now being reviewed to see if there's any negligence on your part. You might have taken advantage of me."

"Taken advantage? Are you trying to kill me?"

"Yes. Taken advantage. You took advantage of a man who had visible signs of distress. You manipulated me. Think back. I seem to remember you putting a contract in my hands when I was on the floor having a psychological episode."

"Are you mad? You called me that day, remember? You needed my help. And what psychological episode? You had thrown out your back."

"Which you then thought could have been psychosomatic, and I hate to admit this, but you were right. It was a near-fatal episode of panic. If my lawyer finds negligence, then you'll hear from him. As of now, the deal remains in place and you'll get your final dispatch. I got a real scorcher for you, Broadwater. President Thieu makes an appearance in this one. So does my fair-weather friend Norman Heimish."

"I can't tell if you're kidding about the lawsuit stuff or not."

"Broadwater, I'm fucking with you. I've been fucking with you for a while now. Why should that have changed?"

He could sense that Broadwater was suddenly filled with relief by his confession, however juvenile it was. Eastman was admitting something real, which he had not yet done in their relationship. Sincere moments were hard to come by in a friendship such as theirs. In truth, he believed that both of them deep down liked battling, the back-and-forth, the slinging of insults. Broadwater was a masochist and Eastman the sadist. When they were students at Harvard it had been the same.

"I've rewritten what you sent. And if I have your approval we're ready to go to print."

"It's approved," said Eastman.

"You haven't seen the changes."

"Read them to me."

Broadwater explained some of the inconsistencies the fact-checkers had flagged in Eastman's first dispatch. "Pencil-pusher stuff," Eastman called it. Broadwater then read to him the last few paragraphs, which composed the bulk of the editorial changes. Broadwater had toned down the assumptions, the melodrama, the self-aggrandizement, the phallic imagery, and had replaced these with solid facts—Eastman's weakest area. This new version was better. Broadwater had done a good job.

"It's fine, print it," said Eastman.

"You don't want to run it by your lawyer?" Broadwater was sparring again. Things were back to normal.

"Don't press me. You're a good editor, and you made it better. That's all I ask in an editor. To keep me from sounding like a jackass."

"I'm sorry? Could you say that again, Alan? You're breaking up."

"You're not bad, Broadwater, once somebody applies a little pressure. You seemed to have shed whatever had been lodged up your ass at the *Advocate*. We'll talk in a few days."

"When are you back?"

"That depends on whether my girlfriend has gotten enough sun out here."

"You met somebody?"

"I ran into an old fling."

Eastman was referring, of course, to Meredith. Since they'd left Saigon he had been referring to her as his girlfriend because it had the effect of making them both feel young again. "Excuse me," he'd said to the stewardess on the plane. "Could you bring my girlfriend an extra blanket?" Meredith had laughed and shaken her head. "Oh, stewardess, my girlfriend here will have the pork loin. I'll have the fish." They giggled together, with great relief.

He knew he shouldn't have admitted to Broadwater about the affair. He'd never done so in the past. Maybe he also knew that Broadwater was aware of his circumstances. Broadwater had guessed it, in fact, at the beginning of all of this. Back when Eastman had thrown out his back and Broadwater had come to his aid with Dr. Dusseldorfer.

"You came through for me this time, Baxter."

"Take care of yourself, Alan."

Eastman hung up.

It was high time he began thinking about the Meredith situation. Honolulu wasn't a honeymoon, it was a pit stop on the way back to a life he wanted very much to return to normalcy. They were now fifteen hours away from Vietnam and about the same stretch of time back to New York. He needed to settle it, where they stood, because technically, though they were both still married, they were free, separated, miles and miles from their spouses. The situation had the makings of a dangerous disaster, duplicitous and ill conceived. They had never both been unattached throughout the affair. He was afraid of any ideas Meredith could be getting, as well as any ideas he could get carried away with.

He found her by the pool with her catlike sunglasses and a silk scarf wrapped around her head and knotted beneath her chin. He stood over her, casting a long, still shadow. Her skin, outside of her one-piece bathing suit, was beginning to redden. Her freckles multiplied. He'd always admired how she'd redden first and then turn to a dark tan over a long weekend.

"I just got off the phone with Broadwater in New York."

"How did it go?"

"The room is on the *Herald*," he lied, because he wanted to create an impression that their stop was not costing them anything. He didn't want her to think later that he'd arranged it all for some premeditated purpose. "They like the piece, it's going to print this week."

"David will be pleased to see it."

He didn't like the mention of her husband, even though he wanted her to go back to him. Bringing Lazlo into it made this harder. It made him aware of how connected they all were. It reminded him of his long overdue book, his career, his debts. This caused him anxiety and worry.

"Why don't you join me?" she said.

He dragged a chaise lounge closer to hers and sat down. "Now that you bring up David, I think we should talk."

"Alan."

"It's a reasonable thing to ask."

"Can't I enjoy myself for this moment? How would you like to talk about Penny?"

"Fine, let's talk about Penny."

"I don't want to talk about Penny. And I don't want to talk about

David. We've never talked like this before—not when we're together—and I see no reason to start. Now lie down. The sun is miraculous."

"We've never talked like this because we've never been in this situation before. And I only bring it up because of what happened in Saigon when you arrived. You implied things. That you left David because of me and I can't have that."

"The only reason I reacted the way I did was because of the look on your face. I was such an unwelcome sight. That was hurtful, Alan. So we had a row."

"I'm sorry."

"You don't have to worry, I'm not asking anything from you. If I had thought about us being together after I left David I was wrong. But how can you hold that against me? Why shouldn't I want to see you? Why shouldn't I think about being with you? It's worked for this long."

"It's worked because it's not a marriage."

"Now you're trying to hurt my feelings."

"Don't be mad," he said. He held her arm. She didn't brush him off.

"I'm not mad. I'm tired."

"I'm going back to Penny." Eastman gave her a probing look.

She didn't miss a beat. "I know you are."

"The man she's seeing, I know who he is."

"She told you?"

"In so many words."

Meredith pushed her sunglasses down and stared at him. She wasn't buying it.

"Okay," he said, "I did a little digging. His name is Arnaud Fleishman."

"Never heard of him."

"He might be an academic. Maybe at her college. They could work together."

"Forget him, Alan. The problem isn't with him."

"Why should I? It's not like she's done this on her own. If he wasn't in the picture how would this have happened?"

"It would have happened with somebody else. Alan, as someone who shares in Penny's struggle with being monogamous, I can tell you he is just a fixation. And he's probably not the first. She's going through a midlife crisis."

"She'll come to her senses."

"Or she won't," Meredith said. "And you have to be prepared for that."

Eastman lay down and imagined the reality of being alone. He thought back to when he had driven Penny to her mother's, the days and nights in crippling pain, reading poetry and somehow not reading it at the same time.

"You're right. Let's not talk about it," he said.

"Order me a drink," she asked. "I'm going to take a nap."

"You're getting red."

He looked into the basket at her feet and found the sunscreen. He put some on his hands and worked up a good cream. Then he rubbed the lotion on her shoulders, arms, and chest. Her skin was hot from the sun. He moved down to the bottom of the chaise to her legs.

"Oh, I can't believe I forgot to tell you," she said.

"What's that, doll?" He was happy again, rubbing the lotion into her thighs.

"I think I may have found a new author. You'll be very pleased."

"Who's that?"

"Take a guess."

"Well, ma'am, as one can intuit," he said with a Texas accent, "I'm busy with these here purty legs."

They laughed.

"Anne Channing," she said. "The reporter you mentioned. I met her over breakfast while you were asleep and we got to talking. We completely hit it off. She has this incredible book she's working on about the war. A book that goes for the heart, not just the politics. It's about the people, Alan. That's what we want to read about, isn't it? The voices of the people of Vietnam. You were right. She really knows her stuff. I can't wait to get my hands on it."

For some odd reason, while he worked his way from Meredith's thighs to her ankles and feet, Eastman grew more and more displeased listening to Meredith's enthusiasm. He didn't remember mentioning Channing to her. If he did, he couldn't understand why he did, because he was intentionally keeping the two women apart. A flush of embarrassment overtook him. He concentrated on applying sunscreen to Meredith's feet, even in between her toes.

"Alan?" Meredith asked.

He was thinking about the night he kissed Channing out on the balcony of the presidential palace. He had punctuated their lousy conversation by forcing himself on her. He let her down. Channing respected him and he let her down. But if Meredith knew, it would ruin him in her eyes. Even though he was desperate to end their affair, it mattered to him that she not know anything like this occurred while she was in Saigon. Those were the rules. He didn't want to be forced to defend himself.

"I'd watch out for her," he said, his voice two octaves higher.

"What do you mean?"

"Well, she's an odd duck, that one. If I can be honest, I caught her in a number of lies on more than one occasion. She's not all that trustworthy. I mean, she's got guts. Don't get me wrong. She goes places I wouldn't necessarily go. Tried to get me to come with her to Cambodia before you arrived. And I had half a mind to go with her, I told you this. But I would never leave you in Saigon alone. Out of the question. I found that not all of her stories added up. She embellishes a lot to make herself seem more accomplished than she is."

"What did she lie about? You know how you can be intimidating. Maybe she wanted to impress you."

"Maybe," he said in such a way as to lend Meredith's idea validity. His tactic seemed to be working, but he knew he needed to push further if he was going to kill Meredith's interest in Channing. Kill, he told himself. Kill this book. "No, that can't be it," he continued. "I can tell these things. I'm a good judge of character. I hate to say this, Meredith, but she's a liar, flat out. It was really disappointing, too, because I thought she had something. I liked her. But if you were to publish that book you'd have to have it fact-checked twice over. Hell, maybe three or four times. I offered her my expertise while I was staying at the Continental. I would have read some of her work, given her notes. But this book of hers, I don't know what she told you. . . . She hasn't written a word of it. And I doubt she ever will. Some people, you just know they have the determination to write a major book and to wrestle with it, right to the end. I don't get that sense with her."

He was trying too hard. Meredith's expression went from disappointment to annoyance. "Well," she said, "I had the most intelligible conversation with her and I got quite the opposite impression."

"That's how I felt when I first met her, too. But she took a turn somewhere."

"This seems hard to believe, Alan." Meredith shook her head and turned off in the direction of the palms just outside the pool area.

Meredith wasn't easily swayed. Having already stepped both feet in a pile of shit with this Channing business, what could he do now? Either cower like a politician caught with his tail between his legs, or finish her off.

"I was trying to put this lightly," he said. "But she came on to me. And I wasn't having it. She was hurt. Naturally. I get it. But she turned into a real cunt after that. Lied to everyone at the bureau. Tried to ruin my reputation. No one believed her, of course."

"When did this happen?" Meredith sat up.

"A couple of days before you arrived."

"I don't understand; you spoke so highly of her."

"I was being nice. Maybe I was thinking about your new feminist imprint. I mentioned her to you, I guess. I wasn't thinking. It wasn't such a big deal, after all. You know I don't hold a grudge."

"Okay, now I know you're lying. You can hold a grudge longer than anyone I've ever met."

"Not against a troubled girl like that, I don't. Anyway, considering you're now interested in her I thought I should mention it. I just don't think she's worth a damn."

"Well, I do. And to make this trip worth a damn, I'm going to make sure I follow up with her in New York and see for myself."

Meredith waved to the waiter for another drink and waited in silence. She was disappointed. Eastman had moved to his chair and took off his shirt while sucking in his gut. He applied the magic lotion to his arms and shoulders, twisting his upper body to reach those most difficult parts, posing in a side twist for her. The waiter brought her drink.

"I thought her book sounded quite interesting," she said.

"In the end, it's your call. Maybe she'll turn around and write something major. Who knows. This is just one opinion." Eastman shifted in his seat and called to the waiter. "Hey, chief. Bring me a Blue Hawaiian. Hold the umbrella."

"You know," said Meredith, "she did blush when I mentioned your name. It made her uncomfortable. I played it down and pretended we weren't together at all. That we were old friends. I mean, she probably assumed I was with you. I was staying in your room. But soon after we talked about you, she rushed off."

"See?" Eastman said. "Odd, that one."

"But what writer doesn't have their eccentricities? It sounds like she had a crush on you is all. And then she was hurt when you turned her down."

"So she smeared my good name? Spread rumors around the bureau. That's some reaction. It's vindictive. She acted like a hateful bitch."

"I don't appreciate your tone. I find it disgusting. You know, Alan, you think you're good at hiding your feelings, but they come out of your mouth and just present themselves as if on a tray."

"What are you talking about?"

"You're threatened by her. You're afraid she's going to write a better book than you and that's frightening to you. You're acting the same way you do with Norman, because in your mind it's a great competition. It always has been. But you know, I've been in this business just as long as you have and those I choose to work with aren't competitors in your intellectual Olympics. And I think you should take a good look."

"Well, there's not even a book, is there? So I don't know why we're arguing like this."

"Because you've insulted me."

"Insulted you how? I was trying to help."

"You've insulted my judgment."

"For that I'm sorry, okay? If there is a book by Channing, then I think you should read it and make up your own mind. I'm always willing to be surprised. Though I doubt you'll ever hear from her again."

Meredith laughed. "When there is a book, believe me, you'll know. And I can't wait to see the look on your face."

That evening they had dinner in the hotel restaurant, overlooking the harbor. Beyond the sailboats he could just make out the lagoon. And over the hill beyond that was Pearl Harbor, at least he thought that's where it was. If he could visit Pearl Harbor in the morning before he finished his second dispatch he could reference it, perhaps as a quick afterword. He could place in the reader's mind that moment in 1941 that he remembered so well. Perhaps he could quote from the poem he penned under the spell of the attack ("Of What May Ne'er Come to Pass"). He still had it somewhere. Wouldn't that be a nice little jab in Broadwater's side? The rejected poem now printed in a far more important publication. No, that was all wrong. Besides, he liked where he and Broadwater stood now. They had a nice editorial relationship; he shouldn't shit on it too much.

For dinner he had the steak and Meredith a salad with pineapple. The house band played ukulele and slide guitar, a simple Hawaiian melody. Together they drank a chilled champagne. He had his with a side of orange juice that he poured into his flute every few sips.

Something about the affair spoke to the little devil inside of him that needed to act out. It was the planning, getting away with it all, even the word "affair" was thrilling. And beyond the word was Meredith. To meet again and again after all these years. He cared for her. They had cultivated a true friendship. She was a powerful, decisive woman who got what she wanted. And Meredith wanted him still. It made him feel sought after, chased. And with Meredith he could talk about books, literature, his work, and feel like he'd been heard. It seemed the opposite of his relationship with Penny, where of late he felt like he couldn't get her attention.

But the affair was dissolving his marriage. The secret life took energy away from his real life. Penny wasn't so aloof either. She had him pegged when he was seeing Meredith again on his trips abroad in the midsixties. She knew by the inconsistencies in his behavior, by his absence. Not answering phone calls, not being in his room until the next morning. She once said she had called him every hour on the hour at his hotel, running up quite a bill, until he picked up at nine in the morning, pretending to have been asleep. "I've been up all night calling you." "I had them hold all my calls. I needed sleep," he said. "Bullshit. I spoke to the concierge. And you know what, Alan. I don't care. Do what you have to if it helps." "It's all in your head. This only happens when I'm away. You become hysterical with jealousy." "I'm not jealous. I'm married to a liar, this is what drives me nuts. And you're not even good at lying, that's the worst part. You can't hear yourself."

To keep the balance inside himself, he thought it best to lead these two lives—one at home with his wife, and then brief excursions outside of it with an affair he could manage.

Was he wrong about himself and the great experiment he'd been conducting with his life?

Over dinner with Meredith, Eastman suggested that they take different flights back to New York, separated by at least a day. She should go first and he would follow. It would be good if they could fly into different airports. Meredith agreed reluctantly. She had wanted to stay a little longer and said he should go first. She needed a few more days out of the city. So the next day he took a cab into downtown Honolulu to a travel agency that was recommended to him at the hotel. He purchased two flights to New York, his own leaving the following evening, and for Meredith's he paid the extra fee for the departure date to be kept open. Let her decide. As far as he was concerned he was almost home.

20

He had that feeling he got whenever he returned from a long trip abroad. It was kinetic, a man renewed from having been somewhere and seen something. He gained a secret experience, and the memory was full, stored up with visions and anecdotes. He had new knowledge from another country, fascinating stuff for those who hadn't gone, and he wanted to share it. He wasn't a part of his old life yet, fresh from a trip like this. No one was waiting for him at the airport. Not his wife or a man hired to hold up a sign. No one knew he was back except for Broadwater, and he thought of the ways he could use this invisibleness to his advantage. Once he got to walking around a familiar neighborhood in Manhattan, he sensed intimations of an alternate existence. Hundreds of people passed him by on their way somewhere and he was a ghost among them. No one recognized him or sought him out. He didn't have any appointments. He had disappeared into another part of the world and daily life continued without him. He had a different awareness now, like being a foreigner in his own city. It wasn't something that would last. It was an edge, and in order to take advantage of it he decided he would stay out of the restaurants and the usual hangouts. He checked into a downtown hotel called the Corlear, close to the Lower East Side. The hotel was seedy, but the rooms were clean. It was the kind of hotel Wall Street types went to with prostitutes in the late afternoons. Pay for the night and stay for an hour. No one here wanted to be recognized.

He chose a corner room on the eighth floor because it had a panoramic view overlooking the East River, the Brooklyn Bridge, and the Promenade, close to where he lived, and where Penny was home with the boys. On the Manhattan side were the tenements, near where his grandfather had the sporting goods company, the proceeds of which had put him through Harvard.

In his suitcase he looked for the few items he had brought back from Vietnam for his children. He'd give Lee the standard-issue Department of Defense Vietnam guide that he'd used while he was there. He fanned through the topics to make sure they were appropriate. AT HOME WITH THE VIETNAMESE, FAMILY LOYALTY, A WOMAN'S PLACE IS AT HOME, THE PROFESSIONAL MAN, VILLAGE LIFE, TOWN AND COUNTRY. For Toby, who was fascinated by the ocean, he bought a miniature, handcrafted fisherman's boat in Honolulu. It was supposed to float in a bath. For both boys he got pilot's wings from the Pan Am flight to Hawaii, but now he could find only one. He checked the pockets in the satin divider of the suitcase, uncovering tickets and receipts from long-ago trips. Instead of the missing present for his boy, he found the matchbook from the Waverly Inn. He still had it. He didn't know he'd brought it with him to Vietnam, but there it was. Inside it, the phone number. He thought he'd burned it at some point, but that was another matchbook, a second one that he got off the bar at the Tic Tac, where he had called his buddy Eddie Sheenan and first heard the name Arnaud Fleishman. It was so perfectly Proustian, finding the matchbook now, and Eastman had to sit down on the bed suddenly because he felt overwhelmed.

He flipped it through his fingers, thinking of what to do about Fleishman. What would happen if he called the number? Would Fleishman pick up? He would assume Eastman was still in Vietnam. So if Fleishman was home, he'd pick up.

His mind felt drunk when he finally called.

"Hello," the man on the other end said. "Hello?"

"Yes," said Eastman. "I'm here."

"Who is this?"

"I've been meaning to call you for some time now."

"Am I supposed to guess?" the man said. "Hello?"

Eastman thought about it. Go ahead, guess.

"It's Alan Eastman."

"Oh," he said.

"I think you know my wife."

He didn't answer right away, and Eastman thought he'd hung up. The silence was excruciating. Eastman held his breath, not quite knowing why. Then, much to Eastman's surprise, the man said, "I've been hoping you would call."

This caught Eastman off guard. "You have?"

"Yes. I suppose I've wanted to talk to you, too."

"You have." Eastman considered the good this would do. Would it be another mishap, like in the middle of a suburban street, pushing Penny further away from him? Or would it bring about vengeful satisfaction, like a strong right thrown into a motherfucker's nose? He considered just hanging up. But against his better judgment, Eastman said, "Why don't we meet. Man-to-man."

"I'd like that."

"You would?" Eastman cleared his throat. "Then let's go somewhere that you both went together."

"Well, jeez. I just figured you'd tell me where to go. There's a hundred places."

"There are. Are you anywhere near the Village?"

"Yes."

"How about the Waverly Inn? Tomorrow at four."

"Okay."

He had a date with his phantom. Eastman could show up or not; he still didn't know what the right thing to do was apropos of Penny, but he didn't have to decide that now. He had time. Go or not, he would inconvenience his phantom just as he had been inconvenienced.

A week had gone by since he had a proper shave and he was growing quite a beard. When the morning came he shaved it in the hotel bathroom but decided to leave the mustache. Next he put on a pair of sunglasses, a T-shirt, and blue jeans. He looked dirty, unhandsome, undistinguished, unnoticeable.

He walked down to the newsstand to check out the *Times* and the *Herald*, and wouldn't you know it, his dispatch made the front page. He bought two copies for now. The *Times* didn't have a Vietnam cover story that day. He felt some satisfaction in this, like he had scooped Heimish and the rest of them. Unfortunately his dispatch had a tabloid subtitle: DISPATCH FROM SAIGON: MURDER AFTER CURFEW. But still, it made him proud to see his byline on the front page and to read the words in print, words he wrote only a few days ago. No matter how small a publication, he never lost the thrill he received from reading his work in print, seeing it out there for the first time. There was a small celebration in his head.

He walked through the Lower East Side, looking for the site of his grandfather's sporting goods company. He heard it had closed, the Hermans ran it under as the neighborhood plummeted in the early sixties. Still, he thought he would be able to recognize the former store by sight. He walked up and down Orchard Street—wasn't that where it was? When he didn't see anything resembling what it looked like in his memory, he went around the block onto other streets that seemed familiar, past stripped-down cars and abandoned buildings. He didn't know which block he was on when he saw a tall tenement that looked familiar. Yes, he knew it from his childhood. He proceeded down the street, which had a small commercial strip of delis and discount clothing stores. People only spoke Spanish. At the end, near a corner with no street signs, was his grandfather's store. It was boarded up, with traces of black smoke on the brick from a long-ago fire. The sign was partially covered with plywood, but still, he could see the name visibly. Eastman. When the Hermans bought the store they kept the name, his grandfather had required it as part of the sale. And since business was good they had no reason to change anything. The storefront, though boarded up, didn't seem beyond salvageable, and the apartment units above were occupied. Air conditioners hung out of some windows and dripped onto the street. Clothing and potted plants were on the fire escapes.

He could sell the house, buy the storefront, and reopen Eastman's Sporting Goods Co. He could specialize in boxing equipment, supply some of the local gyms. There were times over the last decade when the ruts he fell into with stalled books and those flimsy articles he wrote made him believe he could one day walk away from publishing. He would always be a reader, a proponent of the word, but did he have to write anymore? Did anyone still care about what he had to say? The fifties, the height of his talents, were a long time ago. He could revive his grandfather's business and focus on his family. But it was now such a poor area, it would be a bad investment. What the neighborhood needed was a good councilman to secure the resources for recovery. He'd be better off going into politics.

Eastman walked to the edge of Chinatown and the smell of the garbage coming from the gutters reminded him of Saigon. He hailed a cab on East Broadway and told the cabbie to go down to City Hall and over the Brooklyn Bridge toward his home in Brooklyn Heights. In the cab he read his Vietnam article again, which got him thinking about Channing. *It took an honest soul, a pure adept reporter, to do this job. Man or woman, it no longer mattered, and Channing proved this to him as he cowered in his room. He still thought the old guard of American publishing was against her. He expressed this to her a few days later as they toured the shantytowns of Saigon. And he would be wrong. His comments would cost him another friendship— Channing and possibly her alliances at the Saigon bureau—but it was in the service of a realization: that this work, covering a war, had nothing to do with balls or thrills or adrenaline or age, but the exhausting desire for truth.*

He directed the cab to let him off at the corner of Pineapple and Hicks, about a block away from his home. Then he walked down Pineapple Street until he could see his house in perfect daylight. Now he didn't want to get too close, he didn't want to be seen, so he kept a reasonable distance from the house and stood by the bus stop on the corner. This way it looked quite natural for him to be waiting, reading his copy of the *Herald*, waiting for the bus. After some time, with no movement in or out of the house, he decided to get closer and took cover behind a nearby tree. He rolled up the extra copy of the *Herald* he had purchased and tossed it onto the steps of his home. Then he walked back quickly to the corner bus stop to wait some more.

It wasn't long till Penny came out of the house, followed by his beautiful boys dressed in their summer gear. It was hard to watch their routine without being a part of it. Lee carried a brown-bag lunch and Toby a lunch box. As Penny locked the front door, Lee picked up the newspaper—good boy—and brought it up to his mother. Without even looking at it, she unlocked the front door and threw it inside, then they were off.

"Shit," he said. Then she wouldn't see the front page until later.

The boys' summer camp must have begun and he figured this is where she was taking them. He followed, half a block behind on the opposite side of the street. The summer camp was at a nearby church on Remsen, Our Lady of Lebanon. They walked like this for a time, Eastman slowly tailing his own family, separated by half a block. The church was not far at all, and Penny and the boys arrived quickly. She said good-bye to Lee and Toby, gave them each a kiss, and waited by the gate until they checked in with the camp counselor. Once they joined the other children they were out of his sight. Penny waved to them. He felt outside of time and this farcical distance felt impossible to sustain.

Penny didn't turn back to the house. Instead she proceeded along the street toward the bank on Montague. The little detour intrigued him. She was up to something now that she had a free morning. He moved along at the same speed and distance as before.

When she went into the market, he let a minute pass in order for her to move away from the produce by the entrance. *Be patient*, he told himself. Then he went for it, grabbing a shopper's basket on the way in. Inside the basket were pages of coupons from the *Daily Saver*, and for some reason this annoyed him even though he wouldn't be buying anything. He went back to the front door and switched baskets out of habit.

She was in the fruit aisle. She picked several bananas, both green and a few on the ripe end. Some apples, some oranges. Then she moved to dairy for a half gallon of milk. In another aisle, she pulled a tin of the kind of coffee she liked. He trailed behind, an aisle back, before investigating where she had been. He noticed the empty space where she had taken the milk carton and then the coffee can. He grabbed stuff off of the shelves, too, in order not to seem suspicious.

Penny was quick in a market. She didn't waste any time deciding or consulting a list. She knew what the family needed. He stood back and watched her approach the cashier to pay for the groceries. He left his decoy basket on the floor and carefully passed through a closed cashier aisle. As he moved through the aisle Penny looked right at him, and he turned his head away quickly and staggered out. They would have made eye contact were it not for his sunglasses. He waited behind a parked car a few shops down, thinking he was caught. He was hoping she would come out and look for him. But when Penny exited the market she seemed normal, composed, didn't act like anything had happened. What was worse? That maybe she did see him and didn't care? Or that after he saw her he couldn't go up to his own wife and say hello? Both of these possibilities ate away at him. He could hear his heart beating, rattling inside his rib cage.

Penny walked in the direction of home and Eastman followed.

A summer swell of heat, dew in the air, a slight breeze, shade under the tree branches—he was walking in and out of the shadows, trailing behind. His nose and throat felt like he had been crying all morning, and that's essentially what he was doing. He was crying on the inside. Why must he go through this? Why must he follow her? Why couldn't he go home? Of course he could, but if he did so the relationship could be over quicker. He was afraid of this, afraid of what could happen, even though the worst was behind him. Up and down the blocks, men were turning their heads. She smiled politely at the shopkeepers and the people on the street. This is what it was like to be dead, he thought. To have died and have your soul linger around, watching over your family—what horseshit! Ghosts didn't watch over their families. They lived in torture not being able to do anything. They lived with a lump in their throats and fire in their hearts. He almost couldn't take it anymore; he wanted to shout her name.

She stopped at a newsstand and bought a pack of cigarettes. She was smoking again. Picked the habit back up while he was away. He hoped she would see the stacks of newspapers at her feet. The *Herald*, look down. The headline, Penny. She unwrapped the package of cigarettes and yes, something caught her eye. She must have seen the front page and immediately she paused, struck by his name in a byline of bold letters. Her name, too.

She went into her purse for change and paid for a copy of the paper. Then she moved to the corner, put down the groceries, lit a cigarette, and stood there reading it.

He got low and sat down on a hydrant across the street behind a Pontiac that was illegally parked. The article was long, and if she chose to read it all now, he'd need to rest his legs. He didn't know how much longer he could keep this up. And what was the purpose of following her around? To drag himself through more pain? Hadn't he gotten enough?

Penny kept on reading, which made him feel the slightest bit hopeful. Danger, intrigue, fragility, he squeezed it all into that first dispatch. He wanted her to know she could lose him. He might never make it back.

But then she stopped. She'd lost interest. He knew that look.

No, don't stop. You haven't turned the page.

She folded the paper, picked up her bag of groceries, and quickly, without thought or feeling, threw the paper in the trash.

So that's where his work belonged, in the corner wastebasket with the rest of the rubbish. She didn't even have the decency to take it home to show the boys. He was ashamed for her. And he beat himself up because he shouldn't have seen it. Following her was detrimental to both of them. And just how many times had he been bored by her work? Countless occasions. He even drilled her on its validity, criticized her conference papers and academic publications for being too verbose. Tried to push her into writing popular nonfiction and make her let go of academic writing.

He was guilty of the same, or much worse. Guilty of taking her work and discarding it.

Is this what he finally deserved?

Penny kept walking, not in his direction but around the corner, north, presumably returning home. He couldn't bring himself to take another step. He let go. He'd only followed her for a short time that morning, and it was more damaging than helpful. Better to live not knowing. Another unexpected blow would only drive him toward madness. Besides, he had time, she wasn't expecting him home and Eastman had someplace to be.

Eastman thought he would recognize him from their dispute in the street. He never saw the man's eyes, but he remembered that chin, prominent, statesmanlike. Maybe a bit of stubble. And that pimp's mustache made you want to hold the son of a bitch down and shave it off. High cheekbones. A handsome man. Academic type. What did academics dress like in the summer when they didn't have a tweed coat to hide behind? How did he wear his hair? Eastman never got a look at it. Was it fashionable? Yes, it would be. Penny was one who took to modern fashions. She wouldn't fuck just anyone.

He arrived at the Waverly Inn a half hour early, just as the lunch crowd was finishing. He thought it best that they meet at an off-hour, four o'clock. It would be quiet and they wouldn't have an audience. He took a table by the window because the tavern was dark with low ceilings, and Eastman wanted some sensation of air. He sat facing the door so he could see everyone who came and went. The waiter brought him a seltzer, which he sipped. He played with his silverware and resisted the urge to check his wristwatch as he didn't want to appear nervous, not even to the staff.

Eastman scrutinized each man who came through the door. A gentleman with a cane and the kind of circular glasses worn by rare-book dealers. Then a young man, tall, nicely dressed. He was close to what Eastman imagined as his phantom, but a woman followed behind him and they got a booth together in the back of the tavern. Others came in and out. An actor he recognized from movies sat down at the bar and ordered a beer.

He didn't have a list of things he wanted to say. One-on-one he could always improvise. He knew the gist of how he'd play it. He was concerned about whether this meeting was going to get back to Penny, and so he would have to be on somewhat good behavior. Keep composure, sit up straight. Speak with authority. He will revere your authority. Don't try to sound too smart. He has a PhD, remember. He thinks he's smarter than you. Let him. You'll intimidate him by not intimidating him. When you get down to it, present him with options. Tell him there are plenty of ways to make an exit.

If you have to resort to violence—you won't—but if you absolutely have to, first ask him politely to step outside, because you don't want to make a scene. You walk outside ahead of him, somewhere out of the way, and then turn around and ambush him, quickly. A jab into his belly to take the air out of him. If he's wearing a jacket, pull it over his head and continue to hit him in the body—fewer marks in case of a lawsuit. But you won't have to take these measures because you will have a civilized conversation. And remember, all of this will eventually get back to Penny. Don't do anything to make her hate you.

He called the waiter over and ordered something stronger than seltzer. A Tom Collins. Then he changed his mind and switched the order to a white wine, because it was the middle of the day, for Chris-sake. While he struggled to make up his mind a figure appeared next to the waiter. A tall, elegant figure that just sidled up to the table with familiarity.

"I'll have the same," his phantom said to the waiter, sort of joy-fully. He smiled at Eastman and gestured toward the empty chair. "May I?"

He was clean shaven and well dressed, younger than Eastman but not by much. There wasn't anything to scrutinize about his ap-pearance, nothing overly handsome about him that Eastman cared to admit, although he was in better physical condition. The prominent chin Eastman had noticed during their meeting in the suburbs of New Jersey wasn't as pronounced as he'd thought. He had thick eye-brows that lent him some integrity, Eastern European cheekbones, and he was confident, Eastman could intuit, and he got some delight out of being confident.

They shook hands, because that's what one did when meeting for the first time, and the man introduced himself as Charles Lightfoot. It caught Eastman off guard. So who was Arnaud Fleishman?

"I'm sorry," said Eastman. "I thought you would be somebody else."

"Who did you think I would be?"

"Did you shave your mustache?" The man in the car had a mus-tache, and that's probably why Eastman was growing one. He sub-consciously wanted to match his rival.

"I've never worn one," Lightfoot said. "I find them to be gauche. No offense. I see that you're growing one. You know how I knew it was you? I recognized you from television. I knew it was you right away, as soon as I walked in. I said that's him, all right. Alan East-man, the writer."

"You did."

"Oh, c'mon. You must get this all the time. Answer me something. What's it like to be on TV?"

"That's what you want to ask me? Of all things."

"I don't know anyone who's ever been on television. This is exciting for me."

"Does the name Fleishman mean anything to you?" Eastman asked. "Arnaud Fleishman."

"Is this some sort of test?"

"No."

Lightfoot pondered the name for a bit. "It's a German name, Fleishman. No idea what it means. And no, I don't know anyone by that name."

His mind had created another fiction, like it had that night in Saigon at the presidential palace when he accused Channing of somehow being in cahoots with Heimish.

The waiter brought them two glasses of white wine.

"Sorry I can't help you with your missing person," said Lightfoot. "Anyway, I still want to hear all about what it's like to be on *The Dick Cavett Show*."

"You want to talk about television, go talk to that guy. He's been on television." Eastman pointed to the movie actor seated at the bar, drinking a beer.

"Who is that? Is that Elliott Gould?"

"I wouldn't know," Eastman said.

"I don't know either. He's not very recognizable, at least from here. Unlike you. Now you have a very specific face. Your hair, the whole thing. Can't be missed. You must get hounded."

"Are you always like this?"

"Like what?"

"This *up*. This hyper."

"God, I didn't know I was being that way. Sorry, I'm a little nervous. It's not every day you get to sit with a big writer like Alan Eastman. You know, I read most of your books. *To Each His Own* is really one of my favorites."

Eastman took a good swig of his wine. He wasn't going to acknowledge Lightfoot's compliment; it would steer the conversation into the wrong direction.

"Do you know why I called you?" said Eastman.

"Ah, you want to talk about that." Lightfoot had the glass to his mouth and drank quickly. "This wine is excellent."

"Explain yourself," Eastman said.

"Where should I start? It's a long story. You have time?"

"I've got all the time in the world."

"Isn't that a funny concept. Think about it. 'All the time in the world.'" Lightfoot twirled his finger in the air, looking a little loopy, and Eastman thought he could be on drugs. "It's impossible, right? To have all that time."

"How did you meet my wife?"

"I can explain. I thought we'd get to know each other first. Maybe find some common ground before we got into it. But if that's what you want . . ."

"You know my wife. How?"

"I knew we'd meet one day. Somehow I knew it. Like I was waiting for your call. It happens, when you . . . you know. Have relations. Like I have. You spend a good deal of time wondering if someone like you is going to come around knocking on your door. Well, not like you, exactly. You're not angry, are you? It was a long time ago. How'd you find out? Did she just come out and tell you? I bet that was hurtful. But I can't believe she gave you my phone number."

"I'm skilled in the art of conversation, too. You've seen me on TV, you know that. What I see is you slithering around. Delaying. And in delaying you're attempting to weasel your way under my skin. But it's not going to work."

"I'm sorry, this is really awkward for me."

"How do you think I feel?"

"With all due respect, I think you have the upper hand here."

"How do you know Penny?"

"We met a few years ago. I met her at a club. What was the name of that club? God, I can't remember. It was on Fourteenth Street, a private club. People in the scene went there. You know, to meet other people. Married, single, it didn't matter. That kind of thing. Dancing. Drugs. They had everything at this place. Whatever you wanted. The *Vine*! That was the name of it. The Vine."

"Forget the name."

"The Vine. I met her at the Vine. I could tell she wasn't a regular. I think she came along with somebody on a lark or something. One of her girlfriends, I don't know. Just to check it out. So we met, talked. Instead of going upstairs to one of the private rooms—I could tell that wasn't gonna happen with a woman like this. To her credit.—we got something to eat. I think we came here. I don't remember. We talked. Just talked. I really liked her."

"You had an affair."

"We went out," Lightfoot corrected him.

"When was this?"

Lightfoot shook his head, trying to think on his feet. Eastman was bracing himself and he drank more wine because he wanted to numb himself for what lay ahead.

"I guess it was . . . a couple of years ago now," Lightfoot said. "Not a big deal. It was nothing, man. A fling. I figured Penelope was seeing plenty of people. So was I. I was cool with it."

"Penelope, is that what you call her?"

"I mean, yeah. Penelope. That's her name, right?"

"Go on."

"I mean, what else do you want to hear? We went out."

"Did you know about me? Did you know she has a husband?"

Lightfoot wasn't so forthcoming anymore.

"I knew it was you. I mean, c'mon, man. You're Alan Eastman. Everybody knows who you are."

"How many times?"

"How many times what?"

"I want to know how many times you fucked over the course of your affair with my wife. How many times were you together. How often. Give me an estimation."

"Man, I don't get graphic over things like this. You fixate on the details, it's gonna ruin you. I'm not doing this because I want to do that to you. You know, I wanted to meet you."

"Think back after you met her here. When did you see her next? Where and when did you two meet? How regularly?"

Eastman wanted to hear everything as it happened. If they were ever going to get back together he needed to absorb all of the truth, not the fiction in his head. And after a little back-and-forth, Lightfoot provided what he wanted to know. They met in the afternoons at his place in the Village, close to her office at the university. He would make lunch, or have it delivered in advance, and when she arrived they would fornicate first and then eat lunch. Sometimes she wouldn't eat at all, and they would spend the hour in bed. This carried on for a season and then began to taper off, though they still continued to see each other sporadically over the course of a year. Then Penny ended the relationship (he swore). He wanted to continue with the affair, he said, but she was racked with guilt. They never spoke about her family, although he was aware of them. It became a real drag, he said. He was more into "the scene," sex clubs and orgies, and not wanting to bother with the intricacies of a relationship. He agreed they would end it. There was more. A few months passed with no contact and then they ran into each other again around Washington Square Park. Lightfoot asked if she wanted to see his new apartment, he had moved closer to Broadway, and if she still had his number. "I had my number transferred over to the new place. Did you know you can do that now?" That week she called him after work and they met, rekindling their relationship. Eastman pressed for details of the sexual variety. What was it like to sleep with her? What were her preferences? Top or bottom? What were the ways they did it? He wanted to compare, because all this time Eastman was also sleeping with her, about as often as one can with two young children, under the pretense of their marriage. He inquired about choking, asphyxiation, and if Lightfoot had introduced that to her.

"Did you ever choke her?" he asked.

Lightfoot denied it at first and then changed his answer. He couldn't remember.

"Which is it?" Eastman asked. "You didn't choke her or you don't remember?"

"I didn't *and* I don't remember these things."

Eastman knew that Lightfoot was bullshitting him. Everyone kept a sexual memory that they could call to mind, the carnal imagery, whether the experience was pleasurable or not. Of course he had stored in his mind the images of Penny, her body, her breasts, her cunt, all those intimate sexual favors she performed on him. Lightfoot had the memories. And Eastman wanted to reach into Lightfoot's brain and extract them. They didn't belong to Lightfoot; they belonged to him. He was her husband. She had chosen him long ago.

"So what you mean, Lightfoot, is that you were together so often that all the experiences just kind of blur together. Is that your story?"

Lightfoot again took no responsibility.

"I'm not the jealous type, Lightfoot. I couldn't have stopped her even if I knew about the two of you. Nothing would have changed. I would have let it happen. Let it run its course. And with a stooge like you it would run its course. Maybe that's why you're the way you are—the clubs, the orgies, the women, the bisexuality. Because no one wants to be with a person like you for very long. Isn't that the truth?"

"You don't have to insult me."

Eastman smacked the table so that the silverware rattled in place. The wine rippled in the glasses. The restaurant's patrons turned to look at their table.

"Take it easy," Lightfoot said. "We're fine," he said to the waiter. "Can we get another white?"

"Shut up," Eastman said. "You've said enough. I've been listening to you here and I realized something. I've been where you are now. I've had my share of fun. Only I'm not stupid enough to sit down with my lover's husband over a drink. Why are you that stupid?"

"You don't get it. I didn't come here to tell you all those things. You wanted to know. I didn't tell you anything you couldn't figure out on your own. I didn't want to say any of that. That was all your curiosity. You should be thanking me."

"Then why meet me? I don't understand. Make me understand."

Eastman looked into Lightfoot's eyes, trying to see behind them. If there was a soul in there. If there was a sense of morality or plausibility. This meeting had no logic to it, it felt out of time.

"Because," Lightfoot said. "I have something I want to give you." From under the table, Lightfoot produced a manuscript. It wasn't too thick, and he'd had it bound together. He put it on the table in front of Eastman. He wanted him to read it. "You called about a day after I finished it. It was like a sign or something."

"What is this?"

"My memoirs," said Lightfoot.

Eastman pushed it back over to Lightfoot's side of the table and said, "The only thing your life story would be good for is kindling. Burn it."

There was no greater plot against him. He no longer knew if there was even an Arnaud Fleishman. So much of his experience lately relied on misremembered facts and a failing imagination. However, there was a whole truth out there. The night he and Penny split, he waited for her in his study while she packed her things in their bedroom upstairs. She must have gone through everything she wanted to take with her and chose, perhaps deliberately, to leave him a clue. The matchbook from the Waverly Inn. That was the whole hard truth. She wanted him to know about her affair with Lightfoot and didn't even care enough anymore to hide it.

21

It had been a Sunday when she left him and he, the compliant husband, drove her to her mother's. And so he thought it fitting to return home on a Sunday, a symbolic gesture. Had he grown superstitious while he was away? The lost and lonely will humor superstitions. They begin to believe their lives have been left to chance. So they read the horoscopes, consider the alignment of the moon, sun, the revolving planets—as irrational as any organized faith. He couldn't peer into Penny's head, had not a clue as to what she was thinking. All he knew for sure was what he witnessed on the street when he followed her the other morning. The article on Saigon she tossed away. A family, their marriage, she tossed those away, too.

He saw his Saab, parked outside of the house, and noted that it needed a wash. A layer of pollen had adhered to the roof, hood, and windshield.

Eastman hesitated before he went up the front steps. He bought this brick townhouse on the end of Pineapple Street because it was close to his mother's apartment. He could have lunch at her place every day. He was thirty-eight when he decided to put some roots down after years of dealing with landlords—crooks, all of them. His mother encouraged him to buy in the neighborhood of Brooklyn Heights. He was single and told himself it was a major investment in his future with a partner he hadn't met yet. He wanted a home with many rooms. His study he put in the first-floor living room and trans-ferred the living room into what the real estate agent had called a small sitting room adjacent to the large dining area. Upstairs, he had a room for Helen when she came to visit from Mexico, one master bedroom for himself, and another were he to have more children. He had felt so lucky then, young, and full of promise, and the universe was rewarding him already.

It was an early summer evening and still bright out. He used his own key and entered the house. In the foyer was that familiar smell of rubber raincoats and boots; even the tall woven basket that held the umbrellas had a scent he instantly recognized. He entered through the second set of doors and called out, announcing that he was home. The house was still; no one answered. He opened the sliding doors to his study first, and everything seemed to be as he left it. The two reading chairs, his own marked by the indentation of his ass. On his desk, his papers, untouched. He brought his luggage into the study, not knowing for sure if he would be staying the night.

He walked through the rest of the first floor, peeked into the living room. An unfolded blanket on the sofa, the indent of her head on a decorative pillow. On the floor, scattered pieces of a board game, some comic books left open on the rug. Traces of fun while she took a nap.

He was afraid to enter the kitchen. Before he went in, he thought of a few precious things to say were he to find Penny inside, seated at the kitchen table, nursing a cup of tea. But he found no one, only the yellow walls and the white counter tops, clean and polished. It didn't look as if anything had been cooked that day.

He went upstairs to their bedroom, where the bed was neatly made. On the floor were Penny's open suitcases. She'd been living out of them, not even planning to stay for very long. Where was she headed? He could riffle through her things but couldn't put himself through it, not after following her the other morning. He'd rather not find out anything more hurtful. What a sad state the room was in, even with the bed made. How could he stand to live here? Would he have to sell the house? Move into a smaller apartment? Keep a room open for his children? Would that help? He'd been through a divorce before and knew that moving into a new space wasn't a solution to heartbreak.

He had thought of calling her from the hotel to let her know when he would be home, but he didn't want to give her an excuse not to be there when he returned. She could slip out to her mother's or leave for her lover's place. Fleishman? He didn't know anymore. And after his run-in with Lightfoot, he didn't particularly care who she was seeing. It no longer concerned him. Better to talk to her to get everything out in the open. He should have had the strength to do that in the beginning instead of wallowing in his misery and plotting schemes.

He sat down on her side of the bed and opened her nightstand drawer. He threw in the matchbook from the Waverly Inn; he was done with it. Done with his investigation.

He lay down on the bed crosswise. Penny's idea of happiness was now so changed that it didn't include him. All of his best efforts— breaking things off with Meredith, trying to be a better husband to Penny, trying harder with the kids—all were doomed if he couldn't persuade her to broaden her definition of happiness to include him. What was he going to do?

He got up and went into his closet. A line of navy suits, mainly the only color he wore. Starched white shirts. A series of red ties. When did he start dressing so much his age? He'd developed the wardrobe of a politician.

Downstairs the front door opened and he heard his boys rush into the house. He heard Penny say to them, "Wash your hands first. Both of you. You're not getting any unless you wash your hands."

He stood in his closet and flipped through his shirts. In the very back of the closet, he found a black dress shirt that he had bought and never worn. Penny had urged him to get it. It was too young and trendy. He took off what he was wearing and put on the black shirt, buttoned it in the mirror. Tucked it into his chinos. Nothing but red ties. He tried two, a maroon and a lipstick red. The maroon worked, and he tied that one on. He didn't look like himself at all; he looked hip. The shirt fit him well. He had lost weight in Vietnam.

He descended the stairs, and his family didn't hear him at first, but once he reached the front hallway they quieted.

"Is someone here?" Penny said.

"Is it Daddy?" said Toby.

"Yes, it's Daddy," he called into the kitchen.

The kids came running into the hallway, Lee with a chicken bone in his hand, Toby following. They had gotten takeout, a box of fried chicken.

"Don't run with your mouth full," their mother said.

He got low to the ground and met them at eye level. They were all hugs and kissed him with greasy mouths. She stood in the doorway of the kitchen with her arms crossed.

"Why didn't you call?" she asked. "We had no idea you were coming home."

Eastman released the boys.

"What was Vietnam like?" Lee said.

"Yeah, what was the war like?" asked Toby.

"What?" he said to her, avoiding her question. Then to them, "I'll tell you all about it after you finish eating. I brought you some things from the war, men."

They celebrated and ran back into the kitchen past their mother.

"You could have called," she said. "We could have picked you up. They were worried about you."

"It was nothing. I went through hell getting back to New York. I didn't have a moment to call. And I didn't want to bother you. I couldn't ask you to drop everything to pick me up."

"Why are you dressed like that?" she said.

"I thought we could go to dinner. We have a lot to talk about."

"We bought chicken."

"Let them eat it. Let's go get Italian. I've eaten nothing but Oriental food. Pig parts, beef parts. It wasn't bad, but God I'd love something familiar."

"We shouldn't leave them," she said.

"Leave them, Lee's old enough to stay home alone."

"They miss you and want to see you."

"I'll see them when we get back. An hour. Let's go, it's still early."

They didn't touch, or hug, not a welcome kiss on the cheek. She didn't give him any sign that she was glad to see him back in one piece. Had she forgotten? Or were they past all the affectionate gestures of a loving couple?

He entered the kitchen to see the boys in their seats, hovering around a big striped bucket of fried chicken. "You'll be all right, won't you boys, if you let me take your mother for dinner? Aren't you old enough by now to watch over the house?"

Toby looked at his older brother for guidance.

"Of course we are!" Lee said. "We'll watch the house, Ma."

"I don't want to leave them while they're eating, they could choke on a chicken bone."

"They know what to do. Don't eat too fast," he said.

"We won't," said Lee.

Penny wouldn't budge, so he compromised and waited till the boys were done with dinner. They were too excited to eat much anyway and finished up quickly. She wrapped the rest of the chicken and put it high up in the refrigerator, out of their reach.

Together, Penny and Eastman walked to a neighborhood restaurant, a popular Italian place close to home. They rarely visited this restaurant, with its red-and-white tablecloths and checkered flooring. When they entered they found it was busy for a Sunday, but they were able to get seated right away, a table in the back near the kitchen. Eastman faced the kitchen, not wanting to see any of the other customers. All he could see was the kitchen door swinging in and out, waiters coming and going, too busy to pay attention to him if he was to get emotional.

It seemed neither of them had an appetite for anything memorable. She wanted simple, quick, get back to the boys. He wanted to persuade her to slow down, to talk to him. If they didn't have many more nights left together he wanted more out of this one. She munched on a breadstick and he didn't notice anything charming about her now. Had she worked it all out already? The end of their marriage? And when would she present him with her plan if not now?

Drinks came. They ordered. No discussion.

"Okay, how about we cut the shit?" he said.

"What do you mean?"

"You know what I mean. This act, let's get over it. If not over it, then around it. We have too much to talk about tonight."

"Will you be staying?"

"That's what you want to know? The sleeping arrangements? Why, are you that committed to him already? Don't bother answering that. I don't want to fight with you. But we have our children, and our things, and I need to know what's happening here and how we are going to go about it. You've thought about this, I take it?"

Penny looked away from him and held her face in profile. She was about to cry, and she was holding it back. He'd pushed her to emotion, forced her to think about splitting up the family.

"You thought about what you want?" he asked. "Where you want the boys to live? How you want to bring them up? Have you thought about that?"

She faced him. "I'm sorry, Alan. I don't know what I've done to you. It's not like me. I can't see how you could ever take me back."

"Are you asking to come back?" he said. "Because I want that. I haven't considered us fully apart. This is a break, that's all it has to be. I can forget it. It's nothing."

"It's not nothing. I met someone else. Why won't you take me seriously? That's all I ask is for you to take me seriously."

"You're repeating yourself."

"I'm sorry?"

"Next you're going to tell me about the happiness that you can no longer find with us and that's why you've fallen in love with blah, blah, blah. Listen, do you love him?"

Penny hesitated and wiped her swollen eyes. "I don't know," she said.

"Yet you placed everything you have in danger, and you don't know. You don't know? Don't spare my feelings. You do or you don't. If you do love him you have to admit it to me, yourself, and your children. And you should go over to his apartment and tell him that you're moving in, you love him. You should be together. But Penny, you're not taking my boys. You're not taking my boys into someone else's home. If you want to leave, then you leave everything."

"That's not the way this works, Alan."

"It's not? Are you a lawyer? Have you consulted a divorce attorney? I've been through one of these, Penny. If you can prove you're not having an affair then you may get joint custody. If you can't, you get nothing. But you'll have your happiness, won't you?" He was going to get angrier if he didn't stop himself. He was going to make her pay in this moment, and that would diminish his chances of resolving anything. When he was on the verge of losing his temper, it was very hard for him to back away from the edge of the cliff; he simply wanted to push off into the air and plummet.

She wasn't answering him anymore.

"You'll have your happiness, I know how important that is to you."

"Don't patronize me."

"What? You need to be happy. If I can't do it, you must find someone else who can. Because it has nothing to do with you, happiness. It all comes with the person you're fucking. That's where you'll find true happiness."

"Fuck you, Alan."

"Happiness is a warm phallus. I've always thought so."

"Lower your voice."

He was smiling, hiding any sense of pain with bad humor and a phony smirk.

"Anyway, my work is going rather well. The *Herald* ran a long piece I wrote. I don't know if you've seen it. Do you remember Baxter Broadwater? He was a figure from my first marriage. Anyway, Broadwater is the one who sent me to Saigon, paid me loads of cash. Then there's the book I'm going to expand it into. Lazlo's getting behind it. He's gonna pay out more of the advance. Things are going really well for me, Penny."

"I'm glad to hear it."

"I mean . . ." he formed his right hand into a rocket taking off, shooting into space in slow motion . . . "*Pshhhhhhhhhhhh!*"

"Alan."

"*Pshhhhhhhhhhhh.*"

"Alan," she said more forcefully, wanting him to stop.

"*Pshhhhhhhhhhhh.*" His hand was still in the air. "This is a rocket, Penny. A rocket going into space. *Pshhhhhhhhhhhh.*"

"Stop acting like a child. The food's coming."

He still had his hand fully extended into the air, demonstrating the rocket she was not going to be on. The food arrived, and when the waiter put his plate of pasta in front of him he cut it out.

"Let's eat," he said.

They walked home side by side. He found each moment he was spending with her more and more insignificant. He felt her disinterest in him, like she was seeing an old friend she didn't care much for. It was cruel, her behavior, but he understood clearly what she was doing. She was preparing herself for the ultimate good-bye. And her nonchalance was getting to him. Not in the way that made him feel he needed to act out. He had given her enough of that at the restaurant, provided some nice fodder for her and her lover. Eastman, the idiot husband. His behavior only justified her choices. He was handing her to his phantom, wasn't he?

They went home and she immediately went into the kitchen and cleaned up after the boys. He called Toby and Lee into his study to give them the presents he had brought back from Asia. He could sense Lee, the oldest, was keeping up appearances. Lee was good at pretending, like his mother. Toby couldn't ignore the sadness in the house. The lonely sound of his mother doing dishes and Eastman's tiring smile as he fed them their presents. He put his hand on Toby's shoulder and gave the boy a kiss on the top of his head.

They turned in early that evening. Toby, Lee, Penny. He felt out of place in his own life. He wasn't a part of their summer routine and trying to fall into it was taxing. Every time he tried to get near her, she managed to be in another room, occupied with something. Either searching through her bags for something or tidying up. When he went to tuck the boys in, he heard her in the bathroom washing her face. He caught up with her while she was brushing her teeth. He stood next to her and took his toothbrush out of the medicine cabinet, squeezed the toothpaste on the worn bristles, placed it under the running faucet, and began to brush next to her. She had no alternative but to see him in the mirror. She managed to remain expressionless during the whole task. She spit into the sink and returned her brush to the cabinet. He spit his toothpaste out immediately. As she was drying her mouth on a hand towel he reached out and touched her shoulder. She tore it away and left him for the bedroom.

This is what she wanted to put him through. To show him examples of how everything was now different. As they prepared for bed, he asked, "Can I stay in here tonight?"

"Do what you want," she said.

"I'd like to if you're comfortable with it."

"I'm tired, I can't think right now."

It was a warm night and the window was open; no breeze. Normally she would have slept without clothing, but she was still making her point. Penny took off her blouse. Underneath, a beige bra. She took that off, too, resting it on top of the hamper. As she did this she covered herself, held her arm across her breasts, not allowing him to see her. She got the nightgown out of the closet and put it on. Only then did she take off her skirt, beneath the cover of the nightgown.

He, however, would not partake. The night was too hot. He took off all of his clothes, his tie, the black shirt, his pants then underwear, and stood naked before her. She averted her eyes as she got into bed and went under the sheet. He walked around the room for a while, pretending to look for something. A book, perhaps. He went out into the hall to find something to read. In the bathroom was a copy of *Fear of Flying*. He didn't care what it was, he only needed a prop, an excuse to stay up. He got into bed; she had already turned off her bedside lamp. It couldn't have been past nine o'clock and already she was trying to put herself to sleep. Was it that painful being with him tonight?

In bed, he said, "You must be tired."

"I am."

"Awfully early."

"I'm exhausted."

"Me, I'm jet-lagged. I think I'll read."

He let her be for a minute. "Have you read this?"

"Alan."

"I found it in the bathroom."

She turned to look at the novel.

"I thought that was yours," she said.

"Maybe it's Helen's. She must have left it here. She was a great help with the boys before I left for Saigon."

Penny didn't respond. She lay on her back, staring at the ceiling. It occurred to him that she hadn't inquired about Vietnam, whether it was safe, if he'd accomplished what he went there to do. They had had so many conversations about the war, the draft, Johnson, Nixon, Kissinger, the war had stretched out through their entire marriage. And now that he'd gone and seen it she didn't ask. Nothing that involved him interested her.

He tried to read next to her but it was impossible to concentrate. So he put the book down and clicked off his lamp. He lay down on his side facing her. She was awake with her eyes closed. He put his hand on her shoulder. This had worked once before. When she came back from her lost month in London, just before they were married, they lay in bed and he had touched her like this. She confessed to him much later that when she felt his touch she had melted in his hands. Those were good years. He tried to reach for that same power now, not because he wanted to seduce her (though he wasn't against it), but to test himself. He moved his hand over her chest, slipped it under her nightgown and over her breast, just as he had done all those years ago. He'd once been allowed to touch her. Now it felt wrong. Penny put an end to it by turning over to face him. She looked as if she were going to speak, to explain what was bothering her about the two of them. He waited. Then waited for a good two or three minutes more, his eyes open and tearing, desperate to blink. She continued to look at him until he realized there was nothing that would come next.

22

It didn't come to him immediately. He lay next to her, pretending to sleep, aware of a new kind of rejection, his mind working through all the possible outcomes. And once he exhausted his mind, he drifted off.

But as suddenly as he was asleep he was awake again. He thought it was his snoring. He loudly woke himself sometimes. It was Penny shaking him, and he was jolted awake mid-snort. She was in tears.

"Alan, wake up."

"What happened?"

She looked at him, terrified. "Alan, what have I done? I've messed up and I can't apologize. I can't apologize for what I've done."

"Why not?"

"Because it's too horrible. And I've been struggling for so long."

"So have I, Penny."

"No, I've been struggling longer because I was thinking about leaving you for months. I was terrified about what would happen. I couldn't talk to you, and I'm not blaming you again. I didn't want to talk to you. I did it on purpose."

"You can tell me anything, you know that."

"No, no, no."

"When were you thinking about leaving me?"

"Oh, I don't know," she said. "December, last year."

"When? Christmas?"

"I don't know. I told you, I don't know. It was after Christmas. You were so inconsiderate. Wrapped up in your own little world. Always complaining. I convinced myself that this was the only way to be happy. It's too horrible to even think about now."

"It's okay, Penny."

"No, it's not. It's awful. How can you ever take me back? I can't even bring myself to apologize."

He sat up and held her tight and allowed her to cry on his shoulder. The feel of her against his skin, after all this time, was familiar and warm. She looked up at him and came closer. Her face was wet and she kissed him apologetically. She may not have said she was sorry but he knew she was.

After a few brief kisses, he rested her on her back and they simply resumed their respective places on the mattress. He turned over on his side and the bed squeaked.

"We should get a new mattress," he said reflexively.

"Let's buy one this week," she said. "Maybe we should replace the whole bed."

He opened his eyes wide. A jolt of happiness overtook him and it was some time before he could fall asleep again.

In the morning, Penny was up before him, already downstairs making the boys breakfast. He sat up in bed, looked around the room, saw her suitcases were still on the floor with clothes pouring out of them. Blouses and other tops he recognized. He might have hoped she would have put her things away in the closet. But one thing at a time, he thought.

He got dressed. Chose a good pair of pants, an airy summer shirt he'd picked up in Hawaii. He looked and felt good. Everything in his closet fit him now that he'd lost weight in Vietnam.

The boys were seated around the table and he came in and gave them both a kiss.

"Good to be back," he said.

Toby put his arms around Eastman's waist and pressed his ear to his father's stomach.

"What's for breakfast?" he asked.

Penny was frying eggs at the stove and turned around to take notice of him. "I'm making eggs," she said. "Have a seat." She looked tired, her face was swollen from crying, and she wasn't acting overly gracious. The eggs crackled in the pan. She cooked eggs with the heat too high, and normally he would tell her to lower the heat or the eggs would stick to the bottom of the pan. But today he was content to let her do it her way.

"It's good you're back, Dad," said Lee.

"It's good to be back," he said, sitting down. "Let's eat some eggs for protein. Protein builds muscle." He flexed an arm and held it close to Toby. "Feel that." Toby did. His arms were lean and tight, as tight as they'd been in years.

"New shirt?" Penny asked.

"Yes. I got it in Hawaii," he said, and immediately he regretted it.

"You were in Hawaii!?" asked Toby.

"Yep."

"When were you in Hawaii?" said Penny.

"Last week. On a layover back from Vietnam."

"So you flew that way," she said, with implications.

"I don't know. Yes, I flew that way. I stopped in Bangkok on the way there, Hawaii on the way back. The paper has a bureau in Honolulu." He particularly avoided thinking about Meredith. That was over. He ended it and Penny now had his full attention.

Lee chimed in to change the subject, sensing the tension. "What was Vietnam like?"

He told him about how to get there, stressing the length of the flight and the need to stop and refuel. "One can't just fly direct into a war." Then he spoke of the city of Saigon, full of reporters moving in and out, crossing rivers and borders. The hot spots, the curfew, the prostitutes. "Alan!" Penny scolded him. He had a copy of the paper in his suitcase, if Lee wanted to read his dispatch. At the mention of the paper he looked to Penny for a reaction to his work, but she didn't lift her head or say anything. It irritated him, though he attributed her stoicism to being embarrassed for having thrown the paper away in the trash that day he followed her.

"Are we getting the paper delivery?" he asked.

"No, I assumed you had it stopped," she said. She served the eggs, the boys each getting one. He got two, over medium, and reached for the salt. She kept an egg for herself that had stuck to the pan and broken.

"I'll call and have them start delivering it again. The *Times* and the *Herald*."

The boys ate their breakfast with smiles. He was happy to be back, to be around them. He was attuned to their attitudes and feelings for the next few days because his own mood was so connected to theirs. All he had to do was be with his children and he could feel good again. Children were a miracle. Which made him think of Helen. And after breakfast he went to his study and called her at her dormitory at Vassar.

"I'm back and I'm alive. All's well," he said.

"I'm glad to hear it," Helen said. "I got your letter. Did you get mine?"

"No. But everything will be forwarded to me here by the hotel. I'm sorry I didn't receive it in time, but I left in a hurry."

"That's okay. I'll tell you what I said. That I hope you come back safe and sound. That I love you. That I checked up on Toby and Lee while I was in the city again. I called first, of course. Penny was very nice to me. I think she felt bad. I decided whatever happens I still want to be close to my little brothers. And then I wrote to tell you that Bobby Cohen asked me to marry him."

"Well, hold on. You, who don't believe in marriage, are considering a proposal?"

"I didn't say that. And I have good reason to be cynical, don't you think, Daddy?"

"What did you say? And who is Bobby Cohen?"

"Don't worry. I told him no. I barely know him. We went out twice, if *that*. He attends Columbia. My letter explained it all."

"Well, it doesn't seem like you needed my counsel."

She wanted to know how he was and he gave her some details of his trip. He told her that he'd moved home and that they would be working things out. "Prospects are good," he said.

"I'm happy for you. I'm skeptical. But I'm happy. Has she broken it off with what's his name?"

Good question, he thought. "We're working through all the aspects. I'm just calling to say I'm back and that I love you. And I want to see you soon. Why don't I visit or you come down?"

Helen's summer semester had started, plus she was working part time at a record store for $1.60 an hour. She wouldn't be able to get away until August. They settled on his going up to Poughkeepsie for a visit. "I love you, Daddy," she said, and he was again filled with that feeling. Of being rich with love, the kind only children could provide.

For the next week, their house on Pineapple Street bore a faint resemblance to the home they once had. Penny went about the household chores, the boys went to summer camp four days a week at

Our Lady of Lebanon, and he tried to stay out of Penny's way as she cleaned every surface, top to bottom—except for his study. He tried to work, despite the sound of the broom smacking the corners and walls, and the rumble of the vacuum. She avoided his study and any room he was in. So while she was cleaning their bedroom, he approached her.

"Why don't you let me help you," he said.

"This house is so dusty, I'm trying to air it out."

"My study could use a once-over."

She didn't answer. He went over to their bed and began straightening the duvet and fluffing the pillows.

"Are you avoiding cleaning my study? Or is it me you're avoiding?"

In response to what he thought a fair question, she turned the vacuum on once again. He didn't want to get angry, but he saw Penny making very little effort to communicate. He pulled the plug on the vacuum. She looked at him, perplexed, as he held up the cord and threw it on the floor.

"What are you doing?" she said.

"I'm standing here and I want you to tell me what I can do to help."

She didn't think he was interested in helping her and he told her she was wrong. It would be different now. They would be equals and he would do equal work.

"I'm about to do the boys' room next. You can start there."

"Fine."

He went into the boys' room and started picking up dirty socks and T-shirts, their shoes and slippers. He found one of the special pilot's wings in Toby's mattress and he placed it on the bureau. After Penny was finished vacuuming the master bedroom they switched places and he went into the bedroom to tidy up. Her suitcase was closed and placed upright at the foot of the closet. He took it out and saw that it had just been closed, her things remained inside. He would begin here. He spread the suitcase out on the bed and folded her things neatly, laying them out. One pile for tank tops, then undergarments, blouses, skirts, shorts. He hung her blouses in her corner of the closet and put the piles away in their respective places. When the clothes didn't look right in the bureau, he readjusted the piles and refolded some of the items. He even messed up her underwear drawer a little as he remembered it before she left. Her bed slippers he placed at the foot of her side of the bed at a forty-five-degree angle facing out. He wanted to demonstrate that he was trying. The suitcase he put away at the bottom of the closet where he'd found it.

At times, it was hard for them to simply talk. They slept in the same bed at night, though between dinner and bed he went into his study to work on his second dispatch, which still wasn't finished. It reeked of falseness, had little substance, and in truth he might have considered it some of the worst reporting to come out of the war. He took a look at the copy of the *Herald* with his first dispatch, and even though it had some decent parts, mostly regarding Channing, he found it depressed him. And he knew why. He had used Saigon not as a subject, but as a way to sop up all of his misery, ignoring what was at the heart of the misery in front of him. He'd cheated Saigon, but above all, he'd cheated himself. He vowed that it was time to get back to work. He was still intent on making a book out of his dispatches, but to do so, he would have to return to Vietnam in order to do the war justice.

By the time he retired to bed on these nights he was in no mood to talk to Penny and she wasn't pushing for it either.

Friday evening, Penny was late getting home. She'd left for her office in the morning, but didn't call to tell him what time she would be home. If it was a test of some sort, he felt ready for it. So he went to the market with the boys. They would be preparing dinner for their mother to reward her for all of her hard work. They made spaghetti and sauce from scratch. Canned tomatoes, onion, garlic, grated carrots, ground beef, garlic powder, oregano, salt, and pepper. Evaporated milk, too, for creaminess. Lee grated the carrots and chopped the onion while Eastman supervised. Toby was in charge of stirring the sauce from his position on a step stool. For the first time since Eastman was back he was having fun with his boys. He noticed a change in their dispositions, too. They had been walking on eggshells around their parents when Eastman and Penny were both home. They hid in their rooms or played outside in the street. And whenever Eastman entered a room Penny was in, Lee shuffled his little brother out to avoid what they sensed was coming. The children were well aware of the tension in the home. Now with Penny out, they could all relax.

He kept the task of making dinner focused on Penny. They were preparing a meal for their mother. But when he mentioned this it seemed to take the air out of the room.

He had Toby feed him a taste of the sauce over the stove top. It was a touch sour and too salty. "It needs sugar," he said. "Regardless, Mom's going to be very proud of you." The boy made an anxious face. Eastman gave Toby the box of sugar and went to help Lee set the table. Toby yelled, "Dad! Dad!" The boy had poured nearly the whole box of sugar into the sauce.

"Stop, don't stir it in!" Eastman ran over and picked the boy off the step stool and put him on the floor. He got a ladle and scooped out most of the excess sugar into the sink. "There," he said. "We're saved. What happened? Didn't I say just a little sugar?"

"It slipped," said Toby.

"It slipped!? You almost turned the sauce into dessert!" The boys laughed. He put Toby back up on the stool and returned the wooden spoon to his son. "Okay, just keep stirring."

Penny returned, unannounced, just as they were draining the pasta into a colander in the sink. Lee was sitting up on the kitchen counter banging his legs against the cabinets, waiting. The kitchen was a mess, but the dinner was ready. When Penny saw them all working together, she smiled, put her things on the counter. "Down," she told Lee and he hopped off.

"We're making spaghetti," said Eastman.

"I can see that," Penny said. "Do you need help?"

"No, sit. We're making dinner tonight."

Penny sat down and waited while Eastman and the boys served her. She was dressed particularly well and her makeup was extreme. Over the steam and the smell of onion and garlic he could make out her perfume.

It was clear to him in the way she didn't offer an explanation as to where she had been that tonight they would have a major talk. And the meal that he and the boys had so much fun making turned into the worst time they all had eating together. The food was fine. It had been made with love. But the pieces around the table were out of place. He looked to his youngest, Toby, who was tensing his jaw. He remembered Helen pointing this out.

"Hey," he said to Toby in order to distract the boy, "you're eating tomatoes. You never eat tomatoes."

"It's spaghetti," Toby said.

"Yeah, but the sauce is made out of tomatoes."

"It is?"

Eastman looked at Penny to gauge her interest. "He made the sauce."

"It's raw tomato that he doesn't like," Penny said. "He always eats spaghetti, don't you, honey? Now finish your plate."

Toby looked down at his spaghetti and did what his mother ordered.

"All I know is," Eastman said, "the kid doesn't like tomato, never has."

"Let it go, Alan."

"Let what go? I'm only trying to make conversation. If you prefer we eat here in silence—the meal your kids made for you—then all the better."

Penny didn't respond. She wasn't even going to give him the satisfaction of an argument.

Later that evening, in bed, she said to him, "Aren't you going to ask me where I was?" She phrased it as if he had made another mistake.

"I was waiting for you to tell me. Besides, I didn't want to ask in front of the boys in case it was something they shouldn't hear."

"But are you going to ask me now?"

"Are we arguing about whether I am going to act jealous or are you just going to tell me where you were?"

"I was with him. I broke it off."

Eastman nodded his head. Was he to smile at the news? Was he to embrace her with a kiss? He didn't feel like either of those things.

"I thought you would be pleased," she said.

"I am."

"Boy, you're sure acting like it."

"It's a lot to take in."

"You knew, Alan. It's not news that I was seeing someone."

"We have talked about him, once, but you never offered up any details. You kept them from me deliberately. To me he's a phantom. Maybe I don't want any details now because I'd rather not fixate on him and what you did. We're supposed to be working on putting things back together. I'd rather not get upset."

"Lower your voice," she said. He hadn't realized he raised it. And all things considered, Eastman felt justified.

In the past they would have had it out, reconciled, made love, cried, worked through the pain, battled again, and gotten themselves to a place where they felt resilient to what may come. This time, he thought of the children. Would it really benefit Lee and Toby if their parents stayed together? This had been the week from hell; he could no longer ignore it.

All the time he spent brooding over her, rehashing their past, daydreaming of her, and having lustful fantasies didn't seem relevant now. The children were unhappy, and it was because of the dynamic in the home. Penny's feelings for him had changed for a reason. He wasn't picking up any hints from her that she would fall madly in love with him again. And he was too tired to convince her.

Penny furrowed her forehead. Whether she regretted getting back with him or breaking it off with her lover was anyone's guess. She had done something to her eyebrows. Colored them in dark brown to make them look more defined. He didn't prefer it. It was like she had put on a mask and wasn't going to take it off.

Both of them were too drained that night to begin planning the separation. But he went to bed knowing it was the only way to continue.

The newspaper delivery resumed the next day and the papers hit the front door with a thud. He rose early, dressed, and made his way

down to put the coffee on the stove. He went out onto the stoop to collect the newspapers. It was a bright, summer morning with a cool
breeze coming off the water, heading east.

Back inside, he had his coffee in the kitchen, sitting down, flip-
ping through the *Times* to see if there were any relevant stories on
Vietnam. There was one about an accidental bombing by the U.S. in
Cambodia on the Phnom Penh–Saigon Highway, which sounded
close enough to Phnom Penh for him to be concerned. Four hundred
casualties from a 20-ton mistake dropped by their great ally in the
sky. No plausible explanation was given as to why. There was no reported enemy activity in the area.

The *Times* hadn't reported any Americans killed, even though
the bombs were close to a marine barracks, so he shifted to the
Herald to see if they had reported anything different. It was possibly still too soon to know who was killed. He was truly worried
about Channing as he scanned the front page. Then he saw her
byline, front and center, and knew that everything was okay. She
was alive.

Her dispatch was from a place called Neak Loeung, about forty
miles south of Phnom Penh along the Mekong River. He assumed
she wasn't in the bombing, but my God, how quickly she got there
from the capital. He read on about the people of Neak Loeung who
lost entire families, people who wished they were dead, too. She
talked to these men and women perhaps a day after the bombing and
he could feel their anxiety. The article was still damp with emotion.
In his mind he saw the rubble of hospitals and schools, the leveled
homes and debris, the faces caked in dust—all through Channing's
careful eye. Things he would have generalized as "the toll of war"
she stopped to observe. It was a piece of writing that could sway
Washington if the right people were to read it. She knew the power of

emotion, it seeped through her details, got under the skin. The power of witnessing and reporting. The power of empathy. This is what his writing was missing. Not humanity, but humanity's authenticity.

Eastman went to his study and with a pair of scissors he cut Channing's article from the front page. He sat down at his desk and was moved to write a note to Meredith. He got some stationery and a pen, and wrote simply, *You were right. She's the real deal.*

Upstairs, the house began to stir. He could hear Penny awake now, and one of the boys shuffling into the bathroom. He folded Channing's article along with his note into an envelope. Then he walked out his front door with a letter to post.

Acknowledgments

Thanks to the Harry Ransom Center at the University of Texas in Austin and their wonderful librarians for access to the Norman Mailer archive. Thanks to the Norman Mailer Center for their active support. Thank you Gregory Curtis, J. Michael Lennon, Lawrence Schiller, and John Buffalo Mailer.

Deepest thanks to my colleagues at Monmouth University, and to my research assistants, Colleen King and Daniel Murphy.

The figures on page 44 are directly quoted from Gloria Emerson's *Winners and Losers*, a book I am indebted to.

Thanks to the National Book Foundation for their recognition and support in the 5 Under 35 program. Benjamin Samuel, Leslie Shipman, Colum McCann, and Amy Bloom, thank you.

Thanks to the New York Society Library for their generous support in 2014.

Thanks to my readers, Scott Cheshire, Bill Cheng, and my wife, Alexandra Kleeman.

Thanks to my father, Peter Gilvarry, a veteran of the Vietnam War, who planted his stories in my life.

Thank you to all at Viking: Patrick Nolan for keeping me in this business; Beena Kamlani for her editorial guidance; Matthew Klise, Sam Raim, Chris Smith, Lindsay Prevette, Lydia Hirt, Michelle Giuseffi, Kate Stark, Andrea Schulz, and Brian Tart.

Most of all, Seth Fishman.